Named to Kirkus Reviews' Best Books of 2014:
Masters' Mysterium: WISCONSIN DELLS

"One of the best paranormal fantasy releases of
this year…" - *Kirkus Reviews (starred review)*

Masters' Mysterium

WISCONSIN DELLS

R R Reynolds

Masters' Mysterium
Wisconsin Dells

ISBN 9780988679702

Scriptures taken from the Holy Bible, New International Version®, NIV®. Copyright © 1973,
1978, 1984, 2011 by Biblica, Inc.™ Used by permission of Zondervan. All rights reserved
worldwide. www.zondervan.com The "NIV" and "New International Version" are trademarks
registered in the United States Patent and Trademark Office by Biblica, Inc.™

Masters' Mysterium Press

ISBN: 0988679701
Library of Congress Control Number: 2012955438
CreateSpace Independent Publishing Platform
North Charleston, South Carolina

"Do not forget to entertain strangers, for by so doing some people have entertained angels without knowing it."
— Hebrews 13:2

CHAPTER ONE

Trudy Masters didn't feel like movie night. Nevertheless she made the attempt to smile after ringing the doorbell.

"Trudy!" Rachel beamed as she opened the door.

"Why the big grin there?" she asked as the diminutive Rachel continued to block the doorway. Trudy attempted to decipher her frustratingly perky friend. Everything looked in place: long blonde hair pulled back, a freckled face that was supposedly the same twenty-one years as Trudy's but looked somehow less haggard than the one that reflected back at her in the mirror each day, a rumpled Hello Kitty T-shirt and sweat pants … then she spotted them.

"What are those?"

"My fuzzy slippers!" Rachel squeaked. "Do you like them? Reverend Brustad made them for me."

Struggling to hide her distaste, Trudy surveyed the furry brown slippers that gazed back at her, their stuffed little rodent heads staring glassy-eyed up at her. "What are they?"

"Muskrats, I think," Rachel said as she rubbed the toes together. "Look, they're in love!"

"Stop," Trudy grumbled as she pushed her way inside. The living room was a taxidermist's paradise with deer heads lining the walls and various other defunct fauna taking up any flat surface. Reverend Brustad was a closet taxidermist before his wife's death, but Trudy realized his hobby had blossomed into true obsession.

"Is that Trudy?" A voice called from the kitchen.

1

"Hi, Rev," Trudy replied as she walked into the kitchen, closely followed by Rachel. "What's new?"

"Would you like a soda?" Brustad said as he grabbed a Sprecher cream soda from the refrigerator and held it out for her. "Your favorite."

"Thanks," Trudy said, grabbing the cold bottle. She wandered over to a kitchen drawer and surveyed the contents. "Rev, where's the bottle opener?"

Brustad stood there grinning just like Rachel had done before him, his bald dome and Coke bottle glasses reflecting the harsh fluorescent lighting and giving him a mad scientist look.

"What's with you two tonight?" Trudy said, and then she saw it and groaned. "For heaven's sake, Rev, what's a deer's ass doing hanging in the kitchen?"

"You noticed!" Reverend Brustad replied, clearly pleased with himself. "It's my latest creation." He paused and leered playfully at the macabre display on the wall. "Go on. You know you want to."

Trudy didn't move.

"Give it a try," Brustad said.

"Wait, What? You don't mean—"

"Yes! Go on, give it a try."

Trudy walked over to the stuffed deer butt that hung on the wall, tail up and ready. "Why do I feel like a pervert in a minister's house?" she said as she stuck the bottle up the deer's ass and pulled down. The bottle top came cleanly off, fizz from the cola moistening the deer's former sphincter.

"Oh, my…" Rachel gasped.

"I feel so dirty," was all Trudy could add.

"I saw that on a television show and just had to make one," the Reverend chortled. "Guess what? I've got orders for three of them already. It really helps to supplement the salary from our church. Doesn't cost me anything either. Everyone comes to me to have the heads mounted and they give me the rump for free."

"Yeah," Trudy said. "I'm not sure how you pay the bills with what we all contribute. You could do a lot better someplace else."

"And miss out on our friends in Morgan? Not a chance!" the Reverend replied, causing Rachel to blush.

As the microwave dinged, Brustad said, "Well, the popcorn is ready—anyone for a classic film tonight?"

"Sure, what's on?" Trudy asked as she repeatedly wiped the mouth of the soda bottle off with her sleeve.

"*It's a Wonderful Life*," the Reverend crowed. "One of my favorites."

Trudy shot Rachel a glance.

"I didn't pick it out," Rachel replied with a shrug, "but I can't wait to see it again." She added in a voice even meeker than her usual one, "It's one of my favorites, too."

"Masochist," grumped Trudy, plopping down beside Rachel on the lumpy sofa in the living room while Reverend Brustad sank into his La-Z-Boy, clutching the remote in one hand and a bowl of popcorn in the other.

"Do you mind?" Trudy asked as she stood up and went over to the big screen television. Next to it, a stuffed squirrel stood in a pose usually reserved for a bear, on its hind legs with front legs extended and a vicious snarl on its face.

Trudy turned it to the wall. "Thanks," she said as she sat back down. Rachel was now sitting sideways on the couch with her Muskrat feet pointing towards her. Trudy was unnerved by the four glass eyes staring at her but didn't want to say something in front of Brustad; besides, Rachel was so obviously enraptured by them that she didn't have the heart.

Rachel grabbed a big bowl of popcorn off of the coffee table and held it out to her as Reverend Brustad mashed buttons on the remote to get the movie started.

Trudy preferred to concentrate during movies and the constant chatter between Brustad and Rachel was getting on her nerves.

"I was working on my next sermon earlier today," the Reverend said. "I'm thinking of something from the Song of Solomon."

"I love that one!" Rachel said and quoted, "'Behold, you are fair! You have dove's eyes behind your veil. Your hair is like a flock of goats.'"

Trudy ran her fingers through her unkempt bobbed black hair. "I think my hair has been compared to a flock of goats before—at least behind my back."

"Oh, this is my favorite part!" Rachel said as she pointed to the television. "Wait till they open up the floor and they all fall into the swimming pool." Then she tossed a handful of popcorn into her mouth and crunched loudly in her open mouth way.

Trudy continued to watch the budding romance of George Bailey and Mary Hatch with increasing depression. Why couldn't life be like the movies, she wondered? Trials and tribulations, sure, but in the flicks there's always a happy ending—even for the star-crossed George.

"Rachel," Brustad said, intruding on her thoughts. "How are things in Morgan? I imagine this whole scare with the wolf doesn't bother any one of you, but it has us a bit worried over here in Creekside."

"We're keeping an eye out for it. It is a shame what happened to that hunter," Rachel replied. "Wolves look so much like big puppies; it's hard to imagine one doing something like that."

"Puppies?" Trudy marveled. "Maybe to you, but I'm not going to attempt giving one a belly rub."

Jimmy Stewart's impassioned drawling voice drew her attention to the television: "*I know what I'm gonna do tomorrow, and the next day, and the next year, and the year after that. I'm shakin' the dust of this crummy little town off of my feet and I'm gonna see the world.*"

She turned her face towards the ceiling and closed her eyes.

"Trudy, are you okay?" Rachel asked.

"I'm okay," Trudy replied as she looked over at her friend and patted her leg.

Rachel bit her lip. "Do you want to borrow my fuzzy slippers?"

———

After the movie, and having said their goodbyes to Reverend Brustad, Trudy and Rachel began the walk down State Street in Creekside, Rachel having changed back into her tennis shoes but carrying her slippers in a plastic bag back to Morgan. The evening was cooling down as summer surrendered to fall. She could make out the Big Dipper off to the northwest, the moon being but a faint sliver in the sky.

"You know the Reverend really enjoys your visits," Rachel said. "After what happened and all, I think he feels you're like a daughter to him."

"I was thinking about visiting them," Trudy said as they continued downhill towards Main Street. "I'll walk with you to the cutoff to Morgan."

"It's pretty dark out. Would you like me to come with you?"

Trudy smiled. "You're always trying to protect me, aren't you?"

"I'm good at it," Rachel replied matter-of-factly.

As they passed Maggie McKenzie's house on State Street, Rachel asked, "Want to stop in and say hi? Maggie always cheers you up."

"That's okay; she's a dear but we have an early start tomorrow."

Creekside had already rolled up the sidewalks and the main thoroughfare was deserted as they turned onto Main and passed the diner with the hideous name of the Cluck and Grunt.

"I can't wait until tomorrow!" Rachel exclaimed. "To think I'll actually be working there with you!"

"Don't get too excited there, Missy," Trudy chided her gently. "Bill's little establishment is one step below a Waffle House."

"But it's a great honor," Rachel pouted. "None of us from the community have ever had a real job that paid money."

"Trust me, when you see your paycheck you'll find that you are still working for free."

As they crossed the iron girder bridge that spanned a feeder creek into Mill Creek, Trudy slowed to a stop and looked over the side. She could barely make out the stream in the darkness but could hear it as it forced itself around the sharp rocks and towards the river.

"Trudy…" Rachel said, her voice filled with concern.

"Don't worry; I'm not going to jump. It's only ten feet down. I'd break an ankle."

Rachel came up to her and put her arm around her. "Still thinking of *It's a Wonderful Life?*"

"Yeah, sort of…"

"It's not very accurate."

Trudy laughed. "I guess not, but I still feel a bit like George Bailey. I'd like to get out of this crummy town of Creekside, Wisconsin."

"You will," Rachel said as she grabbed her by the arm, pulling her to the other side of the bridge, past the "Welcome To Creekside" sign. "See, you're out of town!" Rachel gave Trudy a lumberjack strength hug. "Remember when we first met? You were standing on this bridge, right over there, with your arms crossed and a big scowl on your face."

Trudy smiled. "Yeah, I wasn't too happy about Maggie and Jonathan's decision for me to keep an eye on you—and you've got to admit you're high maintenance."

"You love it!" Rachel said as she punched Trudy's arm playfully. "Sure you don't want me to come with you?"

"I'm fine!" Trudy said. "See you tomorrow at seven at the diner."

Rachel continued straight down the road to catch the abandoned railroad trestle across Mill Creek and towards the community of Morgan. Trudy made a right and walked up a slight hill to the cemetery. In the darkness it was hard to see anything but Trudy knew exactly where she was heading.

She walked past the fresh gravesite of Paul Sanders, the local haberdasher until he retired thirty years ago. Another fifty feet and she reached her destination. The plots were near each other: Martha Brustad, a few feet away from Trudy's mother, Elizabeth Masters. Fitting, Trudy thought, since they worked through life's turmoil's together, died together in a tragic car accident, and now, in death, would never be separated from each other.

Rachel always told her that separation need never be permanent. She found little consolation in that platitude as she sat down in the damp grass next to her mother's headstone. Running her finger along the letters of her mother's name, she began to cry.

——

Worn brake pads pressing against rickety rotors screamed as the aged Ford pickup came to a stop on the gravel shoulder and the interior light came on. Gavin Young knew it was the end of the line.

"I'm turning off now so I need to drop you here," said the old man in a flannel shirt that gave him a lift from Woodruff. The man squinted a sideways glance at him while his hands continued to grip the steering wheel, large knuckles pointing out like spikes. He raked a forearm across his sleeve, stirring up the mingled scents of Old Spice, cow dung, and motor oil that Gavin had endured the entire ride. "Going to be okay, son?"

"Sure," Gavin said as he realized he was being dumped in the middle of a Northern Wisconsin forest at midnight.

"Crappy weather to be walking in, I know, but I can't spare the time to take you into town," the old man apologized. "My wife is feeling puny and I've been gone too long as it is."

"It's fine," Gavin said as he got out and grabbed his pack from the back of the truck. "Thanks for taking me this far."

The old man gave a faint nod. "There's not a lot of traffic this time of night. Creekside is fifteen miles down the road near Lost Lake but there's a campground about a half a mile away on the right. No KOA or anything fancy like that, but decent enough spots to pitch that tent of yours. Just don't wander off or you'll get yourself stuck in a marsh."

"I'll check it out," Gavin said as he slung the backpack over his shoulder. "Thanks again."

The Ford's weak shocks bounced the truck back onto the road where it hung a sharp left up a gravel trail, leaving Gavin standing in the dark. Fog crept over his shoes and up his thighs as he took in his surroundings. The old farmer was correct, he surmised. Not much chance of hitching a ride at midnight, and it would be morning before he reached Creekside by walking. Resigned to the fact that a damp and probably deserted campground awaited him, he started down the road.

The temperature was drifting downward and the high humidity was adding to the chill. The waning crescent moon provided little light to distinguish the difference between the shoulder of the road and the start of the woods. Marshes crept their way up towards the gravel, the croaking of frogs just to Gavin's right distinguishing the boundary in the darkness. Deciding it was preferable to chance traffic than risk falling into a bog, he followed the yellow line down the middle of the road.

Looking ahead and up above the tree line he glimpsed lightning flashing in the distance. "Oh, great." Still, the rest of the night sky was starry, so he had hopes of reaching the campground and setting up the tent before the deluge began.

The campground was deserted as expected, a dozen gravel plots circling an outhouse. There was a tan signboard that mentioned campground self-registration with soggy pieces of paper packed into a Plexiglas box. Gavin walked past it and tried to find a space that didn't reek of Porta-Potty. The flashes in the distance provided the majority of the light as he assembled his tent. After it was complete he sat down in front of it, pulled off his boots and sniffed them critically, and tossed them in the tent.

The lightning was still far off in the distance from what he could tell, as he heard no thunder. Reaching up, he rubbed the scar on the left side of his head and surveyed the emptiness that surrounded him. If only he had stood up to his mother he would be enjoying the nightlife of a University of Wisconsin-Madison student and not sitting in a northern Wisconsin campground surrounded by poison ivy and mosquitos. He realized his mother was both scared and desperate or she would not have sent him off to a forgotten little village in the Northwoods in hopes of a cure, but it didn't make him feel any better as he sat there alone in the dark.

His head began to protest as he thought about his lack of backbone. Fearing what was to come, he quickly climbed into his sleeping bag and zipped up the tent flap near his head. He didn't want to be caught outside when the lightning came.

He lay there staring up at the nylon and fabric three feet above his head and waited with his fists clenched. He attempted to slow his breathing and calm himself but it was impossible. In the moment of waiting he hoped his mother was right.

When it arrived, the pain was excruciating, his vision turning white—ribbons of light snaking their way through his neurons. He began to sweat and cry. This would be a bad one, he realized, wanting to scream but unable to as his throat tightened. He didn't want to die alone in the woods in a cheap Cabela's pup tent but he wasn't sure he wanted to live through the night, either. Quickly, he shoved the strap of the backpack into his mouth and bit down.

Gavin felt his vision being replaced by lightning, blue and white bands stretching off of the main trunk, curling up and out to his peripheral vision. Mercifully, as the lightning reached its climax, Gavin felt himself passing out. He realized in those few seconds of consciousness that his palms were bleeding, his fingernails digging into his clenched fists. Gavin arched his back as the pain hit him full force, then relaxed as he drifted off into another world that knew no thought.

CHAPTER TWO

Trudy awoke to the drunken braying of The Pogues singing "If I Should Fall from Grace with God." She was able to slap the clock radio off of the night-stand and onto the floor as Shane MacGowan's growls faded into silence.

Sitting on the edge of the bed, she ran her hands through her hair that she had overheard a few people referring to as appearing to have been styled with a hedge trimmer.

She yawned.

The clock said 5:00 a.m., thus began another day of waiting tables at the Cluck and Grunt. How she hated that name. How would that look on a resume? Assuming she ever wrote one, which seemed doubtful at this stage of the game.

The doorbell rang.

"What the hell?" she mumbled as she stood up. "Who is it?"

"It's me," came a cricket-like chirp from beyond the door.

With a grumble Trudy hobbled across the room to the door, feeling much older than her twenty-one years. Adjusting her black T-shirt with The Silencers' *A Letter from St. Paul* album cover in faded white on the front and wrinkled plaid shorts that hung down to her knees, she yelled "Hold on" as she unlocked the twin deadbolts and opened the door.

"Rachel?" she said, yawning at her.

Rachel stood before her in a neatly starched and pressed pink waitress uniform. Her long blonde hair was carefully cocooned in a hair net, and her hands shook in nervous excitement at her sides. She smiled the smile of a gum commercial.

"Whoa!" Trudy said, putting her hands to her eyes. "Way too early for that, and why are you here? You start at seven."

"I'm excited to start my first day of work," Rachel replied in a perky voice that sent a shiver down Trudy's spine. "We can walk to work together."

Trudy paused for a moment. "But Morgan is on the other side of town." She gestured with her thumb. "You had to walk past the diner to get here."

"But our destination is the same. That's what counts."

Trudy sighed.

"Come in," she reluctantly offered. "Don't touch the guitars. Feel free to make some coffee if you want. I'll take a quick shower and get ready."

Trudy's studio apartment sat above a long abandoned liquor store on Main Street and consisted of one small room, seeming even smaller under the pile of dirty laundry, general clutter, and empty Diet Coke cans. A perpetually unmade queen bed took up the bulk of the real estate with four guitars on stands and two Marshall amps located in the corner near a ratty futon and small kitchenette. Two small windows let what light they could in through their unwashed panes.

"Take your time; I'll just admire your artwork," Rachel said as she walked over to the bed and started straitening the covers.

Trudy looked at her and then at the walls of her dilapidated apartment. The room's "artwork" consisted of posters of various bands such as the Pixies, Midnight Oil, Hüsker Dü and the Clash. She had a penchant for the outsider, be it people or bands. Those who didn't fit the mold, who looked at things from a different perspective. Those who many would consider freaks.

"I especially like that one," Rachel said, pointing to a black poster from the group Social Distortion that featured a jaunty dancing skeleton hoisting a martini glass. "I like the name—it's very accurate."

"Yeah, whatever," Trudy said as she walked into the bathroom muttering: "It's going to be a long day."

———

A thump on the tent flap jarred Gavin awake.

"Hey, anyone in there?" a gravelly voice just outside the nylon asked.

It took a moment for Gavin to remember where he was, the stench of new vinyl and damp boots bringing him back. Feeling like he had been kicked by a mule, he still managed to pull his arms out of the sleeping bag and reach over his head to unzip the bottom foot of his tent.

"Didn't you see the 'No Camping' sign?" came a voice located above the black shoes and gray pressed slack cuffs that were directly at Gavin's eye level.

He moved his gaze upward to a holstered Glock securely stowed under the fold of an ample beer belly. "No, sir."

"Well, that's because there isn't one. There should be though. Damn Department of Natural Resources and their 'Love The Wolves' program. Pry yourself out of that cocoon, son, and let me take a look at you."

Gavin clambered out of his sleeping bag and managed to pull his sweatshirt over his thin T-shirt before meeting face-to-face with the officer.

"There are wolf packs in this area, son," the sheriff said, his beefy right hand sitting on the butt of the gun. "About two weeks ago, not a quarter mile from here, a hunter got himself all tore up. They basically ripped him open and spread his guts around. They didn't eat him, more like playing with him. I hear they'll do that sometimes" The sheriff scowled at him. "Play with your carcass. You don't want to be a wolf piñata, do you, boy?"

"No, officer," Gavin stammered. The sheriff looked every inch the middle-aged, gruff and cynical caricature of a backwoods lawman that his graveled voice had suggested. "C. Winston" the badge proclaimed as his shoulder patch identified him as Oneida County Sheriff.

"You're just lucky I was driving by—I can't tolerate the office sometimes," Winston allowed. "I need to get myself some fresh air, from time to time. So tell me, boy, why are you wandering around the north woods of Wisconsin with a piece of fabric for shelter? They make hotels you know." Sheriff Winston squinted his small, porcine eyes at Gavin. "You running from something, kid?"

"No, sir," Gavin replied, growing agitated that he was being questioned for camping in a perfectly legal campground.

"What's your name?" the sheriff demanded.

"Gavin Young."

"You have any identification if I should ask to see it?"

"Yes, sir, in my pack."

"So where are you from, kid?" the sheriff said. "Offhand I'd say you're some kind of skinhead from that close haircut and that big scar on the side of your head, along with those German Army boots sitting in your tent, but that UW-Madison sweatshirt you have on doesn't go together. Are you trying to see the world before they lock you up in some computer lab in Madison?"

"I'm an engineering student at UW-Madison," Gavin replied, then added in hopes the officer would go away, "I'm just trying to get to Creekside."

"Creekside, huh? You have an odd way of picking vacations spots," Winston rumbled and spit in the dirt. "Creekside's not known for getting a lot of visitors. Not that they aren't friendly once you get to know them but they're a bit stand-offish with outsiders."

"I have a relative there," Gavin protested.

Winston looked dubious. "Who's your relative? I live just down the road near Lost Lake, and I know just about everyone in these parts."

"Margaret McKenzie, I'm her nephew," Gavin replied. He noticed the sheriff's demeanor immediately softened and he removed his hand from the butt of his gun.

"You're Maggie's nephew?" Winston said with a big grin. "Young, yeah that was her maiden name. Well, how about that! Why didn't you say so straight off?"

"I didn't think you would know her."

"Believe me, son," the sheriff said suggestively, "I know Maggie very well. All right, Gavin Young, pack up your gear and I'll drive you into Creekside. Better to spend a gallon of gas on you than having to fill out paper work when some dog drags your femur into town. Besides, I can't let Maggie's nephew walk into town, I'd never hear the end of it."

Sheriff Winston made no move to help Gavin pack up. He leaned against his silver and gold Dodge Ram and smoked a cigarette while occasionally giving Gavin a bored look.

Finally he groused, "They don't let me smoke in the Justice Center, and I'm the friggin' sheriff. I swear they're going to make everything a crime one of these days." He flicked an ash off his Marlboro and added, "By the way, if you don't mind me asking, what's the scar on your head, son?"

Gavin took a moment from his packing to touch the crimson scar that ran down the left side of his head to his ear. "I had a tumor. They think they got all of it but I'm not so sure."

Sheriff Winston dropped the cigarette and stomped it out in the dirt. "Why's that?"

"I'm having a lot of headaches now, different than the ones I had before," he replied as he zippered up the backpack. "They don't know why. I just do." As he looked at the ground he added, "And they're getting worse. I'm taking a semester off because I'm not able to concentrate. It's just the not knowing of when another attack will happen. I've had a few in class and it wasn't a pretty sight."

Winston bobbed his big hound dog head. "Severe headaches are not a pleasant thing. My wife had migraines that would stop her in her tracks for days at a time."

"Were the doctors able to help her?"

"No," the sheriff said softly as he walked over and picked up Gavin's backpack and tossed it into the back of the pickup. "Get in."

Pine and birch forest thick with marshlands blurred by as the sheriff's truck made its way along the two lane road to Creekside. Brilliant splashes of autumnal gold amidst the fading green of summer reflected off the stream that the road was paralleling towards town.

"So, where are you from Gavin?" the sheriff asked after a companionable silence.

"Milwaukee, but I'm living in Madison now."

"Go Badgers! I hope they get another shot at the Rose Bowl this year," the sheriff said with a grin. "So, how did you get north of Creekside if you came from Madison? Don't they teach geography anymore?"

"The bus driver said that it was faster to go to Woodruff and then down. Guess I overshot the mark."

Winston snorted. "You can't really blame the driver, kid—not many people know where Creekside is located. Hell, it's not even on my GPS and *everything* is on my GPS. Like I said, I live just a few miles from here so I'm pretty familiar with this area."

To his right Gavin noticed a flock of birds circling off in the distance. It was difficult to see so far back in the woods but he thought he glimpsed a church spire just above the tree line.

"Is that Creekside?" Gavin asked and pointed towards the birds.

"No, that's the Rookery. Or at least that's what we call it now," the sheriff replied, not looking towards where Gavin was pointing. "It used to be the old Morgan Company quarry and the town of Morgan. The limestone played out and the town dissolved back in the mid 1940s. Amish—or whatever they are—have taken it over. They built their own little community. You talk about Creekside not being sociable—they make Creekside look like boozed up coeds in Cancun!"

"So, why's it called the Rookery?"

"The old church there burnt in a fire back in the sixties," Winston explained, adopting a somber tone. "The town was long since dead so it was never rebuilt. It became a home for wildlife. Lots of birds roost there now, mostly blackbirds and crows. When the religious community moved in they never rebuilt it. In fact, the bird population has grown significantly since they arrived."

Gavin cocked a curious eyebrow. "Odd that they wouldn't rebuild a church—I mean, a religious community and all."

"Not strange for them," said Winston, shooting the boy a meaningful glance. "You'll often see them in Creekside. Quiet people; *peculiar* people—always polite, but they give me the willies sometimes. You know how it's possible to be *too* nice? But we never have any trouble with them so we basically let them be."

The sheriff shifted his bulk and went on. "I can't remember the last time I've been out to the Rookery. Nowadays I'd recommend staying away from there altogether. The wolves around here have gotten a taste of human flesh, and it's a long hike down a skinny dirt road to get there. I'm surprised that the folks at the Rookery haven't run into them yet, but I imagine it is just a matter of time. Damn protected species nonsense! If it whuddin' for all the government bullshit I'd take a group of hunters out there, and we'd have the problem solved."

Sheriff Winston pointed forward. "Well, we're coming up on the metropolis of Creekside. Don't blink."

The stream continued south but the road made a gentle bend to the left, then veered south again over a rusty metal bridge that spanned a feeder creek to the river. A metal sign bolted to the span proclaimed "Welcome to Creekside," and just below scattered bullet holes it continued: Population 346. *Tutela Lux Lucis*

"Sign's wrong," Winston said. "It's 345 as of last week. Old Paul Sanders passed. Ninety-eight years old! The old buzzard chalked it up to healthy living and good morals. Sounds like a boring way to live your life to me, but he was a stand-up guy."

Gavin surveyed the town as they drove down Main Street. "Not much here," he mumbled.

"Got that right." Winston glanced over at Gavin. "How old are you, kid?"

"Twenty-two."

"Well, forget about drinking in this town. Dry as a desert here. Not even a bar. There's no law against it; the yokels just don't imbibe so there's no market for it. Any bar here would go broke within a month. The last one folded about five years ago for lack of patronage. Imagine a town in Wisconsin without a bar!" Winston said with snort.

"Here, I'll give you the grand tour. It should take about a minute," the sheriff continued. "Over on the left you have Ed Graff's Buick Roadmaster lot. He's the largest dealer in Northern Wisconsin, as he never fails to remind me. Now I ask you, who the hell would buy a forty-five hundred pound tank of a station wagon from the nineties? It ain't my business, but it should be a crime. Next to that is the dollar store, which used to be a Woolworth until that folded. The Cluck and Grunt on the right is an okay diner for bacon and eggs but stay away from the chili. I tried it once and farted like a sick dog for a solid week. There's Caroline's Bed and Breakfast up State Street, which is the happening place on Friday nights for sheepshead, if you like card games. At the end of Main you have your Citgo, in case you decide you're done with walking and buy one of Graff's Roadmasters, or just pop in and listen to Josh Barber sling the bull if you're completely bored."

Looking down a cul-de-sac to his right that backed up on Mill Creek, Gavin noticed a large cream brick church. The steeple seemed similar to the one he had seen poking above the forest at the Rookery. The sign in front of the building said Evangelical Lutheran Church of Creekside. The notice board below it, with its black clip on letters over a faded white plastic backing, proclaimed with startling irreverence: JESUS SAID, BRING ME THAT ASS.

Gavin could feel Winston looking at him. "That is the place to be on Sunday's," the sheriff said. "They pack it to the rafters; everyone in town will be there. Are you a churchgoer?"

"Uh, no, not really, never saw the point of it."

Winston eyed Gavin ruefully. "Oh son, don't say that in front of Maggie or she'll kick your ass! First time you say you don't need to go to church your butt is hers!"

"Now you have me worried. Last time I met her I was twelve and don't really remember that much about her."

"Understand," the sheriff replied in a serious tone, "she is by far the best woman you will ever find on God's green earth. Didja notice that motto on the sign coming into town—*Tutela Lux Lucis*? It means *Protecting Light*, and they take that very seriously here; Maggie most of all."

Margaret McKenzie's house was a two-story Victorian wearing peeling white paint over gingerbread woodwork. It sat just up the hill on State Street with a commanding view of the Hansen Mini-Mart's roof. Sheriff Winston swung his truck around and pulled up in front of the home. "I'll see you to the door. Make sure you don't get lost."

"Thanks," Gavin replied as he opened the car door and stood up. A wave of dizziness and nausea stopped him, and he had to cling to the car roof as his vision turned Creekside into a lightning storm.

"Are you alright, kid? You're pale as a ghost."

"Yeah, sure," Gavin lied bravely, wiping the sweat from his forehead, as the lightning slowly started to disperse from his vision. He felt as if he were back in Madison with his professor looking down at him, asking if he needed to see the school nurse.

The walk up the stairs to the front door left Gavin out of breath, even though Winston was carrying his backpack. The sheriff put it down and rang the doorbell.

After a few moments the door opened and a woman in faded jeans and a blouse of gold and red flowers answered the door. Her face was tan and chiseled, but her childish dimples and crooked smile framed by locks of red hair softened her demeanor. Although late middle-aged, she had a girlish charm that immediately put Gavin at ease. Unfortunately it did not seem to have the same effect on the Sheriff, who returned an awkward smile.

"Why, Clarence, what a wonderful surprise!"

"Maggie," Sheriff Clarence Winston replied as he stared at his shoes. "I brought you something I found alongside the road."

She turned her gaze upon Gavin and beamed at him. "My, my, my, it's Gavin! Welcome! You've grown into a man since I've last set eyes on you, and you're the spitting image of my brother. Your mother said you would be dropping by to visit for a while. I have a room all set for you." She returned her attention to the sheriff. "Clarence, please come in."

"I really should be getting back to work, Maggie," said Winston, fidgeting like a schoolboy. "Creekside is a cesspool of crime, you know."

Margaret cocked her head and laughed. "Get yourself in here Clarence Horatio Winston Jr.! I've never known you to be rude to a lady."

As they walked into the living room Gavin noticed that the house was decorated with what could best be described as time-warped, hippie-inspired Nepali Scottish fusion. On one wall of the living room was a large silk banner with the word Kathmandu spelled out in the embroidered roots of a marijuana plant. Below that was a recliner with a plaid tartan quilt on it. Notable by its absence was a television.

Maggie observed Gavin's forlorn expression and commented, "Guess you noticed—not a lot of fancy technology in this house. I'm afraid I've been passed by as far as modern conveniences."

"Maggie is what's left of the hippie movement, Gavin," Winston put in.

She grinned. "And fortunately I can't remember much of it."

"Gavin, you're flushed!" she said with concern, putting her hands up to his cheeks. "Your mother filled me in on your condition. Why don't you go upstairs and rest a bit. Your room is the door down the hall and to the right, directly above where we are now. I put out some fruit and candy, and there's a mini-fridge with some soda and juice in it. Don't bother about us. I need to spend some time catching up with Clarence here anyway."

"I think I will," Gavin responded, slightly embarrassed that it was only ten in the morning and he needed to rest, but passing out from pain didn't really count as sleep. Reaching down by Winston's feet, he lifted his backpack and climbed the stairs.

———

"Clarence, come with me," Maggie ordered as they walked into the kitchen that was wrapped around a picnic-style table that was far too large for the room. She grasped his hands and said, "It's been too long. We see each other so seldom nowadays."

Seeing that she was embarrassing him she let go and added, "Would you like some coffee?"

"No thanks," Clarence replied and then exhaled loudly. "I'm concerned, though, about the kid being here. This isn't exactly a welcoming town as you know."

"I realize that, but his mother practically begged me to take him for a while. She knows my story, and she thought something similar would happen here for Gavin—some turning point. When you are a mother you want the best for your boy, and I can't refuse my brother's wife."

Maggie paused. "Gavin has problems—"

"I know," Winston cut in. "He told me about a brain tumor."

Maggie nodded. "They say he's cured but he keeps getting worse. His mother says he has headaches and dizziness quite often nowadays."

Clarence folded his arms. "So, what do you expect to happen here? Wouldn't it be better if he were in Madison with doctors instead of out here in the middle of a godforsaken Wisconsin forest?"

Maggie gestured vaguely with her head towards the town of Morgan. "Perhaps the community can help."

Winston sighed. "Maggie, you know how I feel about that sort of thing—"

"Don't try to tell me what I know and what I don't know!" she snapped. "I'd be dead without them." Her voice rose. "Dead and buried in some shallow grave in Pokhara, Nepal, if it weren't for those people whom you so easily dismiss as crackpots. Don't you ever tell me that I don't know what's possible."

Winston threw up his arms, "Okay, do what you think is best. Just watch out if you bring him around the Rookery. There are wolves out there, and they don't care if you're on a mission of mercy, they only care if you taste good. I'd hate to see either of you hurt."

"Understood," she said curtly.

Sheriff Winston had started to leave when Maggie touched his arm lightly. "Why do we always end up in an argument? There was a time when we didn't."

The sheriff looked in her eyes an infinitesimal moment, smiled weakly, and walked out.

CHAPTER THREE

The setting sun passed through the scratched windows of the Cluck and Grunt, reflecting off an aluminum pie stand that held a slice of crystalizing lemon meringue and directly into the eyes of Trudy.

"So ends another day in paradise," she said while walking over to close the blinds.

"I'm beat," Rachel added as she collapsed on a stool in front of the cash register. She reached up removed her hair net and shook out her long locks and put her forehead on the counter with a sigh. It was closing time and the hectic day clearly had worn Rachel to a frazzle. "I never realized how difficult it is to work for a living."

"Welcome to my world," Trudy said as she came over and patted her on the back. "You did well for a first day. How were the tips?"

Rachel raised her head and looked at her. "They gave me a lot of money for just doing my job. Why is that?"

"How much does Bill pay you per hour?"

"Two dollars and thirty-five cents," Rachel replied proudly. "That's a lot of money, isn't it?"

"Uh, no," Trudy said. "So there you have it. They feel sorry for you."

"A lot of them don't have much money either," Rachel said. "I don't want them spending it on me."

"They tip you because they are happy with your service," Trudy said. "Just thank them and don't worry. It's what's expected."

"They're happy with what I did?"

Trudy sat down next to her at the counter. "Why are you so surprised?"

"Because I don't know what I'm doing! This is all so new to me. A man ordered his eggs over easy—what is that anyway? Bill gave me some eggs that didn't look like they were fully cooked. I didn't know if I should give them to the customer or send it back. Can't you get sick from eating them that way?"

Trudy scowled. "You can get sick off of anything we serve here. Look, you're a kind and caring person. People sense that. You'll get the bigger tips. They tolerate me, but they like you. Plus, they respect you."

Rachel paled. "Are they are giving me money because of …?"

"*Pfft.* No! Get over yourself," Trudy snorted, causing Rachel to stare back open-mouthed. Then, turning to look through the pass to the kitchen, she hollered to the cook, that seemed more closely related to a bear than a human: "Hey, Bill, what do you think of our new server? How's that skill set they taught her over in Morgan?"

Bill looked up from the grill he was cleaning, wiped his nose on his sleeve, and gave a bored, "Meh."

"Well, there you go," Trudy said, hugging Rachel. "Hey, we're family here, remember? If anyone is going to treat you like crap it will be your family. Now, go on, get yourself back to Morgan and put your feet up—we're going to have another busy day tomorrow."

———

The sun was setting as Gavin awoke and realized that he slept through most of the day. How long had he been out? There wasn't a clock in the room but it didn't surprise him that umpteen years later, his aunt was still on Nepali time. The headache had receded, its force not nearly as bad as the night before.

His mother had told him that everything had a purpose. This he doubted as he stretched and walked to the window. There certainly was no purpose to being in Creekside. As far as he could ascertain there wasn't even a purpose *for* Creekside.

He came downstairs and found his aunt on the floor in the living room, looking through a photo album. "Sorry, I overslept," he yawned.

Maggie smiled up at him. "Don't be sorry. You needed your rest. Do you feel any better?"

"Much."

"Glad to hear it. I was just looking over some old photos of mine, friends that have come and gone. Sentimental old woman memories, I'm afraid. Nothing you'd be interested in." She closed the album and held it to her chest. "So, what would you like to do tonight? I bet you're hungry."

Gavin sat down in the chair next to Maggie. She looked frail, sitting there on the floor, clutching her book of memories—very different than his first impression of her. "Why am I here?" he asked.

"Your parents didn't tell you?"

"My mother rattled off something in her own stream of consciousness way that didn't make much sense. Whatever it was, my dad certainly wasn't impressed. He sat on a folding chair out in the garage that first night drinking Leinenkugel until he passed out."

Maggie smiled. "My brother is a stoic one. He'd prefer to sit by himself and drink rather than open up."

"So why *am* I here?" Gavin asked again.

She patted his knee. "Because your mother loves you; your father, too, in his way—unless, of course, it conflicts with one of his cherished beliefs."

"That doesn't really explain why she tosses me on a bus to the middle of nowhere, saying things about miraculous healings," Gavin replied. "So I get up here, expecting to see a giant circus tent with some preacher in a white tux tossing crutches onto the stage and passing the hat. Instead I see a sleepy little town surrounded by forest that looks like it hasn't had the slightest sliver of anything interesting happening there for at least two centuries."

"Gavin," his aunt said gently, "we often take the extraordinary for granted, perhaps none more than the residents of Creekside. If I were to tell you how truly interesting this town is you'd be on the first bus back to Milwaukee to tell your mother that I've lost my mind. Sometimes it is better to discover on your own. Once you get settled I'll take you to a dear friend of mine who once saved my life. If he could do that for me, then a little headache"—her tone suggested she was trying to downplay the seriousness of his illness—"shouldn't be so difficult."

Maggie worked her way off the floor. "It's hell getting old," she grunted, grasping the chair arm for support. "So, what would you like to do? Our only restaurant is closing up right about now but I can make you something."

He thought for a moment. "I grabbed an apple upstairs. I think right now I'd just like to take a walk and spend some time alone." He added, "I don't mean to be rude."

Maggie smiled. "Not rude at all! You're not a prisoner here. Go see Creekside. Stop by Mill Creek and enjoy the beauty. There really is beauty here if you look for it."

"I'll be back soon," Gavin said as he walked towards the front door.

State Street sloped down to Main and Gavin let gravity do its work. He stopped at the corner of Main and State next to the mini-mart and pondered which way to go. Either direction only lasted for several blocks, and from his vantage point he could see the NOW LEAVING CREEKSIDE signs to the south and north. He decided to go north and started walking up Main. From the cornerstones he surmised that most of the buildings were built in the mid eighteen hundreds. The drab brick walls, coated with the soot of long abandoned factories, gave testament that a pressure washer had never entered the town.

Gavin stopped midway down the street. He glanced over at the diner with the awkward name of the Cluck and Grunt as it went dark. A moment later a young woman with bobbed black hair and a rumpled pink uniform closed the door and locked it. Head down, she proceeded south on Main.

He continued walking until he was at the iron bridge that Sheriff Winston had brought him across earlier in the day. The sun dipped below the horizon and the first stars had begun to appear. The manmade lights of Creekside faded as he crossed the bridge out of town. It became another near moonless night, and the darkness quickly enveloped him as he sat down in the grass next to Mill Creek.

Gavin watched the creek as it made its way over the worn granite rocks that at one time, many thousands of years ago, were crushed under the weight of glaciers that covered the Midwest. His aunt was correct. There was beauty here. Not the manufactured kind that he was used to in the city but a natural beauty that helped him to relax. He felt the stress from his shoulders release as he listened to the creek, which was really a lot wider than he imagined anything with the name "creek" should be, and looked up at the night sky.

As the night grew darker he noticed a band of lightning to northwest, causing him to stand up and look off to the distance.

This lightning seemed different than what he was used to, so Gavin climbed up on the bridge railing to get a better view of it. Holding on to one of the girders he scanned the distant forest. It was coming from the Rookery area, and unlike normal lightning it did not change position, fade, or create thunder. It was a solid, glowing tower of light, larger near the treetops, and becoming finer and more delicate as it rose into the sky. Filigrees wrapped in and out of the column, twisting off into horizontal branches as it pushed further into the sky. It continued unabated, its blindingly bright central core writhing with power as it threw out bluish ribbons of light.

Gavin could feel the electricity in the air as the static charge pulsed against him and then began burrowing its way through his flesh. The hair on his arms bristled at the pulse as his scalp began to itch. The lightning that he carried with him in his brain began to cycle in cadence with the external horizontal flashes, blending into one. The amazing thing for Gavin was that, for the first time, the lightning brought no pain.

Gavin jumped down from the rail and sat on the ground with his back against the bridge, fascinated by the light show before him. He never knew that lightning could be so beautiful or that it could be so precise. It didn't seem possible, and yet there it was before him.

Eventually, he stood up. Not a car had passed since he sat down, which was a testament to how forsaken Creekside was. Slowly he headed towards Maggie's, not knowing how much time had passed, with only the occasional backward glance at the light show scintillating in the distance.

Gavin quietly opened the door and looked inside. The light was on in the hallway but Maggie was nowhere to be seen. Locking the door behind him he crept upstairs, trying to be as quiet as possible.

Reaching his room, he walked over to the window and opened it. The lightning was still visible in the distance—bluish white arms twisting in the night sky, almost as if it were a living being. Dragging a chair over to the window, he sat down. He could still feel the electricity coming off of the lightning from behind the wall. Gavin grabbed an apple out of the basket on the table and leaned back, putting his feet on the window sill. For once, he felt at peace.

CHAPTER FOUR

The Reverend Jay Masters cut off yet another car as he maneuvered his way to work. The Wisconsin Dells tourist traffic picked up in the late morning as visitors from around the Midwest flocked to the roller coasters and indoor water parks that made the Dells a low budget Disney World. Tourists wandered out of restaurants and began their trek towards the many famous and infamous attractions that the Dells presented. He took a moment to continue a decade-long tradition as he swerved his BMW X5 off of the road, over the sidewalk, and onto the damp grass in front of the Tommy Bartlett Water Ski Show entrance, in the process almost running over a family in matching Branson, Missouri, sweatshirts. Glaring at the Bartlett sign that proclaimed twenty-five hundred seats under cover, he lifted his hand, stuck out his middle finger, and flipped it off.

"Here's your morning bird, o' Tommy boy," he shouted as he spun his tires in the mossy grass near the sidewalk. He swerved back onto the road and continued a quarter mile to the Hilton and hung a right, down a once quiet street that used to be a sedate neighborhood near the lake but now was a vast expanse of asphalt with perhaps a dozen cars lined up, almost all of them belonging to his employees. His building, a 50,000 square foot corrugated metal warehouse, sat at the rear of the property. The facade was embellished with curved fiberglass panels of dark black that reached up into the sky on steel poles, projecting the look of a Goth circus tent. The exterior maintained its sinister appearance except for a yellow and orange neon sign that proclaimed without subtlety MASTERS' MYSTERIUM.

The Reverend drove around to the back of the building and honked his horn. A large metal garage door lifted open, and he drove inside. Extracting his super-sized frame from the vehicle and adjusting his H. Huntsman tailored suit, he motioned for the door to be lowered. The repo man was on the prowl, and he couldn't expect the pimply high school students he employed as lot attendants to properly guard his vehicle.

"Good morning, Reverend," the nineteen-year-old maintenance manager said as he ran over to close the door.

Masters didn't acknowledge his existence as he left the musty smell of the garage and entered the Mysterium proper. He usually began the day by inspecting his kingdom. The Mysterium was a collection of every oddity, rumor, hearsay, improbable event, and conundrum created by nature or man. Although the *Milwaukee Journal Sentinel* once called his empire "the remnants that the Believe It or Not museums refused to take," it was the culmination of Reverend Masters' dream.

Ambling past a display of New Guinea penis sheaths, Masters reflected upon his journey. More like reveled in it. He had started just out of high school in the early nineties on the Southern faith healing circuit, making a good dollar off some slick lines, a microphone hidden between the bosoms of his convincingly concerned and comforting assistant who worked the crowds and transmitted directly into Masters' earpiece for those all-important words of knowledge and a cheap diploma from an unaccredited seminary that he found an ad for in an issue of *Popular Mechanics*. His true success was followed ten years later by the exposé and the subpoena.

Upon moving back to the Midwest ten thousand dollars in fines poorer, an idea hit. He remembered that state fairs were popular with the yokels and a buck could be earned by giving the populace an oddity to ponder. He toured through the Corn Belt for several years with Gertrude the Giant Horse—a popular attraction because, unlike most of the competition, it was not a hoax. At almost nineteen hands high and 2,500 pounds, Gertrude was indeed a giant horse. Unfortunately, the overhead was extreme, for Gertrude also ate like a giant horse. Months later he abandoned the attraction when the old mare fell over and nearly crushed a pensioner. Masters put her down and stuffed her the very next day.

He approached the turntable that now held the mammoth beast's lifelike carcass. She still awed the suckers, but now the old girl only required a dusting once a month. He used the reflective black Plexiglas of Gertrude's rotating turntable to preen as he straightened his Versace tie and admired the sparkle of his diamond pinky ring under the spotlight. Times had been tough lately, but he still prided himself on his appearance. At six and a half feet tall, he made for an imposing figure and used it to his advantage. A fine pinstriped suit accentuated his height while simultaneously intimidating those around him. Masters glanced down a final time only to be greeted by the reflection of a horse's ass.

"Jay!" came a muffled shout from the corner. "Get your ass in here now!"

The Reverend turned to face his well-endowed administrative assistant.

"Holly, that isn't a proper way to speak to your employer," he reprimanded her as he openly ogled the thirty-year-old's ample manmade cleavage and two-sizes-too-small dress. "I do like the dress though."

"Yeah, well, so does your appointment. I can't keep one of them from grabbing my boob," she retorted sharply. "I slapped his hand away, but he just grins and tries it again."

"Well, that's why I hired you, isn't it?" Masters rebutted as he walked over to her. "Office work isn't your forte now, is it?"

"I can entertain the normal lowlifes you bring through here, but not these crackers. Where did you find them anyway? It's like they crawled out of a swamp or something."

The Reverend smiled. "Not a swamp," he replied. "Better—a bog in the Upper Peninsula, which means they're perfect for the job. Go have a smoke or something, I'll deal with them."

Masters waved Holly away to compose herself while he went upstairs to meet his newest employees. He noticed that the white Berber carpet of the stairway had muddy footprints on it. "Damn," he growled.

As he entered Holly's work area he noticed three men rummaging through her desk.

"Hey, assholes!" he shouted. "What are you doing?"

The tallest of the three stood up and said, "Just looking to see if the little lady kept any of her unmentionables in the desk. It gets a little lonely out in the woods, if you know what I mean."

A feeling swept over the Reverend which he seldom had: disgust. The man who spoke had the confidence of the leader of the group. Masters assessed them as they continued rummaging. All three seemed as if they dropped out of *Deliverance* into the family-friendly Wisconsin Dells. They all looked to be in their mid-thirties, two with stringy mullets, one bald.

The probable leader held up a thong. "Jackpot!"

"I hope you didn't scare any of my customers when you came in," Masters said through gritted teeth. "Get into my office. We've got a lot to go over."

The Reverend's office was on the second floor of his Mysterium with a row of windows overlooking Lake Delton. Off to the right he could see a glimpse of the water ski show stadium. The view was beautiful, but also a bitter reminder that he was not king fish on this lake. Tommy Bartlett may be long gone but his vision remained to torture Masters each day as he subsisted on the overflow that the famed water ski show—replete with gaudy old-fashioned showmanship and unabashed patriotism—created.

The Reverend's glory was back in 2008 when the lake was eroded by flooding to the point of draining out entirely. It put the water ski show out of business for all intents and purposes for about a year. A year of pain for Masters' business as well, as the muddy lake bed sprouted weeds and stank of dead fish. The Mysterium may have suffered decreased attendance but there was joy in knowing it hurt the so-called Greatest Show on H20 even more.

"So, gentlemen," the Reverend began sarcastically as the mullets started towards two plush chairs lined up in front of his desk. "Don't sit. It takes time to get a burning permit in this town."

Then the leader spoke. "I'm Theodore Winslow, and this here is my brother Pervis." He pointed to the second mullet. Then, motioning to the bald bumpkin that was swigging from a bottle of Jack Daniels found on Masters ornate oak cabinet, he said, "That there is Buck."

Buck smiled a gap-toothed grin and offered a liquor soaked belch.

"Am I supposed to care?" Masters said impatiently. "Do you know why I hired you three hillbillies?"

"Yes," Theodore said. "You want us to trap something for you."

Masters slapped a hand on his forehead. "Not trap, you idiot. I want it dead. Live is expensive. Dead is more cost effective in my line of work."

Theodore smiled. "Well, that's what we do best. Killing is our specialty."

"Finally some good news today," Masters continued as he waved his hand about. "Here's the deal. Up north above Rhinelander there is a little town called Creekside. Due to an unfortunate circumstance called marriage, I spent a year in that place. It's a hemorrhoid on the ass of our fair state. I bet you boys will like it."

"What do you need killing up there, the wife?" Theodore snickered.

Masters didn't find the humor. "No, she's already dead, thank you very much. There have been rumors of something in the woods for the last few months. The locals think it is either a lone wolf or a pack. There have been rumors coming in from northern Wisconsin, Michigan, and Minnesota that something much larger and more interesting might be out there, so I sent a hunter up there a while back. Turns out the hunter and my wife now share the same graveyard."

"So, what is it then?" Pervis asked, seemingly interested for the first time.

"I'm not sure, but if it's something out of the ordinary, even a massive wolf, I can market it to the suckers. Trust me, I can market anything to the rubes. If you bring it back dead, and it's something I can use, I'll pay you ten grand for your efforts. Bring back nothing, you get nothing."

"But we'll have expenses," Theodore countered.

"What kind of expenses?" Masters grumbled. "You guys don't look like you stay at the Ritz, and I doubt any of you have come in contact with a shower in the last month or two."

Theodore's eyes narrowed threateningly.

Unfazed, Masters paused, a finger to his pursed lips in thought. "Look, I'll give you a couple hundred for the necessities—food, booze, and *Hustler* magazines. If you are as good as I was told—and believe me, after looking at you guys I'm not feeling it—then it shouldn't take you much time to do the job. You probably won't get past the centerfold before you're back in civilization."

"Sounds fair to me," Theodore spoke for the group.

"Okay, then get out of my office before I have to fumigate." Motioning to Buck, he added, "And take that bottle of Jack with you. I don't think even alcohol could kill whatever backwash you put in that bottle. Oh, and if you see Holly on your way out, keep your hands off of her. She's mine."

"Yes, Mr. Masters," Theodore replied.

"*Reverend* Masters," Jay growled. "I worked hard for that title, boy."

———

Gavin bounded down the stairs and greeted his aunt in the living room. She was reading a book on the couch just underneath the six foot wide banner of Kathmandu.

"Well," she said, looking him up and down with a smile. "You look a lot fresher than that poor thing Clarence dragged in yesterday. Sorry I couldn't stay up for you. I trust you didn't get into too much trouble last night?"

"It's a wild town I must admit," he said, even though he was distracted by the drug-promoting banner.

She looked up behind her, "My one souvenir from a previous life," she said. "I was fresh out of college, and I wanted to see the world before being relegated to being a pharmacist in a Walgreens. So a girlfriend and I bought a Europass and planned to tour Europe for a couple of months. Turns out, we didn't get out of Amsterdam."

Maggie leaned back on the couch and motioned for him to have a seat. "The drug culture was prevalent in Amsterdam, and we dove in head first. Fitting, I guess, for a pharmacist to be fascinated with drugs. From our contacts there with other youths supposedly trying to find themselves, we heard that the drugs were better and cheaper in Asia, so I had my parents wire me some more money so that we could visit the museums in Germany. Actually, we hopped the Magic Bus heading down the drug trail. We spent a few months in Afghanistan and then moved down to India for about a year, and finally to the end of the drug trail in Nepal."

Maggie hesitated for a second. "Your mother knows this, but don't tell your father—I'm afraid my brother wouldn't be very receptive to his sister's former debauchery. Anyway, I spent two years in Kathmandu, mostly in upstairs rooms on Freak Street selling myself for drug money. Rich European hikers would come through on their way for Everest or Annapurna treks. Most didn't want to take their chances on Nepali women so I was quite popular."

Gavin was shocked by such a forthright declaration from her. He couldn't grasp that his aunt was once a prostitute. "I—I had no idea," he stammered.

Maggie looked down with a pained expression. "I lost Nancy there. She died from an overdose on a back street in Kathmandu. People just walked around her like she was a piece of trash. I had long ago sold my passport for drug money, so there was no going back to the States without doing a hefty jail sentence. Instead I took the bus to a more remote spot to hopefully curl up and die. I was lakeside in Pokhara, basically trying to beg for food from the westerners and competing with the water buffalo that wandered the streets for table scraps. It was there that I met Jonathan, the person I'll be introducing you to. It was an awkward meeting; I offered myself to him for ten dollars."

Maggie smiled sheepishly at the incredulity in her nephew's eyes and continued. "He said no, of course, and would have been overpaying if he did; my body was completely shot by that time. Instead, he offered to bring me back to his community that was located on a hill with a beautiful view of Machapuchare, which is part of the Annapurna range of mountains. I was malnourished and an addict, really in bad shape. I didn't trust them at first, this cult on a hill in the middle of nowhere, but they took care of me nonetheless.

"Even with the love they were showing me I felt like my life had no worth. I left the community one evening, intent on using one of those spectacular vistas to end my life. I figured a thousand foot drop should do the trick." She looked at Gavin with moist eyes. "Jonathan saved me that night from certain death in a way that was so astounding that I could never again live the way I once did."

"What did he do?"

Maggie smiled. "Don't you enjoy cliffhangers? Right now you wouldn't believe me, so let's just say that miracles still happen, and I expect one for you as well.

"Want to grab some breakfast at the Cluck and Grunt?" she asked, and then, perhaps sensing Gavin's apprehension, quickly added, "I promise that it's better than its name."

"Sure," he said, still wishing that she would share more but not wanting to push like a little boy asking for more stories at bedtime.

The walk to the diner was a short one: down the hill on State Street, across Main Street, and to the right. The Cluck and Grunt was a hole in the wall that looked like it had been part of Creekside for decades. Creekside's architecture would have been very novel in its pre-Civil War day, he realized. Most of the buildings were constructed of Cream City brick that must have been railed in from Milwaukee. The porous bricks would have been a light yellow color and quite lovely when new but now have picked up decades of accumulated smoke, smog, and grime, turning them nearly black. As they entered he noticed that the interior consisted of nicotine-encrusted fake wood paneling with faded photographs of the *old* Creekside, all of which looked depressingly like the current Creekside just outside the windows. There were only two distinguishing features of the restaurant that Gavin could see. One was the lighted fiberglass sign above the counter showing a cannibalistic chicken and a pig dancing amidst a landscape of eggs and bacon. The other was the waitress behind the counter with wild brunette hair and piercing blue eyes. Gavin smiled absently as the glint from her faux diamond nose stud reflected in his vision.

The waitress looked up from behind the counter to glower at him. Then her eyes went to the right as she noticed Margaret. She broke into a wide smile. "Maggie! How the hell are you?"

"Trudy," Gavin's aunt said as they approached the counter, "I'd like you to meet my nephew, Gavin Young. Gavin, Trudy Masters. Trudy's the only woman in town that understands me."

"Yeah, the outcasts flock together," Trudy said while motioning towards the bar stools at the counter. "Take a seat." She jerked her chin to a perky blonde waitress taking an order at a booth across the restaurant. "Speaking of outcasts, look what I've got for help."

Maggie looked over her shoulder and gasped. "Are you serious? I don't understand…"

"Rachel wanted to work in a *real* job." Trudy shot her hands up, making quotation marks. "Be like the *real people* she says. Grouchy over there"—she pointed to the large man behind the grill—"he's desperate for help. Not a lot of menial laborers around here to choose from. Since Clara left I've been trying to cover two shifts. Unsuccessfully, I might add."

Rachel came around the counter to put her order in at the pass and Trudy motioned her over. "Don't be so nice to the customers, you're creeping them out."

"I just want to make sure that they are being taken care of," she said with a pout.

Trudy exhaled a derisive breath. "If you're too nice they think you're trying to cover for the food or something. Be a bit slow and inattentive, but not too slow and inattentive because the food *is* crap. Look at this place. This isn't a Michelin-starred restaurant or anything."

Rachel stared back at her blankly.

"Never mind, just go take table eight's order," Trudy said in an exasperated voice.

Margaret pulled close to Trudy. "I know she's your friend and all, but is this going to work? Their social skills when they are new are shall we say ... lacking."

"She's okay," Trudy said. "She's getting the hang of it. It's only her second day. She just needs experience. I'll look out after her."

For the first time Trudy looked at Gavin. "So, what brings you to the lovely village of Creekside?"

"I'm not really sure," he replied, not willing to kill his chances with one of the few women his age in town by telling the truth.

"Well, I guess you'll fit in. None of us are really sure why we are here, either," Trudy admitted.

Rachel came back to put another order in. This time she stopped and spoke to Gavin's aunt. "Maggie, how are you doing? Brother Jonathan was hoping to pay you a visit sometime. He enjoys talking with you about Nepal."

"He knows he's always welcome," Maggie replied. "He's my dearest friend around here."

Gavin couldn't help but ask Rachel, "You're from the Rookery, right?"

All three women gave him a simultaneous stink eye.

"What?" he said defensively, looking around at them.

"Yes, I'm from Morgan," Rachel said evenly as she picked up the coffee pot to make her rounds.

"Rachel, this is my nephew, Gavin Young. He hasn't been informed of the sensitivities that go along with that name."

"Gavin," Maggie informed him, "The Rookery is a bit of a derogatory term that was used of Morgan when the community that Rachel is a part of first moved in. A lot of people in the area are very set in their ways and couldn't understand why the church was not rebuilt. A number of people welcomed Rachel's community to the area, thinking that the lovely cream brick building would be restored. It didn't sit well with some of them when it wasn't."

"I apologize," Gavin said to Rachel, which also seemed to serve the purpose of softening Trudy's stone-like countenance.

"Last night," he continued, "I saw some lights off over the—uh, Morgan. It was like lightning but larger and more defined. It was just a continuous pulsing white trunk with bluish sparks coming off the sides."

Rachel paled while Trudy and Maggie looked at him with confused expressions.

"Do you know what that was?" he asked.

"You—you saw the lightning?" Rachel said in a shaky voice as she lowered the coffee pot onto Trudy's arm.

"*Ow!*" Trudy yelled, as Gavin noticed the side of her arm already swelling.

Gavin instinctively put his hand towards the burn and a static spark flew between his finger and her arm.

"*Ow!*" Trudy yelled again as she batted his hand away.

"Gavin!" Maggie exclaimed. "What was that?"

"Sorry," Gavin said, looking at Maggie in bewilderment. "I don't know."

"I'm so sorry." Rachel said. "Trudy, here, put it under cold water." She dragged her friend over to the sink and turned on the faucet.

"This day isn't living up to even my meager expectations," Trudy said as she held her arm under the stream.

Rachel took off her apron and looked at Trudy with a panicked expression. "I've got to leave."

Trudy attempted to calm her. "It's okay, Rachel, accidents happen. I'm not mad."

"I know," Rachel said as she turned to stare at Gavin. "It's something else. I've got to get back to Morgan now."

"Are you going to leave in the middle of a shift?" Trudy complained. "Granted, it's not busy but I'm the injured one here, remember?"

"I'm sorry," Rachel said. "I'll be back later if you'll take me but I've got get to Morgan now." With that, she ran out the door.

Trudy sighed as she watched Rachel leave. "And people think I'm strange."

CHAPTER FIVE

Reverend Masters stood before the floor to ceiling windows that overlooked his empire. He hoped beyond all hope that the three men that he had sent into the woods the previous day would perform better than the single one who couldn't even manage to keep his own heart beating. There were a lot of hunters in Wisconsin, and he was prepared to run through all of them if need be to bring back his trophy.

Looking down to his desk, he pushed the intercom button. "Holly, get your fat ass in here, please."

Holly Stenberg skittered into his office as quickly as her skintight dress and four-inch heels would allow. "What is it, Jay?"

"Those hunters the other day—"

"Tell me you sent them packing."

"They're doing a job for me," he replied. "You'll be getting calls from them from time to time with a status update. If they get fresh let me know, and I'll deal with it."

"Thanks," she said, obviously relieved. "They scare the bejesus out of me. Something's not right with them. The bald one that doesn't speak much, he's the worst."

"That's exactly why I hired them," Masters declared. "I'm guessing that this thing is predictable. It has its own routine and habits. Introducing those crazies into the equation might be just what we need."

He opened his desk drawer and pulled out a battered cell phone. "I haven't shown you this before. When that first hunter died, the sheriff department performed slipshod crime scene investigation. This was covered up in the dirt by the, shall we say, enthusiastic play habits of the creature. A bit of wandering and calling the guy's number on my part turned this baby up." He leered at his prize, adding, "The idiots missed the most important evidence of all."

Masters pushed a couple buttons and handed the phone to Holly. "Here are the last moments of the hunters encounter with the so-called wolf."

Holly took the phone and looked at the screen as Masters hovered over her shoulder as she watched. The scene looked like something out of *The Blair Witch Project*: trees spinning in circles, and then a shot of the ground. There was the sound of a man screaming in terror. With a jerky frame-rate the phone played back video of the last moments of the hunter's life. The hunter fell to the ground and the phone hit the dirt, camera up. The last seconds of the video showed the Beast.

It wasn't a wolf—that much was clear. Masters put a hand to Holly's waist and could feel her tensing up as she watched. The creature was huge, much larger than a wolf, and the features were not those of a recognizable animal. Not a creature that had ever been seen before on Animal Planet or at the zoo. What he found so unnerving were the eyes. The eyes were intelligent, and the eyes were filled with hate.

Holly screamed and dropped the phone, then began to cry.

"That's exactly what I was hoping for!" Masters said, pleased with her response as he picked the phone off of the floor. "Can you imagine what people will pay to see this thing? People pay to go to horror movies and see recreated evil. What if they can come here and see the real thing? That demon-possessed little bitch from *The Exorcist* is nothing compared to this! What if they can come here to see evil in its purist form?"

"What is that thing?" Holly whimpered. "What are you hunting?"

"It is our ticket to riches once I get it stuffed and posed in one of the galleries."

"If that thing comes here, I'll leave," she said in a soft tone, like the wind had been knocked out of her. "I love you, but I'm not staying if that monster is around."

"It'll be dead," Masters attempted to calm her. "It won't be able to hurt you."

"I don't care," she cried. "Did you see those eyes? I don't want to be in the same town with it, let alone the same building, dead or alive."

"Well, we'll cross that bridge when we come to it. For now I need those three nitwits to do their job."

———

Brother Jonathan sat on the steps to his porch in Morgan and contemplated the dull throb in his right knee. The community had been hoeing potatoes for nearly a week and it, he had to confess, was getting the better of him. A field to tend may look bucolic and peaceful but he had long ago found out that it was a painful and potentially dangerous place. His respect for farmers grew with each passing day as he pulled thorns and thistles from his garden, not to mention that the ragweed made him sneeze.

Looking across the open grass to the bright yellow gathering house on the opposite side of the square, he watched the inhabitants of Morgan going about their daily chores. It had taken a lot of time and sweat to rebuild the old quarry town into a habitable state. There wasn't much when they settled Morgan other than stone foundations and a few cracked chimneys. To see the scattered houses now with their freshly painted exteriors and flower pots hanging from their porches gave him a sense of accomplishment. Another lesson learned.

Morgan was not a large community, only about three dozen homes scattered amongst the woods. The main square was a grassy park with the large gathering house on one corner and the abandoned Morgan Lutheran Church on the other. The church had been vacant and in disrepair for several decades before the fire swept through to finish the job. Its once lovely cream brick exterior was now soot-stained and covered in bird droppings. The charred roof had a gash in it that ran down through the collapsed west wall, large enough to allow access to the local bird population—something they did with great frequency to nest and rear their young. What made the abandoned building an oddity was the blinding white column of light that shot through the torn roof and into the stratosphere.

Jonathan contemplated that for a normal religious community the rebuilding of the church would have been first on the list. He wondered if their neglect would bring up questions in the future similar to the scorn they first received as they arrived in Morgan, but he couldn't rebuild it with what it now contained. Besides, the birds had made it their nest, and he didn't have the heart to destroy what they had built with such labor a twig at a time.

The hair on the back of Jonathan's neck stood up. He had felt that same feeling many times before, but never at Morgan.

Slowly, Jonathan stood up and walked down the steps of the porch onto the fresh cut lawn.

Something was not right.

———

The Beast moved through the woods with an ease that belied its bulk. It had learned to live in this cursed forest and use it to its advantage. Now it actually preferred the forest darkness and the hidden places to that of the rice paddies and the woods-denuded hills of Nepal where it had last dwelt in this form.

It had finally located them, and its hatred burned within towards them. They had hidden themselves well this time, but they could not hide forever. The Beast had to be within a few hundred yards to sense them, and that meant months of roaming through the Midwestern woods in search of the loyalists. Now that they have been found, the Beast knew it would be rewarded.

Slowly, it crept near the center of Morgan. Padded feet kept it quiet, with only a slight clacking sound and a small spark when its claws hit upon a rock. Its death gray skin clung to its ribs as massive muscles moved it through the brush upon lion-like legs. How long had it taken to find them, five or six years? Time blurred for the Beast. It had been on the hunt for so long.

The Beast crept just inside the tree line in back of the abandoned church. There was no need for it to advance closer, as it could see that the building was dark and deserted, nothing more than a burnt out shell. Nothing worth wasting time on to explore.

Continuing around the outskirts it approached the rear of a house and could see a man standing next to it, gazing into the forest. The Beast cursed itself that it had been sensed. Crouching to the ground it froze in place, pulling its four bat-like wings of tattered skin close, and contemplated the next move.

A crashing through the woods to the Beast's right distracted the man as another figure came into view. The Beast could not help but enjoy how uncoordinated the bipedal forms were. Why have two legs when four work so much better?

"Brother Jonathan!" a blonde-haired girl shouted as she emerged from the forest.

The Beast's ears perked up upon hearing the name, as it remembered it had seen the male once before.

"Rachel!" the man said to the girl.

"I have news, brother," she gasped.

"Slow down, Rachel," he said. "Control, remember."

Bending over and resting her hands on her knees for a moment seemed to help calm her down. Raising back up, she proceeded. "There is a new boy in town. He sees the ladder."

With this news the Beast's attention rose, and it crept as close as it dared to the two.

"Surely that can't be," the one called Jonathan said. "It's impossible."

"This one can. I'm not sure how or why, but he described it perfectly to me."

"Who is he?"

"Gavin Young, he is a relative of Maggie."

The man looked up in the direction of the Beast. "We should go inside," he suggested.

The Beast slowly crept back into the deep woods. Was it possible, it thought? If so, then multi-year searches could be narrowed down to months, weeks perhaps.

The Beast had heard of this Maggie before. She was a pet of Jonathan's in Nepal. The Beast had many opportunities to pounce upon her but for some reason, never did. So many chances to rip her apart and have it blamed on a Yeti or whatever boogeyman the superstitious villagers could concoct to best describe a giant creature with claws and fangs. At the time it didn't understand why it couldn't gut her, but now it was glad. If she was dead in Nepal, then the Beast would have missed the choice opportunity before it.

Clearly it needed assistance to decide the best course of action going forward. Its masters would be pleased with the news. Perhaps one day they would let it out of the forest to feast upon Creekside.

CHAPTER SIX

Train's "Calling All Angels" blasted over the cheap speaker of Trudy's clock radio until it hit the wall. Trudy groaned as she lay in bed, looking up at the popcorn ceiling and cobwebs.

The doorbell rang.

"You're doing this on purpose," she said to the ceiling as she rose and staggered towards the door. "Who is it, as if I couldn't guess?"

"Rachel," was the perky reply.

Trudy batted her head against the door and said, "It's five in the morning. You don't start until seven."

"But I need to talk to you," Rachel pleaded.

Opening the door, Trudy was again presented with the immaculately uniformed blonde.

"I hope I still have a job," Rachel asked.

"Yeah," Trudy sighed. "Bill said that he needs the staff, and that after dealing with me his expectations are pretty low. But what's with running out and leaving me to deal with this burn?"

"What burn?"

Trudy looked down at her arm and the red swollen mass that ran for three inches down the inside of her arm was gone—completely gone. "Well, I'll be—it hurt like hell when I went to bed." Her eyes narrowed. "Rachel? Explain, please?"

"Not me," Rachel replied as she barreled past her and into the apartment. "I've got nothing to do with it."

"Well, how else would it heal so fast? It could only be someone from Morgan and I haven't been around anyone else from the community lately."

Rachel bit her lip. "I think I know, but I'm not sure that I like the answer."

Rachel sat on the corner of the bed as Trudy pulled uniforms out of the clothes basket and sniffed them before choosing one that appeared to be the least repugnant.

"So, Rachel, what's your theory on my miraculous healing?" she asked as she stripped down to her underwear and wiggled into the waitress uniform.

"Remember after I burned you how Gavin shocked you?" Rachel replied.

"Yeah, I can't forget a moment of that glorious day."

Rachel got up and walked over to Trudy and stopped her "You're not wearing that, you'll be stinky."

Trudy sighed. "I like to stink; it masks the smell of Bill's food." Upon seeing that Rachel was not backing down, she relented. "Okay, thanks to you I have time to give this a quick wash but tell me about the healing."

"I think he did it," Rachel replied.

"Gavin?" Trudy laughed. "I don't think so. He doesn't impress me as the sort with a special talent—or any talent for that matter."

"Oh, he has a talent," Rachel said. "One that probably nobody else on earth has."

Trudy was in the process of rooting through her dresser for clean underwear when she stopped and looked at Rachel. "Really, what is it?"

"Do you remember when he asked about the lightning?"

"Yeah, what's with that anyway? I've never seen any lightning over Morgan."

"That's the point," Rachel said. "Nobody has, except for him."

Trudy leaned against her dresser and asked, "So there really is lightning out there that nobody in this town has ever seen?"

"It's not really lightning," Rachel replied. "It only looks like lightning—if you can see it, that is. Only our kind can see it ... and Gavin. When he comes into the diner to ask you for a date, can you let me speak with him for a few minutes?"

Trudy made a face. "Date? What are you talking about?"

"You're not as observant as you make out," Rachel said with a mocking smile. "I noticed the way he was looking at you. He'll be back."

Josh Barber was stocking the end cap with a fresh shipment of generic lemon snack pies when a pickup pulled up to the front of the Citgo.

The truck was one of those lifted mid-eighties Chevys that had spent far too much time in the woods. The camo-painted body could not disguise the Bondo and rust beneath it. Primer-painted brush guards and roll bar both carried a hefty assortment of KC HiLiTES off road auxiliary lighting. The mudders that vehicle rolled on were actually cleaner than the three occupants that jumped out of the vehicle.

Instinctively Josh moved behind the counter and towards the Smith & Wesson that he kept loaded just under the register.

Josh could smell the men before they entered the store, their odor sifting its way through the cracks around the glass doors.

"May I help you gentlemen?" Josh forced out as the bell over the door chimed.

"Yeah," the tall one said as he approached the counter. "Need to pick up some supplies. You got any whisky?"

"No," Josh replied as he looked at the bald one, who was making a mess of the fruit pies that Josh had so precisely placed in order.

"Beer then?" the tall one asked. "Buck, what kind of beer you drink these days?"

"They got any Old Milwaukee, I'll take it—or Schlitz," the bald one replied as he dropped a pie on the floor.

"No beer," Josh informed them.

"Well, hell, what do you drink up here anyway—your own piss or what?"

Josh observed that the tall one must be the group's spokesman. "We're a dry town. Sorry."

"Damn, I ain't never heard of no dry town in Wisconsin. Isn't that against the law or something?"

"No law, we just choose to have it that way."

"Then how about some titty magazines? Got anything in plastic behind that counter you're hugging there?" the tall one said in a more agitated tone, causing the others to look towards Josh as well.

"Nope," was Josh's curt reply.

"Well, hell, boys, it looks like we pulled into a damn church camp here."

"Plenty of other towns have that stuff—just not this one," Josh said in an attempt to make them go away. His hand moved closer to the counter.

The tall one motioned to the others, saying, "Pervis, Buck, let's go into town and see what the choir looks like. The pastor here keeps sliding towards something under that counter, and I'm sure as shit it ain't no Bible."

———

Trudy's walk to work had always been quiet in the past. Now, with Rachel, it was a nonstop question and answer period.

"I'm currently fascinated by the underlying social economic underpinnings that developed into the nihilistic punk culture and its relation to the music of, say, the Sex Pistols," Rachel opined.

Trudy stopped dead in her tracks and looked at Rachel. "Seriously? You've got to be kidding, right?"

Rachel shrugged. "I know you like that music so I'm attempting to understand it."

Trudy started walking again. "Do me a favor: *don't*. Stick to your television addiction." As she said that she noticed a beat-up Chevy pickup driving slowly down Main Street just behind them.

"Rachel," Trudy said.

"I see them. Let me take care of it."

Trudy looked around and stole a glance at the seedy trio ogling them from the cab. They were definitely on the prowl.

"I can handle it," Trudy said. "I'm used to this type. Besides, you have a tendency to overdo things."

"Hey, sweet cheeks," called out a mullet from the driver's seat, craning his head out the window. "What are you two cuties doing out so early in the morning?"

"None of your business, I think," Trudy returned. "Rhinelander has a very nice soup kitchen if you need a meal."

"Oh, honey, you wound me deeply," the man said as the truck pulled up beside them. "I'm Theodore and this here fine specimen of manhood is my brother Pervis. The quiet and hairless one over there is Buck. Who might you be?"

"No one you need be concerned with," Trudy said.

"Well, I don't think so, ma'am." Theodore continued. "You see, I like brunettes and Pervis here likes blondes. Buck isn't too particular but leans towards redheads. Guess he's out of luck."

"You three are all out of luck as far as we're concerned," Trudy said, keeping her eyes forward.

"Now, sugar baby, don't be hostile. Why don't you two jump up here in the truck and we'll give you a little ride?" Theodore gyrated his pelvis lasciviously and winked at the girls as his companions laughed raucously.

"I'm sure it would be very little," Trudy shot back as the pair continued walking.

The driver didn't take the hint and gunned the truck up and onto the sidewalk, a giant tire blocking their way.

"Now look here, boys," Trudy said. "Let us go to work and you can go take a cold shower. It's all good."

Theodore wagged his butt-ugly head. "Don't think so, honey, See, the Citgo don't carry no porn and there ain't any rotgut in this piss-pot of a town. We can't spend our time hunting in this damn forest if we don't have a little rest and relaxation to go with it."

Rachel nudged Trudy and whispered. "Let me help."

"Just hop up here in the cab, little lady," Theodore continued. "I'll show you a good time." With that he reached down and grabbed Trudy's right arm and pulled her roughly towards the truck.

Rachel scampered forward and in front of Trudy until the top of her head reached the door handle. She looked up at Theodore. "Leave her alone," she said in a stern squeak.

"Or what?" Theodore mocked. "I'm not seeing anything but a couple of little sluts with far too many clothes on."

Rachel looked at him, her eyes narrowing to slits. "Then you are not seeing reality," she said quietly.

The first tremor was small, hardly noticeable. But it made Theodore let go of Trudy. The shaking built, growing with each successive wave as Rachel and Trudy backed away from the truck. If it were California it would definitely be an earthquake, but this was the far North of Wisconsin. Pervis and Buck looked equally alarmed.

The first wave hit the truck on the side, caving in the driver's side door and sending Theodore flying into Pervis and Buck. The force of the blow moved the pickup five feet down the sidewalk. The second came from above, crushing down like an invisible fist, bending the bed into a "V" shape. The third came from underneath, flipping the Chevy completely over and onto a fire hydrant, the force shearing it off and causing water to shoot twenty feet into the air.

"Let's go!" Rachel said as she snagged Trudy's arm.

They made it inside the Cluck and Grunt and locked the door behind them.

"Sorry," Rachel said sheepishly as they went to the windows to see if there was movement from the pickup.

"Why aren't you two doing prep?" Bill grumbled from behind the counter. "What did Rachel screw up now?"

"She did a little bodywork on some creep's truck," Trudy said as she continued to look out the window. She could see Bill's reflection shake his head and walk back into the kitchen.

After a few minutes the lights of the sheriff's pickup flashed by the windows, followed by an ambulance and fire truck.

"Not surprising someone called 911 about that," Trudy said as she shakily sat down. "Very subtle there, Rachel. You can't go all Jedi on some jerks just because you can."

"I'm sorry," Rachel said, lower lip trembling. "I'm still new to this."

Trudy felt bad for correcting Rachel. She was right: It takes them time to learn control. Taking her hand she said, "Well, you know the town will cover for you. They always do. They'll just say that it was drunken hunters run amok, but you need to be more careful. We're lucky it's the sheriff responding and not one of the regular patrols. Sheriff Winston is a friend of Maggie, but he isn't from Creekside. We don't want outsiders interfering in our business. Besides, I could have handled it."

"No, Trudy," Rachel corrected. "I can't read minds but I can feel hearts. It sort of brought out my protective instincts when I felt the violence that was in his soul. What he was planning most likely would not have been survivable."

———

Sheriff Winston was finding it difficult to come up with charges for the three hunters that sat handcuffed at his feet. They reeked of sweat but not alcohol or weed and a search of the upside-down pickup didn't yield any stash. It had taken some time for the fire department to get the hydrant capped off, and the street and pickup were soaking wet, along with the trio before him.

"Do any of these assholes need to visit the emergency room?" Winston asked one of the paramedics.

"Nah, they just are a bit bruised. The bald one has a small cut on his arm but it doesn't need stiches or anything, and the guy said he's had a recent tetanus shot."

A number of Creekside residents made it a point to come out and give their versions of what happened, each in glaring contrast to the proceeding one. But they all agreed on one thing: The three hoodlums should be tarred and feathered and soon as was found convenient by the local magistrate.

"We didn't do nothin'," Theodore protested. "That little witch thing did it. The blonde one that Pervis liked."

"I didn't like her," Pervis retorted. "I prefer someone more intellectual."

"You know what, officer," Theodore said in a whisper, "I think she's a space alien."

"Really?" Winston said with mock seriousness.

"Sure," Theodore replied. "How else could she flip a two-ton truck? Makes sense, don't it?"

"Only one problem with that theory," the sheriff said. "None of the witnesses said anything about a blonde girl being anywhere's near the scene of the accident. The only woman mentioned as being on the street was Mrs. Petersen and her hair, what is left of it, is an off shade of blue."

Winston relaxed as a squad car pulled up. He was simply trying to get to work in Rhinelander when the radio dispatcher gave him the heads-up. He was close by so he took the call. He gave into a brief moment of introspection, realizing that he also kept an eye out for Creekside because he wanted Maggie to be safe, but quickly emerged from the reverie as he watched the patrolmen squeeze the three into the back seat of the car.

"So, that's it?" Theodore complained. "You'll take the word of a bunch of hicks and not us?"

"Look, boys," Winston said. "I'm not happy about having to waste my morning filling out paperwork on you numbskulls, but you caused property damage and the locals accuse you of erratic driving. I'm taking you in where I can sort this out with a cup of coffee and my feet up. My bunions are killing me."

———

Gavin was on his way to the diner and had to walk past Sheriff Winston and the accident scene. A crowd of about ten people stood in a large puddle discussing the over-turned pickup while bored firemen and EMTs packed up to leave as a tow truck made its way down Main.

"Sheriff Winston," Gavin smiled. "I thought you said there wasn't any excitement in Creekside?"

"Yeah, this will probably be talked about for months. Maybe even a song written about it," he said as he slapped the roof of the squad car goodbye. "How are you doing, son?" he continued as he waddled over to him.

Gavin didn't break stride. "Bored out of my skull," he replied honestly, which caused the sheriff to laugh.

As Gavin continued down the street, Winston called out. "Hey, Gavin, hold up a minute—I've got a question for you."

"Sure," he replied, coming to a stop next to the upside-down truck.

"Uh, you—y-you see ..." Winston stammered as he came close. "How do I put this? Your aunt and I used to be an item around here back in the day."

Gavin grinned. "You and Aunt Margaret were lovers?"

Winston's face flamed tomato-red. "Well, maybe we were. We both lost our spouses around the same time, and we just naturally gained comfort from each other. Problem is that now I'm on her shit list—have been for some time now."

"Why's that?" Gavin asked while also wondering why the sheriff was confiding in him.

"I just don't buy into all of that metaphysical mumbo-jumbo hooey she subscribes to. I've been in law enforcement for thirty years, and I've never seen anything supernatural or unexplained in all those years of duty." Winston leaned against the overturned pickup. "Everything can be explained."

"Is that what you call it to her face, mumbo-jumbo hooey?"

Winston shook his head briskly. "No, of course not—well at least not intentionally. It just makes me so damn mad that she falls for all of that bunk. But it means a lot to her, and I have probably been a bit insensitive at times."

"Have you told her you're sorry?"

Winston stared blankly at him.

"You know, apologize?"

"But I don't believe in that crap," Winston protested.

"But you did say that you were insensitive. Apologize for that."

Sheriff Winston grumbled, "Well, I guess I could do that …"

"She won't bite you," Gavin reassured him.

Winston placed a fatherly hand on Gavin's shoulder. "You don't know Maggie like I do, son. She used to be quite the biter," he said with a smile and wink.

Gavin whistled to cover his embarrassment. "Okay, okay—too much information for today."

Gavin continued walking down Main, still trying to shake the unwholesome vision in his head of the sheriff and his aunt in *flagrante delicto* until he reached an almost empty Cluck and Grunt that had just opened for the day. As he entered he noticed Trudy and Rachel staring at him from behind the counter.

"Told you!" Rachel said as she punched Trudy in the arm and walked off towards the food locker in the back of the kitchen.

"Hey, Slim," Trudy said as Gavin sat at the counter. "Come to enjoy the fine dining experience?"

"Maybe a cup of coffee," Gavin replied. "Did you see the mess out there?"

"Yeah, we're smack dab in the middle of crazy hunter land, nothing unusual about that," Trudy said as she put a mug on the counter and poured him some coffee.

"Your burn!" Gavin said, amazed upon seeing that it was healed. "It's gone."

"Good as new, must be the water here," she said, putting the pot back on the warmer.

Trudy turned back to him and huffed, "Are you going to ask me out or what?"

It took a moment for Gavin to recover. "Actually, I *was* wondering if you would like to go out sometime?"

"Whatcha got in mind there, Slugger?" Trudy said as she put her elbows on the counter and cradled her head in her hands. "Dazzle me," she cooed as she batted her eyes at him.

"Now, that's where I need a little help." Gavin said. "I know there isn't anything in Creekside but I have no idea what else is in the area. I've got no car, and very little cash."

"Now you just know how to sweep a lady off her feet don't you, Big Boy?" Trudy said in a breathless vamp voice that would do Mae West proud.

Gavin essayed a lopsided grin. "You're not going to make this easy, are you?"

Trudy righted herself and said, "Okay, Sport, I have wheels, and there's a concert in Rhinelander on Thursday night that will make your ears bleed until you're anemic. I've got the tickets covered. You buy dinner but it cannot be here—*anyplace* other than here. Got it?"

"Yes, ma'am." Gavin saluted. "So, where do I pick you up?"

"I'm the one with the car, remember?" Trudy corrected. "I'll pick you up at Maggie's at eight."

Gavin looked over at the open food locker with Rachel peeking around the corner with a grin from ear to ear.

Trudy apparently couldn't resist putting her friend on the spot. "Oh, and Rachel also wanted to speak to you about something."

The poor girl dropped her load of flash-frozen hamburger patties and waved meekly at him.

CHAPTER SEVEN

"What do you mean you're in jail?" Reverend Masters bellowed as his martini danced in his glass. "What did you assholes do now?"

"It wasn't us," Theodore argued. "It was a space alien."

Masters sighed; he had such hopes for these three. "You're disturbing a business meeting. What do you need?" He motioned to Holly that the meeting was over. Having located her thong she shimmied herself into it and headed back to her office in a huff.

"We need a new ride," Theodore said. "Ours is all busted up."

"Can't you get it fixed?"

"Naw, frame's bent like a pretzel. It's from when the space alien used her invisible hammer powers on it."

Masters zipped his fly and collapsed into his leather chair. "Where did it happen? What were you doing?"

"In Creekside," Theodore answered. "We were just trying to be friendly with a couple of the local girls, who are not really girls at all, and then one of them used her alien powers on our truck."

"I've heard enough," Masters grumbled; he could feel the veins on his forehead standing out. "What are you doing in Creekside in the first place? You're supposed to be in the forest doing what I damn well am paying you to do!"

"We needed to get supplies," Theodore replied. "Then we were going to head right out."

Masters thought for a moment. "Okay, here's what's happening. I'll pay your fines and I'll make some calls and get you a rental. After I set that up I expect you to go directly into the forest and do your damn job. I'm not sure what happy juice you guys are using to see space aliens but I want it to stop until the job is done. Understood?"

"We're dry as a bone here. We're not using anything," Theodore protested.

"Understood?"

"Yes, Mr. Masters."

"*Reverend* Masters, you moron!" With that, he hung up. "And to think I was just speaking to the smart one."

Sitting there and contemplating how slowly things were moving was agitating him further. For a man whose very existence was predicated on the pursuit of instant gratification, the wait was agonizing. Now, to hear that his employees were not doing their job—and were delusional on top of that—did not bode well.

He had been on this hunt for months, following sightings and rumors of a large, previously unknown beast traipsing through the deep woods of the northern Midwest. He realized how dire his situation was at the Mysterium, the specter of foreclosure ever threatening. He needed a new centerpiece that would bring in some quick cash and allow him to catch up. To fail would be the end of him. A backup plan must be put into place.

Masters spun through his contact list on his cell phone and dialed.

———

Dieter Jaeger stood in line outside of the Milwaukee Art Museum, waiting for the doors to open. The traveling Vermeer exhibit was highly rated and Dieter was looking forward to seeing *The Milkmaid*, a painting that he had previously seen in the Rijksmuseum in Amsterdam fifteen years ago.

The massive roof wings of the museum's Santiago Calatrava addition began to open slowly above the building, signaling the start of another day. Perhaps a bit too showy for Dieter's tastes but it certainly made for a landmark downtown, its futuristic shape and angel wings having been used for everything from a backdrop for expensive German car commercials to *American Idol* auditions and major motion pictures. He turned off his Kindle and began the shuffle indoors to the next line for tickets.

Dieter heard Beethoven's "Ode to Joy" reverberating off of the marble floors and realized his iPhone was ringing.

"Yes, how may I help you?"

"Dieter, its Jay Masters. I need your help, buddy."

"May I call you back, Jay? I'm about to buy my ticket to the Vermeer exhibition."

"The what? Listen, I need to talk to you now. I've got three crazy shitheads out hunting in the forest north of Rhinelander and I'm afraid they're going to fuck me up the ass."

"Now Jay," Dieter scolded, "you know I do not appreciate such language."

"Sorry, I forgot your delicate constitution," Masters growled.

"I am far from delicate, Jay," Dieter protested. "Did you know that the painting known as *The Milkmaid* was considered highly erotic in its day?"

"Not that I care," Masters replied, "but why?"

"Maids were seen as connoisseurs of sex and temptresses of men of higher status. *The Milkmaid* painting contains symbols of a cupid, as well as coals burning inside a foot warmer, which, when placed under a woman's skirt, heated her nether regions. There is also a wide mouth jug that symbolizes a certain portion of a woman's anatomy."

"You do realize they have porn on the Internet, right?"

Dieter sniffed. "Yes. Quite."

"Look, Mr. Fancy Pants," Masters continued, "I need you to go there and clean up the mess for me. Get me back on schedule."

"You know I'm retired from such things. Why don't you try Nigel or Joseph?"

"I need you. I need the great white hunter to go out there and bag my game."

"I prefer my city life now, Jay," Dieter said. "Have I told you? I'm getting married next month. We have a condo lined up in downtown Chicago within walking distance of the art museum."

"Wonderful. I'm glad for you. That doesn't help me any."

"Besides," Dieter added, "you have gentlemen in the field now. If I were to go there I might hit one of them by accident."

Masters gave a snort of disgust. "Shoot all three by accident if you want. Believe me, you would be doing the world a favor. Tell you what, Dieter, if you do this for me, I'll cover the entire cost of your honeymoon."

Dieter paused, weighing the possibilities. "We are going to Tahiti. We have reservations at the InterContinental."

"You're busting my balls, buddy! Look, I promise I'll treat you right. If this thing is as big as I think it is, I'll buy you your own island."

"What is it that I would be hunting?" Dieter asked. "There is little other than deer and an occasional bear in that section of the state."

There was a pause before Dieter heard Masters proclaim, "Evil, pure undiluted evil."

"I do not understand."

"Go find yourself the most evil, depressing painting in that fancy art museum and multiply it by a hundred, and you'll still be a long way off from what I'm talking about."

"Let me think about it," Dieter replied as he hung up.

He bypassed the temporary exhibition space that contained *The Milkmaid* and continued down the white hallway that resembled a futuristic corridor on the starship Enterprise, past the gift shop, and into the older building of the museum. Turning left, he entered the Old Masters section of the gallery. It hung against a plain white wall: Charles Le Brun's 1685 painting of *The Fall of the Rebel Angels* on loan from a museum in France.

He sat down on the padded vinyl bench to study the work more closely. It was cracked with age and the style was one he did not prefer. His tastes ran towards the seventeenth-century Dutch masters, especially the precise architectural paintings of Berckheyde or the bawdy renditions of daily life provided by Jan Steen.

He looked closer at Le Brun's simplistic view of the rebellious angels being forced out of heaven. A churning column of light filled with the writhing of countless fallen angels was at the center, while angels wielding shields and lightning circled those being cast out. While some of the demons appeared as men, interspersed with them were strange beasts with horns and goat-like bodies, lion-like heads, and bat-like wings. He was about to dismiss the painting and move on until one detail caught his eye—the limb of a giant Beast with massive claws reaching out at the center of the painting. Dieter compared the corrupted Beast to that of the lightning-wielding angel's, clothed in white, with glowing wings. To believe the stories, the creature with the claws and hatred in its eyes was once like the angels it fought. Could evil change a being so completely? If so, what would it look like?

He felt that Le Brun actually did a fair interpretation and his respect for the artist grew, but he realized that if this were true, the claw only hinted at the evil that would have entered the world. Later, downstairs in the Calatrava Café, with a plate of scallion-studded mahi-mahi before him, Dieter reached into his pocket, pulled out his iPhone, and dialed.

"Yeah," Masters replied.

"I will do it," Dieter said dryly and hung up.

CHAPTER EIGHT

The Black Crowes began belting out a spirited rendition of "She talks to Angels" until the clock radio arced across the room and hit the wall.

The doorbell rang.

Trudy ignored it, attempting to burrow deeper under her covers.

It rang again.

"What?" she shouted.

"It's your big day!" was the response from behind the door.

Trudy managed to make it across the studio apartment and open the door to glare at Rachel, who, not noticing, pushed her way inside.

"Are you excited?" Rachel chirped. "I would be."

"About what?" Trudy tried to comprehend. "That's its five a.m.?"

Rachel looked at her in wonder. "About your big date tonight! I always love it when life bonds are formed."

"Whoa, now waitaminnit there, Missy," Trudy strenuously objected. "It's just a first date. Probably a last date as well."

"Nonsense," Rachel said as she began to rummage through Trudy's dresser drawers. "What are you wearing?" She tossed aside items deemed inappropriate and moved on to the closet.

"I haven't decided yet," Trudy replied, snatching a brown skirt away from Rachel.

"I would love to attend the wedding," Rachel said, giving a black blouse the once-over. "Do you have an iron?"

Trudy rolled her eyes heavenward and said through gritted teeth, "It's just a date, remember?"

"Ooh, what's this?" Rachel said as she got on her knees and started burrowing towards the back of the closet. Pulling out a rumpled red dress, she stood up smiling, holding it up before her.

Rachel pouted as Trudy pulled the dress out of her hands and tossed it on the bed. Then she latched onto Trudy and was nearly bouncing up and down with excitement. "Where are you going? What are you doing?"

Trudy broke loose and went into the bathroom, where she turned on the water and stuck her head under the faucet, taking a mouthful of tepid water and gargling. "I can't hear you," she said around the swishing liquid.

"Please!" Rachel moaned.

Taking a towel Trudy wiped her face, then went over and sat on the bed. "Well, I'll pick him up at Maggie's and then we're going to dinner down in Rhinelander. After that we're going to a concert at the Jailhouse."

Rachel looked pained. "That's it?"

"Well, what do you want?" Trudy replied, flustered at the question. "I'm certainly not going to bed with him tonight!"

Rachel looked ashen. "I don't mean that! I mean the romantic part. Does he bring you flowers? Do you look into each other's eyes? Hold hands? Do you … kiss?" Trudy could see that Rachel was almost beside herself at this point, "How—how do you know that you have bonded?"

Trudy smiled, patting the bed for Rachel to sit down next to her. "You really haven't learned to live in your skin, have you?" Trudy said, putting her arm around Rachel. "You're overthinking things. It's not a formula. You just know when you've found the one."

Rachel put her head on Trudy's shoulder, whispering to herself as she stared at an AC/DC poster. "You just know."

———

The Hyundai Accent roared down the logging road, its muffler having been ripped out by a rock a quarter-mile back.

"Watch it, Theodore," Pervis shouted over the rumble. "I hit my head on the roof—again."

"Cheap ass Masters couldn't rent us a truck," Theodore fumed. Pervis and Buck were starting to get on his nerves with their constant complaining—especially his brother Pervis, who had a nasally drawl that set him on edge. Pervis was technically his half-brother as his father had a penchant for spreading his seed around Escanaba, Michigan, and surrounding Delta County. Hell, he imagined he had siblings throughout the Upper Peninsula, but Pervis had lived most of his life with his family and was considered kin despite his uselessness.

"When are we getting out of this thing?" Buck asked from the back. "With the gear, there is hardly room to breathe back here."

"Stop your bitching, I'll pull off in a minute or two," Theodore spat. "Road's getting kind of tight. We can stash the car in the woods and then move on by foot."

"Just asking, man," Buck replied. "Be glad you're not stuck back here like a sardine."

"Over there," Pervis pointed. "There's a good spot."

Theodore pulled the car off of what remained of the road and bounced down a slight slope before coming to a stop in the middle of some young birch.

"This should do it," he said, confident that his partners would shut up now.

"I'd prefer to just leave it here and walk back," Buck mumbled as he attempted to extricate himself from the car. "Let Masters eat the charges. It's in his name anyways."

Theodore got out of the car and noticed the long scratches in the paint, where tree branches had etched their imprints. "Nothing doing, I'm looking forward to that rental car bitch's expression when she sees this thing."

The titular leader of this little expedition opened the trunk and started tossing gear on the ground. "Okay boys, here's the plan. We're gonna parallel the road and head towards that Amish town people have been telling us about. I want to have a little peek at it and see what we've got to contend with there. After that we'll start moving out in a circle around the town until it finds us."

Pervis blinked stupidly like a cow chewing its cud. "Finds *us*? I thought we were hunting *it*?"

"It's a man-eater. I think the best bait you could have is a man," Theodore said. "So, I'll be the bait and you two ladies can watch my back.

He turned to Buck and said, "Got your big bowie knife ready? Might end up having to do some cuttin' and guttin'."

Buck tapped his hip fondly and grinned a shit-eating grin. "I don't go any-place without Miss Behavin."

"So why is it again you named your knife after a stripper?" Pervis asked.

"Pervis, you've heard that story a hundred times," Theodore said. "It's because of her sharp wit."

Buck laughed like a hyena in heat. "She was holding th' knife to my belly when I tried to say hello in the parking lot. After I flashed her a few hundred her mood changed. When I was getting dressed afterward I slipped the knife down my pants. The knife was worth a few hundred so I came out even and got some free poontang out of it."

Theodore felt a measure of comfort with Buck being along; he was cer-tainly more competent than his brother. He suspected that all the beatings his father gave Pervis over the years must have knocked something loose at some point. He was okay with a rifle but had the common sense of a rock, and would forget his own name if he didn't keep reminding him of it. Buck was the one he depended on. Back last year the three of them were out poaching black bear in the Upper Peninsula. And Buck brought one down single-handed with his Bowie.

Theodore looked upon their assembled accoutrements of death with satis-faction and announced, "Well, we got everything—let's move on out!"

———

He waited in the woods until the three had left the vehicle and moved off to the north. He realized that he wasn't dressed to be hiking through the woods, but then he always wanted to look his best. Adjusting his Dolce & Gabbana double-breasted wool coat, he stepped over some brush and into the clearing near the car.

Opening the passenger side door, he reached down and pulled open the glove compartment latch, removing the rental agreement from inside.

A shadow crept over the man but he did not turn to look. Instead, he remained intent on the documents in his hands. He could tell from the stench that his associate had arrived.

"Welcome," the man said finally as he turned to face the Beast. The Beast towered over him, the size of a minivan. He was pleased by how well the Beast maneuvered through the forest despite its bulk. The Beast's skull-like human face pointed forward and it revealed the rotted meat of a mouth wanting to speak as humans do, flapping open and closed on loose hinges, the tongue sending spittle in every direction. The face gave a frustrated expression, then the Beast rotated its feline head towards him and roared.

The man looked at the Beast with a smirk. "Cat got your tongue? You have four heads on that neck of yours. I would expect you to be four times as intelligent."

The Beast rotated its vulture head at him and regarded him icily as its wings spread out threateningly. The man smiled in seeing that he had upset his associate. It was always important to keep the subordinates aware of their status. "You have not presented to me the head that you know I truly appreciate. Do not hold out on me."

The Beast swiveled its neck again and the head of a bull now faced forward. Angry red eyes framed by massive horns that curled up and away to end in saber sharp points. The Beast gave a loud snort and lowered the front of its body in a gesture of submission. The man patted the decaying gray skin with one hand while he held the rental agreement up to read in the other.

"This vehicle was rented by a Reverend Jay Masters, from Wisconsin Dells," he said. "I overheard the bald one say that it was Masters who had the rental, so the three out there are just hired hunters. I'm going to Creekside to see if anyone knows about this Reverend Masters. He may have some local connections. I'll also look up this Gavin Young that you told me about."

He patted the Beast on its feline head, which resembled a pox-ridden saber-toothed tiger, causing its spiked tail to wag. "Soon I will give you the order to kill the hunters, but make sure that you leave the tall one, the driver, alive. He may be useful."

The man gave the Beast one last affectionate stroke. "You have done well. Your superiors are pleased. Soon you will be allowed to enter Creekside."

———

"So, what's your story, Gavin Young?" Trudy asked from behind a breadstick at the Rhinelander Olive Garden. They sat in booth near the window, which gave them a prime view of a statue of the Hodag, the mythical beast that was the official mascot of Rhinelander. With its almost goofy, humanoid face and outsized tushes, horns, and dorsal spikes from neck to tail, the green-painted concrete sculpture looked vaguely liken a furry iguana on steroids as it sat on a rough steel base in the middle of a traffic circle. The statue was an object of whimsy that greeted tourists and basically made them more willing to spend their bucks. As Gavin knew, the Hodag of legend was reputed to be decidedly more fearsome in appearance and disposition.

"Not so fast," Gavin replied. "I'm supposed to be the mysterious stranger here." Gavin thrust his hands out, palms open, in a gallant manner. "You first, milady."

Trudy sighed. "If you insist, but it's not going to be pretty."

"Should I order a stiff drink before you begin?" he smiled.

"Well, I live in Creekside. That should be worth a drink right there."

"Family?" he asked.

"My mother died in a car accident when I was seventeen. I've been on my own since then. My scumbag father, and I use the term *father* loosely, knocked her up, found religion, and decided he was a great healer. Obviously so great a man of the cloth couldn't take care of a wife with a bun in the oven so he abandoned us as expected. I've never met him, but I do indeed hate him." Trudy scowled at Gavin and snapped the breadstick in two for emphasis.

"What?"

"Rachel said you can heal. Are you a scumbag in the making?"

"Look, I don't know what she's talking about. I don't believe that stuff is even possible."

"Rachel told you that she thinks you zapped me with your electric personality and healed me, right?"

"You think I did that?" He reached out and ran two fingers down the inside of her forearm, causing Trudy to relax a bit under his touch. Gavin continued. "Rachel said she'll take me to see a Brother Jonathan at the Rookery in a few days. Who is this guy anyway? I picture some old dude with a long beard busily crafting buggy whips. Is he the leader over there? Rachel thinks he'll be able to explain what's going on."

Trudy gave a soft whistle that made the nearby waiter turn towards them. "You must be important there, kiddo," she said, waiving the waiter off.

"Invites to Morgan are rare. I've only been out there once myself, and I have connections."

Gavin played with his eggplant. "Are they all like Rachel? I know she is your friend and all but she's kinda—"

"Ditsy?" Trudy laughed. "No, Rachel is unique. She's more like a baby bird, all awkwardness and sharp angles. It's like she's still trying to figure out how everything works out in the world. She's also, by the way, the purest soul I've ever met. There is no guile with Rachel, which is rare these days." She looked hard at Gavin. "And she is my dearest friend. But enough about me, what about you?"

"Well, I'm in my last year at UW-Madison as an engineering major."

"Got any family?"

"Well, there's my parents. My father is a truck driver and my mother works at a florist shop."

"Do they get along?"

"They love each other but are polar opposites. For example, she goes to church regularly and he thinks she's crazy."

"Well, they say opposites attract," Trudy said as she shoveled another fork-ful of lasagna. "It's nice to hear that there are still some normal families out there. So, what brings you to Creekside? Maggie's a gem but I doubt you came here just to visit."

"My mother. She wanted me to come here. About a year ago I was diag-nosed with a tumor near the frontal lobe of my brain. They operated, as if you couldn't guess." He tapped the scar on the side of his head. "Anyway, they're sure they got it all, and that I should be fine now. But should be is different from *being*."

"What's the matter?" Trudy said with genuine concern; she hadn't realized that Gavin was ill.

"About four months ago I started getting severe headaches. Like someone putting an icepick in my ear and trying to push it through to the other side. I'd also lose my vision and just see lightning going off in my brain."

"Lightning again," Trudy mumbled.

"My mother thinks that the people over at Morgan can help me."

"Heal you, you mean?" Trudy replied. "I'm picking up a theme here. Lightning and healing. Funny, since you don't believe in all that so-called crap."

"Like I said, my mother pushed me to do this," he said, raising his hands helplessly. "Funny thing is, since I've been here my headaches have gone away."

"Maybe you'll have to stay in Creekside for life?" Trudy said as she leaned back in her chair. "Personally, I'd take the headaches."

———

Sheriff Winston rang the doorbell as he fidgeted with his tie.

Maggie opened the door and beamed. "Well, Clarence! What a surprise. Come on in. You're looking all spiffy. Is that a new suit?"

"I just wanted you to know that I do wear more than khaki uniforms."

"Come on back to the kitchen, I have some coffee ready."

He stiffened as he entered the kitchen and noticed another man already sitting at the table. "I didn't realize you had guests, Maggie. I'll come back later." He turned to go.

"Nonsense," she said, grabbing his arm. "You remember Jonathan from Morgan? We were just talking about old times."

Jonathan stood and held out his hand, which Winston reluctantly shook. Jonathan stood a head taller than him and his lanky frame was in contrast to the good sheriff's own slightly rotund torso. He immediately felt on the defensive.

"Have a seat," Jonathan said as he pulled out the chair next to him. "We were just discussing our time in Nepal."

Winston sucked in his gut and eased into the chair. "Maggie has told me a bit about that time. How your community helped her when she was in need."

"Saved my life is more like it," she said as she poured each of them coffee and then sat down across from Winston. "You didn't know me back then, Clarence. Probably wouldn't have liked me if you did. You would have arrested me I'm sure."

"Now, Maggie," he scolded.

"It is true," Jonathan interjected. "She really was a different person. We met lakeside in Pokhara. She tried to sell herself to me."

Winston glared at Jonathan for being so bold. "She's told me about what she had to do to survive," he said in her defense.

"Jonathan!" Maggie said with a laugh. "You could have left that part out!"

"You didn't know what you were doing," Jonathan said.

Maggie continued. "Jonathan and his community brought me back from the precipice, literally, and they cared for me until I was well. They showed me that the world was much more amazing than I ever imagined, and that I had a place in it. They helped get me back to the States."

"So how did your community end up here?" Winston asked Jonathan. "Sounds like you prefer out of the way spots for some reason."

Now he felt Maggie digging into him with her eyes.

She spoke up. "There was a rough time near the end. People were being killed in the hills nearby the community. Some of the locals ascribed it to a Yeti. People were being torn apart like some giant animal was at fault."

"Interesting," Winston said, eyeing Jonathan, "that now we're seeing something similar to that here."

Maggie scowled him. "Now you're starting to sound like the Nepali villagers. They started saying that none of this happened before the community arrived. That they brought the evil to them."

Jonathan sipped his coffee. "Perhaps we did."

"Nonsense," Maggie snapped. "Eventually they drove them out. They forgot all of the good the community had done in the area."

"Jonathan," Winston pressed, "how did you end up here in the middle of nowhere?"

"Maggie's to blame," Jonathan replied with a wink to her. "We kept in touch over the years, and she suggested that Northern Wisconsin was a perfect spot for our next community. Morgan was available, and we do like a challenge. As soon as we were allowed we planted a seed here. It's grown now into Morgan."

Winston blew on his java and took a hearty gulp. "Well, you certainly had a challenge with that town. But, I've got to hand it to you—you did a good job with it. Last I remember it was coming along well."

Jonathan nodded. "We have added a new gathering house since you've last been there. It can hold our entire community for meetings, and we also use it as a craft area."

"What about the church?" Winston asked. "Any plans to rebuild it? From the photographs I've seen it used to be a pretty little building."

"We're always discussing it but have decided not to," Jonathan replied. "After all, it's given our town its nickname."

"The Rookery," Winston said. "I always get a dirty look from folks when I use that name—including Maggie."

Jonathan managed a faint smile. "It's an apt name but we prefer Morgan. We want to pay homage to those who lived there before us, and to the work they put into their homes and community."

Winston cleared his throat. "Maggie, can I speak to you alone for a moment?"

"Sure. Jonathan, would you excuse us?"

"Certainly. I'll just step out on the porch and enjoy the evening for a bit."

As Jonathan left the kitchen Maggie leaned closer to Winston. "What is it? Is everything okay?"

"Sure, sure. I just wanted to say something to you that I've been putting off for a long time due to my pigheadedness. I wanted to say that I'm—I'm sorry."

"Sorry for what?"

"For being insensitive to your beliefs and belittling them."

"Don't be sorry," she said as she cupped his hand in hers. "The one you are hurting the most is yourself."

"How are you so certain of all of this? How can you be so very certain of what you know?"

Maggie's blissful smile said it all. "Because I've lived it Clarence. I've lived it."

———

Trudy brought her ancient Toyota to a rattling stop in front of a boat slip at Thunder Lake. The concert venue, otherwise known as a bar, was obviously packed to the rafters from the number of cars, trucks, and motorcycles that circled the small building.

She looked over at Gavin; he was holding his forehead. "Are you sure you're okay? You look a little ragged around the edges."

"I'm fine."

"Okay, here's the deal. This is a bar, a very nice bar, but a bar. This is also northern Wisconsin. Put the two together and that means the most modern music you will be hearing is"—she cupped her hand to her ear as Led

Zeppelin's "Immigrant Song" coursed through the wood walls of the building and out to the parking lot.

"Classic rock?" he suggested.

"You got it, kiddo," Trudy said as they got out of the car and started walking towards the building. "I'm sure this isn't what you sophisticated boys in Madison listen to. Think you'll be able to cope?"

"I'll try not to throw beer bottles at the chicken wire."

———

Gavin was surprised by how inviting the bar was, decked out in wood paneling with a view of the lake, and also how crowded it was. A makeshift stage was in one corner, the bar in the other, and the space between was filled to capacity with beer swilling patrons. The band hired for the evening was a quartet of cocksure twenty-somethings doing a respectable job of cranking out—at earsplitting decibels—classic rock anthems that were growing mossy on FM radio even before they were born. They seemed more interested in scanning the crowd for willing "groupies" to score with after the show than paying homage to rock dinosaurs.

The headache had started during the concert and Gavin had just ascribed it to the 120 decibels that were accosting him in the claustrophobic venue. The wood paneling ricocheted the sound around the room while his beer vibrated with the resonance. The familiar narrowing of his vision, and the lightning that set fire to his brain, let him know it wasn't just the band that was causing it.

"We've got to leave," Gavin said in a panic.

"What?" Trudy shouted.

"WE'VE GOT TO LEAVE NOW!"

Once they were outside the bar, Trudy pulled him aside on the parking lot and put her hand to his forehead. "Is it your headache? You feel clammy."

"It's back," he said, wobbling on his feet. "We need to get back to Creekside. I'm too far away."

"What do you mean?"

"I felt better when I was in Creekside, near the lightning."

"Okay, sure," Trudy said with concern. "Can you make it to the car?"

"I think so," he rasped.

Trudy's aged Toyota gasped in agony as they made their way north towards Creekside.

"How are you feeling there?" Trudy asked as she glanced over at him. He seemed to be doing better but she was kicking herself for taking him so far from Creekside for a stupid date—not that she would have predicted the repercussions.

"It's getting better. I'm sorry for ruining your concert."

"Don't be silly. Stupid hack band anyway. I know the bass player. He tried to grope me backstage one time. That's why he sings falsetto now."

"STOP!" Gavin yelled.

"What?" Trudy cried as she punched the brakes with both feet and him with her fist at the same time. "Don't do that! Do you want to get us in an accident?"

"Back there," he said. "There was something along the road."

"I didn't see anything," she protested. Backing up and pulling over into the gravel, she put on the hazard lights and looked at him. "Well, let's go find out what you spotted, Mr. Eagle Eye."

"It was right back here," he said as they got out of the car and started walking south along the road. "I saw a flash of white in the headlights, and it moved. Over there," he said, pointing.

Illuminated by the flashing warning lights, they could see movement on the ground in front of them: a skunk that had been hit by a car. The impact had knocked it just onto the shoulder but didn't kill it. It squealed in pain as it attempted to stand up, not knowing that it's back legs were crushed beyond recognition.

"Poor thing," Trudy said. "We should put it out of its misery. I'm going to look for a stick so we can club it."

"Don't," Gavin said in a hushed tone.

"We can't just leave it here to suffer," she protested.

"Rachel says I can heal. It's a good time to find out if it is true or not."

"Look," Trudy said, grabbing his arm, "now might not be a good time. You're still a long way from Creekside. What if you can only heal there? Besides, you'll have to touch it, and we don't know if it has rabies or not. A cornered or frightened animal will almost always bite. And in this case, you'll get sprayed with a perfume that smells like the butt end of hell."

Trudy watched as Gavin observed the panic-stricken animal. He looked intent on testing Rachel's theory, which scared her. What if she were correct? Why couldn't she find someone *normal* to date?

"Nothing ventured, nothing gained," Gavin said and proceeded to reach down and touch the skunk's flank.

A bolt of electricity traveled between Gavin and the skunk, knocking him back on his heels. Trudy caught him as they both looked down at the wounded animal.

For a moment nothing happened. The skunk appeared dazed but at least had stopped its mournful cries.

Then there was a sound of cracking that Trudy couldn't pinpoint until she realized that it was the bones in the hind legs of the skunk that were being pushed back into place. The skunk still seemed in shock and didn't move or make a sound. Slowly the legs reformed back into their normal positions and the fur closed up over the gaping wounds.

"Still don't believe in healing, Mr. Smarty-pants?" Trudy said as she continued to hold him.

The skunk seemed to regain its consciousness and looked around as if it was trying to figure out what had happened. It was able to stand up this time as though it had never been hurt.

"Well, that's amazing," Gavin said.

They stood there in awe, staring down upon the small woodland creature.

The skunk shook out its fur, and then, returning their gaze, turned, and sprayed.

———

Trudy and Gavin sat together in the tub, underwear being their only modesty as Maggie dumped tomato juice over their heads in a failing attempt to mask the smell.

"Bet you didn't think you'd get me undressed on the first date," Trudy said as she turned her head and squinted up at him. "Or at least you better not have."

"It was a bad idea," Gavin sighed. "You were right—I shouldn't have tried to heal it."

"Well, you proved that it's possible," Trudy replied. "Maybe you can confine your healing to less fragrant critters from now on."

Maggie commented, "Here your mother sends you up here to be healed, and it turns out you can heal others. Have you thought about trying to heal yourself?"

"Sort of like electroshock therapy?" Gavin said. "Uh, no thanks."

Trudy bit her tongue and looked at the ceiling, "Gavin Young, Supernatural Pet Vet. You could have your own reality show."

"I've been on dates that have gone awry," Maggie snickered, "but nothing approaching this."

"How's your headache?" Trudy asked.

"It's gone. Guess I am trapped in Creekside."

"There are worse things," Trudy said. "Oh, wait a minute … uh, no there aren't."

"Oh hush," Maggie said. "You know this is the most exciting place on earth. Or do I need to have Rachel remind you?"

"That's okay," Trudy replied. "I remember Rachel's last little stunt all too well."

"Gavin," Maggie said, "we'll find out how to help you. From the sound of it you have received a great gift. Jonathan was here earlier. He's looking forward to meeting you.

"I'll be right back with more tomato juice," she continued as she walked to the door. "Mr. Hansen was not happy about me waking him up at three a.m. to open up his store. I was hoping he'd have some hydrogen peroxide so that I could concoct my miracle skunk stink remover. He didn't have any so I went with the next best thing—Mott's Tomato Juice. It won't fix the issue but at least you'll reek of tomato juice instead of skunk."

Trudy leaned up against Gavin in the tub and he wrapped his arms around her.

"You know, this would be romantic," Trudy said, "if it weren't for your aunt pouring tomato juice over us—and the ungodly stench."

Gavin looked at her with repentant puppy dog eyes. "I'm sorry."

"Yeah, you said that before. It's going to take a week to air out the Corolla. So, do you believe now?"

"Guess I don't have much choice."

"That's the Creekside way," Trudy said as she put her head against his chest. "Creekside bludgeons you over the head with the fact that the way the world sees itself is totally ass-backwards."

She looked up at Gavin. "The weirdness has just begun for you, Gavin my dear. You've have been officially warned."

CHAPTER NINE

The brisk morning air refreshed Reverend Brustad as he gently adjusted the worn letters on the sign outside the Evangelical Lutheran Church of Creekside. It was a nice change from the summer heat. The black plastic letters were becoming brittle due to the constant exposure to the sun, and he had already accidentally snapped off part of a B, which was actually fortunate, as he needed a P for this week's message. He always preferred some quip or play on words that might catch the passing motorist's attention and draw them in. This week: GOD SHOWS NO FAVORITISM, BUT OUR SIGN GUY DOES—GO PACK GO!!

"Good afternoon," came a voice from behind him.

Brustad turned to see a man in his mid-fifties dressed nattily in a suit that he guessed to be tailored by its perfect fit, although he himself could never afford such luxuries. "Hello, May I help you?" he ventured.

"I'm looking for a pastor and thought you might know of him," the man said. "His name is Jay Masters, Reverend Jay Masters."

Brustad looked at the ground as he attempted to pull distant memories out of the back of his brain. "Yes, I know of a Jay Masters. I'd hardly call him Reverend though."

"Why is that?" the man asked.

Brustad's blue eyes flashed, but his tone was even. "Masters is probably one of the most despicable human beings on the face of the earth."

The man in the suit visibly brightened at this revelation. "Indeed! I thought all people were equal in God's eyes?"

"We're all sinners, that is true," the reverend replied. "The difference is Masters revels in it. He raised it to high art."

Brustad closed and locked the glass of the church sign and continued. "He came here fresh out of school and married a local girl. She gets pregnant, and suddenly Masters is looking for a way to escape. He buys himself a diploma and starts calling himself a pastor. Says he can heal people. He ends up running down south with some carnival that called itself a miracle healing conference."

"Do you know where he is now?"

"He hasn't been around here for twenty some odd years, which is fine with me. I don't know where he is now and don't wish to."

"What happened to his wife?"

"She never remarried. It broke her heart. She died a few years ago in a car accident, along with my wife. The only Masters around here now is his daughter Trudy, who is a waitress at the Cluck and Grunt. She has never met him, which is probably a good thing."

Brustad eyed the man, trying his best to project incurious detachment, but he wondered what his real purpose—benign? Sinister?—could be. He hated Masters for what he did to his wife and daughter; he realized it was not a very Christian feeling, but he figured that God would give him a pass on this one.

"Are you law enforcement?" he said at length. "Are you going to lock that son of a bitch up? Excuse my Latin."

With a long thin hand, the stranger flicked away a bit of fuzz on his lapel. "He will definitely get his just reward. Thank you for your time."

As the man started to walk away in the direction of the diner Brustad issued a parting admonition: "If you mention Jay to Trudy, you better be fast on your feet. There's liable to be a cleaver heading your direction."

———

Gavin and Rachel walked along the abandoned railroad trestle that crossed Mill Creek. They were heading out of town and towards Morgan. It had been a day since his date, and only now was he beginning to shed the pungent reek of skunk and tomato juice. The lightning was flashing and twisting off in the distance, marking the direction to Morgan.

"So, why am I the only one who sees that?" Gavin asked. "It's like the sky is ripping apart and reforming continuously."

"You have special talents—Trudy told me that you healed a skunk."

"Yeah, it was a memorable first date."

"That was very kind of you. From my experience I would say most people wouldn't have risked it."

"It probably didn't help my chances any with Trudy."

Rachel looked at him and smiled. "She likes you, you know."

"Did she say that?" he asked hopefully.

"Trudy says she hates everything, but I know better."

"Well, if we have another date it will have to be in Creekside—seems like I'm trapped here. Did Trudy tell you that my headaches return if I'm at a distance from here?"

"Don't worry—Brother Jonathan will be able to help us figure this out," Rachel said as they started down a dirt path that headed into the woods. Impulsively she grabbed his hand. "Stay close to me. The woods are dangerous."

———

Pervis and Buck were in the process of packing up their tent when Theodore traipsed out of the woods and into the clearing while zipping up his fly.

"Anything?" Pervis asked. "I'm sick of this place already. Masters said we'd be back by the centerfold. I've already blown my wad on that and come to the ads in the back for pecker enlargement pills."

"Wouldn't hurt you none to order some," Theodore spat. "Maybe grow some bigger balls while you're at it. I'd thought we find some signs for sure by now. I'm leaving plenty of markers around but I guess it doesn't care."

"A fuckin' poor excuse for Dan'l Boone you are," Buck grunted as he hefted his backpack, "you said this thing would find us. So far it seems not to be too interested in you or your piss."

Theodore skeeted a vile stream of Red Man at Buck's feet. "Keep your shirt on, dickweed. The plan is still in place; we're moving in a circle around Morgan. I took a gander at the town—nothin' to be concerned about there, just a bunch of country bumpkins farming their land."

"Good," Buck said. "We don't need any trouble while we're out here."

"Theodore," Pervis asked. "Do we know what this thing is? I might be looking for something the size of a bear and a little killer rabbit will pop out of bushes and go for my neck."

Theodore displayed his set of rust colored teeth with a huge grin. Putting up with his brother sometimes was worth it just for his unwitting comedy. "Masters thinks it is huge, so we'll go with that until proven otherwise. Let's give it another day and see what turns up."

———

The Beast sat on its haunches just inside the tree line near the one of the cultivated fields of Morgan. The inhabitants were busy pulling potatoes out of the ground. It looked like back-breaking work. There they were, hunched over with their potato forks and buckets, moving slowly down the rows, sweat dripping off into the mud.

Why did they do this? The Beast pondered. They were better than this, higher than this. Why did they insist in groveling in the dirt? They didn't come from the dirt like the ones in Creekside. What was the appeal?

The Beast decided that the reasons need not be made clear to it. It was in the woods to do particular tasks assigned to it. It hated Azael. The pompous fool thought he was so much better than it. Someday it would rise above him, and then they would all see who was the greatest. But for now …

It rose and stretched; time to return to the hunt. The Beast wanted the quarry to become complacent as it made their final moments more exquisite. Now was the time to pounce.

———

He entered the Cluck and Grunt and chose a table that faced the counter. Behind it he could see a young woman with short-cropped black hair and a wrinkled uniform stained with grease. In the back he could see a hairy cook in white T-shirt who was having a coughing fit over a dented steel pot.

The woman came over to his table, holding a coffee pot. "Afternoon," she said as she handed him a menu. "Would you like some coffee?"

"Yes, please. Black is fine"—he looked at her name tag—"Trudy."

"Specials are on page three," she said as she turned over his coffee mug and poured. They both looked up at the sound of the cook's phlegmy gagging in the kitchen. "Uh, you might want to pass on the chili. I'll give you a few moments to look it over."

As she went back behind the counter the ringing of the bell over the door signaled another customer. This one came directly over to the counter and spoke to the waitress.

"Hello, Trudy."

"Oh, hi, Maggie, how's it going?"

Upon hearing Maggie's name he pretended to study the menu and listened intently.

"Have you heard anything from Gavin and Rachel?" Maggie asked.

"Not yet," Trudy replied. "I don't expect to for a while. Rachel can be fast by herself, but with Gavin it will take them some time to get down that old logging road and back."

Maggie sighed. "I know. I'm just impatient to find out what can be done for him. Thought if anyone knew it would be his girlfriend," she laughed.

He could not help but look up from the menu. Trudy took this as a signal to approach and take his order. "I'm not his girlfriend," she said as she sauntered around the counter. "I'd hardly take getting sprayed by a skunk as the capper of a decent date."

"Did you decide?" she asked him.

"Yes, I'll have the grunt burger and fries."

"Anything else?"

"No, thanks."

"I'll go ahead and put this in. Let me know if you need anything."

When Trudy was back behind the counter, Maggie continued. "I saw the way you two were in tub. I wish I had dates as hot at that. You two might have stunk to high heaven but there was definitely chemistry between you."

Trudy smiled and looked off to the distance. "That was pretty nice, except for the part where I wanted to vomit from the stench."

He sat at the table, drinking his coffee and pretending interest in the passing traffic outside the window. If this Trudy Masters was the girlfriend of the Gavin Young the Beast had informed him of, then an opportunity had just opened for him. As he well knew from many ages of experience, the first rule in situations like this was to sow discord. It appeared that optimal discord had just been handed to him in a dirty coffee cup with free refills.

He decided that he must pay this Reverend Jay Masters a visit.

———

"Rachel," Gavin huffed. "Are we lost?"

"Of course not, this is a short cut. The road takes a long curve to the west. This is shorter and also more scenic."

Gavin clambered over a fallen tree only to have a birch sapling slap him across the face. Rachel seemed unfazed by the terrain and grabbed his hand again to lead him down a gully and up the other side. She was wearing blue jeans and a green knit sweater with her hair pulled back with a scrunchie. Gavin realized this was the first time he had not seen her in her waitress uniform. She seemed more relaxed in the woods. In town she always appeared to be a fish out of water, not knowing how to behave or what to do.

Good thing they were not hunting anything, Gavin thought. Rachel was sure-footed but noisy, crunching the fall leaves underfoot and panting like a bellows through her mouth.

———

The Beast had started its hunt. Moving silently through the woods, it listened for the prey. It wasn't long before it heard noises in the distance. The three hunters were not being careful, and that would bring doom upon them. Following a small ridge line it moved towards the sound. When it determined that it was directly in front of their forward movement, it crouched and waited.

———

"Theodore," Pervis said, "maybe we're going about this wrong. Maybe we should be settin' traps."

"I thought about that," Theodore said. "I still believe that since this thing is a man-eater we are the best bait. I'm thinking if we keep traipsing through its territory for long enough and pee on everything we can find, eventually it will find us. Saves us a bit of work, don't you think?"

"Your call, bro," Pervis replied. He shot Buck a dubious glance. "I just hope that when it finds us, Buck there is ready with his Bowie—an' as good as he claims he is with it."

"I'm always ready, and I'm always good, you little prick," Buck answered. To prove it he grabbed the knife from its sheath and threw it one deft motion. It sunk into the bole of a young birch with a *thwanng*. "I'll try to make it nice and clean though. Something the taxidermist won't have too much trouble fixin'."

———

The Beast heard their approach although it could not yet see them. It knew that with its stride, it was a jump and a short pounce away from the prey. It remembered that the tall one must live; beyond that, the kills were its to enjoy.

Now was the time.

It sprang.

As it came out of the woods it was on a clear trajectory to its target.

"Gavin!" a female screamed as the Beast came down upon a young male.

What? thought the Beast, knocking the boy to the ground, *this is not right.* Even as a claw dug into the human's shoulder it realized that it must not kill this one. Where were the hunters? What were these two doing in the woods? Then it sensed it, as its sparse hackles rose: something it had overlooked in its bloodlust. Something extremely dangerous was nearby.

———

Gavin lay on the ground in agony as hundreds of pounds of what-the-hell sat on his chest, cutting off his air. A claw was deeply imbedded in his shoulder; he could feel it scraping against bone. Through his blurry vision he could see the Beast. He had never witnessed anything like it before: a body of a nearly hairless emaciated feline with mottled gray skin covering bones and muscle, a long tail spiked at the end, and four massive wings of tattered flesh. The Beast had four heads upon one neck, each facing a different direction. The one to the right was a cat with massive jaws and saber-like teeth projecting downward.

He could barely see the one in back, but he thought it was that of a bull with giant horns curling up. To the left a vulture-like visage, with bloodshot eyes scanning the forest. The front-most face that was directed towards him was almost human, if you could consider a corpse buried in the earth for a month human; deep set eyes and the remnants of skin and muscle were still capable of expression and the expression it held now was one of confusion, rapidly changing to fear.

Behind the Beast the forest brightened into white as he witnessed Rachel begin to glow. If anything comparable existed in the world that Gavin had previously known, it would be that of a caterpillar metamorphosing into a Monarch butterfly, only indescribably faster and incredibly more beautiful.

Gavin screamed.

As he lay there in shock under the Beast, he understood now why the animal was in fear. The being that Rachel was becoming was too bright, too beautiful to comprehend. Gavin watched in stupefied terror as Rachel transformed. The gentle if a bit unusual girl began to grow and glow as her feet lifted off of the ground. Lightning coursed around and through her as her sweater and jeans changed into silver armor that hissed and crackled in time to the electric bolts that hit the ground, sending up puffs of burnt foliage. In her left hand the lightning coalesced to form a solid rotating circle, the sound of it that of a large turbine engine spinning up, as the charged particles became a shield. In her right hand lightning bolts lengthened out into the shape of a sword spreading the smell of ozone through the woods.

Behind her back, bluish-white wings sprouted and rose above her head. These were not like the drawings of angel wings in the heavy family Bible that Gavin had unfortunately used as a coloring book as a child. These were menacing forms not used for flight as she stood there fifteen feet tall and already six feet off the ground. The wings on what once was Rachel were weapons, sharp-edged and lethal.

As her brightness became nearly intolerable, Gavin heard and felt Rachel's wings beat, sending a deep *whomp* through the forest like a sonic boom, blowing golden leaves off the nearby birch. She then turned towards the Beast and swatted it with a wing, sending it into a pine tree that shattered into splinters.

The Beast took a moment to shake off the impact. It took another moment to decide whether or not to fight. The boy must live, and it knew the loyalist that stood in front of the crushed human was far more powerful. There was nothing for it to do but concede this fight and slouch back into the forest.

The shame was almost too much for it to bear. To make such a mistake would not be tolerated by its superiors. It hoped the boy lived through the wound it had inflicted. If he were to die, the punishment it would receive would be terrible indeed.

———

Gavin continued to lie on the ground. His shoulder was shattered he knew, but it didn't seem to matter. Rachel, or what was once Rachel, filled his vision. Looking at her was like staring into the sun. He thought he would go blind from the brightness, but he was also unable to take his eyes off of her. The other feeling he had was one of shame. He felt dirty and corrupt when compared to the seraphic being that stood before him. He was but a filthy rag to be tossed aside. Why did this powerful being fight for him? Why did it even care?

Before slipping into unconsciousness he heard Rachel saying, in a voice at once remote and intimate: "Do not be afraid."

And he was not.

CHAPTER TEN

"Good morning, Sunshine!"

Gavin pried open his eyelids to see Rachel, the *human* Rachel, staring down at him.

"Pancakes?" she asked with a crooked smile.

"Where am I?" Gavin groaned, trying to get his bearings.

"At Brother Jonathan's house. We have some real maple syrup. Not that cheap imitation stuff that Bill buys for the diner."

Gavin propped himself up by the elbows and surveyed the room. He was on a double bed in a room furnished with simple but functional furniture. The walls were painted bright yellow, and the quilt that covered him had a loud yellow and brown checkered pattern, which made the surroundings much more festive than he felt.

"My shoulder," he said, reaching his hand over to feel it.

"Good as new," Rachel grinned. "Luckily, one of our community is a healer. He fixed you up."

"Thanks," he said, rubbing what had previously been a down-to-the-bone gash that would have required multiple stitches in the "real world." Sitting up in bed, what had happened in the forest all came flooding back to him.

"What was that thing back in the woods?" And then backing himself up against the headboard, he looked at Rachel in mingled wonder and terror. "And what are *you*?"

"That was one of the Fallen, and I'm just plain ole Rachel, silly. I'm not Fallen." She bit her lip and added, "We have bacon!"

"What? I don't understand," Gavin said, shaking his head. "What nearly killed me?"

"A Fallen one. You know them as demons, and it didn't try to kill you. If it wanted to, it could have done so before I was able to stop it."

Gavin considered this. "It looked confused, like it didn't know what was happening."

"It stopped when I yelled your name. It knows who you are."

"*What!* Why would it know *me?*"

Rachel gave a worried look. "Brother Jonathan can tell you more. You need to get dressed first."

Gavin realized that he didn't have any clothes on and pulled the quilt tighter around himself.

"I washed your clothes—you soiled yourself." She said sheepishly, "I also mended your shirt." Rachel motioned to the other side of the room. "I put them on the chair. Take your time and come downstairs when you're ready." She left the room and closed the door behind her.

Gavin sat in bed awhile longer, not fully understanding what was happening. Rachel's story was so farfetched, but he had seen it with his own eyes. He was suddenly mad at Maggie, who obviously had known all along about the angels, and also at Trudy. After all, Rachel was her best friend; there was no way that she would not have known Rachel's true identity. He suddenly felt stupid, like the last person in a room to get a joke.

Gavin slowly stood up and teetered toward the chair. The wound to the shoulder may have healed but being knocked down by something the size of a van had left him sore and bruised. "They could have healed *everything*," he grumbled as he slipped on his pants.

Gavin stopped and looked around the room; it was extremely bright, even though there were no lights on. He also felt the hairs on the back of his neck rise and a prickly sensation start to cover his body, similar to when he watched the lightning before, but this time it was much stronger. He walked over to the window and opened the sheer drapes.

Morgan was hardly a town, just a grouping of houses around a central park-like area. Behind them he could make out barns, sheds, and other outbuildings characteristic of farm life. There was one large building directly across from him that looked like a meeting hall. The wooden structure was painted in a cheery yellow with a wide veranda sheltering a number of rocking chairs. To his left he could see the façade of the church. Opening the window he stuck his head out to get a better view of it and had to grasp the window sill to keep from losing his balance when he realized what he was seeing.

The old church that stood forlornly at the far end of the park was covered in soot and bird droppings, and was also notable for a sizeable hole in the roof. The charred timbers of the roof beams were slowly falling in, and with time there would be no roof at all. But what made Gavin almost fall was the sight of the column of churning white light that shot out of the church roof and disappeared into the sky.

Birds flew in and out of the gap in the roof, blithely unconcerned with the breathtaking phenomena continually unfolding. Gavin could understand why they would consider the church prime roosting territory. Sheltered but with easy access to the sky, it truly was a rookery.

The brightness of the column grew and Gavin had to turn away. He felt the electricity coming off of the lightning as it passed through him, cleansing his soul. Was this what a nuclear blast victim felt in his last moments? The feeling was akin to his flesh peeling away, leaving nothing but dust. Gavin stifled a scream as the burst of energy receded just as suddenly to manageable levels.

Opening his eyes, he turned back to the church in time to see a woman coming out of the building and gently closing the door behind her.

———

"Have a seat!" Rachel said as he came down the stairs. "I've got coffee ready."

"Thanks," he wearily replied. The kitchen was small but functional, just a wooden table and a bench seat up against the wall.

Rachel pointed to the middle-aged man in front of the stove and introduced him. "Gavin, this is Jonathan."

Jonathan turned around and held out his hand. "Welcome! I've heard a lot about you, Gavin." He wore a pair of faded jeans, white sneakers, and a T-shirt with a silk screen of a '57 Chevy—not the guise Gavin would have picked for the leader of a strict religious community populated by earthbound angels; but after knowing Rachel for a while he wasn't quite certain what to expect. "Are you ready for some breakfast?" Jonathan added.

"I've sort of lost my appetite," Gavin said. "Probably from almost being killed by a demon."

Jonathan's friendly face bloomed in a benevolent smile. "But it didn't kill you. That is both glad and troubling news."

"How do you mean?" Gavin asked. "Rachel said it knew me."

"Yes," Jonathan replied as he plopped a plate of stacked pancakes on the table. "That is my fault, I'm afraid. I sensed something in the forest on the day Rachel came to tell me the news of you seeing lightning over Morgan, but I didn't act on it, and that brings us to where we are today."

Gavin sat down, stunned. "I don't understand."

"If they could use you or control you, then it would make life much easier for them," Jonathan said, placing a cup of warm syrup on the table that caused Gavin to suppress his gag reflex. Under normal circumstances he'd dig right in, but the idea of being a demon's puppet made his stomach churn.

"Rachel told you what we are?" Jonathan asked.

Rachel giggled. "I don't think he believes it, even though he saw it with his own eyes."

Gavin scowled at her. "Rachel, said you are angels or something, right?"

"Exactly right," Jonathan replied as he sat down opposite Gavin. "We are messengers of the most High, and the lightning you see is the gate or ladder to the throne."

"Okay, slow down there—ladder to the *what?*" Gavin asked, equally perplexed and scared.

"Because of the way the lightning appears with its horizontal spikes, it has been spoken throughout history as a ladder," Jonathan explained patiently. "Gate, portal, whatever you wish to call it, it is our access point between realities: the world where you dwell and the world of angels."

"You mean heaven?" Gavin questioned. "But I thought you could just zap yourselves anyplace you wanted to be if you're angels, after all—right?"

Jonathan laced his fingers atop the table and leaned in close to him. "Despite what you may have heard, we are not omnipotent and omnipresent. There is only One who is. We can only be in one place at a time, and our knowledge is limited, just as your own. If you were going to travel from Milwaukee to Madison each day you could take country roads through the forest and farmland, or you could hop on I94 and have a direct route. That is what the ladders are for us."

"Hopefully without the traffic jams," Gavin replied as he put his head in his hands. "I don't even believe I'm talking about this. Angels don't exist."

"That's exactly what Maggie said when she first found out." Jonathan said. "When she jumped from a cliff in Nepal intent on killing herself, I was the one who cradled her with my wings and protected her from harm."

"For that matter," Rachel put in, "A college boy shouldn't be able to heal a pretty girl's burn, or mend the broken bones of a poor skunk, either."

Gavin looked up. "Point taken. So, is my healing power related to the ladder? I know I feel better when I'm closer to it. My headaches go away."

"Perhaps," Jonathan said as he sipped his coffee, "but then it might be something else. You shouldn't be able to see the ladder, but thousands of years ago it was quite common for humans to see them. It's a bit of a lost art, I'm afraid. As your species has deteriorated over the millennia, the ability to see heaven has been lost. This world is in decay. Humans once lived for hundreds of years; now it is only through medical advances that your life expectancy is creeping up once again." He pointed towards Gavin's scar. "I think the surgeons must have jostled things in there pretty good. It seems like you've picked up a few talents in the process of having that tumor removed."

"The Fallen ones," Rachel added, "have no ability to see them. They are so far corrupted that it isn't possible for them to even glimpse a ladder."

Jonathan looked at Gavin. "And that's why they would love to have you. Each of our communities on earth has a permanent ladder in place. They can sense our kind, but they need to be in close proximity. Finding a little village such as Morgan out in the woods is not an easy task for any of them. You have an ability that they greatly covet."

Jonathan stood up. "Would you like to see our ladder up close?"

———

Masters surveyed the empty room off to the side of the Mysterium. It had previously held packing crates full of shrunken heads and two-headed goats but he had ordered it cleared out. The five hundred square foot space would be adequate for herding the rubes through to see the Beast but not allow enough space for them to dawdle. Get them in, shake out their pockets, and get them out was the plan. Having a separate room and admission fee would be the most profitable. The gift shop at the exit to the Beast's lair would be open to all. Masters had contacts in China that could churn out cheapjack, probably lead-based (not that he cared) souvenirs modeled on the creature's likeness by the shitload. He got goose bumps just thinking about the fortune to be made.

"Reverend Masters?" a voice said.

He turned to see a man in a business suit of a quality seldom seen in the tourist trap town of Wisconsin Dells. He was flattered that his correct title was used but put off by the man's eerie resemblance to an IRS agent. "Depends who's asking."

"My name is Mr. Azael. I hear you are looking for a creature in the forests north of Creekside."

"What makes you think I'm looking for some Beast? I've got more oddities than I can handle right now."

The man looked around the empty room. "I see that," he blandly stated. "You have three hunters in the woods right now that are woefully ill-equipped to deal with what is out there."

"How do you know that?" Masters grumbled. "Are they trying to work both sides of the street? Anyway, I'm not going to lose any sleep over those dipshits if they end up dead in the woods. I've got a professional coming in."

"You need more than a professional hunter," the man said. "I can deliver the Beast to you without a shot being fired."

"Oh, and how is that?" He didn't know what this grifter was selling but he was always willing to listen to a good spiel.

"Let's just say that the Beast and I are on a first-name basis."

"And your first name is?"

"All in good time, *Jay*. You see, *Jay*, you are not on a first-name basis yet with me, but that will be rectified soon. I can feel it in my heart."

Masters stiffened upon hearing the man's condescending words. "And how much is this service going to cost me?"

"Why, absolutely nothing!" Mr. Azael said with a smile. "Nothing of monetary value at least, just a little of your time."

"Yeah, go on."

Azael came closer to him, until he could smell the man's cologne; Kilian Straight To Heaven, White Cristal; over two hundred bucks for less than two ounces—expensive taste for a grifter. During his faith healing days he used to practically bathe in the stuff, but under the current economic circumstances he was drifting dangerously into Old Spice territory. "There is a young man in Creekside that is of great interest to my associates. We need to get on his good side, let him know that we are his friends."

"How does that affect me?"

Azael smiled. "He's dating your daughter."

Masters rolled back on his heels. "Daughter? I don't have a daughter," he said as firmly as possible.

"Think back, Jay," Azael said. "You left a pregnant wife in Creekside. You had to have known that she'd produce a male or a female. There aren't really any other choices."

"I told that bitch to get an abortion," Masters snarled.

"I'm guessing that you didn't give her any money to pay for it. Besides, I doubt she would have done it anyway. It sounds like she really loved you. She probably was hoping you would return to your family someday. Well, now's your chance."

Smirking, Azael slapped Masters on the back. "Your negligence has come to fruition. Your daughter's name is Trudy, and she works at the diner in Creekside."

Masters didn't appreciate Azael touching him so familiarly, but there was something menacing about this interloper that let him permit it. "So what am I supposed to do? She probably doesn't like the fact that I left her mother."

"Actually, I'm fairly certain that she hates your guts."

Masters threw up his hands. "Well, there you go! Nothing I can do then."

"Reverend, you are not giving yourself much credit. You're a smooth talker or you wouldn't be in this business. I'm sure in a week or two she will be calling you Daddy and sitting on your lap."

Masters rubbed his jaw in thought. "So, assuming I humiliate myself and show up in Creekside and get to know this long lost brat of mine, then what?"

"Leave that to me," Azael assured him. "Once she trusts you, then she will give her precious boyfriend into our care. Don't worry, we do not seek to abduct him or anything crass like that, but it is very important that we always know his location. You need to have your daughter trust you enough that she will always confide in you as to where he is."

Azael started towards the door. "Misguided love, Jay—you've worked that angle before."

Masters called out: "So, when do I get my Beast?"

"Patience! The faster you get to Creekside and make nice with your daughter, the faster you'll receive your pet."

———

Gavin followed Jonathan across the courtyard towards the Rookery. He noticed a number of people staring at him as they walked by.

"Should I be concerned?" he asked.

"It's been a long time since there's been a human who could see a ladder. You're a subject of fascination," Jonathan said as he waved people back to work. "Ladders are quite rare, and to be in the presence of one is a great honor. We have seven communities such as this one in the world at any one time— always seven. When one is removed, another in a short period of time will take its place in a different location."

"Seems kind of redundant."

"Even with seven in place, only a small fraction of our kind can partake of them at any one time. Our numbers are far greater than all humans currently alive on earth. So you can see it is a great gift to be allowed to join a community such as this."

Gavin stopped and kicked frustratedly at the sod. "I don't get it! Why do you even need these communities in the first place?"

"A ladder doesn't start out the way you see it now," explained Jonathan in his patient, avuncular way. "It doesn't light up the night sky and scatter energy to the four winds. It begins very small—just a tear or rent in the fabric of space-time; a small sliver of light that comes out of the earth and reaches towards the sky; a narrow crossing from your existence to ours. It barely allows for the passage of one of us, and travel is quite difficult for the first few through. Most importantly, it always begins with a friendship created, a bond between one angel and one human."

"Maggie?" Gavin asked, already knowing the answer.

Jonathan smiled. "Yes, in a way you could call this Maggie's ladder, as she planted the seed. How I wish she were capable of seeing what she has created. Trees are perhaps the best analogy for the ladders, as they are alive in their own fashion, much as trees are. As more of our kind joined the Morgan community and began to build friendships, the ladder has grown taller and stronger. What once was a sapling has now sunk its roots deep into Morgan and Creekside, feeding off of the relationships that have been built."

Jonathan fixed his friendly but penetrating eyes on him. "As for why they are here, it is for our benefit for the most part. You must understand, we were there at the creation of your universe before time as you know it even existed. And we were there at mankind's fall and rise throughout your history. But despite this intimate witness, we do not always understand you."

"Join the club! We don't understand ourselves most of the time," Gavin said.

"Exactly!" Jonathan exclaimed. "To live and work as you do helps us to understand a bit more of what you go through, the joys and sorrows of your existence in this creation." Jonathan paused and held up a blistered palm. "In my own case, farming makes me a better servant."

He opened the church door for Gavin and they stepped inside.

The narthex was unexpectedly clean and tidy. A pair of whitewashed doors separated it from the sanctuary proper, a small wooden table with a crystal vase of white roses being the only ornamentation. Once through those doors the scene changed dramatically. The building was littered with charred wood and ashes. Bird droppings covered everything except for a small path to the center of the building. In the middle a circle, some twenty feet in diameter, was filled with churning light, the electricity coming off of it causing Gavin to step back a foot.

"The Fallen always attempt to find these portals between the space-time continuum as they have been exiled to this world," Jonathan intoned, obviously enraptured by the awesome sight. "They have been cast down and no longer have entrance to the throne. Their hatred burns, and their twisted joy consists of wreaking havoc in the lives of those that are joined by this ladder."

Gavin also could not take his eyes off the light. "So the demons can't use these ladders to return to heaven and fight there? That's good, right?"

"The Fallen are not allowed access, but if one were to touch it they would destroy the ladder immediately. We are on constant guard against them gaining access to this area. Birds, as you can see, and even humans who do not see the ladder, are not affected by it, but the demons were once angels as myself. Their touch is capable of destruction." Jonathan turned and looked at Gavin. "Since you can see and feel it, I would advise you not to touch the ladder, as you might not live through it."

"Not heaven material, I guess."

Jonathan nodded gravely. "Not yet, but I have high hopes for you. Seldom do the Fallen have to resort to direct assault upon a ladder. They can feel our presence if they are within a few hundred yards, but that still doesn't tell them the exact location. Instead, they usually work in the darkness, sowing deceit, mistrust, and fear. Relationships are broken and the ladder weakens, slowly starving for love. Eventually it shrivels and dies.

"But if that fails," Jonathan went on, "then they will attempt to close it through force directed upon the human community nearby. Violence is also their way. In Nepal they assumed physical forms designed not only to terrorize the villagers but also to kill. The fact that they have one in its corrupted Beast form here is not a good sign."

Gavin looked up into the sky and lost the ladder amongst the clouds. "Why only seven of these?" he asked. "If there are so many angels you'd think these thingies would be all over the place."

"The reason there are only seven ladders in the world at any one time is because this world is not capable of withstanding more," Jonathan explained. "More than that could rip the fabric of space permanently. While humans and demons go merrily along their way, neither can see the violence that accompanies being within close proximity of a ladder opening. I'm telling you this to prepare you, since you are able to see the ladders, you will also be in the unenviable position of seeing what a rip in the fabric of space and time truly is. It is one of the mysteries of creation that such a violent reaction goes unnoticed by almost everyone"—Jonathan looked at the boy with extraordinary compassion—"except you. Cover your eyes, lad, the ladder is about to open."

Again, Gavin felt it before he could see it. The hair on his forearms bristled as the first static wave hit him. From this distance the blast from the ladder was almost intolerable. He didn't feel pain, as his body was not being harmed, but what he knew as himself, the inner Gavin that lived in this body of his, was being assaulted by the pureness that passed through him, ripping him to shreds and rebuilding him by the second. Admitting defeat, Gavin had to close his eyelids, and even then the brightness came through and seared itself into his retinas.

Gavin screamed and fell to his knees.

As quickly as the lighting came, it vanished to leave him stooped before a woman that had emerged from the ladder.

"Greetings, Angela," Jonathan said with a smile, "welcome to Morgan. This is a guest of ours, Gavin Young."

The woman held out her hand and helped Gavin to his feet. She had an elegant yet warm persona that relaxed him instantly. "Gavin, I've heard all about you. Nice work with the skunk."

"Angela is a healing angel," Jonathan observed. "I imagine you are quite the topic amongst her kind."

"Great," Gavin replied as brushed down his clothes "I'm in the gossip columns of heaven!"

———

"Theodore," Buck said as he used his big Bowie knife to whittle on a birch branch, "I'm tired of being bait. We've tried this and it ain't working. We need to do some real hunting because this thing sure ain't looking for us."

"Yeah, you might be right." Theodore said, shooting a shit-colored projectile of Red Man at the Coleman stove. "You'd think a man-eater wouldn't pass on the opportunity to gnaw on Pervis's leg."

Buck sniffed the air. "Smells like rain too. It's gonna be about as much fun as tryin' to screw a one-legged whore out here by tomorrow morning."

"No shit," Theodore spat. "Let's pack up and move. We're gonna find this thing old school style."

———

The Beast was still in a rage, crashing through the woods and shattering trees as it went. The more it thought about its mistake, the more its anger grew. It had almost ruined everything. The fact that the boy was in the protection of one of the loyalists infuriated it even more.

As its anger grew, it felt its limitations more keenly. It could not venture into Morgan, as it would stand little chance against those who hadn't rebelled. It also could not go into Creekside, as it had strict orders to stay away. There was only one opportunity to satiate its hatred and regain a measure of control. The three hunters were still in the woods and two were fair game. The third might just possibly die by accident.

———

Dieter Jaeger watched intently as the mechanic made the final adjustments. He realized that he was annoying the man by hovering over him but he wanted to make sure the work was done to perfection.

"Should be good as new," the mechanic said as he patted the side of the Newell Coach. "This is one beautiful bus you have here."

Dieter was relieved because the nearly new RV's living room slide-out was making scraping noises, which was totally unacceptable for a vehicle costing upwards of a million dollars.

The cell phone in Dieter's pocket began to chime.

"Yes, may I help you?"

"Hey, this is Jay. Where the hell are you, buddy? Are you heading my way?"

"Soon. I just wanted to make sure the RV was in proper mechanical order."

"Well, you old goosestepper, when you get that land yacht of yours put together, swing by the Dells and pick me up. I'm going with you."

"You do not understand, Mr. Masters," Dieter replied, purposely leaving off the title. "I work alone."

"That's fine," Masters grumbled over the phone, obviously having understood the slight. "I'm going to stay in town while you're out bagging the game. It appears I have some unfinished business in Creekside."

CHAPTER ELEVEN

The knock on the door rattled the deadbolts and set Trudy's teeth on edge. Even though the clock radio was silent it still flew across the room, its duct-taped plastic case hitting a poster of Jimi Hendrix.

"It's Sunday, Rachel!" Trudy yelled from the bed. "No work today!"

"It's Gavin," the voice on the other side of the door responded.

Trudy's eyes flashed open. "Just a minute."

She leapt out of bed and raced to the mirror for a quick inspection and was shocked by what she encountered. Her short black hair was sticking up in every direction without even the help of a gel. Her wrinkled T-shirt and shorts had seen better days. Frantically she rummaged through the closet, looking for her robe.

"I need to speak with you," Gavin said, "it's kinda important."

"Hold your horses, Champ, I'm working on it."

Finally in a state that she deemed barely acceptable, she opened the door. Gavin stood before her with one hand on the door frame. Her first instinct was to hug him and then slug him for not updating her as to what was happening. *Doesn't anyone know how to use a cell phone in this town?* she thought.

"Do you want to go to church?" he asked.

"Wow," she said in wonder. "I told you this place would screw with your mind. What's with the sudden change there, mister secular college boy?"

"Kind of hard to argue when the supernatural sits on your chest. May I come in?"

"Sure, make yourself at home."

Gavin surveyed the room and stooped to pick up the clock radio. "You're kind of hard on this poor thing, aren't you?"

"My nemesis in the morning. That, and Rachel. By the way, how is she?"

"The human Rachel or the angel Rachel?" he asked as he put the radio back on the nightstand.

"So you know?"

"We were attacked in the woods by a demon. Rachel turned into this huge glowing warrior thingy, just like in a comic book." Gavin sat on the bed. "She saved me, even if she doesn't take credit for it."

Trudy shot him a worried look as she sat down next to him. "A demon? Are you okay?"

"I'm fine now. So, how long have you known that they are angels? And why didn't you tell me?"

Trudy sighed. "I've known ever since the community started over in Morgan. We've all known for years. I was paired with Rachel about two years ago. Some of us are assigned an angel to help with their immersion into human life, although I admit she's been a little more work than most," she said with a smile. "There are always new arrivals in Morgan so eventually everyone in town will be paired with an angel."

"Everyone? The whole town? Everyone will have an angel as a buddy?"

"Yep, well, perhaps not Bill—wouldn't want to do that to an angel. Anyway, Maggie got the ball rolling and informed us one at a time. It's not a big town so it didn't take long. We went through all of those stages that you probably just went through: disbelief all the way through to acceptance. They're like our family now, and we protect them from the outside world. Sometimes, as you have seen, they protect us as well."

"That's a pretty big secret to be keeping," Gavin said.

"I wanted to tell you but I decided you'd think I'm even crazier than I normally appear. Besides, Creekside is known to be standoffish with outsiders; wouldn't want me to break with tradition, now would you?

"So," she continued. "Did they have any ideas about your headaches and that little skunk incident?"

Gavin let out a long, cleansing breath. "They think the surgeon zigged when he should have zagged inside my noggin—basically said my brain is better than new because of it."

"Then it's not a problem?"

"Oh, it's a big problem. Now I have demons hunting for me."

"What?" Trudy said in shock. "I don't understand."

"Apparently the lightning is a portal that they use in Morgan. We can't see it because we've fallen since creation. The demons can't see it because they have fallen even further. Since I'm able to see it, they will try to use me to find the locations of the ladders and shut them down."

Trudy stared at him. She thought she heard what he said but for some reason her brain was unable to process it. She knew the angels came into the world through some kind of portal, but demons were something new, and the idea that they would want to use Gavin to find those portals frightened her.

"Look," Gavin explained, "the demons don't want the angels to understand us better. They believe that their kind is far higher than humans, and it is disgraceful for them to associate with us. It's also a little jab at God to mess with his servants. Whenever a community is formed the Fallen ones try to shut it down as quickly as possible. Not knowing where the ladders are causes them to search for months, or even years, before they find one."

Trudy gasped. "And if they have you, they can find them faster?"

Gavin shrugged embarrassedly. "Guess I'm kinda like a dousing rod for angel ladders. If this one is removed, my headaches will start again and get worse the further I am from one. They'll also get better as I move closer. Naturally, I'm going to move closer to the next one."

Trudy studied him, her brow knitted. "And they'll follow you."

"Exactly," he said with a sigh. "And so on and so forth, always moving and always being followed."

"Did they have any suggestions?"

"If they have any ideas, they haven't told me about them yet. As far as the healing, they don't know if it's related to some residual power from the ladder or if it's a natural talent of mine. The angels are too polite to just come out and say that I'm screwed, but I could see it in their eyes."

Trudy put a hand on his knee. "We'll figure this out. Rachel may be a country bumpkin in her human form, but she has thousands of years of experience and is one of the most powerful beings in the universe. She'll help us. She's the closest thing I have to a sister in this world." She repeated, "She'll help us."

Gavin looked at her and put his hand on top of hers. "It shouldn't be 'us,' Trudy. It's my problem. No reason for you to get involved."

"Hey, kiddo, so far I've only seen the good side of having angels as neighbors. So now their crazy relatives from Michigan show up and start causing a ruckus. We'll deal with it." She smiled and put her lips to his cheek. With a gentle peck she whispered, "Let me get cleaned up and then we'll go to church."

"Are you sure I'm dressed okay?" Gavin asked Trudy as they entered the Evangelical Lutheran Church of Creekside. "When I packed, church wasn't really on my to-do list."

She looked him over, slovenly appealingly in Levi's and a sweatshirt. "You're in Creekside. Minimum standards for church here are bib overalls—shoes are optional." She wrapped her arm around his. "You'll be fine."

Trudy noticed Reverend Brustad beaming at Gavin from the front of the little church as they entered and found their seats. She knew it was the Reverend's blessing as well as his curse that his congregation believed 100 percent in his message. There was no one to save from hell. There was no doubt in the building; the residents of Morgan had assured that long ago. His signs out front became increasingly outlandish in hopes of luring some passerby or tourist driving through town to stop and attend a service, yet nobody came. The altar steps were dusty from lack of knees of the converted, and the membership stayed constant, but she knew he always maintained hope.

They found a pew about midway down the sanctuary and five rows behind Maggie, who sat near the front. Trudy noticed Gavin fidgeting. "You okay?"

"Sure. It's been a long time since I've sat down in church. Is Rachel coming?"

"No," Trudy whispered. "Church is for humans, not for angels. They don't want to intrude. They have their own worship time in Morgan."

Gavin looked down at the mimeographed order of service he held in his hand.

"High-tech stuff, isn't it?" she jested as they read the bulletin. The title of today's sermon: *Angels – God's Army.*

"Oh, freakin' great," Gavin sighed.

The service began with a hymn "Beautiful Isle of Somewhere," which the bulletin said was written by one Jessie Brown Pounds in 1897 and was sung at the funeral of assassinated president William McKinley. Trudy held Gavin's hand while they stood and sang the last verse:

> *Somewhere the load is lifted,*
> *Close by an open gate;*
> *Somewhere the clouds are rifted,*
> *Somewhere the angels wait.*

The scripture reading for the service was from the Book of Revelation 12:7: *And there was war in heaven. Michael and his angels fought against the dragon and the dragon and his angels fought back. But he was not strong enough and they lost their place in heaven. The great dragon was hurled down—that ancient serpent called the devil, or Satan, who leads the whole world astray. He was hurled to the earth and his angels with him.*

Reverend Brustad stepped up to begin his sermon but stopped suddenly, his mouth hanging open as he looked to the back of the sanctuary.

Everyone, including Trudy and Gavin, turned to see what held the Reverend's gaze.

Standing in the back of the building was Brother Jonathan.

"Reverend," Jonathan said, "I apologize for this intrusion, but may I address the congregation?"

It took a moment for Brustad to regain his speech. "Certainly brother, it is a great honor."

Jonathan approached the pulpit. "I wish I were here under better circumstances," he said to Brustad as he patted his arm and then turned to address the congregation.

"War is coming to Creekside."

The congregation looked in dismay at one another and whispered, unsure what Jonathan meant. Trudy's grip tightened on Gavin's hand.

"A demon has been sighted in the woods outside of Morgan. It is, we believe, what killed the hunter several weeks ago. I expect it will kill again."

The room became silent, waiting for him to continue.

"Where one is, many will follow. They seek to shut down Morgan. They consider the world their domain and do not want us here. If we stay, I'm afraid that they will take out their wrath upon your town. I'm proposing that we leave Morgan and avert this war."

The congregation began talking loudly amongst themselves.

Josh Barber stood up. "Jonathan, what do you mean 'leave'? You made your homes here. We've invited you into our homes, our lives. You can't just up and decide to leave."

"I understand the pain involved in this," Jonathan replied. "But I've seen this before." Jonathan looked towards Maggie, who sat several rows back. "A lot of good people died needlessly."

Maggie stood up, visibly shaking with anger. "Jonathan!" she scolded. "Do you mock what we have as our town motto? *Tutela Lux Lucis*. Protecting Light? That is what our existence is here. If people do not stand up and protect the light, then darkness will follow. It happened in Nepal after you left. The darkness that descended was unspeakable. I was safely back in the States but I read about it. I heard of the atrocities when the Maoist rebels came through the area that I previously called home. Certainly the killings by demons ended, but the deaths at the hands of other humans grew."

"Are you saying it was a mistake for us to have left?" Jonathan asked.

"Of course I am! You were a force for good in the area. You often say how the community is for your benefit, your chance to try on human skin and live like we do. But if you were truly human you would know that you cannot just pack up and leave when circumstances turn against you. It's part of being human to realize that you are in a bad place and there is no way to avoid it. You must go through it."

"If we stay," Jonathan said gravely, "then some of the people sitting here in this congregation will not be here at the end."

Brustad placed a hand on Jonathan's shoulder. "You don't know that, brother. You are a powerful being but you are not God. One of your kind thought he was higher than God, and he now roams the earth in disgrace. Unless God has told you that we will die, do not assume it."

Jonathan lowered his head, clearly distraught by what Maggie had said. "I am at a loss for words. You show great love for us, even though we are so unlike you. I see again why He calls you His sons and daughters. I will bring your request before the community of Morgan."

———

Theodore bulled his way through the underbrush as a light rain began. He proceeded down a slight hill as Pervis and Buck followed behind him.

"How do you know if we're going the right way?" Pervis asked. "I don't see no signs of that whatchamacallit, and we been walking for hours."

Theodore slid a couple feet down the muddy hill. "Hey, get down here, boys. I've got something to show you. I think I've found that sign you've been bitching about."

"You found some broken branches?" Buck asked.

"Uh, in a way," Theodore said. "Come see for yourself."

Pervis made it down the hill and could only stare in disbelief.

Buck spoke for all of them: "Holy mother of shit."

"Well, boys," Theodore said proudly. "Looks like I found us a sign—hell, a whole damn highway."

"Shit the bed! Looks like a herd of elephant's been through here," Pervis said as he surveyed the broken timber that stretched from east to west.

Buck knelt down to observe one of the footprints. "It's definitely no elephant. Prints as big as one, though, but elephants don't have claws."

"Hell with this," Pervis spat. "I didn't sign on to hunt some monster. I'm glad it's going that direction. I say we go find that piece o' shit Hyundai and get out of here."

"Not so fast," Theodore replied. "It won't expect us to be following it, so we have the element of surprise. If we can stay behind it and get close enough for a shot, we can collect an easy ten grand from that sumbitch Masters. Besides, if it's something really interesting we can probably force the tightwad to shell out more than that—a lot more."

"Or," Buck suggested, "we can sell it to the highest bidder."

Theodore grinned and a trickle of tobacco ran down his chin. "Now you're talking. It'd serve that cheap bastard right if we did. Well, what do you girls say? Want to go find us that overgrown bear or whatever it is?"

Buck put his booted foot in one of the tracks; the print was a good four times bigger. "We're gonna to need some help hauling this mother out. A lotta help."

"Once we have it down we'll have people begging to come out here and help us, just to catch a glimpse of the thing." Theodore said. "Masters is right. It will be quite the show."

The Beast swiveled its heads back down its improvised trail. With its eight ears, its hearing was precise, which served it well in the forest. What it heard now was the sound of fortune blundering towards it.

This time it was determined not to make another stupid mistake. It decided to move off of its route and parallel the shattered trees in the direction of the sound. As it approached the hunters, it crept closer to the trail. The ridiculous trio moved past the Beast without noticing. Once it was behind them, it decided to strike.

Bounding out of the brush and into the clearing, it did not attempt silence. It wanted the fools to see it, to fear it, just before their deaths.

The men turned, and the Beast soaked in the shock and horror that was on their faces. Before any of them could lift their rifles, the Beast covered the twenty yards to the men in a half dozen strides.

First to die was the hunter with the matted hair that the Beast was allowed to kill. The look of surprise on the human's face pleased it. It reveled in the human's dumbfounded expression—not even knowing it was being killed as a claw swiped across his torso, making a clean wound through the jacket, into the tender white flesh; it rejoiced at the geyser of blood that painted the pine needles and leaf mold red. The human made a valiant but unsuccessful attempt at holding in his spilling guts before collapsing face first into the dirt.

The Beast howled in pain as a knife plunged deep into its forelimb. Instinctively it swatted the human away, sending the hunter crashing into a tree ten yards away. The Beast was going in for the kill but then noticed the tall one raising his rifle. This was the one that it had orders not to kill. Conflicted, it stood motionless for a moment, but then decided to obey its masters. It covered the few feet to the man while turning its neck so that the cat head would face the doomed hunter. Clamping its massive jaws on the hand holding the rifle, it felt the pleasant taste of blood. The gun fired but not towards the Beast. The aim was off and the round hit the human sprawled against the tree square in the forehead, spraying blood and brain matter all over the trunk. The human sank to its knees, the top of its head resembling a burning match, with a few bone fragments sticking out grotesquely.

The Beast used the pressure from its immense jaws to sever the hunter's right hand. The rifle fell to the ground, its stock cracked in two, with the blood-dripping appendage still clutching the trigger.

The human yelped in agony, which only fueled the Beast's rage. The man staggered off into the brush, blood leaving a red trail behind him and as the Beast fought with the urge to finish the prey. To make a mistake was bad enough, but to openly disobey its masters would be foolish indeed. There were unspeakable places the Beast could be relegated to, and punishments it could receive that made the forest seem like paradise. But still it was in a rage; it wanted to kill again. It needed to kill again.

—

Theodore staggered through the woods for several hundred feet before realizing that he was badly injured. Tearing a strip of fabric off of his shirt he made an improvised bandage and covered the mangled flesh that was his wrist. The bleeding was not as bad as he would have expected, but he kept pressure on the wound and tried to elevate it as much as he could and still run through the uneven terrain of the forest.

He had to find the Hyundai and get to civilization before he went into shock and bled out. The car was still where they had left it. The difficult part was getting the keys out of his right front pocket with his left hand. Once this was accomplished, he started the car and attempted to get it out of the ditch, all the while keeping an eye out for the Beast.

After what seemed like an eternity he was able to get the car backed out onto the road and headed down the logging trail towards Creekside. The Hyundai lost its passenger side mirror to a tree as Theodore's vision went in and out of focus.

The Hyundai became airborne as it shot out of the forest and landed in the center of the road leading to Creekside. His driving was erratic, and he knew that he was starting to lose consciousness, but that only increased the panic he felt and the need to get to help.

—

Gavin and Trudy exited the Evangelical Lutheran Church of Creekside along with the rest of the congregation. The sky was overcast; a slight wind prompted him to zipper up his jacket.

"Gavin," said Jonathan, placing a hand on his shoulder just as Maggie approached them, "you need to stay away from Morgan. The Beast didn't kill you, but we do not know what it is allowed to do."

Maggie looked hard at each of their faces in turn. "Is it that serious? Gavin, what happened out there? You ran out of the house today before I could even ask. Are you all right?"

"Don't worry," Jonathan said, turning to Maggie. "I'll fill you in on the events."

He turned back to Gavin. "I'm going to assign Rachel to watch over you until we figure this out."

Gavin was about to protest until Trudy put a calming hand on his arm. "Thank you, Jonathan," she said.

A red Hyundai roared into Creekside at least thirty miles per hour over the posted twenty-five miles per hour speed limit. The rear suspension was obviously shot, as it caused the back bumper to drag the ground, throwing up sparks as it went. The mailbox on the corner of Main was the first victim. After the impact, the car veered to the left, crossed the street, and just barely missed a street light.

Bouncing over the curb, it continued down the sidewalk until it ran into a fire hydrant across the street from the church. The white billow of the airbag could be seen through the windshield even as it cracked under the folding of the chassis. The hydrant was sheared off at ground level, and a plume of water shot twenty feet into the air.

The congregation ran towards the car to check for injuries.

Josh Barber reached it first and was able to grab hold of the door handle, and, by putting his right foot on the side of the car, force it open.

Gavin and Trudy were next to reach the car.

"It's him!" she said while shielding her eyes from the fireplug's artificial rain.

"Him who?" Gavin asked, gazing a little nauseously at the man with the bloody stump slouched over the steering wheel.

"The guy who was hitting on me and Rachel when we were walking to work. I think he said his name was Theodore."

"Is he alive?" Reverend Brustad asked.

"Looks like he's breathing," Josh Barber said. "He lost a lot of blood though. Did anyone call 911?"

"I did," said Ed Graff, who had just come puffing up. "But it's going to take them awhile to get here. Do we move him?"

Jonathan moved closer and looked at the man in the driver's seat. "He needs medical attention *now*, Gavin."

He looked skeptically at Jonathan. "You've got to be shitting—uh, I mean, I can't. You do it—you're an angel and all."

Jonathan's face was as bland as a stone. "It is not my role, and I have not been given permission. It is for you to do this."

"But—but it's not like a skunk."

"It's exactly like a skunk," Trudy countered. "And I'm probably insulting skunks by calling him that."

Gavin looked down and knew that the blood-soaked driver was probably in shock and close to death.

"Ah, shit," Gavin sighed as he reached out his hand.

Gavin's middle finger brushed Theodore's shoulder and a spark flew between them. Gavin exhaled in relief; he was expecting at least a skunk-sized shock. The driver looked like he was regaining consciousness as his eyes briefly opened and looked at Gavin.

Then it hit, a blinding white bolt went between the two that knocked Gavin to the ground. The crowed made no move to help him up, but just stared on in incredulity.

"Look!" Trudy said as she absently attempted to help Gavin to his feet while keeping her attention on Theodore.

Theodore groaned and moved his head. For all intents he looked the same as before Gavin touched him except for one detail: The stump of his wrist was growing. The bloody bandage had come loose, and it moved apart as the change took place.

The crowd gasped. Trudy clutched Gavin's hand, gouging her nails into his flesh.

What had been bloody mangled meat was becoming whole again. Gavin could make out the back of a hand that soon sprouted fingers and fingernails. The flesh, ashen at first, soon turned pink with restored blood flow.

Theodore moaned. "Where am I?"

Trudy leaned down towards him and asked, "Where are you friends? What happened to them?"

"Dead. It got them both."

"What got them?" Josh Barber asked.

"I think it is clear what did," Jonathan ventured. "It's starting."

The ambulance and an Oneida County Sheriff's Department pickup pulled up next to the crash. Sheriff Winston got out of the truck as the paramedics approached Theodore.

"What happened?" Winston bellowed, then he noticed the driver. "Oh, this guy again. He has a fetish for fire hydrants. Is he injured?"

A paramedic responded, "Lots of blood but I'm not seeing any wounds—has to be from somebody else."

"He said his two buddies are dead," Trudy contributed.

"Okay, get him ready to transport." Winston barked. "You can get him fixed up enough for a nice stay in my jail."

Winston turned to Trudy. "Did he say anything else?"

"No, nothing."

"Okay," the sheriff said. "Fire Department and local police are on their way." He looked over to Josh. "I'm going to need to ruin your Sunday, Josh, and have you tow the car to impound if you don't mind." He turned and looked down the street. "Guess I need to inform the post office as well. I swear, I need to start avoiding this town—too much commotion for my taste." He looked over to Maggie, who gave him a disapproving look that he had probably seen countless times before.

When the sheriff regained his composure he addressed the group that had formed. "Did anyone see the accident?"

All hands went up.

"Was he driving erratically?"

All nodded their agreement.

"Anything unusual about this whole thing?"

They stood there with blank faces.

"Just a guy with somebody else's blood all over him driving into a fire hydrant, then?"

Gavin heard Maggie give a disgusted *humph* and walk away.

Winston scratched his growling belly. "Okay, nothing more to see here. Move along!" He continued to mutter to himself. "Looks like I get stuck with trying to sort this mess out. A blood-soaked redneck without a scratch on 'im—just what I need, an apparent murder case. Well, nothing for it but to call the lab rats in—and I haven't even ate yet."

CHAPTER TWELVE

Reverend Masters sat in his office at the Mysterium, looking at the clock. "Where is that Kraut anyway?" he groused, then gazed out the windows of his office. People said that Lake Delton was beautiful. All he could see was water and trees. Water and trees didn't make money. The black tent of the Mysterium blocked out the prime view of the lake from arriving customers, but he had little interest in giving them freebies anyway. The beautiful thing, the thing that mattered most, was just below him in the Mysterium proper. His future—probably his life—depended upon the success of what went on below him.

That was what made the wait for Dieter so damn infuriating. Perhaps the rich German didn't have a care in the world, but he did. It was a mountain of care piled up on his accounts payable manager's desk. Then he remembered that something remained to be packed. Opening his desk drawer he removed a Ruger P95. The black 9mm pistol felt comfortable in his hand. He rooted around in the desk until he found two full clips of ammo.

His suitcase was packed and sitting on the couch against the wall. He walked over to it and unzipped it, placing the weapon safely inside and closing it again.

He decided to walk out to the reception area. Holly was sitting at her desk, watching Netflix re-runs of *So You Think You Can Dance* on her computer. Her skirt was far too short for appropriate office attire at any business, the possible exception being a strip joint. Masters was pleased.

"Holly, have you thought about coming with me?"

"Not on your life," she said. "You're going to find that thing, and I want nothing to do with it."

"You're going to leave me with Dieter for company?" he pouted. "That isn't showing much compassion for your employer."

Holly took her hands off the desk and crossed her arms while glaring at him. "My employer shouldn't be hunting for that thing in the first place. Leave it in the woods. Why do you even want that monster?"

He thought for a moment. "It reminds me of my father," he said as he sat on the corner of her desk. "I can't just let it go, Holly. If you actually performed your administrative assistant duties you'd know we're going broke. We need a spectacle to bring in the tourists."

"I'd rather be broke," she grumbled.

"I'm not letting everything I've worked for vanish in bankruptcy court. My father was a supreme asshole. Never worked a day in his life as far as I know, and he had the nerve to tell me that I'm worthless! I've built more here than he could even dream of in one of his alcohol-fueled delusions. We're, not folding Holly. *I'm* not folding."

Holly put her hand on his thigh. "You can always make a fresh start. I'd help you."

He looked at her and gave a genuine smile. "You're a good girl, but there are some paths we can't go down. That is one of them. We'll make this work just as it is. Do you remember when I first met you?"

Holly brightened. "Sure, you came to see me dance."

"That I did. I was in Minneapolis, and who would have thought that a young woman from Pole Cat Crossing, Wisconsin, would be dancing in the evening show at Sinners."

"You were quite the charmer back then," Holly said wistfully. "Said I had a place in the entertainment business and was meant for more than being gawked at by people who don't realize my real talent."

Masters smiled, remembering that she was so uncoordinated that she could barely hold onto the stripper pole. "I'm still a charmer. And I still mean what I said back then, but in order to do that we need to have the business. This creature, or whatever it is, can be our way of keeping it and maybe even expanding. Wouldn't you like to see a Masters' Mysterium in every mega tourist trap? Las Vegas, Orlando, Niagara Falls? Of course that would mean travel for you."

"Branson, Missouri, don't forget Branson!" she chimed in. "I love that place. If only I could sing, I could probably work some of the shows there. They have wonderful Christmas shows …"

"That's my girl," he said, happy to see that he smoothed his way past the issue. "I'll get you some vocal lessons. Most of those big stars are auto-tuned or lip-synching anyway." Holly really was a good sort but also easily distracted. He could see that she was now picturing herself donning some outrageously tacky outfit and dancing three shows a day at the Andy Williams Theater in the hillbilly Mecca of Branson.

There was a knock at the door. "May I come in?"

"Dieter, is that you?" Masters yelled. "About fucking time, get in here!"

"You must learn to curb your vulgar language if you are to travel with me," sniffed Dieter upon entering.

"Yeah, bring some soap along to wash out my mouth. Holly, watch the shop for me. If those three bozos call, give them my cell number."

Holly stood up, her arms poised slightly away from her body, but she seemed unsure if she should hug him goodbye in front of the visitor. She settled for a little wave and a "keep safe, Jay."

———

Sheriff Winston sat in the interrogation room with Theodore, listening to his improbable story. The detectives had already gone over it a dozen times, but anything to do with Creekside was a special case for him. He thought of Maggie for a moment, then snapped out of it.

"Let me understand this," Winston said. "A giant monster killed your friends and bit off your hand, didn't like the taste of it, and spat it out. The right hand that you are currently holding that cigarette with. Which, by the way, is not allowed in the Justice Center, but I'm making an exception this once because I'm a nice guy. The blood in the car is really yours and that a kid in Creekside zapped you with a lightning bolt and healed you. This is after the space alien girl tossed your pickup around like a Tonka toy. Am I missing anything?"

"You don't believe me?" Theodore protested.

Winston got in the man's face, spittle flying. "Hell, of course I don't believe you! Who in their right mind would? Now, the way I figure it, you go into the woods with your buddies to poach this wolf. A while into it you're arguing and drinking, drinking and arguing, until a fight breaks out. You're the only one that survives the altercation, dazed and blood soaked. You drive into town but are so overcome by the circumstances that you accidentally crash your car."

Winston and Theodore were now eyeball to eyeball. "Now doesn't that make more sense?"

"If it was true," Theodore said unblinkingly, "But it ain't."

Winston rocked back in his creaky chair. "Then why don't you lead us out there into the woods and show us where your brother and your friend are? You know we're going to find them sooner or later. Sooner is better for you. We value cooperation with the authorities here. It will make life a lot easier for you. Also, if that monster is out there like you say, we don't want to risk anyone getting hurt needlessly as they search the woods."

Theodore huffed. "Now you're—what's that word?—patronizing me."

"Wow, four syllables—very good." Winston smiled.

"Look," Theodore said, "I'll take you out there so I can show you my hand. It's got to be in the woods still. You can run the prints. They'll match. Also, it's my own dear brother's mangled body what's out there. Blood of my blood. I want to see him get a proper burial."

"Well, it will be dark by the time we get out there so it's best to wait until first light," Winston said as he stood up. "Looks like you get to enjoy our accommodations for the evening. We'll regroup tomorrow and find that extra hand of yours." He looked at Theodore as he motioned for the deputy to take him away. "And you better hope we find one."

Theodore was led away, and Sheriff Winston returned to his office to find one of the lab assistants waiting for him. He sat down in his chair and sighed. Oneida was a sparsely populated county and the murder rate could usually be counted on one hand, minus the thumb. Creekside and Morgan were starting to play hell with his statistics for the year.

"So what did you find out at the crash site?" he asked.

"Interesting," the technician said. "The front seat was covered in blood, and there was a bloody bandage on the floor. The driver didn't have any cuts or bruises on his body. They took a blood sample at the hospital and we ran one on the blood in the car. Both are AB negative—an extremely rare blood type; only about one percent of the population have it. It would be extremely rare to have more than one out of three with this blood type."

"What about the brother? Couldn't he be a match?"

"Half-brother we found out. That makes him a long shot for a match. We'll know more when we get the bodies in for autopsy. In the meantime we can do some DNA matching from the white blood cells if you like."

"No," Winston said after thinking for a moment. "Keep the samples in case we need to do them later, but I'm not spending taxpayer money based on what this asshole's saying. I can predict what they would say at election time: 'Sheriff wastes taxpayer money on space alien hunch.'"

———

"Can't you drive any faster than this?" Masters said in disgust.

"I prefer safety over speed." Dieter said. "I'm confident your will-o'-the-wisp will still be there when we arrive."

"Yeah, but I may be dead from old age," Masters growled as his cell phone started ringing.

"It's Holly," Masters smiled. "Maybe some good news. What's up, babe?"

"Jay, I received a call from one of the hunters—the drooling one, Theodore. He said he needs bail money: five hundred grand bond to get him out."

"Shit!" Masters swore as he glanced over to see Dieter's scowl. "A half-mill? That's going to cost me fifty grand to have a bail bondsman spring him. He isn't worth fifty grand. He's out of his mind. What did they do?"

"Sounds bad this time. He says the other two are dead, killed by that thing in the woods. Police think he did it because his story is so whacked." Masters thought he heard her whimper before she went on. "Jay, be careful, darling. I'm scared."

"It'll be okay," he replied. "Don't worry. I'll deal with that numbskull when I get up there. Where's he being held?"

"Oneida County Jail in Rhinelander."

"Okay, he can just sit there and watch his fellow inbred retards on Springer on the prison television for a while. I'll deal with that later. We're still on plan to reach Creekside tonight—if Dieter can find the gas pedal, that is."

"There's more, Jay," said Holly. "He said they're taking him out to the woods tomorrow to find the bodies."

"Double shit!" he yelled again, oblivious to his driver's sensibilities. "Just what we need, the authorities traipsing around in the area. I was afraid this might happen."

Masters hung up the phone.

"Well, Dieter, looks like you're the man now. The other three are out of commission, two of them permanently."

"What happened?"

"Just what I thought would happen. I bent over and they fucked me up the ass."

Dieter hit the brakes with both feet, locking the brakes and sliding the RV to a screeching stop. Before Masters could say anything, Dieter had slipped the vehicle into park and removed his seat belt. With athleticism that belied his age Dieter bounded from his seat and onto the Reverend's chest, pushing the passenger seat all the way back. Masters looked down to see a twelve-inch knife up against his throat.

"I thought I had made my position regarding vile language clear," he hissed. "The spoken word is sacred to me; I will not tolerate cretins who cannot express themselves civilly without resorting to crudities and outright vulgarity. Not in my recreational vehicle. Not in my home. You will do me the courtesy of remembering that. Are we clear?"

Masters gulped. "As rain."

———

Trudy sat on the counter at the Citgo station, munching on cheese curds out of a plastic bag. There was nothing like fresh cheddar cheese curds from the dairy state with their characteristic squeak when chewed, due to trapped air within them, something the *New York Times* once described as the sound of "balloons trying to neck."

"That was really something," Josh kept saying to Gavin, who stood near a display of bean dip. "How'd you do that?"

"Wish I knew," Gavin replied.

"Well, it was really something …" Josh trailed off. "Oh, that redneck," he added. "He was in here with his friends a while back. A real piece of work, that one; all three for that matter. He got mad when I couldn't sell him booze and porn. They got a little flighty when I started reaching for the bodyguard under the counter." Trudy and Gavin stared at him blankly. "My Smith and Wesson Bodyguard 380," he explained. "They decided to take off."

"That's probably when Rachel and I ran into them," Trudy said. "Rachel pimped their ride for them, but not in a good way."

"Ha!" Josh smiled. "I had to tow that thing away. That little lady really knows how to lay the smack down."

"Speaking of which," Gavin said, "I'm not sure that I want Rachel following me around like a hired gun."

Trudy looked at him. "Kiddo, you're like a celebrity for the demons now, so you need a little security detail just to keep the groupies at bay. Who's better than an angel for the job?"

"So, what am I supposed to do now?" Gavin said as he grabbed a bag of chips and dug in his pocket.

Josh waved his calloused hand. "Your money isn't any good here son. You're a celebrity, remember? Besides, I feel like I should pay you for today's entertainment."

"You're supposed to stay in Creekside until Jonathan comes up with the next move. Staying here isn't such a bad thing is it?" Trudy asked, batting her eyes at him comically.

Gavin smiled. "True, but I just feel like I'm not contributing to my own destiny."

The bell over the front door rang. All three turned to see who it was.

"Hello!" Rachel chirped. "Sounds like I missed all of the excitement." Her blonde hair was braided into a ponytail, and she wore a blue-checked long-sleeved shirt with blue jeans and a rope belt.

"Have you been watching *The Beverly Hillbillies* again, Elly May?" Trudy quipped. She leaned toward Gavin and confided. "She's addicted to that show."

Rachel blushed. "How did you guess? Reverend Brustad had it on the tube the other day. It's a fascinating story about a rustic group of people being transplanted into a rich, materialistic world they do not fully understand."

Trudy sighed. "Only Rachel can wax philosophical over a hayseed sitcom."

"Jonathan told me to watch over Gavin," Rachel said. "I'll be moving over to Maggie's house for a while." She looked at Trudy. "Don't worry, I will be unobtrusive. I'm not going to get in the way of your bonding with Gavin."

Trudy's mouth dropped open like a barn gate as Gavin stared at his feet and Josh turned away to laugh.

CHAPTER THIRTEEN

The first rays of light shone upon a very unhappy Reverend Masters. Dieter had insisted that they camp overnight at a luxury RV park just shy of their destination. Chastened by Dieter's outburst, and having lost the power of the expletive, Masters was unable to adequately convey the urgency of the situation.

He had also never realized how much work was involved in the recreational aspects of such a vehicle. Setting up camp took upwards of three hours, and the breakdown looked to be about the same. "What the hell, Dieter." Masters said, wrestling with a folding chair. "Uh, I can use the word 'hell,' can't I?"

"That is acceptable, if you feel that way," Dieter replied as he precisely rolled up the AstroTurf in front of the coach. "There is actually a small town on Grand Cayman that is named Hell. It has some very interesting rock formations."

"What about 'damn'?" Masters chided. "They used that in *Gone with the Wind.* As in, 'Frankly, my dear, I don't give a damn.'"

"If you insist," Dieter blandly replied as he stowed the carpet in one of the massive storage lockers under the bus.

"'Shit' should be good," He pushed, "Bodily function, right? As in, 'Does a bear shit in the woods?'"

Dieter pushed a button to retract the awning into the side of the vehicle.

"Reverend Masters, I only ask for the respect that is due when you are in somebody else's home. The occasional expletive is permissible, if the circumstance allows. It is gratuitous swearing that I cannot abide."

Dieter climbed up into the coach and sat in the driver's seat. "I believe we are ready."

The hunter pulled out of the campground and approached the main highway leading north. Masters sat in the passenger seat, nursing a cappuccino that Dieter had prepared in his marble and stainless steel wonder of a rolling kitchen.

"What's the holdup?" he groaned. "It's going to take us all day to get twenty miles if you can't even get out of the campground."

"Look to the south," Dieter said as he motioned to his right.

Two police cars, followed by two unmarked vans, were making their way up the road, heading in the direction of Creekside. The two vans pulled off into a BP station across the street, but the two squad cars continued north. As they passed, Masters could make out a passenger in the back seat of the first car.

"Theodore!" Masters gasped. "That son of a bitch is going to take them out there to find the bodies." He struggled to use his now limited vocabulary and not spill his coffee at the same time.

"Let me out," he said at a whisper.

"Reverend?"

Masters stood up. "Let me out," he slowly repeated.

Once Dieter opened the door, Masters hopped down onto the gravel skirt of the road and threw his coffee mug against the nearest tree. He then walked about thirty feet away from the RV to make sure that he was outside of the prudish German's mobile homeland.

"Shit!" he shouted. "Fuck you, Theodore, you asshole, I hope you burn in hell!"

———

The clock radio belched out Robert Plant's "Angel Dance" until Trudy swatted it off the nightstand, dislodging several rubber bands that held the masochistic thing together.

The doorbell rang.

"Monday already, Rachel?" Trudy grumbled as she got out of bed and staggered to the door. Reaching down her shorts, she attempted to adjust the elastic of her underwear, which had grabbed her thigh in its viselike grip. Opening the door with her other hand she had time to let out a giant yawn that quickly turned into a gasp.

Rachel, in her starched pink uniform, greeted her with a big smile; to Rachel's right was Gavin.

"*Arggh!*" Trudy yelped as she slammed the door shut. "What's he doing here?"

Rachel gently knocked on the door. "I had to bring Gavin. I'm responsible to watch out for him, but also for my work."

"Believe me," Gavin was quick to add, "it wasn't my idea to be here at five in the morning."

Pulling her arm out of her pants, Trudy found her robe and ran her fingers through her spiky hair as she looked in the mirror. She rubbed her sleeves across her eyes in an attempt to remove whatever grossness had congealed there during the night. When she decided that she looked a little less like the Creature from the Black Lagoon, she opened the door.

"Come in," she sighed and motioned them inside.

Rachel bounded into the room and sat on the bed and looked at Gavin and Trudy with a grin.

"Sorry," Gavin whispered to Trudy. "I couldn't stop her."

"Rachel," Trudy said, "what are you grinning about? You're creeping me out."

"Ohh, just admiring you two—you're the perfect couple."

Trudy scowled at her hopelessly Pollyannaish friend. "Settle down there, Little Miss Matchmaker. I know you don't have any experience with such things, but don't push it. *Please* don't push it. I told you it doesn't happen that way."

Rachel looked stricken. "I didn't realize …" Her lower lip quivered as she appeared ready to cry. "I just want the best for both of you. I'm sorry."

Trudy walked over and kissed Rachel on the top of the head. "It's okay." She looked at Gavin. "I guess sometimes we need a little angelic help to get out of our ruts."

A noise was coming from the street.

Gavin looped his way around the dirty laundry piles to the window.

"What's going on?" Trudy asked.

Gavin parted the drapes and said, "There's a coupla sheriff cars on the other side of the street. Winston is in one of them, and I believe it's the guy from the crash in the backseat—hard to tell. Looks like they're waiting for something."

Trudy went over to the other window. After a few moments two unmarked vans pulled up in back of the cars. Once the caravan was assembled the convoy headed off north in the direction of Morgan.

"Looks like they'll be searching for that guy's friends again today," Gavin said. "Hope they have better luck this time."

Trudy sat down beside Rachel. "Has Jonathan said anything? Any ideas on what we are to do?"

"Not yet, but he will," Rachel said. "I have never lived in a community before, so I've never experienced what it is like when the Fallen ones arrive, but Jonathan has. He'll know what to do."

"Well," Gavin said, "it doesn't sound like my aunt was too impressed with his last idea."

"It's different here," Rachel replied. "In Nepal, the local population turned against them. I can't really blame them; they were terrified of what was out there. Here, everyone knows what we are, and they accept it. They don't allow us to be here because they want something. They want us here because we're friends."

Trudy took Rachel's hand and patted it. "Family, remember—family."

———

The road down towards Morgan was in even worse condition than normal due to an overnight rain. Sheriff Winston watched the vehicles behind him in his mirror. The cars bounced along, scrapping their undercarriages and causing Winston to mentally recalculate the allocated repair budget for the year.

"So, where did you leave your car when you came down here?" he asked Theodore, who sat dejectedly in the back seat with his arms handcuffed behind him.

"Just down yonder a bit more—I'll tell you when," Theodore huffed. "Do I need to be handcuffed, Sheriff? Every time we hit a rut I bump my head on the roof."

"Might knock some sense into you," Winston replied. "Only sense you've shown so far is to take us to the crime scene."

"Hey," Theodore said. "Over there, see the little path off to the right? That's where we parked."

"Okay," Winston said as he came to a stop. "How much further is it from here?"

"You've gotta go by foot," Theodore said. "It's about five hundred yards straight ahead to the trail with the shattered trees, then go west on the trail about another hundred yards—can't miss it."

Winston got out of the car and motioned for the others that they were walking from here on. Opening the rear passenger door he motioned to Theodore. "You up for a walk?"

"Well, I sure as hell don't wanna be left here with that monster in the woods."

After a few hundred yards of maneuvering through the thick underbrush, Sheriff Winston wished he had actually used that treadmill he'd bought with the best of intentions for something other than a hat rack. Sweat was quickly staining his once pressed uniform. "Only monsters I see out here," he said while swatting at his head, "are mosquitos.

"So, where is this trail?" he asked Theodore.

"Just up a bit further. Believe me you can't miss it." Theodore slipped in the mud and came down hard on his knees. "Do you think you can let me out of these handcuffs so I don't kill myself on a rock?"

Two officers grabbed Theodore by the arms and lifted him back to his feet. "Don't think so," Winston said. "You're doing fine."

He could see light up ahead, like the forest was clearing a bit. They worked their way up a slight rise and surveyed the area.

"About time," Theodore groaned.

"What did they bring through here anyway," one of the team members mused, "a bulldozer?"

"Looks like a firebreak," another conjectured.

"Okay," Winston said. "Let's get down there and take a look."

Most of the party successfully slid down the muddy slope and into the clearing. Winston noticed a trooper giving Theodore a shove that sent him sprawling in the mud.

"Hey!" Winston yelled. "We treat everyone with respect here, even him."

"Sorry," the trooper said, grabbing Theodore under the arm and hauling him back up again.

"Settle down," Winston said, holding his hand against a pine tree that had been split in two. The trunk went up about five feet to end in a jagged tear while the rest of the tree lay off to the side of the trail. He looked east and then west; everywhere the destruction was the same. A path about six feet wide was lined with broken and splintered trees while anything in the path was either trampled or uprooted.

"Believe me now?" Theodore snorted as he tried to shake mud out of his shoes.

"It is curious, I admit," Winston said. "Hardly proves your monster story though. Or your space alien story, or any other cockamamie story you might have. Which way now?"

"West," Theodore said. "Not far."

Making their way up the trail, they soon found what they were looking for: two dead bodies, one face down in the mud and the other leaning against a tree.

"What a stench!" one of the investigators said.

"Yeah," said another. "Too bad we didn't find them when they were fresher—easier on the nose."

"Here," said the first investigator, digging into his pocket. He produced a jar of Vicks VapoRub, smeared a little under his nose, and tossed the ointment to his partner.

As they stood there a few feet from the crime scene, Winston pulled Theodore over by the arm. He could see him staring at his brother's corpse, visibly shaken. "Tell me about it son, what happened?"

Theodore gagged a bit and then proceeded. "We was following the trail and the footprints, thinking we was behind it. It musta known we was coming because it went off the trail and circled back behind us."

"No chance we'll find any tracks in this mud," An officer said as he looked down. "Even our tracks our filling in."

"Anyway," Theodore said, glaring at the deputy that interrupted him, "we got to this point when it decided to attack us. My brother here"—he pointed with his head to the man face down on the ground—"he didn't have a chance. The monster gutted him with one claw swipe."

With no little surprise, Winston noticed that Theodore was crying.

"He was a good kid," Theodore said. "He didn't deserve to go with his guts spread out in the mud. Buck over there, well, he got his Bowie out and was able to stab the thing once in the shoulder. But that only made the creature mad as hell. It tossed him against the tree like he was a rag doll."

"Where were you during all this?" Winston asked.

"I was back there a few feet. The monster was coming for me next," Theodore said, his voice rising slightly. "I was trying to bring my rifle up but it decided to chomp on my hand. My shot was off and hit Buck there, but I think he was dead already anyway."

"Is that your rifle on the ground over there?" the sheriff asked.

"Yeah, that's it. The thing chewed my hand off at the wrist. It was still holding the rifle, and they fell right over there—rifle and my hand."

"Funny thing," Winston said. "I'm not seeing a hand attached to the firearm."

The other officers laughed.

Theodore bristled. "I swear to God I ain't shittin' you! Why would I lie? I bet some varmint ran off with it."

Winston walked over and looked down at Pervis, who was attracting flies. "Bart's right, we're not going to find any tracks in this mud. Looks like there has been some animal activity though—something was pretty interested in your brother's liver."

Theodore bent over and hurled.

"Sorry," Winston said. "I didn't mean to upset you." He then swiveled around to look at Buck. "Nice clean shot through the forehead," he said. "So that was accidental? Pretty accurate for someone who just watched their brother die."

"I swear it was," Theodore said.

Winston whistled appreciatively. "Large caliber. Took most of his head off."

"Seven millimeter," Theodore offered.

The sheriff walked over to look at the rifle. "Browning. Nice scope on it too. Not something you'd leave in the mud if you didn't have to."

"So you do believe me?"

Winston spat and then took out a cigarette. As he lit it, he answered. "I admit the whole broken tree thing is strange. You've got me on that, but how's this for an alternative to your Brothers Grimm story: What if you three bumpkins were traipsing through the woods, looking to poach that wolf, and stumble upon this trail? We'll need to check into who came out here and cleared it—might be those folks at the Rookery hired someone, since the current road they have is beat to hell. Far as I'm concerned, you're only doing something like this with heavy machinery—and that, my friend, the Rookery folks don't have.

"Anyway, the three of you are arguing and drinking, not necessarily in that order, and maybe you're starting to imagine monsters in the woods. That would put anyone on edge. So it gets really tense between you guys; real jumpy. Buck over there pulls his Bowie and guts your friend. Blood splatters all over—all over you. In the struggle he falls against the tree and drops his knife. You see that as an opportunity and put one between his eyes."

Theodore was shaking his head violently. "No, no, that's not how it was!"

"So," the Sheriff went on, "you're freaked out because of what just happened and that you just killed your friend and your brother is dead. You drop your rifle and run off. By the time you get to Creekside, you're beside yourself with panic and run your car into a hydrant."

Winston exhaled and dropped his cigarette on the ground, grinding it into the mud under his boot. "My version makes a whole lot more sense, doesn't it? In fact, it even works out better for you. Less than a murder rap if you were trying to save your own life from a man who just killed your brother. You might even be able to walk away from it completely if a jury feels kindly towards you. You should probably get a haircut before the trial though."

"I didn't kill him!" Theodore cried. "He was already dead or dying. I swear on a stack of Bibles!"

"Well, our boys here will go over the crime scene with a fine-tooth comb," Winston said. "We'll see if they can turn up that third hand of yours."

———

"Ah, so this is Creekside?" Dieter said. "It is a quaint little hamlet. Reminds me somewhat of a Bavarian village. I quite like it."

"It's a hellhole," Masters replied. "Drop me off downtown and then go set up camp wherever you can find."

"Certainly. Would you like me to pick you up in a little while?"

"Yeah. Unhook your Explorer and come get me in an hour or so."

Dieter looked dismayed. "It is a Mercedes G55 AMG."

"Whatever," Masters said as he got out of the coach, "as long as it has four wheels."

Reverend Masters could not help but shudder when he stepped onto the sidewalk of Main Street. He had vowed never to return, yet here he was. When he was last in the area to check on his fallen hunter, he purposely went out of his way to avoid the town. Watching Dieter drive off prompted Masters to contemplate for a brief moment what he was about to do.

Turning, he began walking towards the Cluck and Grunt.

Entering the dingy restaurant, he quickly surveyed the room. Hardly any tables were occupied, but it was well after the breakfast rush that a dump like this would cater to. He spied a disinterested fry cook picking his nose in the kitchen, a cute blonde waitress shooting the breeze with a guy in the back booth, and a waitress in the front who looked like hell. He surmised that was her.

Moving up to the counter in front of her, he sat down.

———

"Coffee?" Trudy asked, putting on her best phony smile.

"Why, yes … Trudy," the man said.

Trudy grunted in acknowledgement. "Here's a menu." She always hated when guys used her first name off her badge when they didn't know her. It was usually the prelude to a bad pickup line.

When she returned with the coffee, he asked, "So, what's good? The place has changed a lot since I was last here."

Trudy looked around. "Unless you were last here in the nineteenth century, I doubt it. Can't go too wrong with the bacon and eggs," she added, pointing to the garish sign above her of livestock dancing over their fallen kin.

He looked up from his menu. "Actually, it's a little over twenty years ago. I lived here for a while."

"Wow, not many people will admit to having lived here. Know what you want?" she rushed him.

The man smiled back. "How about the phone number of the pretty blonde back there?" he said with a leer.

"Her?" Trudy pointed with her pencil and couldn't help but laugh. "Not your type—trust me on this one. Not even close."

"That her boyfriend?"

Trudy concluded that she was probably number two on the creep's to-hit-on list and attempted to dissuade him. "No. Actually, he's mine."

The man looked over at Gavin with an interest that seemed odd. "Good for you," he said. "Nothing like young love."

"Know. What. You. Want?" Trudy repeated.

"I'll go with the bacon and eggs you recommended. Over easy with rye toast."

"Works for me," she said, scribbling on her pad and walking over to the pass to shout at Bill. "One Cluck and Grunt special: flop two, whisky down." She turned to her customer. "Sorry, he makes me say that."

Bill snatched the ticket off the wheel and coughed on it.

———

A little later, when Trudy brought Masters his food, he initiated more small talk.

"Tell me, Trudy, is there a hotel in town?"

"No hotels. There's a Motel 6 about ten miles south of here. We do have a bed and breakfast just up State Street. I'm sure they have rooms. Not a lot of traffic around here this time of year. What makes you want to stay—?"

"In this godforsaken place?" he finished for her with a smile.

"Well, we are anything but forsaken by God, but you catch my drift."

"Have you ever been to the Dells?"

"Nope. I can't swim, so water parks are out, and I vomit on rollercoasters. Other riders tend to frown on that."

Masters smiled. Despite himself, he was starting to like her. "There are a lot of other attractions at the Dells: beautiful scenery, shopping, good restaurants, casinos, and the Mysterium." He shoveled a forkful of eggs into his mouth.

"Okay, I'll bite. What's the Mysterium?"

"It is my attraction," he said proudly before chomping on a piece of toast. "I built it from the ground up. It houses a collection of the most fabulous wonders from all over the earth."

"Sort of like Ripley's?"

"Nothing like them!" Masters said as he gagged on the rye. "They have the name and all, but not nearly the wonders that my museum houses."

Trudy cocked one skeptical eyebrow. "So, what's there? Two-headed goats and shrunken heads?"

Masters started to reappraise his initially positive feelings for the girl. "You'd have to see it to understand. When you get down that way let me know. I'll give you a free tour."

"Thanks," she said unenthusiastically. "So, what are you looking for up here? The Johnston family had a foal with five legs a while back, but they had to put the poor thing down."

Masters leaned in and whispered. "There's something in the forest—something big."

Trudy paled. "I don't know you, mister, but I'll give you this advice. Stay out of the woods. It's not safe."

"Exactly," he smiled. "That's why I'm interested in it. I've brought help along, someone who is skilled in hunting large game animals."

"You don't understand. You are way out of your league, even with a professional hunter."

"Oh, and why is that?"

Trudy glanced away, which he filed under the heading of she's-hiding-something. "Just tryin' to help you out, mister. Take it or leave it. It's no skin off of my nose."

"Well, if you see the creature wandering down the street, give me a call." Masters reached into his jacket pocket and removed a business card and held it out for Trudy.

She took the card and examined it. Her face flushed as she looked up at him. "What is this, some kind of joke?"

Masters stood up and reached for his wallet. "No joke."

"The hell it isn't!" Trudy exploded. "Used to live in Creekside, last name Masters. Reverend Fucking Masters!"

The blonde and Trudy's boyfriend couldn't help overhear the outburst and approached them. Masters smiled at both of them and then looked back at Trudy. He removed a one hundred dollar bill from his pocket and tossed it on the counter.

"Keep the change," he said as he turned to leave. "My daughter deserves a better haircut."

———

Later that evening, Trudy followed Rachel and Gavin through the back of the diner and out to the alley that bordered Mill Creek. Located next to a dumpster and under a full moon was a table with a red checkered tablecloth and two chairs. A candle blazed romantically on the tabletop next to a vase of seven red roses.

Trudy smiled as Gavin held her chair for her. As Gavin sat down, Rachel ran back into the kitchen and came out with a heaping plate of spaghetti and meatballs that she placed between them.

"You've been watching *Lady and the Tramp*, haven't you?" Trudy groaned. "I'm not pushing a meatball to him with my nose."

"Of course not, silly," Rachel beamed. "*He's* supposed to do that."

"Perhaps," Trudy suggested with exaggerated politeness, "you can get us a couple of plates and silverware, like a good little waitress?"

Rachel smacked her forehead with her palm, dashed to the kitchen, and returned a few minutes later with a tray. She had the plates and silverware, but also a bottle of wine and long-stemmed glasses.

"How'd you get the wine?" Trudy demanded. "You know Creekside's as dry as a bone."

"Angel, remember?" Rachel smiled. "Let me leave the two of you alone. I'll be in the kitchen if you need me."

Trudy bowed her head and prayed. "Thank you, Lord, for bringing us an angel and for this food. Amen."

"Been a long time since I've heard prayer at dinner time," Gavin said. "It's not that popular at the Capital Café at UW-Madison."

"Creekside sort of gives you a different viewpoint about it," Trudy said as Gavin filled her plate with spaghetti and poured her some wine.

"Trudy," he asked, "was that really your father who showed up today?"

Trudy made a face and blew noisily across her lips. "Apparently. At least the story matches what I know of him. He still has that cheap-ass reverend title that he got just before he abandoned his family."

She looked down at her food. "Guess he decided he'd drop in and say 'hi' to his little girl after all these years."

"Why now?" Gavin asked.

"He runs some kind of sideshow in the Dells. He came for the demon. Not his daughter."

"How would he know there was a demon in the woods?"

"I don't think he knows what it is. I think he believes it's some kind of undiscovered animal that he can put on display."

She grew pensive as she rolled a meatball around on the plate with her fork. "A while back there was a hunter that came in bragging that he sighted some kind of monster in the woods," she said quietly. "It was too far off for him to take a shot, but he said he knew of someone that would pay big money for it when he did. I bet I know who the big spender was."

Trudy put a shaky hand on her wine glass, but before she could bring it to her lips she started to cry.

Gavin put his hand on her arm.

"I'm sorry," she sniffled, pulling her arm away. "It's just so discouraging that when my father does finally decide to look me up, it's only because I'm in the same area as something he is more concerned with. Guess he couldn't be troubled to come by just to see me."

She took the napkin from her lap and attempted to dry her eyes. "Not that I shouldn't expect it. Who would come to see a freak like me? I've got a shit job, no education other than my GED. I didn't have any friends in school, and now that I'm on my own, my best friend isn't even the same species that I am. How pathetic is that?"

Gavin put his hand up to her and wiped a tear from her cheek; he then leaned in and kissed her on the spot where the tear had previously been. She turned towards him, but in the process her elbow knocked her wine glass to the ground.

"I'm the same species," Gavin said, then he kissed her on the mouth.

Trudy pulled away just an inch and smiled. Putting her arms around him she kissed him back.

Trudy looked up while still kissing Gavin as Rachel ran out of the diner after the glass shattered, only to stop quickly near the doorway.

In Trudy's peripheral vision she could see the petite angel biting her lip and wringing a towel in her hands. Then, giggling happily, Rachel crept back into the kitchen.

After a few moments, music drifted out of the kitchen: Dean Martin singing "That's Amore." Trudy closed her eyes and cried.

CHAPTER FOURTEEN

Holly had her head inside the refrigerator of the Mysterium's employee break room. Her muffled shout of, "Did someone steal my Lean Cuisine again?" drew no attention.

"I swear," she said as she extracted herself from the appliance and slammed the door, "you'd think people here would be more considerate."

She was about to go interrogate the gift shop girls on the whereabouts of her missing lunch when the television that hung from the wall caught her attention. A mug shot of a disheveled Theodore appeared on the noon news.

"Well, I'll be," she said as she ran over and turned up the volume.

From his comfy studio perch, a smarmy news anchor with a bad rug and a cockeyed smile was speaking with a female reporter with a spray-on tan outside the county jail in Rhinelander.

"So, Barbara," the anchor asked, "what can you tell us about the recent deaths to the north of us?"

"Well, Tom," the reporter replied, flashing her pearly veneers, "two are dead in the forest near the village of Creekside. One man is in custody"—she glanced at her notes—"a Theodore J. Winslow from the Upper Peninsula. He has not been formally charged as yet."

"Oh, shit," Holly said as the graphic of Theodore again filled the screen.

"Barb, these are not the first deaths in the woods in that area, are they?" the anchor read off of the teleprompter.

"That is correct, Tom. A hunter was killed in the same area less than a month ago. That death was attributed to a wolf attack. These latest attacks appear not to be animal-related."

"Have we heard anything from the suspect?"

"We have heard from a source familiar with the case that the suspect is saying there is a large Beast in the forest north of Rhinelander."

"A Beast?" the anchor said, no longer looking at the teleprompter. "You mean the wolf?"

"No, the suspect apparently believes it is some sort of giant, previously unidentified species," Barbara said with a bemused grin.

The anchor gave a subtle smile that let viewers know he felt the alleged murderer was grasping at straws. "Perhaps he stumbled upon that mythic creature of Wisconsin lore, the Hodag?

"Thanks, Barb, keep us updated as the case unfolds."

"I will Tom. This is Barbara Kern outside of the Oneida County Jail for Channel Seven News."

"Oh, crap!" Holly said as she rushed out of the break room while attempting not to break her neck by falling off her nosebleed heels. She didn't even hear the whistle from the security guard as he admired her tight jeans.

Finally, kicking her shoes off, she ran up the carpeted stairs to her office and directly to the phone.

———

Masters picked up his cell and heard Holly's screech before he could even put it to his ear.

"Yeah?" he said.

"Where are you? Have you seen the news?"

"I spent the night in Dieter's rolling palace but I'll be moving into town later today. He's having satellite problems so, no, I haven't seen anything."

"The shit has hit the fan!" Holly said so quickly that it almost became one word.

"What has? Slow down and tell me."

He could hear Holly taking a deep breath and exhaling. "The news just showed a mug shot of that creepy Theodore guy. They talked about the deaths in the woods."

"That's not so bad. I was expecting there to be something out about it. Two deaths is something they would consider news, even in a backwater like this area. Not to worry: Teddy'll take the fall for it."

"That's not all, Jay. They started talking about a creature in the woods. The anchorman was joking that maybe Theodore had found the Hodag."

Masters didn't reply.

"Jay, are you still there?"

"Yeah, I'm here. I'd be swearing now but Dieter is in the kitchen hovering over a soufflé. I'm supposed to be keeping a civil tongue in my head. Or he'll cut it out."

"Come back here," Holly said in a worried tone. "We can take what cash we have and move to St. Thomas. You said you used to like to fish."

After another pregnant pause, Holly added, "I'll make you tropical drinks and dance for you in a string bikini. Please, Jay."

"I've got to go," he said quietly. "Be a sweetheart and take care of business at the Mysterium. I'll be back soon."

Masters set the phone down on the kitchen table.

Dieter looked at him. "Problems, my friend?"

"The guy they have locked up for the two other deaths out here, he's started to blab his story around that there's a large creature terrorizing the woods. It was just on TV."

"It was perhaps foolish for you to have hired someone so inexperienced," Dieter said. "Being frugal is commendable, but sometimes it costs more in the end."

"At least they were out there looking for the thing," Masters said angrily. "You're in your million dollar estate on wheels pretending to be Gordon Ramsay. At least he swears." He grumbled some more. "Now every crazy loon that hunts for Bigfoot or Mothman will be out in the woods. I've seen it before. This whole campground will fill up with idiots looking to get their fifteen minutes of fame on MonsterQuest."

Dieter turned to him and placed the two perfect soufflés on the kitchen table. "You must eat it quickly. As they say, 'Kings wait for soufflés: Soufflés do not wait for kings.'"

The German sat down across from him and picked up a spoon. "I believe you are overestimating the amount of interest one random news broadcast from a small, local market station will bring."

"Perhaps if there were no prior mythos, but they linked this to the Hodag. That's the same as saying it was a Bigfoot sighting. The crazies will be out in droves."

Dieter savored a mouthful of soufflé and then asked, "What is this Hodag you refer to?"

Masters marveled at Dieter. "How long have you lived in Wisconsin?"

"Ten years." Dieter said as he carefully organized the soufflé on his spoon. "The culture of Milwaukee brings back fond memories for me of Hamburg, but I have not studied the history of Wisconsin in great depth."

"Well, it was all a flimflam back in the 1890s," said Masters. He leaned back in his chair, fingers laced behind his head, warming up to a good story. "A guy said he found the Hodag in the woods of northern Wisconsin. It looked something like a dinosaur with claws, big teeth, and a spiked tail. Supposedly its favorite food was white bulldogs that it only partook of on Sundays. He said it took dynamite to finally kill it, and then he photographed the remains. Later they captured a purported live one and put it on display. Like I said, all flimflam. There never was such a thing." He leaned back further, hands still behind his head. "I sometimes wish I lived back then. I'd make Barnum and those other guys look like amateurs."

Dieter granted him a small smile. "Yes, I believe you would."

Masters belched loudly. "Excellent soufflé by the way."

———

The gathering house of Morgan was a simple structure inside, bare wooden beams holding up a whitewashed ceiling. Sanded but unstained pine planks served as flooring, as this was also a work area during the day. When not being used for community meetings it was the main craft area for the group, giving them plenty of space for quilting and woodwork, canning and sewing. Today all of the tables and equipment were pushed to the outside walls, and a number of benches were placed in front of a roughhewn podium near the back of the building. Jonathan stood behind the podium as the group slowly took their seats. He fidgeted as he waited. Why did angels always act like they had all the time in the world?

"As you all know," Jonathan shouted above the hubbub, "one of the Fallen is somewhere just outside our community. We know that where one is, more will follow. They are most likely already here." This appeared to get the flock's attention, and they quickly found their seats.

"They will attempt through whatever means possible to close us down," Jonathan continued. "We all know their hatred towards us and the humans—especially the humans. They hate that we associate with them and wish to understand them better. They especially hate that we call them our friends.

"In the past we have always closed our communities and moved when it became too dangerous for our human neighbors." Jonathan looked around at the hundred people gathered together, their anxious faces watching him expectantly. "This time our family in Creekside has asked us to stay."

The flock looked at each other and began to whisper amongst themselves. Finally one of the male community members, a messenger, rose and spoke. "As you said, we move when it becomes too dangerous for our neighbors. Why should we put our friends at risk this time? Jonathan, I implore you to announce to the other ladders that we are closing and seek shelter. I will carry the message myself. There is no shame in protecting the innocent."

Jonathan contemplated his words before answering, "We do not leave our family when things become difficult. This is what the humans told me, and I know in my spirit that the sons of Adam and daughters of Eve are correct. They call us their family and will not part with us."

Elder Tomas, a respected member of the community, stood and addressed Jonathan. "We love these humans as well, but we cannot put them in such a position, no matter how painful it may be. We have been through similar situations many times before."

"What makes this different," Jonathan continued, "is that there is now a human who can see the ladders. Many of you have seen Gavin Young when he was here in Morgan. He is a good man and deserves our help. We know from the demon's behavior that they, too, are aware of his ability and seek to use it for their own ends."

Jonathan held his hands out to try to settle the restless gathering. "I've assigned Rachel to his care. He is being protected from harm."

"But if we leave," another voice from the crowd suggested, "the boy will not be able to easily find us, even though he can see the ladder."

"His gift causes him severe headaches when he is at a distance from a ladder," Jonathan reassured the gathering. "It goes away when he draws near. He will instinctively move in the direction of the next ladder to seek relief. The Fallen will follow. We cannot allow them to follow him to another community, and we cannot remove the ladder, as it will cause great pain to the boy."

Elder Tomas' rich baritone rose over the babel of the crowd. "Jonathan, you are the leader of this community so it will be as you command, but it is so much easier when we are not in this form and not on this world, as the Most High directs us in all that we do. Here it is so much more difficult to discern His will. Our human friends are in the same situation. Their asking for us to stay, is that His will or their wish?

"I must admit," the elder continued, "I am worried. It has been a long time since I last appeared as one of the sons of man. Perhaps things have changed over the millennia, but I still vividly remember Lindisfarne.

"I was new to the human world, much as our sister Rachel is today. What I knew so certain from afar I now questioned at every turn. What is the saying the humans use? 'Do not judge a man until you've walk in his shoes.' The human experience left me both baffled and frightened. My condition allowed me to understand better why He had to truly become one of them.

"When we came down to England, to Lindisfarne, we found a welcoming community. The Bishop of Lindisfarne, Eadfrith, knew what we were, but let us settle nearby. Many of the community, such as I, were new, and he helped us to adjust to our new home and new lives. He shook his head with a smile at our mistakes and directed us as a gentle parent would a child."

Elder Tomas paused for a moment, perhaps afraid his oratory was too obscure. When he saw his audience was rapt, he went on.

"Eadfrith was a wonderful artist and his illuminated manuscript of the gospels survive to this day, but the monastery does not. Eadfrith now communes with the saints, waiting for our Master's return. He does not blame us for what happened, but I cannot help but feel at fault and have told him as much on many occasions. I read something much later in the Anglo-Saxon Chronicle that was so very true, I committed it to memory. It speaks of the year 793. Eadfrith had been dead for about seventy years. I was finally learning to live in the world and feeling confident about my abilities. Our love for the people of Lindisfarne was unquestioned. They in turn loved us.

"Please pardon my long digression," the elder said with sadness in his voice, "and permit an old man to recite what he memorized about that time:

"In this year fierce, foreboding omens came over the land of Northumbria. There were excessive whirlwinds, lightning storms, and fiery dragons were seen flying in the sky. These signs were followed by great famine, and on 8 January the ravaging of heathen men destroyed God's church at Lindisfarne."

The elder blinked away tears. "The people thought the Vikings came to pillage them. They were wrong. The Vikings were only instruments used by Abaddon to come against the Light.

"Came against it they did," he said angrily. "And darkness descended across the land."

The elder looked at Jonathan with wet eyes. "I know what it is like when humans see us for what we are and still call us their family. My family was wiped out in 793. We fought alongside them and held the evil back as long as we could but in the end, it didn't matter. We remained but our human family did not."

"That is the question we always ask ourselves," Jonathan solemnly replied. "Are we doing more good than not when we form such a bond with our mortal friends? Might I suggest, though, that you have taken on the perspective of our human friends, but we must always remember that they do not see clearly as yet. You speak of the pain of separation, but are they not still with us? Can you not visit them whenever you wish? Can you not speak with Eadfrith this very moment if you so desire?"

"You know what I mean," the elder grumbled. "This thing called death is an unnatural state that I wish upon no one. And I feel the pain keenly each time I must see one of them transition and leave those they love behind."

"Yet it is the current state in this fallen world." Jonathan said, "but it is not the final state. Remember that, brother. You speak of the failure to keep evil at bay. Those that separated themselves from us have been cast down. I do not need to remind any of you of our own history. Everyone in this room fought in that battle so many millennia ago. It is their world now, not ours. We know when we come here that we are invading their territory and to expect war.

"During your community's existence in Lindisfarne the priory became a beacon of light throughout England and Scotland. It was known not only for the beautiful illuminated gospels that the monks produced but also for evangelism, missionary activity, and the great love they showed to the surrounding people. You cannot tell me that you did not help inspire them to this, and that many more now share the Kingdom because of it.

"The rulers of the darkness of this world do not want us here," Jonathan concluded. "That is all the more reason for us to stay."

———

Winston sat at his desk at the Oneida County Sheriff's Office, waiting for the phone to ring. The lieutenant of the investigative division was due to call him with their findings on the Creekside case. He stared at an ashtray with the witty inscription "the butt stops here" that was presented to him upon his twentieth anniversary with the force. It only made him want to have a smoke.

The phone rang.

"Like clockwork," Winston said, snatching up the receiver. "Winston."

"Sheriff, Lieutenant Lange. I've got the preliminaries on the double homicide."

"Go ahead."

"Uh, it's very strange." Lange paused. "The coroner went over the bodies. The one with the bullet hole—that was from the Browning found at the scene."

"Nothing strange about that," Winston said. "That's what we were expecting."

"I'm not through. He also had three broken ribs—one that punctured a lung—a broken collar bone, and five cervical fractures. All appear to be a result of impact with the tree. The coroner is pretty sure he died from a broken neck, not the gunshot wound."

Winston was quiet.

"It gets stranger," the lieutenant continued. "The guy with the guts hanging out, it was not from the Bowie knife. The coroner believes it was from an animal claw. There was a fragment of the claw found embedded in the man's jacket. It apparently got snagged on the zipper. It's small, barely larger than a fingernail, and they're still running tests, but at this point they can pretty much confirm it isn't human."

Winston leaned back in his chair. "Anything else?"

"The rifle had trace amounts of blood that match the suspect. Interesting thing is the stock is cracked in two with what appear to be bite marks on either side. Like a lion was using it as a chew toy."

"Okay, thanks," Winston said as he started to hang up.

"Once last thing," Lange said. "Blood typing from the car accident does not match either of the guys in the woods. Unless the suspect had a really bad nosebleed we still can't explain where the blood came from."

Winston sighed. "Next you're probably going to tell me we should believe this asshole's story."

"I'm just saying—"

"Lange, go ahead and run the DNA testing. I want to know for sure what is going on before I make a fool of myself in front of the district attorney."

CHAPTER FIFTEEN

Masters hated his room. It was all doilies and flowers, reeking of lavender and moth balls. It confirmed his suspicions that Creekside was hell on earth. He was not looking forward to an extended stay at Caroline's Bed and Breakfast.

He was in the process of unpacking when there was a knock on the door. Masters assumed it was the busybody owner, Carol something-or-other with her clingy desperate ways, coming to tell him about the nightly sheepshead game in the parlor. He was surprised when he opened the door to be greeted by Mr. Azael—first name still unknown.

"Reverend Masters," Azael said with a smile. "So good to see you again. I trust you had a pleasant journey."

"Just like going to the dentist," Masters grumbled. "Come in."

"Thank you," Azael said as he entered the room and glanced around. "Cozy." He turned to Masters. "So, have you met her yet? Have you resumed your long neglected parental obligation?"

"I went to the diner," Masters said as he put his socks in the dresser drawer. "Perhaps it wasn't the most pleasant of reunions—for either of us."

Azael patted Masters on the back. "Well, we were expecting a rocky start, weren't we? You'll get her to come around."

Hoping to appear a little more competent than he was sounding, Masters added, "I saw that boyfriend of hers."

Azael brightened. "Did you now? Tell me, what is the lad like?"

"He was sitting at the back of the restaurant, yakking with one of the waitresses. He's a tall drink of water with a scar on the side of his head. My daughter can do better."

"Let's hope not, Reverend, I think that relationship is perfect the way it is."

Masters shot Azael an impatient look. "Okay, I'm doing my part. When do I get my exhibit?"

"Patience. You still have much fence mending to do with your lovely offspring."

"How do I even know you can deliver? I'm hearing a lot of fancy talk from a man in a fancy suit, that's all."

Azael's nostrils flared slightly. "Tell you what—I'll drop by tomorrow and we'll take a little hike. I can introduce you to the Beast. Until then, spend some quality time with your daughter."

Azael made his way back to the door. "Oh," he added. "Try not to be an asshole when you're with her."

———

"A chaperone?" Trudy sighed. "Really?"

"I must protect Gavin," Rachel pouted as she zipped up Trudy's dress. "Jonathan is at Maggie's now while I'm over here."

"Have you ever heard the old human saying, 'three's a crowd'?"

Rachel spun Trudy around and pronounced, "You look beautiful!" and then spun her around to face the mirror.

Trudy looked at the reflection of someone she was pretty sure she had never seen before. The mirror still displayed in the background the messy apartment with the overflowing trashcan as it always had, but the woman that stood directly before it was unrecognizable.

"You clean up well," Rachel smiled.

Trudy continued to look at the woman in the mirror with the perfect makeup and impeccably styled hair. The reflection wore a red dress that had previously spent years on the floor in the back of her closet, only to be rescued by an angel.

"Wow," was all that she could say before turning to Rachel. "Is this going to be okay? I mean going out of Creekside?"

Rachel nodded enthusiastically. "Sure! The restaurant is only ten miles out of town, and Gavin really would like to do this."

"I know he's going stir-crazy here, but don't we all?" Trudy said. "I just don't want him hurt on a silly date. And don't tell me that it's all his idea. I see the workings of a certain angel behind the scenes."

Rachel threw up her hands helplessly. "I only suggested the restaurant because it's at a manageable distance, although I hear it's really romantic *and* they give you a free dessert with every entrée."

Trudy went over to the dresser and tried to balance while putting on her heels. "Who invented these things anyway?" she grumbled. "I'm sure they pass them out in hell."

———

Gavin sat on the edge of his bed surrounded by boxes of clothing and items from his room back home. He had spoken with his mother on the phone several days ago when it became apparent that his quick run to Creekside would become a marathon. The timing of the arrival of her care package was perfect, and Gavin was able to find a pair of slacks and a sports jacket for tonight's dinner.

He went over to the dresser, where he had placed a small LCD television that was able to pick up three local channels. His mother had thoughtfully included it to help protect his sanity. "Better than nothing," he mumbled.

As he stood there looking out the window, he was able to make out the ladder flaring in the distance. He thought about Maggie and Trudy and how they were unable to see the wonder just outside of Creekside. Still, they were friends to angels and protectors of the light that they could not see. Gavin smiled at his own medieval imagery. What a strange world it was turning out to be after all.

———

Masters stopped halfway down the stairs of the B&B, listening for any sign that the owner was nearby. He heard her teapot whistling in the kitchen and deemed it safe to sneak the rest of the way down and out the front door.

The Mercedes was idling at the curb. Masters went over and got in.

"How was the first day of the hunt?"

"Uneventful, I'm afraid." Dieter replied. "I did find the clearing where your other—and I use the term loosely—hunters were killed."

"Oh, anything interesting?"

Dieter tossed a plastic bag at Masters.

"Shit!" the Reverend yelled as he jumped in his seat. "What the hell is that?"

Dieter overlooked his non-cursing edict under the circumstances. "I would say," he calmly replied, "two and a half fingers."

"From who?"

"Your guess is as good as mine. I found them further up the trail. They were protruding inconspicuously from a burrow. It would have been very easy for someone less skilled than I to miss. I believe a badger consumed the rest of the unfortunate hand."

Masters put the fingers in the glove compartment. "Let's get out of here. I need a drink."

Dieter started to pull away from the curb when Masters said, "Stop! See that boy who just came out of the house over there? I need to speak with him."

Obligingly, Dieter drove down the street and pulled up next to the pedestrian.

———

Gavin noticed the SUV roll up in front of him and the passenger window roll down.

"Hello, you're Trudy's boyfriend, right?" the stranger said. Gavin recognized immediately who he was.

"You're her father?"

"Yes," Masters said with a smile. "She's my kid all right."

Gavin stuck both hands in his pockets and walked over to the car. Leaning his lanky frame down, he said, "You know she thinks you're a scumbag?"

"Yeah, I get that a lot," Masters replied. "I'd like to explain to her what happened. Try to make it up to her. Have a new start."

"She says you are here for something else. That you didn't come for her."

Masters got out of the car and pulled Gavin over a few feet away from the vehicle. "Look, I admit, I'm here because I want something that is out in that forest. But I could have just as easily not have introduced myself to Trudy. She would never know that I was her father. I wanted her to know."

"Or perhaps you just wanted to screw with her mind." Gavin suggested. "That seems to fit you better."

Brother Jonathan walked out onto the porch. "Any problems Gavin?"

"No. He was just leaving."

Masters walked back to the car and got in. "Just give me a chance, son. Everyone deserves a second chance. Put in a good word for me with Trudy. You won't regret it."

The Mercedes rolled down the hill and made a right onto Main as Jonathan walked up next to Gavin.

"What was that about?" he asked.

"Trudy's long-lost father," Gavin said as they started to walk down the street towards Trudy's apartment. "He's really here to capture the demon."

Jonathan broke into laughter. "I assume he doesn't know what it is?"

"Not a clue. Just thinks it's some big animal is my guess." Gavin smiled. "Well, he's going to have a big surprise."

Jonathan furrowed his brow. "We need to find a way to keep him out of the woods. I wouldn't want to see him hurt because of his ignorance."

"I wonder if Trudy would say the same thing," said Gavin, shaking his head.

———

Trudy studied Rachel as they stood just outside the upscale restaurant. While Trudy felt a bit understated in her modest red dress and heels, Rachel was if anything overdressed. She was wearing an orange underskirt with a beaded sheer vest that looked vaguely Victorian in style. "Okay, what television show is that getup from?"

"It's from a movie." Rachel replied. "*Titanic*"

"You're wearing a dress from a movie about a sinking ship to our dinner date?"

Rachel pouted. "But it's a great love story."

Trudy sighed. "Have you ever been to a restaurant before?"

"The Cluck and Grunt," Rachel replied with obvious pride. "Oh, and a banquet in ancient Mesopotamia overlooking the Euphrates River. It was very beautiful."

"You don't get out much, do you?"

"No, but I've seen other people at restaurants—on television."

"As you are well aware, seeing is different than being," Trudy observed wisely. "If you need any help with the menu, just let me know."

"I was going to sit by myself, so I don't disturb the love birds."

"Oh, no, you're not," Trudy replied as Gavin opened the door for them. "I'm not having you sit on the other side of the room and stare at us during the entire meal." As they approached the podium, Trudy stepped up and barked, "Table for three!"

———

They were seated at a booth, Trudy and Rachel on one side and Gavin opposite. Gavin could see that Rachel was beaming as the waiter brought warm bread and butter to their table and filled their water glasses.

She nudged Trudy and asked, "Why can't we do that at the diner?"

"Because Bill is a cheapskate," Trudy said as she looked over at Gavin. "How's the noggin?"

He touched his head gingerly. "So far, so good I feel a little pressure around my skull but it doesn't hurt. Funny thing, though—there's one area that doesn't have any pressure."

Trudy leaned in curiously. "Where?"

"It doesn't stay in any one spot. As I move around, it changes position, but it always points in the direction of the ladder."

"Well," Trudy said as she sliced the bread, "at least you'll never get lost."

"They have ravioli!" Rachel exclaimed as she flipped through the menu. "Oh, this is so romantic! You two should hold hands."

Trudy shot her friend a sideways glance. "I thought bodyguards were the strong silent types."

Gavin felt he needed to break the tension. "Rachel, Jonathan mentioned that the communities can only allow a tiny fraction of angels to participate. How were you chosen?"

"I am a protecting angel." Rachel said as she flipped to the dessert section. "Ooh, tiramisu! Pardon me, got carried away. God knew you would need protecting. That's why I'm here."

"And here I thought," Trudy put in, "that it was only to wake me up at five a.m.—"

"Protecting angel? Are there different types?"

"Sure, silly," Rachel said. "There are different classes, such as the seraphim, cherubim and the archangels. We're all created differently, with our own distinctive personalities. I'm not the same as Brother Jonathan."

"Yeah," Gavin said. "I sort of figured that one out already."

"We have different ministries and opportunities for service as well," she continued. "Some are messengers, some encourage the despondent, and some heal." She looked up from the menu for the first time and met and held Gavin's eyes with a fierceness that told him the transformed angel he previously witnessed lurked just under the surface of the gentle blonde girl. "*I* protect."

The waiter approached the table, his stiff and overly formal manner looking like he never removed the coat hanger from his jacket. "Are we ready to order?" he asked in a monotone while staring over his glasses at Rachel.

Having to order first threw her into panic mode. "Ravioli, please!" she blurted out much too loudly.

"I am sorry, miss, but the ravioli is only on the children's menu."

Rachel continued to stare at him.

"He means," Trudy cut in, "that you can't order the ravioli. Here"—she flipped quickly through the menu,—"try the eggplant parmesan. I hear it's very good."

"Okay." Rachel looked back at the waiter. "I'll have one of those."

"Excellent choice. Soup or salad?"

Rachel looked back at Trudy, eyes wide.

"She'll have the house salad."

"Dressing?"

Gavin noticed that Rachel had dug her nails into Trudy's forearm.

"Blue cheese," Trudy said.

"And to drink?"

"Wait, I can do this." Rachel quickly scanned the drink menu. "A Bahama Mama!" she said confidently.

The waiter's patience was clearly wearing thin. "May I see your ID?"

"My idea?"

"Your identification, miss," the waiter said in an exasperated tone.

Rachel looked back at Trudy. "I—I don't have any."

Trudy cut in with, "She'll have a Safe Sex on the Beach. I will as well," causing Rachel to blush.

After the orders were taken and the waiter stomped off in an imperious huff, Gavin exhaled loudly. "I didn't know if we were going to make it through that."

Rachel gave a sheepish grin. "Sorry. I never realized how difficult that is. The people who order in Cluck and Grunt are very brave."

Trudy pried Rachel's hand from her arm and patted it. "You need to be brave to order any of Bill's cooking."

Gavin noted, "Well, I never thought I would see someone that is thousands of years old carded."

"I don't like the idea of following the youngsters like common degenerates," Dieter said as he and Masters sat in the Mercedes outside the restaurant.

"Hey, I'm anything but common." Masters said. "We've got to eat, too, and there aren't a lot of choices around here." He reached for the door. "Let's head on in. I'm starving."

As they entered the restaurant Masters quickly scanned the room and found his daughter sitting at a booth near the back. "Give us a table over there someplace," he told the hostess, while pointing to the opposite side of the room.

"Certainly," she said as she grabbed a couple of menus. "Follow me."

As they walked to their table Masters knew that he was spotted by Gavin but not by his daughter. He sat down facing the booth, with Dieter attempting to sit opposite him.

"Move," Masters said. "Sit over here to my right. You're blocking my view."

He noticed whispering between Gavin and Trudy, and then she looked over and spotted him. Even from across the room he could see her face flush in anger as she attempted to get up. Gavin grabbed her arm and motioned for her to sit back down. The cute blonde was there as well, and even she was glaring at him.

"It looks like you made quite the impression, Reverend," Dieter said.

"I'm not sure where all this latent hostility is coming from. I'm sure her mother didn't raise her right."

Dieter shook his head as he called a waiter over. "Reverend Masters, you are a— how do you Americans say it?—a piece of work?"

"Yeah, well order me a double bourbon and some sort of dead animal." Masters said as he stood up. "I'm going over there."

———

"Shit," Gavin said, "here he comes."

"Will anyone notice if I slug him?" Trudy asked. She was hoping for a quiet dinner with Gavin and had just come to accept the fact that Rachel would be the third wheel, when a fourth rolled into her view.

Masters walked up to the booth, smiling unctuously. "Gavin, nice to see you again," causing Trudy to look at her date for any sign of how they knew each other.

"And Trudy, you look lovely. Took my advice about the hair cut I see." He then looked at Rachel and held out his hand, "And who do we have here?"

It took a moment before Rachel shook his hand. "I'm Rachel. I work with Trudy."

"That's right!" Masters said. "I remember you at the diner." He pushed his way into the booth next to Gavin, "May I have a seat?"

The Reverend was facing Trudy. She scowled at him with open contempt, hoping he would notice and leave. "Did I mention that I don't want you in my life?" she said icily.

Masters received his bourbon from the waitress and thanked her. Ever the charming rogue, he sipped and nodded cordially at a man at nearby table. "Look, girl," he said to Trudy, "I could tell you I'm sorry for leaving you and your mother, but I'm not. You live in Creekside. You know what a stinking pile of crap that place is. It's filled with holier-than-thou Bible-thumpers that think they know everything."

Trudy could sense Rachel bristling at the comment and patted her knee under the table.

"But," Masters added, pointing his finger at her, "they're actually a motley collection of knuckle-draggers and mouth-breathers. That's what they really are. I was glad to get out of there."

"You left your wife and child behind," Trudy growled. "I don't know what she saw in you to marry such a sack of shit."

"You think your mother was such a saint, don't you?" Masters said, his voice rising. "She wasn't. Trust me."

"What do you mean?"

"I mean, your mother wanted to get out of Creekside and she wanted out bad. Enough to marry a boy she didn't love just because he was from a big city. She tricked him into falling in love with her just so she could leave."

"That's not true." Trudy countered. "She never left. And she always loved you."

"She never loved me," the Reverend said, putting his drink on the table hard enough to slosh some bourbon onto his fingers. "I had big dreams. I wanted to become something. Do something amazing with my life. She loved my dream. Not me."

"So why didn't you two leave together?" Trudy asked. "You hated Creekside and she wanted out too. Why didn't you just go together?"

Masters licked the bourbon off his fingers. "I found my gift in Creekside." He leaned over the table closer to Trudy. "I have the gift of the grifter. The ability put on a show that delivers nothing."

"So she thought you were a crook and wouldn't come with you?"

"Not at all. She didn't have a problem with my idea of ripping off the rubes. Her problem was with my choice of how to do it." Masters leaned back. "You don't get it, do you?"

Trudy shook her head slightly.

"I decided to become Reverend Masters. There was money and adventure to be found on the Bible Belt tent circuit. I became a healer."

Trudy and Rachel glanced at Gavin.

"For your grandparents, this was the one thing I couldn't do. They felt I was disrespecting God or something and my dear wife would burn in the pit of hell because of my sins. Her parents turned their hypocritical hatred towards me, and she was forbidden from leaving with me even though I was her husband."

Masters took another sip. "So I left on my own. I would have taken her if she wanted to. I knew by then she didn't love me, but we did the whole 'till death do we part' thing so I was willing to have her tag along."

"So," Trudy said, "if she hated Creekside as much as you say, why did she spend the rest of her life there? Nothing was stopping her from leaving on her own, especially after my grandparents died."

"Nothing has stopped you, either, yet here you are. I guess the apple doesn't fall far from the tree. You can't imagine the life you could have had with me out on the road. Growing up, seeing the world, and learning the art of the flimflam."

Masters stood up and grabbed his drink. "Look, I know you don't trust me. In my line of work not many do. But I do want to get to know you. As I told Gavin when we ran into each other this evening, I didn't have to introduce myself to you. I could have completed my business in Creekside and left without you knowing."

He looked at Trudy, smiling wanly. "I have no other family. You're my daughter, whether you like it or not, and I would really like to get to know you."

Trudy looked down at the table while grinding her teeth.

"Think about it." Masters said as he started back to his table. "I'll be in town for a while."

CHAPTER SIXTEEN

The doorbell rang.

Trudy slapped her hand down upon the empty space that once contained the despised clock radio. Remembering that she had sent the cursed thing to the ninth circle of hell, she sat up in bed.

"Rachel?"

"Yes, and Gavin."

"Nice of you to tell me this time," Trudy muttered as she found her robe on the floor and opened the door. Rachel was once again in her starched pink uniform. "Is there a dry cleaner in Morgan I don't know about?" Trudy asked sarcastically. "Come in," she added, holding open the door. "Make some coffee if you like. I'm going to go shower."

———

While Trudy went into the bathroom, Rachel prepared the coffee and Gavin examined the four guitars—a Rickenbacker, a Fender, a Gibson, and a Steinberger—on their stands in the corner of the room. He didn't know much about guitars, but he could see that Trudy probably had more money tied up in the instruments than her apartment furnishings, wardrobe, and car combined. "Does she ever play these?" he asked.

"Not that I know of," Rachel said as she sniffed the coffee before measuring. "She's been depressed for a while now. She's pretty much stopped doing everything that used to interest her."

"She always seems too feisty to be depressed." Gavin said, surprised by Rachel's comment.

"She uses her sarcasm and wit as her security barrier but look around," she said, waving her arm around the room like a game show hostess; Gavin surmised she had probably been studying *The Price Is Right*. "She loves music but doesn't play it. She doesn't take care of her health, and she's a slob. The only time I've seen her care about how she looked was the other day when we went to the restaurant. You make her care about something. She cares about you."

"So is that why you have been so—"

"Pushy?" Rachel smiled. "Angels can only do so much on their own. I love Trudy, and I want to see her happy. I'm still trying to understand myself in this form, and everything is so new and exciting. I admit I get carried away sometimes. Angels have no experience with romance, as that concept is reserved for mankind, not my kind." She sighed. "It is such a wonderful gift humans have been given! I just would like for Trudy to experience it fully."

"Trudy told me," Gavin said, "that you're her best friend in the world. You are the sister she never had."

Rachel blinked and looked away. "I'm honored."

When Trudy came out of the bathroom Gavin was startled to see that her uniform was clean and unwrinkled.

"What?" Trudy said.

Rachel composed herself quickly, smiled beatifically. "You look ... very clean."

———

Reverend Masters was not fond of traipsing through the Wisconsin forest behind Azael. "Do you always wear Armani and Allen Edmonds when you go hiking?"

"One should always look their best," Azael replied. "You're in a business that understands this. I can tell you have refined tastes. The look of success spawns success, does it not?"

Masters grunted in response as he tripped over a root and almost fell on his face. "Couldn't you have brought the Beast out to a parking lot or something?"

"It is not much further," Azael said. "And you will be glad that you went to the effort."

After another fifty yards they entered a clearing and Azael stopped. "Right here, this is where we wait."

"Wait?" Masters grumbled. "How long?"

"Patience my friend. I have summoned it, but it is still has its own mind. It will come when it desires to come. No sooner."

As they stood in the clearing ringed with pine trees, Masters looked at his Patek Philippe watch, the one thing that remained from his faith healing days. It cost him twenty grand of suckers' money back in the day—worth every penny of it. "Well, I hope its schedule doesn't overlap lunch."

"Do you hear that?" Azael said, cupping a hand to his ear. "That is the sound of your fortune approaching."

Masters strained to hear but couldn't. But he started to smell something. He was once told that bears smell like old garbage cans. What was heading his direction smelled like the entire dump. Then the forest became quiet, and he could hear a cracking sound of brush being pushed aside and stertorous breathing, like an asthmatic was working its way through the woods.

"Come here, my darling." Azael called out. "Come to me!" Slowly, the woods to the north became dark as a shadow descended upon it. "Come meet Reverend Masters."

Masters could see it now and was startled by how large it was, bigger than a pickup. He stood upon shaking legs that refused to move and attempted to stifle his gag reflex. Even though he had seen the video on the phone numerous times, it hadn't prepared him for the behemoth before him.

"I'll need a bigger room," he gulped.

The Beast came slowly into the clearing, its massive body moving with feline grace as large clawed feet dug into the leaf-layered dirt. The neck that held the heads was constantly moving as the faces rotated to scan the surroundings. Then the decayed human face turned its attention to Masters, and the expression even on such a corrupted being could only be described as hate. The Beast stopped in front of Azael. He put a hand on its shoulder, and it sat down on its haunches, very much like a cat.

"You will not be able to display it," Azael said.

"What do you mean?" Masters said in surprise. "That's our deal. I'll make nice to the kid, and you'll give me—whatever that thing is."

Azael scratched the Beast near the belly causing its hind leg to start moving in rhythm to Azael's rubs. Masters was surprised that the ugly-as-hell Beast was wired very much like a dog. "I am going to give you something even better."

"Yeah, what's that?"

"Publicity!" Azael said with a little laugh. "I have a plan that, when put into motion, will make Reverend Jay Masters a household name across North America—perhaps the world. You will be on everyone's lips, in every newspaper, on every talk show. You might even author a book—with a ghost writer of course."

Masters was becoming agitated. "How's that? Why can't I just *have* it? What do you *call* it anyway?"

"It's a freed cherub, no longer subservient to the tyrant. You can't stuff it, Reverend, like that horse in your museum. It's not of this world. It doesn't die, at least not by human hands."

"Cherubs have dimples and diaper rash," Masters said, "and everything dies." Azael was beginning to get on his nerves. He was starting to feel that he was being played.

"Spiritual beings do not."

Masters stood perplexed. "I'm not understanding—it looks real to me. You just rubbed its belly and it practically peed itself in joy."

"Your trophy," Azael corrected, "is actually in this form to serve a specific function that has nothing to do with becoming an exhibit that kids will climb on and have their photos taken."

"So, how do you know so much about it?"

"As I said, we all have our forms for a purpose."

Masters eyed the creature's tremendous size, its arsenal of natural weapons, its expressive, intelligent faces. "I think the Beast got the better deal," he said. The Beast apparently understood and snorted at Azael in agreement. "So, what is this some pact with Satan?"

"You honor me, but no. I am just a lowly servant; no signatures in blood or anything crass is required." Azael smiled. "Let's just say it is a gentlemen's agreement between likeminded individuals."

148

"Shit," Masters said, taking only a moment to decide that his fortune lay with Azael and the Beast. "I've still got a hunter out there. I should tell him to stand down. I don't' want him taking pot shots at my ticket to fame and a private island."

"He could not inflict permanent harm. As I said, a spiritual being can only be killed by another spiritual being, and even then it is not death as you would know it: It is a movement from one form to another, from one place to another—a place that we prefer not to think about.

Azael paused. "This hunter of yours, is he any good?"

"The best," Masters bragged. "He's worked for me before. Back in the day he was in the GSG 9, which is the German equivalent of America's Special Forces. Then he decided to freelance. Later he started a munitions factory and made a tidy fortune selling illegal, and not quite quality controlled, ammo to various guerrilla forces around the world. He sold the business to a Laotian company and settled into big game hunting to keep himself occupied. In certain circles, he's a legend. He's a bit of a highfalutin dandy, but he always gets his man—or his Beast."

"Perhaps," Azael said. "We should let your valiant hunter continue upon his quest."

"Why? You already said he can't kill it."

"I wasn't thinking about him killing it …"

"Now wait a minute, I don't know if I like your thought process here. I admit the guy has a stick up his ass, but he's been a good friend, in an annoyingly my-shit-don't-stink way, over the years."

"I'm just saying, Reverend Masters, it would be quite the headline, especially if it should be documented."

"Documented?"

"Perhaps," Azael said as he patted the Beast's head, "you would like to accompany your hunter tomorrow. I trust you have a camera."

———

Sheriff Winston walked into the interrogation room and sat down opposite Theodore. "Enjoying your stay?"

"My lawyer says you're charging me with involuntary manslaughter."

"Probably for that excellent 7mm shot between the eyes."

"I didn't aim to do that."

"That's probably why you are up on manslaughter charges and not first degree."

"The lawyer says you didn't find my hand."

"That's right. But we did a DNA match and the blood in the car is yours."

"That's what I've been telling you!"

Winston leaned back in his chair. "So, how did all that blood get in the car if you didn't have any wounds? And don't go telling me about a miraculously third hand that sprouted after you were hit by a lightning bolt by some kid."

Theodore said nothing.

Winston continued. "So, were you carrying around a bag with your own blood? Is it some kind of vampire cult? My niece made me go see *Twilight*, so I know all about that sort of hooey. What's the real story?"

"You watch too many movies," Theodore snorted. "I know you think I'm as full of shit as a Christmas turkey, but the whole thing happened, just the way I said it did. It ain't my fault if you don't believe in the supernatural."

Winston perked up. "A former girlfriend often told me that. I didn't change for her, so I'm certainly not going to change for a punk like you."

Theodore grinned his decaying jack-o'-lantern grin. "Smart lady to dump your sorry ass then."

Winston had both hands on the arms of Theodore's chair before he could blink. "Look," he blustered, "because of your stupid little story getting out I'm certain we're due for some looney tunes showing up in the Creekside area to try and capture your mythical Beast. Now my department will need to spend extra man hours to keep them safe. You're interfering with my budget during a recession. I hate paying overtime."

Winston backed off. "One last thing. You mentioned during your interview with our team that a guy from the Dells hired you. Is that true?"

"Yeah," Theodore said. "He wanted us to go out and shoot whatever the thing was in the forest so that he could display it in his freak show."

"How did he know there was something in the forest?"

"He said that another hunter of his went out to try and kill it and ended up dead himself."

"What was your employer's name again?"

"Masters. Jay cheap-ass Masters, although he likes to go by the title Reverend. He couldn't even afford to get me a decent lawyer. I'm stuck with the public defender."

"I know your lawyer," Winston said. "She's very good."

He walked over to the door. "Maybe I'll look up this Reverend Masters. Make sure he doesn't send anyone else out into the woods."

"You can try," Theodore said as the guard came to take him back to his cell. "He won't listen though. He don't care about anybody's life 'cept his own. My only brother and my buddy down in the morgue can attest to that."

"If dead men could talk," Winston couldn't resist adding. "Take him away!"

CHAPTER SEVENTEEN

As Masters drove Dieter's hundred grand SUV towards the campground, he was grateful for the loaner—not only for the ability to quickly leave Creekside but also that he was able to swing by the twenty-four hour Wal-Mart in Rhinelander last night and purchase a halfway decent digital camera. The Panasonic Lumix was waterproof and able to shoot in low light, which might come in handy in the thick woods. He had slight buyer's remorse as he stood at the only open checkout counter—why was there *always* only one open?—clutching the small box but was able to quickly shake it off. He was now making his way down the gravel road to the campground to join the prudish hunter for eggs Benedict before beginning the day's momentous hunt.

"Fuck!" he swore aloud, grateful to use the word without Dieter's censure. Half of the campground was now filled. Dieter's million-dollar palace was surrounded by battered Airstreams, thirty-year-old Winnebagos, pop-up trailers, and a sea of tents. One of the Airstreams had an Area 51 sticker plastered to its burnished aluminum side with a strange antenna structure poking out of the roof. A fifth-wheeler off in the back had a Wisconsin Bigfoot Science Center banner tied to the canvas awning. Someone with a modicum of talent had scribbled a not-bad chalk drawing of a Hodag on the concrete in front of their tent.

"Well, it's started," he grumbled. "I hope that Azael is right."

Dieter opened the door of the Newell Coach as Masters pulled up. "They started arriving last night."

Masters stifled a laugh as he looked upon the big game hunter, who was wearing a safari shirt and shorts along with an honest to God pith helmet straight out of a Three Stooges short. "Look around, Dieter, this ain't Africa, and these ain't hunters—they're the first flock of loons flying in for the season."

"Come in," Dieter said, shaking his head. "Breakfast is ready."

Masters entered the RV and sat down at the kitchen table, while Dieter poured him coffee. "I have spoken to a few of them," Dieter said. "They heard the reports of a Hodag on the news."

"Crazy assholes," Masters grumbled.

"Not crazy at all. Misguided, perhaps, but they are quite sane. They love a good mystery. The thought of something undiscovered just beyond the trees thrills them. We must feel the same or we would not be here either, correct?"

Masters slurped his coffee and gave a satisfied *ahh*. "You might have a good cup of Joe, Dieter. But can the philosophical bunk. I'm here for myself. You're here because I'm paying you."

Dieter smiled as he sat down across from him. "You are indeed jaded my friend. Do you know the reason I am here? It is not for the money, that is certain. You, however, are—how do you say?—parsimonious."

"Trust me," Masters said. "Nobody calls me that—whatever that is."

Dieter paused, his jaw muscles working. "A cheap bastard!" he said at length, pointing a bony finger at him. "Yes, that is what you are: a cheap, penny-pinching tightwad of a bastard."

"Okay, I'm impressed with your command of the English language; you're even dipping your toe into the sea of profanity. I must be rubbing off on you, but can we go now?"

Dieter took a sip of coffee and continued, "I took this job because of what you said to me while I was at the museum."

"That I'd pay for your honeymoon?"

"That you wanted me to hunt true evil," Dieter said quietly, leaning back in his seat and folding his arms. "Reverend, I do not consider myself evil, yet I have done many unspeakable things over the years. So, the question is: What is true evil? Hitler was undoubtedly evil. He destroyed entire countries, including my own, killed untold millions of innocent souls, but was he evil incarnate? Was he the evil that despises everything and everyone? It is said that even Hitler loved his dog. What if we go beyond Hitler and Stalin and Pol Pot—who, incidentally, I am quite embarrassed to say, I sold arms to when he was in power in Cambodia—beyond the most notorious mass murderers in history, to a time when evil began."

Masters squirmed uncomfortably as Dieter looked at him. Could he sense what was to come?

"Reverend, I know what you seek. You seek the one who shakes his fist at God and swears to never bow, the Prideful One whose hatred is total and complete, who loves no one and nothing other than himself."

"You know?" Masters said, nearly certain the thump he heard was not his coffee cup jostling, but his jaw hitting the table. *Does he know that it is a demon?*

Dieter smiled. "Don't look so surprised, my friend. I am not the ignorant immigrant that you sometimes treat me as. I actually have great admiration for your decision. I never fully believed what everyone said about you. I knew that somewhere in that corrupted being of yours, you were Don Quixote preparing to joust at windmills. It is a noble quest you are on to confront evil and defeat it."

Masters relaxed after realizing that the crazy Kraut had entirely overestimated his moral standards. "I'm glad you understand," he said, almost saddened by the imminent demise of his friend.

"Still, you should not come with me this morning," Dieter said rigidly. "I do not believe it is a good idea to bring someone so inexperienced into the woods. It is counterproductive to your goals and also potentially dangerous, especially with the others that are out there now looking for the creature."

"Look," Masters said. "I just want to see what it is like out there. You're probably right, and I'll scare off the Beast with my huffing and puffing, but that's okay. I can deal with a day's delay. The better I understand the terrain, the better I'll be able to make my display back at the Mysterium."

Dieter stood up and walked over to a closet. He pulled out a blazing orange safety jacket. "Well, you can wear this. I do not want someone mistaking you for a monster and taking a shot at you."

Masters eyed the thing with disgust. "How considerate of you."

Gavin stood in front of the deeps sinks at the Cluck and Grunt, spraying water onto the egg-encrusted plates of prior patrons. The twelve-foot-high walls painted in guacamole green and bathed in harsh fluorescent lighting caused the dried yokes to take on a dark orange color that left him somewhat queasy. He sighed as Trudy came in with another full tray of dirty dishes.

"How's our new unpaid employee?" she asked.

"I guess it beats sitting in the dining room and drinking coffee until I float away."

"Bill really likes you and is thinking about doubling your salary," she laughed. "So, how does my engineer like manual labor?"

"Bill's food looks bad enough when it's hot off the grill. In here it looks like warmed-over road kill."

Trudy grabbed him around the waist. "That's why he's lucky to have a monopoly around here." All at once, the hanging work lights in the room started to sway back and forth as flecks of dust rained down from the ceiling.

Gavin stopped spraying the dishes and looked at her. "Earthquake?"

The tremors became more violent as dishes rattled in their stacks and hanging pots clanged together.

"I don't think so," Trudy replied as a tray of silverware skittered across the metal counter and threw itself over the side. "Is Rachel still in the dining room?"

"I think so, I haven't seen her."

"Oh, shit!" Trudy yelled as she burst through the swinging doors and into the dining room.

———

Trudy stopped short. In the middle of the room, Rachel faced a man in a pinstriped suit about fifteen feet down the aisle. Tables were bouncing across the floor like Mexican jumping beans as customers scurried out the front door or ran around back through the kitchen. Old photographs on the walls that had not moved an inch since they were hung forty years ago crashed to the floor.

A shout came from the kitchen. "You bust up my dining room, Rachel," Bill yelled over the commotion, "and you're fired!"

Trudy paused for a moment to assess the situation. Gavin came up beside her and she put out an arm to block him. Rachel had begun her transformation; a soft aura of light was around her, but it was brightening quickly.

Trudy stepped up and put a hand to her shoulder. "Rachel, easy, honey, calm down. What's the matter?"

"He's a Fallen one," she said, her voice a little stronger, louder, more forceful than her normally pleasant lilt.

Trudy looked at the man in the suit. "He's a demon? I thought he was a banker."

"I prefer freedom fighter—the name is Mr. Azael," he informed Trudy, and then turned his attention to Rachel. "You may stop bristling, Rachel my dear. My visit is one of peace."

Slowly the rumbling in the room quieted and Rachel's glow faded.

"That's better," Azael smiled. "It was just like old times there for a moment." He raised his arms and proclaimed in a stentorian voice, "I am always killing boars, but the other man enjoys the meat."

"That quote! I know it. Do I know *you*?" Rachel asked, her voice returning to its normal squeak.

"Do you not remember your old adversary?" he replied, lowering his arms and looking slightly hurt. "Surely you remember the Diocletianic Persecutions? It seems you do remember Diocletian's saying." He smiled. "Ah, those were the days. Thanks to Emperor Diocletian, and my kind of course, protecting angels such as you were never at a loss for work—true job security. You should thank me, as I was leading the slaughter."

"It's you!" Rachel said. "We came against you. We defeated you."

"Many years and much loss of life later. I'm afraid that happy period in Roman history ended, that is true, but I would hardly call it a victory. But I come to speak of other things. You need to inform Jonathan that the community should disband and the ladder should close. You are ill prepared for what is to come. I would tell him myself but I doubt he would invite me over."

Azael eyed Trudy with raw contempt. "Rachel, your kind is so much higher and greater than these mere formations of dirt. I do not even know how you can stand being in that disgusting human form of yours! I can barely tolerate this bipedal mass of meat I must wear for my duties, but to do so willingly?

Unthinkable! But for some unknown reason you care for them. I'm sure you would not want one to come to harm."

Tremors started again in the restaurant, prompting Trudy to whisper to Rachel, "Cool your jets. He enjoys it when you're pissed."

Slowly the room returned to normal as Azael looked behind them to Gavin. "Is that Gavin—the young lad we have heard so much about? Come here son; let me get a good look at you."

Gavin stepped up alongside of Rachel and Trudy.

"I hear you have a great gift," Azael said. "The ability to see the ladders is a wonderful thing; wonderful indeed. I wish I were able to do that, but alas, it is not my bailiwick, I'm afraid."

"Your business here is over," Rachel said.

"Certainly! I would never overstay my welcome." Azael gave a little salute to Rachel. "Always a pleasure, whether it be in battle or in friendly conversation. Please convey my request to Jonathan. He's a stubborn one; do try to impress upon him the dire consequences if he does not comply.

"Gavin, my boy," Azael added as he walked towards the door. "I hope we meet again under friendlier circumstances. Don't be a stranger."

———

"You should be more careful," Dieter said to Masters for the third time. "You make more infernal racket than an elephant in a bamboo forest."

"They should pave this whole place and build condos," Masters said in disgust. "You do this for fun?"

"Why, yes. The opportunity to be in nature and to challenge oneself—I cannot imagine anything more rewarding."

"You're a freak," Masters grumbled. "I should have you stuffed and put on display at the Mysterium. I could bill you as the Rare Nazi Tree-hugger. Nobody would believe it though."

Masters stumbled over another root. "Give me a smoke-filled casino with flowing liquor and a good lap dance, and I'm happy."

Dieter waved for Masters to be quiet and get down.

"What is it?" Masters whispered as he kneeled next to Dieter.

"I think we may have gotten lucky, despite your noise. Up ahead I can see some movement." Dieter turned to him. "Reverend, stay here while I move on ahead. I do not want you to scare it away."

Masters waited until Dieter was about ten yards ahead before he began reaching into his pocket for the camera. If this was the Beast and not a crazed Bigfoot zealot, he wanted to be ready.

Dieter disappeared down a ridge obscured by a fallen tree.

The forest was quiet for a moment, and then it was pierced by a scream.

Masters stood up and ran as best he could towards the fallen tree while holding the camera out in front of him. Approaching at a fast trot, he could see the back of the Beast rising slightly higher than the ridge. He moved closer and snapped his first shot: a blur of badly focused gray skin.

Dieter winced in pain under the Beast, his rifle having been knocked several yards away. The demon had him pinned with one foot, a claw deeply imbedded in his stomach.

The Beast watched Masters with its sickly buzzard face as he made his way down the slope of the ridge and, in a careful sidestepping motion, walked around to the front to stand near Dieter's rifle.

Standing six feet away he started snapping photos of the scene. Dieter was still alive and obviously in great pain. He attempted to move but the Beast just dug the claw deeper into his flesh. "Help me!" he cried in a gurgling gasp, pointing towards the rifle that lay at Masters' feet. "Reverend, the rifle, please!"

Masters raised his camera and took another photo.

"Fuck you!" Dieter yelled as his face registered understanding of his fate. "You fucking bastard!"

The hunter said not another word as the Beast ripped him apart, splattering blood onto Masters' shoes.

The Reverend snapped several more photos before shakily putting his camera away. He had never seen such violence up close and the scene was disturbing.

"So, what now?" he asked the creature.

The Beast turned the face of a bull towards Masters, and he felt the burning hatred behind the red eyes. He took a step backwards as the Beast snorted in rage and lowered its horns.

Like quicksilver the demon pounced forward and slashed Masters across the left sleeve of his jacket with a rapier-sharp horn. Before his mind could even register pain, the Beast had disappeared into the forest.

He looked down at the ripped orange fabric of the jacket and felt blood running down his arm to puddle in the cup of his hand.

"God, it hurts like a motherfucker!" he cried as he inspected the wound further. The blood was considerable, and he knew that he needed to slow down the bleeding if he expected to make it out of the forest alive.

With his good arm he was able to remove his belt and cinch it around his arm to slow down the blood loss. Staggering back the way he came with his improvised tourniquet, he just hoped he could make it back to the Mercedes, which was parked on the shoulder of the highway. Dieter might have been full of himself—and shit—and he got what was coming to him. But he had to thank the dearly departed Jerry for insisting he don that ridiculous pumpkin jacket. He hated to think how much worse the wound would have been if he hadn't worn it.

Pulling his cell phone out, he attempted to call for help. "Don't they have cell towers out here?" Masters grumbled as his phone went to roaming.

Masters hand was becoming numb and starting to turn blue as he reached the highway. Fortunately the Mercedes was still there, along with a state trooper's car.

The officer was peering into the passenger side window of the vehicle as Masters struggled up the lip of the road.

"Help me," Masters coughed as he stumbled on the gravel shoulder.

The trooper ran down and grabbed him by his good arm and pulled him up to the road, while at the same time calling in the incident to the dispatcher.

"What happened?" the officer asked, temporarily loosening the tourniquet to allow some blood flow back into the hand.

"The Beast," Masters said, then remembered what he had rehearsed. "The Hodag! The Hodag, it killed my friend."

"Where? Where is your friend?"

Masters was able to point in the direction of the woods before passing out.

———

Sheriff Winston had just pulled up in front of Maggie's house when the radio buzzed with news of another death near Creekside. He was conflicted about pulling away from the curb because he wanted to see her again but was also afraid of impending arguments when he inevitably disagreed with her deeply held beliefs.

Perhaps a murder scene would be more pleasant, he thought as he put the pickup in drive and hit the gas.

Fifteen minutes later he spotted the Mercedes and the squad car along the left shoulder of the road. Swinging around, he pulled the pickup in front of the SUV and got out. Walking along the gravel shoulder to the passenger side of the car, he found the trooper kneeling beside the injured man.

"What happened?" Winston asked.

"This guy says a monster, or Hodag I think is what he called it, clawed him and killed his friend. He was able to get away but he's pretty weak." The trooper looked down at Masters. "He's lost a lot of blood."

"Where's the friggin' ambulance?" Winston demanded.

"First one blew a tire," the officer replied. "Another has been dispatched but it's at least a half hour out."

Winston swore lustily underneath his breath. "Half an hour? What the hell are they doing, driving from Kenosha? Okay, get on the horn and tell them to meet me in Creekside on Main Street. That will save about fifteen minutes." He bent down, saying, "Help me get this guy into my truck. What's his name, trooper?"

"His driver's license says Jay Masters. From the Dells."

"Well, looks like this saves me a little drive after all," Winston said as they carted Masters to the back row of the sheriff's pickup and carefully loaded him.

"How long until the investigative team arrives?" Winston inquired as he closed the passenger door and went around to the driver's side. "And don't tell me a half hour."

"They should be here in the next twenty minutes or so."

"Okay. I'll be back after I transfer him to the ambulance. Don't start without me."

—

Trudy was sweeping up the dust loosened by Rachel's mood swings when she noticed the sheriff's pickup, lights flashing, as he pulled up in front of the Cluck and Grunt.

"Uh-oh. Bill, you didn't call the cops did you?"

"Course not," came a greasy wheeze from the kitchen. "I'm not gonna turn in a little girl that can kick my ass if I say I don't like her pink uniform."

"Smart thinking. I'm going out to see what the commotion is. Rachel, want to come along?"

"Sure," said Rachel. She called over her shoulder, "Bill, you do like my pink uniform, don't you?"

"You bet, little girl. I'd wear one myself if they came in my size."

As they walked out on to the sidewalk Trudy could see Sheriff Winston on the other side of the pickup, a frown on his jowly face.

"What's the matter?" Trudy said as they walked around to the pickup's open door. She paled when she recognized the bleeding man in the back seat.

"Guy was out in the woods and got mauled by something. We're meeting the ambulance. It should be here any minute now." Winston looked at her with an odd expression on his face. "Trudy, are you okay? You're white as a sheet."

"That's my father," she said shakily. "Is he going to be okay?"

"You're father? Masters! Of course—I never associated the two of you. He's lost a lot of blood and may lose that arm if we can't get him some help fast."

Trudy looked at Rachel. "Get Gavin."

When Rachel didn't move, she said again, louder: "Rachel, get Gavin NOW!"

Snapping out of it, Rachel finally ran into the restaurant and a minute later she emerged with Gavin.

"Oh, crap," Gavin said as he looked at the man in the back of the truck. "That's your father."

"Yeah, that's the scumbag," Trudy replied. "You've got to do your little Tesla coil thingy on him—he might not survive otherwise."

"What are you taking about?" Winston said.

"Can't describe it," Trudy replied. "You just need to watch." She looked back to Gavin. "Please, he isn't much, but he's the only father I have."

Gavin took a step to the truck and grabbed the door frame tightly. Reaching down, he touched the Reverend on the shoulder. A bolt flew between Gavin's hand and Masters, sending up a little puff of smoke and the smell of burnt nylon. Gavin was pushed back, but he continued to hold onto the truck even as the lights and siren went off of its own accord.

Winston was thunderstruck and his face showed it. "What the hell just happened?"

Trudy moved up and grabbed Gavin around the waist to steady him as she watched her father begin to regain consciousness.

The ambulance pulled up and two paramedics got out. "What's the situation?" one said.

"I-I'm not s-sure." Winston stammered as he looked at Gavin. "What *is* the situation, son?"

Gavin shrugged with exaggerated innocence.

Masters looked up from the backseat of the truck. "My arm! It was all tore up." He reached out feebly, trying to touch his injured arm. "What happened? I feel like a horse just kicked me." Then he seemed to be able to focus on them. "Trudy? Gavin?"

One of the paramedics approached Masters and inspected his arm. The color had returned, and now the bluish hand was a bright pink. "Lots of blood, but I'm not seeing a wound. The jacket is all tore up, so I would expect there to be one here but … nothing. Why'd the hell did someone put a tourniquet on a healthy arm?" he said disgustedly as he proceeded to remove it.

"Better take him in for observation at least," Winston said to the EMT.

Masters looked up at the sheriff in a panic. "My friend! He was killed out there by a giant Hodag. You've got to find that creature and kill it before it kills someone else."

"Easy, sir, we're going out there to recover your buddy," Winston said. "Believe me, if there is man-killer in that woods, we'll find it."

Winston and the others followed along as the paramedics put Masters on a stretcher and wheeled him towards the ambulance. The sheriff said to the paramedic in the driver's seat, "I'm going to need you to contact the Rhinelander police on your way in and have them meet you at the emergency room. I need him to stay at the hospital under supervision until we can question him about the death."

"Sure, no problem, but we're going to Tomahawk, not Rhinelander."

"Tomahawk—great." Winston sighed. "That's a friggin fifty-mile round trip from Rhinelander."

As the ambulance drove off, Winston turned to face them. "So," he said, "which one of you is going to be explaining this to me?"

Masters sat in the back of the ambulance, refusing to lie down. "I'm perfectly fine," he grumbled to the paramedic as he stuck his now healed hand into his pocket. Pulling out his cell phone he selected the Mysterium and hit dial.

"Sir," the EMT said, "I can't allow you to do that, and you need to lie down. It's for your own safety."

"Yeah, make me. What are you going to do, injure your patient while attempting to keep him safe? That will look good in a lawsuit."

"Holly." Masters said into the phone. "Get those stilettos moving and get up to ..." He looked at the paramedic. "Where the hell are we going?"

"Sacred Heart in Tomahawk."

"Tomahawk? Why not Rhinelander?"

"It's closer, sir."

"Did you hear that, Holly? These assholes are taking me to Sacred Heart Hospital in Tomahawk. Yeah, it will take you two or three hours if you don't stop for a pedicure or another Coach bag at the outlet store. I'm in an ambulance. No, I'm not hurt. Just get up here!"

Winston pushed his belly into a booth at the Cluck and Grunt opposite Trudy, Rachel and Gavin.

"The dining room's a lot dustier than I remember it," he commented, wiping the table off with his palm. The three youths sat stoically like the Three Wise Monkeys. "Well? Let's have it!"

The three looked at each other. Trudy finally replied, "Gavin here has the gift of healing."

"Yeah, right." Winston shot an appraising look at the lanky Gavin, who looked to him no more remarkable than any other slacker twenty-something. "That right, son?"

"I don't know if I would call it a gift, sir. I discovered that I could do it after coming up here. Jonathan, from Morgan, thinks it has to do with my surgery. That they messed something up when they were in there."

"Or fixed it," Trudy put in.

"And Jonathan is an expert on these sorts of things?" Winston said, slightly annoyed by hearing Jonathan's name. "Did you by any chance happen to heal anyone else around here lately?"

"The guy in the car wreck," Gavin replied, staring sheepishly down at the table.

"And a skunk!" Rachel added. "Oh, and Trudy's arm—I burnt her by accident."

Winston shook his head. "So that asshole was right about growing a new hand?"

"Uh," Gavin said. "Yeah …"

"Why didn't you tell me when we were all there at the scene?" Winston demanded.

"Would you have believed us?" Trudy asked.

Winston blew exasperatedly across his rubbery lips. "Of course not," he said, fixing Gavin in his unblinking gaze. "Son, your aunt is always spouting off about all the miraculous stuff around this area that I'm missing out on because I refuse to see it. Is she right about any of it?"

Gavin looked back at him unflinchingly. "All of it. Every single word of it."

"Next you'll be telling me this restaurant is full of supernatural beings or something."

"No," Rachel replied. "Just me."

Winston turned an annoyed eye on the mousy girl, who blushed.

Trudy crossed her arms on the table and looked at him. "Sheriff, here's the thing. The shit is about to hit the fan around here, and we need someone we can rely on to help us. Maggie trusts you, and that's good enough for me."

She pointed to Rachel. "Yeah, she's an angel. She's the one that made a pretzel out of that creep's pickup when he started to screw with us. Over at

Morgan, they're all angels; not a human in the bunch. They came here to be like us so that they could love us more completely."

Winston fell back in his seat, stunned. "You don't expect me to swallow this hog swill do—"

"Oh, it gets better," Trudy cut him off. "The Beast in the woods. It's not a Hodag, whatever the hell a Hodag is supposed to be. It's a demon. They search for these communities of angels and attempt to disrupt them and ultimately shut them down because they think it's beneath an angel to want to understand or sympathize with us. God loves us; therefore they hate us, and they hate all who attempt to protect us, including Rachel and her brothers and sisters at Morgan."

Winston was about to speak but Trudy held up her hand. "Better be quiet. I'm not done screwing with your mind. We had a visitor in the diner today: a Mr. Azael—polite guy in pinstripes. Someone you would get a mortgage from. He's a demon. He is out to close down Morgan but he is also after Gavin."

Winston had to admit this girl was articulate and convincing. He decided to hear her out. "Why?"

"Because he can see the portals the angels use to come into this world. He feels the location of them in his head. The demons can't, and they want to use him to gain knowledge as to where the other portals are."

Winston looked wonderingly up at the ceiling. "How am I supposed to believe something so farfetched?" he said through nervous laughter. "And that the little lady here is an *angel?*"

"A protecting angel," Rachel corrected.

"That crazy bastard with the new hand thought you were a space alien." He leaned back in his seat and regarded the diminutive Rachel. "You can understand my disbelief. You're probably ninety pounds soaking wet. And I'm supposed to believe you crushed a full size pickup with some kind of angel voodoo?"

Trudy bumped Rachel with her shoulder. "We need him, so it's time to put on a little show for the good sheriff. But not too much."

"Sheriff," Rachel said as she pointed out the window, "you may want to tie your pickup down before it floats away."

Winston turned to see his truck hovering about five feet off the ground just outside of the restaurant. A couple that he recognized as residents of

165

Creekside walked by it as if it were an everyday occurrence. "Shit! Oh, holy shit!" he said. "Okay, put it down! Put it down! But put it down gently—that's taxpayer's money out there."

Slowly the pickup descended, all four wheels ever so gently touching the asphalt at the same time. The shocks didn't even budge.

Winston sat in the booth, not saying anything for a few moments.

"Are you okay?" Gavin asked. "Hello?"

The sheriff snapped out of it. "Does everyone in town know about this?"

"Yep." Trudy then yelled back to the kitchen. "Hey, Bill! What is Rachel?"

Bill spit into a coffee cup he had been using. "A pain in the ass."

"No, the other part," she yelled back.

"Messenger of the Most High, herald, protector, angel, blah, blah, blah. A little girl in a pretty pink uniform that should be working instead of sitting in a booth."

Winston sat completely stunned by what had just happened. Everyone was so blasé here about what he found so amazing. Admitting defeat he said, "Tell me what you need, then I guess I better go over to Maggie's for a dinner of crow."

———

The sheriff was shaking as he drove back towards the scene of the last hunter's death. The sight of his truck floating in air disputed everything he had known and taken for granted about the how the world behaved. The woods on each side of the road had now become something to fear, because now they contained demons.

As he rounded the bend in the road he couldn't believe the amount of vehicles that had assembled. There were two cars for the investigative team, the squad car of the trooper he had spoken to, an ambulance, and the Mercedes being loaded onto a tow truck. In back of that were three television news vans with their dishes poking into the sky. Further back still was a motley assemblage of vehicles ranging from an aged VW bus with a crudely painted Hodag on its side to an allegedly eco-friendly Prius splattered with petroleum-based plastic stickers incongruously protesting big oil. Their passengers were all milling about the shoulder of the road, their postures stooped under the immense weight of their camera's telephoto lenses.

Winston parked on the other side of the road and walked over to the trooper. "Where's the team?"

"They're already at the scene. The reporters were getting on their nerves."

"Anything so far?"

"It will take them awhile. They'll need to get their shovels out to scrape up the guy who's out there. Sounds like quite a mess. Oh, by the way, sheriff—the Mercedes is registered to a Dieter Jaeger out of Milwaukee. And there was an interesting find in the glove compartment."

"Yeah?"

"A plastic bag with a couple of mangled human fingers in it."

"Well, after the prints are run we'll try to find their rightful owner," Winston said, even though he believed he already knew whom they belonged to.

"Sheriff!" One of the reporters huddled near their trucks called out.

Winston turned to see it was the Botox blonde from channel seven. Barbara something-or-other. "Sheriff, this is the fourth death in a matter of weeks for this normally quiet area," she shouted at him. "Is it true that a large, unidentified animal roams these woods and is responsible for the deaths?" She held out her microphone for his reply.

Winston stalked away into the woods.

He had grown up in the woods. His father was an avid hunter and never missed a deer season, and he always brought his boy along. Previously he had always been comfortable in this environment, but now he was spooked.

When he reached the scene he had to stop for second and turn around, feeling he would vomit.

"Yeah, we had the same reaction," one of the investigators said.

"What the hell?" Winston said. He had been unprepared for the carnage.

"Pretty much confirmed it was an animal attack," another investigator said. "We've got prints in the dirt twelve inches across. This sucker's huge."

"Makes that guy's Hodag story look more plausible now," A third investigator chimed in.

"Let's get this straight," said Winston, angered by what he now knew. "We're not using the H-word. There are no Hodags wandering around in the woods here. The gawkers out on the road are nothing compared to what would happen if this cock and bull story gains credibility. More people will get hurt. All we know is a large, dangerous animal is in the area and that people need to stay away." Winston looked at each of them in turn. "Got it?"

"Yes, sir," came the scattered mumbles.

Winston turned away. *Signs and wonders!* he thought. *Protecting angels. A punk kid who can regrow hands. A demon in the woods.*

He looked at the gently swaying trees. *More things in heaven and earth, Horatio.* After today, he wouldn't be surprised to find the Hodag in there, munching on a bratwurst.

CHAPTER EIGHTEEN

Masters was propped up in the hospital bed at Sacred Heart, flipping through channels on the television. He paused briefly at a show where three women were fighting over one guy that looked vaguely like the recently deceased Pervis Winslow, greasy mullet and all. "Why are people such assholes?" he groused, pounding the remote and finding only similar lowbrow fare.

He had spent the night for observation, but also for safekeeping until the police could talk to him, a fact confirmed by the officer he could see standing outside his door whenever a nurse entered the room.

Masters' mood brightened at the sound of a familiar voice in hallway. The officer opened the door with a smile as he let Holly through. From the officer's expression Masters judged he was mentally peeling her skintight jeans off, and who could blame him. One of Holly's very few talents was the ability to charm any male into doing just what she wanted.

"Jay!" she screeched. "Are you okay? I was so worried about you."

"I'm okay," he managed to get out before she launched herself onto him.

"Are you hurt?" she said as she straddled him and grabbed his crotch. "Does everything still work?"

"Get off of me!" Masters said, as he pushed her to the side and turned up the television volume at the same time. "Listen …"

"This is Barbara Kern reporting from the woods north of Creekside. There have been numerous reports of a large, unidentified animal roaming the forests outside this once peaceful village. So far, there are four confirmed deaths that appear to be the result of innocent hunters being attacked by the fearsome Beast. The latest attack was yesterday afternoon, when famed big game hunter Dieter Jaeger found himself no match for the ferocious Beast lurking just inside the tree line."

"Come on," Masters urged the television. "Say it. Say it."

"Some," the reporter continued, "say that the deaths are the handiwork of the legendary Hodag of Wisconsin folklore."

"*Yes!*" he exclaimed and then remembered there was a cop just outside the door.

"Okay," he said to Holly conspiratorially, "here's the deal. Look over there in my jacket pocket, the left one."

Holly went over and removed the camera.

"Here's what I need you to do," Masters said. "I need you to take that camera to this Barbara Kern person at Channel Seven."

Holly cocked her head in a question. "Why?"

"Because it has something on it that she needs to see, Einstein. Give it *only* to her. Don't let anyone else see it. This broad looks like the desperate middle-aged female reporter type, someone who could use a major story to extend her shelf life."

Holly stared at the camera. "Jay, tell me that what's on here isn't what I think it is."

"Don't look at it. It would only upset you. The good news for you is that the Hodag won't be coming to the Dells."

Holly brightened a bit at that. "Thank God, that thing gives me the willies."

"Now be a good girl and hide that camera between those ample bosoms and get out of here."

———

"Gavin told me that Clarence had an epiphany thanks to Rachel," Maggie said to Trudy as they stood outside of the Lutheran church.

"Rachel is never subtle," Trudy said. "I think he was more freaked out than he let on. Has he spoken to you yet? Sounds like he was dreading having to say you were right."

Maggie laughed. "He hasn't stopped by yet. I'll try not to say, 'I told you so,' but it may be difficult."

Maggie scanned the sign out front of the church, which the pastor had updated for the week: WHY DIDN'T NOAH SWAT THE TWO MOSQUITOES?

"I worry about the Reverend sometimes," Maggie said with a sigh. "Well, shall we go in? Rachel and Gavin are going to Morgan this morning. Gavin was pretty shook up. He hardly ate anything at breakfast."

"I imagine so," Trudy said. "It's not every day you find out that a demon would like to be your best buddy. Let's get some coffee. As they say, Christians' drug of choice."

———

Gavin walked behind Rachel as they neared Morgan. "So it's out there somewhere?"

"Yes," she replied. "But don't worry. It knows who you are now so it will not attack."

"That's exactly why I'm worried. I don't like the idea of demons knowing who I am and wanting to use me. I didn't even believe they existed not that long ago."

Rachel grinned. "Funny, they've believed you existed for a long time."

They came up to Brother Jonathan's house and climbed the steps to the porch.

Jonathan opened the door on the first knock. "Come in, Rachel, Gavin. Gavin, can I get you anything?"

"No, thank you," he replied as Jonathan motioned to a chair. "I've lost my appetite lately."

"Understandable," Jonathan said as they sat down in the simply furnished living room.

"Brother," Rachel said, "a Mr. Azael came to the diner yesterday. He wanted me to tell you to disband the community and close the ladder. He says that not to do so would be disastrous."

"He also said," Gavin added, "that he hoped he and I would become better acquainted."

"I imagine he would," Jonathan said. "You're the only human who has been able to see an open ladder in thousands of years. It makes you quite valuable to them."

"How could they use me? I'd never tell them where a ladder is," Gavin protested.

"Not willingly, no." Jonathan looked at Gavin. "I've met Mr. Azael before on the battlefield. He is cunning and filled with deceit. Never believe anything that he says."

"What do they plan?" Rachel said in a worried tone. "They made threats and I'm afraid they might hurt Trudy." She quickly added: "Or others."

"We must be vigilant," Jonathan said. "Morgan is out of the way. I do not expect them to attack here. Our numbers are more than adequate to defend the ladder." He turned to the girl. "Rachel, I believe that they will concentrate their efforts on Creekside and our friends there. Destroying Creekside will cause the ladder to shrivel and die."

"We can't allow it!" Rachel said, her voice rising in concern. "We must do something ..."

"Hush, dear one." Jonathan said. "We will not sit idly by, I can assure you of that. I will call reinforcements to guard the ladder. The group that is here is well known to the residents of Creekside. We will create a perimeter around the town. I will not let Azael casually stroll into Creekside again."

———

Holly sat in the waiting room of Channel Seven News, looking at the photos in a three-month-old *People* magazine for nearly a half hour until finally a tall blonde walked in and greeted her.

"Hi, I'm Barbara Kern. Sorry for the wait but it's been a busy news day. How may I help you?"

"Do you have someplace to talk?" Holly asked. "A little more private?"

Barbara looked around the empty room. "I'm sorry but I have a deadline I need to keep. Can you tell me what you've got right here?"

"My boss, Jay Masters," Holly started. "He runs a place in the Dells, Masters' Mysterium."

"Oh, that tourist trap," Barbara snapped. "My kids hated it. Total rip-off."

Holly bit her tongue. "Yeah, well. My boss is the one who has been sponsoring the hunters that are winding up dead in the woods north of Creekside. He was there when the last hunter was killed."

She shakily removed the camera from her purse. "There are photos of the Beast on this." Then she remembered. "Oh, Jay says it should be called the Hodag in any newscast. He maintains full rights to the images, but you can use them for your broadcast without charge as long as the Mysterium is mentioned, uh—profusely."

"Why isn't he here himself to specify his requirements?" Barbara asked as she grabbed the camera out of Holly's hand.

"He's currently in the hospital under police custody."

"Hmm," Barbara said as she turned on the camera and started to bring up the stored photos. The first one was a blurry shot of what looked like dirty carpeting. She flipped to the next photo.

Barbara let out a bloodcurdling scream and dropped the camera.

The bitch's stricken look buoyed Holly's spirit. "I haven't seen those. Jay says I don't have the constitution for it."

Barbara ran to the waste paper basket in the corner and vomited. When she stood up there were tears in her eyes. "We still have time to put them on tonight's news."

———

Sheriff Winston walked into Masters' room at the hospital. The window blinds cast the light from the setting sun into bars across the room, giving it the appearance of a prison. Someplace he hoped Masters would become familiar with.

"I've heard that Detective Waters interviewed you and that you'll be allowed to leave if you feel up to it," said Winston. "The doctors have given you a clean bill of health."

"So, you believe me that it was an animal?" Masters asked.

"It wasn't an animal. You and I both know that. Stop sending people out into the woods. We don't want any more deaths, and for heaven's sake stop calling the *demon* a Hodag."

Masters flushed. "So, you are smarter than you look, sheriff."

"Yeah, I know. Now prove that you're smarter than *you* look. People are getting all spun up that they can be the first one to capture a legendary Hodag. They're just taking a needless chance that they will be hurt or killed."

Masters drummed his many-ringed fingers nonchalantly on the nappy hospital blanket. "I'd like to oblige, but it may be a little late for that."

He pointed to the television and increased the volume.

"This is Barbara Kern with a Channel Seven exclusive. The Reverend Jay Masters, proprietor of the world famous Masters' Mysterium in Wisconsin Dells, was with his friend, legendary big game hunter Dieter Jaeger, in the woods north of Creekside when they were savagely attacked by what Masters insists is a living, breathing Hodag—seemingly sprung straight out of Wisconsin lore and into this sleepy part of the state.

"Masters had the quick thinking to snap several photos of the Beast before he himself was attacked and nearly killed. We are going to show these photos to you, but we need to make you aware of their graphic nature. Parental guidance is strongly advised.

"These incredible photos depict Dieter Jaeger being held on the ground by the giant Beast. We have blurred out Mr. Jaeger out of respect for his relatives."

Winston shot Masters a glance. "You asshole."

The screen filled with an image of the Beast. It was looking directly at the camera, and one could see in its eyes its all-consuming hatred and contempt for its prey, for humanity … for everything.

Winston averted his eyes from the screen while attempting to settle down a wave of nausea that a mere image of the Beast produced.

Masters, unfazed by the sight of the thing that held his "friend's" life in its claw, was almost giddy with joy. "Now that right there is gold. Fucking G-O-L-D!" Masters said, pointing to the screen and kicking his feet up and down in the bed while giggling like a child. "I'm going to be both rich *and* famous, I tell you!"

CHAPTER NINETEEN

Trudy wasn't prepared for the onslaught. Being the only restaurant within ten miles had its disadvantages. Even Bill was fuming at having to work so hard.

"What on earth is going on?" Trudy grumbled to Rachel as they both brought dirty dishes into the back room. Buried underneath the mountain of crusty plates, Gavin looked frazzled.

"It's been on the news," he said, turning towards Trudy. "I didn't want to tell you, but your father released photos of the demon to the news."

"He did what?" Trudy said, her voice rising, "After what we did for him? What you did?"

Rachel put a hand on Trudy's arm, which she shook off.

"You should've let that son of a bitch bleed out!"

"Now, this is *exactly* why I didn't want to tell you," Gavin said.

"Trudy," Rachel said calmly. "You don't mean that. He's your father."

"I do mean it," Trudy insisted. "What has he ever done for me except contribute his sperm?"

"That's just it," Rachel said. "You're Trudy Masters; there is only one like you, and there will never be another. You're my best friend in the world, and I have your father to thank that you are here and alive."

"Personally," Gavin observed wryly, "I'm pretty happy that he donated his sperm as well."

"This does present a problem though," Rachel said.

"How so?" Gavin asked.

"Jonathan's plan was for our kind to protect Creekside from the Fallen ones. Everyone in town knows what we are. Now, there are a lot of people at surrounding campgrounds. People we can't protect easily, people who don't know what is happening here."

Gavin nodded. "You know they'll be traipsing through the woods looking for the thing."

"We can patrol the woods, but there is no way we can protect everyone," Rachel said sadly. "This may mean the end of Morgan."

Trudy was stricken. "All the more reason to hate that so-called father of mine."

———

Maggie opened the door and smiled. "Clarence, come in."

Winston entered the house, hat in hand. "I'm sure you heard by now that I've had a little bit of a change of heart about the existence of … well, miracles."

"Why, Clarence, whatever do you mean?"

Winston stumbled over the words. "Rachel has shown me that things are not always … what I think they are."

"And?" Maggie continued to watch him with a cat-that-ate-the canary smile.

"Maggie, you're enjoying this way too much."

"Damn right, I am! It's been too many years coming."

"I'm sorry. You were right all along. Satisfied now?"

"Very. Now, why don't you come on over here and give me a kiss?"

———

There was a knock on the door of Masters' room at the B&B.

As quickly as he unlocked it, he found himself on the floor with Theodore on top of him.

"Thought you'd seen the last of me?" Theodore said as he whisked a knife to Masters' throat. "They let me out because your photos proved I whutn't crazy. They even found my fingers in the glove compartment of your hunter's SUV. They don't know how to explain it, so how can they charge me?

"Besides, I'll be wanted for murder in a little bit," Theodore sneered. "They can probably charge me for this one but it will be a pleasure anyways."

"Now just wait a minute!" Masters said as the blade scratched the surface of his skin. "I didn't know that thing was going to attack you."

"The hell you didn't!" Theodore spat. "That thing practically posed for them photos. No way you didn't know what was going on."

"I'll pay you," Masters said, feeling blood trickle down his neck. "I'll have a lot of cash when this thing plays out. I could make you wealthy as well."

"I've been poor my whole life. Had a brother most of my life too," Theodore said. "No sense getting rich on the graves of my own kin and a good friend. Well, it's time to meet your maker Reverend Masters, though I doubt if St. Peter will even let your sorry ass in."

Masters closed his eyes to wait for his death. Instead he heard a sound similar to an egg cracking and the weight of Theodore falling upon him.

The Reverend opened his eyes to see Theodore's face two inches from his own. The anger was erased from Theodore's features and replaced by unconscious blankness, his tongue sticking out as blood flowed down around his ear. Masters pushed him to the floor beside him and looked up to see Trudy holding a poker from the downstairs fireplace.

"Carol, call the police" she said to the goggle-eyed woman busy wringing her hands behind her. "It's just what I thought would happen."

"How did you know?" Masters said as he shakily got to his feet.

"I saw this jerk," she said, nudging Theodore with the poker, "walking past the diner, so I decided to see where he was going. When he went in here I knew what was going to happen." She adopted a mocking little girl voice. "Why, Daddy, you just inspire all these warm fuzzy feelings in people."

"Well, thank you," Masters said. "You saved my life, for a second time. I'm doubly indebted to you."

"Gavin saved it the first time," Trudy corrected him. "And this was more payback to him"—she pushed the poker into Theodore's side again, a little harder—"than to save you."

"Well, either way." Masters said. "I thank you." Then, looking down at Theodore: "Is he dead?"

"No. My aim was off. I just grazed him. Head wounds always bleed a lot. At least that's what I read once on WebMD. Although I imagine he'll have one hell of a headache when he comes around."

———

Holly made it back to the Mysterium to find the parking lot, normally a desert of asphalt, filled to capacity and a line snaking from the remotest space to the ticket counter.

"Why is it so crowded?" she asked Wilford, the lecherous security guard as she came in the employee entrance.

"That whole Hodag thing has gotten around," he said, his eyes roving helplessly to her bust.

"Hey, my eyes are up here!" said Holly, more out of habit than annoyance.

"Sorry, Miss Stenberg. People are curious and want to see something about it. Some of them are getting a little rambunctious when they find out we don't have an exhibit and that our famous Reverend's not around."

"Okay, I'll get a hold of Jay and see if we can figure out what to do."

As Holly entered her office, she noticed the voice mail light blinking furiously and a pile of sticky notes littering her desk. She quickly scanned the notes left by the admissions office. Almost all were requests for interviews.

She picked up the phone and called her employer.

———

"Yeah," Masters answered.

"It's Holly."

"Holly, I'm in the middle of spending some quality time with my daughter," he said as he looked down at the prone Theodore, looking like something the cat drug in. "Can this wait?"

"Uh, I don't think so. The parking lot is full of people wanting to see the Hodag. My desk is filled with notes with requests from the media to interview you." Masters heard her rummaging through papers. "Oh, wow! NBC, CBS, CNN, Fox News—all the big boys. There's even one from the producers of

MonsterQuest on the History Channel—they want to do a segment on you! And I haven't even gotten to the voice mails yet.

"You've got to get back here," she said with panic in her voice. "I don't know what to do."

"Okay, okay, keep your shirt on—for now. I'll take care of the media frenzy when I get back to the office. If anyone contacts you, take their number and tell them I'll call them back. What I need you to do is to call around the tourist traps in Rhinelander and see if you can score some Hodag merchandise. If anyone has it, they will."

"Sure, Jay."

"Do you still have the camera? Did Barbara what's-her-puss give it back to you?"

"Yes, I've got it."

"Good girl. Drive over to the printer we always use and have him make up some posters using the photos. We'll put them up as a temporary exhibit until we can put something better together. Get Stan Grazinsky to help you; his number's in my organizer, he'll know what to do with the space. He's the best set decorator in town and owes me a favor for covering up his little jailbait escapade. Remind him of that if he gets uppity."

"When are you coming back Jay?" Holly asked. "I miss you."

"I should be back later today. My daughter will drive me."

He looked over at Trudy, who was shaking her head vigorously and emphatically mouthing the word "NO!"

As Masters hung up, Trudy verbalized it. "*No*, I'm not driving you to the Dells."

"But I don't have a car." Masters pleaded. "I was borrowing Dieter's, and the police impounded it."

"Why is that my problem? There's a Roadmaster dealer at the end of Main."

"The sooner I get back to the Dells, the sooner I'm out of your hair."

They could hear Carol down below, letting in the police and EMTs as Theodore came to, making moaning sounds.

"Please, Trudy," Masters pleaded with the most mournful voice he could muster.

"Shit, *okay*. As soon as we get done with this mess"—she poked Theodore none too fondly one last time in the small of his back—"I'll take you to the Dells. But don't try to be fatherly or I'll kick you out of a moving vehicle."

———

Gavin and Rachel were standing at the door of the Cluck and Grunt when Trudy finally returned.

"What happened?" Gavin asked. "You were here one moment and then gone the next. Then we heard the police car."

Trudy looked at Rachel. "Remember that creep in the pickup that you remodeled? The tall one who grabbed me? He walked by the window heading towards State Street."

Rachel looked at her blankly. "Sure, I remember him. But it was good that he didn't come in here, right?"

"Not really," Trudy said as she went behind the counter and poured herself a cup of coffee. "He was one of my father's hired guns. Like anyone who deals with Big Daddy Masters, I assumed he held a grudge."

"You should have told us," Rachel said. "We should have gone with you."

"What, and leave Bill here all alone?" Trudy said as she waved and smiled to Bill in the kitchen. "You know all he does is grunt at the customers."

Bill acknowledged her assessment by scratching his armpits and farting.

"So, did the thug go to visit your father?" Gavin asked.

"Yeah. Carol allowed me to borrow the fireplace poker. Good thing, too. When I got upstairs the guy had my father on the floor with a knife to his neck."

"Trudy!" Rachel said. "You should have gotten me. You could have been hurt."

"It's okay, the guy wanted me to bang him, so I did. Just in a different way than he expected. Which leads me to the next item: I'm going to drive my father back to the Dells tonight after we close."

"Well, we're coming with you," Gavin said.

"And who's going to babysit Bill?" Trudy replied. "It'll be late when we get there, so I'm probably going to spend the night and come back tomorrow. I need you to help Rachel with the morning service. With all this Hodag mania, the breakfast trade's picked up you know."

"Guess you're right," Gavin sighed.

"I usually am."

———

Trudy watched her father shove empty food wrappers aside with his foot in the floorboard cum trashcan of the aged Corolla. "Is that a mouse?" he asked with a start as something small and furry emerged from underneath a Snickers wrapper and skittered to safety under the seat.

"Could be ..."

Trudy was hoping for silence throughout the trip, and they made it as far as Rhinelander before it was uncomfortably broken again.

"My father was an asshole," Masters said apropos of nothing to jump-start the conversation.

"Wow, so is mine," Trudy replied as her hands tightened on the steering wheel. "Or at least that's what I hear. I wouldn't know, of course, because he wasn't around to be a parent to me."

"Look, I told you why I left. It wasn't about you."

"Yeah, I'm sure you didn't even think about how it would screw up your soon-to-be daughter for the rest of her life."

"I don't think you are screwed up," Masters said while looking out the window. He then looked over at her. "Even if you are, there are a lot of well-adjusted people who didn't have a parent. You can't blame me for that."

"You left me in Creekside," Trudy said as she swerved around a pothole. "With a mother who couldn't function as one. She had a hard time functioning at all, let alone taking care of me." Trudy shot him an angry look. "But at least she tried."

"I'm sorry," Masters said. "I wasn't even thinking. I just knew I had to get out, and that I couldn't take your mother or you with me."

Trudy drummed the steering wheel with her fingers, interested in spite of herself. "So, you became this big time healer and conned a bunch of suckers. Was that worth it?"

"Hell yeah!" Masters grinned. "Those were good times, the gravy years. I always loved the road, the different towns every week. I put on a good show. Nobody left disappointed."

"But all a fake."

"Sure. I never thought anyone could actually heal until I ran into your boyfriend Gavin. He's the real deal." Trudy could feel his eyes on her, studying her. "So how does he do it?"

"I don't know. He doesn't even know."

"Well, the boy's got a gift. He could make a fortune off of that."

"Contrary to you, he doesn't rip people off."

"You see, that's the beauty of it. He wouldn't be conning the rubes. Like I said, he's the real deal."

"I see where that conniving brain of yours is going and just forget it. You're not going to put him in your freak show."

"I'm just saying," Masters pressed, "it's a shame to waste talent like that when he could be helping so many people."

Trudy shot him a look. "You know I never met my grandfather on your side of the family; the one I knew on my mother's was a sweet gentle man who brought me Tootsie Rolls as a surprise when he got home from work. So, riddle me this—is this the way he was an asshole, or is this something new that you've created?"

"My father would never have seen the possibilities in anything," Masters grumbled. "The guy was a loser and only made himself feel better by letting me know that I was an even bigger one. Be glad you didn't know your grandfather, kid. I wish I could say that."

Masters slumped further into his seat and continued, "I grew up in Chicago and he spent most of his life, at least the part that I can remember, on the dole. While he wouldn't work a lick, he did manage to drive my mother to an early grave with working two jobs, raising a family, and taking care of his sorry ass. He even had me working after school since I was twelve, but not for my own money. Everything except what I could sneak on the side went to him for his next round at Paddy's Pub. He caught me a few times holding back on him and he would take his belt off and whip the daylights out of me."

He sat there wearily. "Let's change the subject. How was growing up in Creekside? Was there any good in it at all?"

Trudy thought for a moment. "Yeah, sure, there was good there. The town is like a big family. A bit dysfunctional, but they mean well. There are worse places to have grown up."

"Yet you're restless now. I can almost smell it. I know how that is myself."

She sensed something surprisingly sympathetic in her father's tone. "Sure, I don't belong there anymore. The sideways glances I get from people let me know that every day. Everyone else my age has moved on. They went off to college, got their degrees, and are working in fancy jobs in big cities. Everyone in town is so polite, but I know they see that big L plastered to my forehead. They think I'm some failed rocker loser."

"So, why didn't you go to college or a music school?"

Trudy sighed. "When I was eighteen I found an ad on Craig's List posted by this drummer in Green Bay who was looking for a guitarist for his band. The guy was a total prick, but a talented one and his band was halfway decent. I used what little cash my mom left me and moved out there. For a while it was working out. We played some gigs around the area and a couple of the local festivals. We even started to receive a little recognition—until the cops picked him up on an open warrant. Seems his side job was jacking cars for a local chop shop. He went to prison, the band dissolved, and I came back to Creekside broke.

"Bill gave me a job at the Cluck and Grunt even though I had no experience. I know he looks like the offspring of Grizzly Adams and a vagrant, but behind that chili-encrusted apron he's a big softy. I felt like a complete failure when I returned. Gavin's Aunt Maggie knew what it felt like to be an outsider as well and she supported me and kept me going."

Masters smiled at her. "You can't give up on your dreams after one try. Look, life is a monkey that occasionally slings shit at you. You live with it and move on. After this group in Dallas that snoops on televangelists and faith healers got some video of the way I worked a crowd and ratted me out to *60 Minutes,* I thought my life was pretty much over… But if that didn't happen I wouldn't have the Mysterium now.

"Look, you're a grown woman and can do what you want, but don't forget you are a Masters. A Masters never gives up on their dreams. Maybe it would be better if you did get out of Creekside. Make a fresh start. Besides, that creature in the woods is dangerous. I saw it face-to-face."

"By the way," Trudy asked, "how did you get away from that thing? It looked like it was close enough to reach out and swat you."

"If you remember," Masters said as he reached to his shoulder, "it did. I got lucky—something must have spooked it. Too bad. If my hunter had lived up to his reputation and bagged the effer—"

"You don't know what you're messing with," Trudy fumed. "Or maybe you do. Either way you're trying to profit off of something evil, and unknowingly you might destroy something beautiful at the same time."

"Climb down off your soapbox, little girl—"

"Shut up! You've got daddy issues, I get that, but you don't need to bag the Beast to prove him wrong. Your puss on a *Time Magazine* cover isn't going to change his opinion of you. He's dead."

"Does that go the same for you?" Masters asked. "The shadow of a Masters spreads wide."

"Maybe," Trudy said. "You know, I've been living too long under the dark shadow of my father. I can't change where I come from, but I can change how I respond to it."

"That's a good philosophy. You sound like my daughter now."

"What did I say about being fatherly?" Trudy shot back. "Just remember that this is a piece of crap car and that passenger door you're leaning on doesn't always stay closed."

———

Winston threw his small stash of fake money down in disgust and glared at Maggie, who sat across from him at her kitchen table. "How can I win against an angel?"

"I'm not cheating," Rachel said with a pained expression. "I'm just very good at *Jeopardy*—I'll take quantum physics for eight hundred please."

"You've lived through all of human history," Gavin added while flipping up the question. "That might be considered a bit of an advantage."

"Now don't pick on Rachel," Maggie scolded. "She can't help it that she was created long before we were."

"We are all created for eternity," Rachel said. "I just had a little head start. I bet that in ten thousand years we'll all be laughing about it." She giggled. "Ooh! What is Schrödinger equation? I win!"

"I'm still trying to wrap my mind around all of this," Winston said. "Everyone around here is so blasé about angels and the supernatural." He looked at Maggie. "The world isn't supposed to work this way."

"This is the way the world has always worked, Clarence," she said airily. "You just haven't noticed it."

"The communities are an oddity," Rachel admitted. "We're usually where you cannot see us because our work doesn't require us to be known to you, and this world is yours, not ours." She looked at Winston with a twinkle in her eye.

"But the Bible does say that you should show hospitality because you may be entertaining angels unaware."

"But it doesn't say that I should let them beat me at board games," he griped.

"Well, I'm going to call it a night," Gavin said as he stood up, yawning. "I'm going to have a busy morning trying to help with breakfast service at the diner. I don't know if I'm cut out to be a waiter."

"You'll do fine," Rachel said. "If I can get the hang of it then you shouldn't have a problem."

———

When Gavin entered the bedroom he felt a chill and remembered that he had left the window open. He walked over to close it but stopped when he felt the refreshing electricity emanating off of the distant ladder. He stood there watching for a few moments until the ladder flared again into the night sky. From this distance the description was correct: The horizontal spikes coming off the main branch of the bolt made it look like a giant ladder reaching into the heavens.

Rachel came up beside him. "Beautiful, isn't it?"

"It is. But it's flaring more than most nights—I can feel it."

"More of our brothers and sisters are coming down the ladder." Rachel said serenely. "With the ladder strong and secure it allows many to arrive, and many will be needed I'm afraid."

Gavin's face was questioning.

"Reinforcements to defend the ladder, I mean, while we will spread out through the community and the campgrounds."

"Do you really need reinforcements?" Gavin asked. "I thought there was only that one Beast in the woods."

"You forget Mr. Azael. He is a well-tailored Beast—the proverbial wolf in sheep's clothing of scripture—that has commanded legions into battle. It would be unlike him not to call more Fallen to his side. Most of our battles are fought in a realm that you cannot see, and be glad of that. Unfortunately, this one I'm afraid will be fought in the open."

"Can you kill the demons?"

"We cannot condemn them to a death like you experience. But we are able to send them into the pit—something they fear more than any death. Our Master was once begged by a group of demons to send them into a herd of swine as they were so terrified of the alternative." Looking pained, she continued. "It is not something we rejoice in when they are sent away; they were once my family, but unlike humans they have made a choice that can never be undone."

"What can they do to you, Rachel?" Gavin asked, not sure he wanted to hear the answer. "Can they hurt you?"

Rachel put her arm around him. "Don't worry. As with any war, there is pain and suffering but they cannot permanently hurt us. They can slow us and disrupt what has been built but ultimately they are already defeated. God always wins. How can you defeat the undefeatable? You can shake your fist and Him and hate Him but in the end it does nothing. It is their failure to understand this that has caused their downfall."

She laid her head on his arm. "Don't worry. I will protect you and Trudy."

CHAPTER TWENTY

"Wait!" Masters said, pointing out the window. "Pull up over there."

"What? Where?" Trudy asked blearily.

"Up on the grass, near the sign. I've got a tradition to uphold."

"It's ten frickin' p.m.," Trudy carped as she pulled to the side of Wisconsin Dells Parkway, over the sidewalk, and onto the grass in front of the Tommy Bartlett Show's empty parking lot. "What kind of phony healer ritual could you possibly need to perform now?"

"This one," Masters said as he rolled down the window and flipped a double bird at the vacant parking lot. "I've finally bested you, Tommy boy!" He yelled. "May your parking lot be forever empty!"

"You're one sick puppy," Trudy marveled. "Hasn't Tommy Bartlett been dead for, like, nearly fifteen years?"

"It's a symbolic act, sweetheart, and it felt damn good," said Masters, easing back in his seat. He flicked his hand vaguely. "Just up the street and hang a right at the Hilton."

Trudy bounced the Corolla back onto the asphalt while looking in her mirrors, hoping they hadn't been spotted, and drove in the direction her father pointed. She made a right at the Sprecher restaurant and headed down a quiet side street.

"This used to be all residential until I took a bulldozer to it," said Masters pridefully. "Turn right, up there. You'll see the sign."

The entrance to the parking lot was glowing an eerie yellow from the light put out by the two stories tall Masters' Mysterium sign. The yellow and orange neon would have been considered tacky in Vegas but in the Dells, amongst the family-friendly attractions, the sharp lettering and silhouette of a black circus tent hidden in the woods was downright creepy.

Trudy pulled into the Mysterium parking lot. "Wow, this is bigger than I expected," she said, catching sight of the warehouse with the black fiberglass circus tent covering it like a funeral veil. "And I thought circuses were scary even before seeing this. I suppose they don't really like you over at the Circus World Museum in Baraboo."

"You know about that, eh? I'm impressed." Masters' eyes roved over the complex. "My life's work," he beamed. "I have a grudging respect for the circuses of old but I have surpassed them all. We can park fifteen hundred cars when needed. Fifty thousand square feet of exhibit space, gift shop, café—only the best for those dear, deep-pocketed rubes. Keep going around the side to the office."

"Over there," he said as he scribbled something on a piece of paper. "Here, I got you a reservation at a hotel for tonight. It would be nice if you stuck around long enough tomorrow so that I can buy you breakfast and show you the Mysterium."

Trudy grabbed the paper from him and took a look. "You're kidding right?"

"Sorry," Masters replied, "The national organization of dental hygienists are in town and they've taken most of the rooms. This is the best Holly could come up with."

"Well," Trudy said as she pulled up to the office door. "I guess you owe me a decent breakfast then."

"I'll pick you up at nine," Masters said as he got out.

———

Trudy easily found the motel thanks to the garish neon sign out front that proclaimed the establishment as the CHUBBY CHERUB MOTOR LODGE AND RESTAURANT. Beneath a rotund cherub whose butt cheeks wore a pinkish glow thanks to its flashing neon wings, the sign mentioned free HBO and "visit our world famous petting zoo."

"Only the best for daddy's little girl," she mumbled as she got out and approached the office.

The musty lobby was half filled with stands for brochures and cheap wire stands filled with postcards. Nobody was behind the counter, so she pushed the doorbell button attached to the pine-paneled siding of the desk.

She could hear the buzzer in the room adjacent to the lobby and a moment later the door opened. A well-fed woman in a purple muumuu emerged from what was obviously her living room, as she could see a man, decked out in a wife beater and boxers that left too little to the imagination, snoring in a La-Z-Boy as the opening strains of *The Late Show* theme blared from the television.

"Sorry," the woman said. A soggy Virginia Slims dangled from her wet bottom lip, "We're full up. The 'no' part of the 'no vacancy' sign burnt out, and we haven't gotten someone out to fix it yet."

"I have a reservation," Trudy said, halfway hoping that the troll was correct and she could go sleep in her car.

"Oh, well that's a different story then." She toddled up to the counter and put on her cat-eye specs. "What name is it under?"

"Masters."

"Oh, yes!" the woman said and her face brightened under the neon glow. "From the Mysterium. And your name?"

"Trudy. Trudy Masters."

"Are you related to the owner?"

"I'm his daughter," she replied sheepishly, not sure if this would cause her to be ejected from the premises.

"Really?" the woman said. She leaned in conspiratorially. "Is he married—Reverend Masters, that is?"

"Not that I know of," Trudy replied. She glanced into the living room where the woman's worse half was still asleep, a hairy hand involuntarily scratching his balls.

The woman glanced in the same direction. "Now Fred there," she whispered, "he's a real bump on a log. Your father, on the other hand, is out there risking his life trying to capture wild animals. I wouldn't mind giving him a ride," she said with a wink.

Trudy stared daggers at her. "I'm his daughter."

"Oh! Yes, of course," the woman said. "Sorry! I didn't mean—"

"If I can just get my room key."

189

"Certainly," the woman said. "It's 23A just on the other side of the petting zoo. Easiest way is to go directly through the enclosure but be careful of the goats. They get a little temperamental when someone is traipsing through this hour of the night."

———

Trudy pulled her bag out of the trunk of the Corolla and looked once again at the sign. Moths were flocking around the pink cherub's ass as the blinking neon wings flapped and hummed above it.

In the center of the L-shaped motel, where normally there would be parking and a pool, there was instead a fenced-off area of dirt that stank of dung and old straw. Trudy walked up to the gate that was lined with dispensers for animal food. In the dim light it was difficult to see the clearest path to the other side, and she was certain she would need to burn her shoes in the morning.

She made it thirty feet into the enclosure when a gang of deer approached her, sniffing her clothes and craning their long necks at her for a handout.

She kept walking.

One of the deer shoved a nose into her kidney.

"Hey!" she said and kept walking.

Another deer came up directly in front of her and stopped, blocking her while another started to chew on the corner of her jacket

"Stop that!" she said as she yanked the jacket out of the animal's mouth.

Another grabbed the strap of her bag and was attempting to steal it.

"Back off, Bambi," Trudy growled, hugging the strap on her shoulder tighter.

Trudy stepped around the blocking deer and ran for the far gate, with six ravenous whitetails in hot pursuit. Out of the corner of her eye she could see the goats waking up and starting their run towards her as well, bleating to beat the band. She made it through the far gate and was able to shut it just in time before being mugged by the angry menagerie.

The room was dingy and stank of hundreds of past cigarettes, while the wall air conditioner groaned in decrepit agony, but Trudy didn't care. She fell onto the bed and dug in her jacket pocket for her cell phone.

She dialed Gavin. "Hey big boy."

"Trudy! You made it. How was the trip?"

"Not as awful as I expected but I still wouldn't say it was pleasant. The old man's still an ass but I can tolerate assholes. I'm having breakfast with him tomorrow and then touring the freak show that he's so proud of. So, how's life in Creekside?"

"Same as always. Rachel's gone to bed. I didn't realize that angels snore like lumberjacks. I walked by her room a few minutes ago and thought the door would blow off."

"Ha!" Trudy laughed. "Oh, guess where I'm staying? The Chubby Cherub Motor Lodge! Did I mention I hate cherubs?"

"No, you didn't. Is it similar to my fear of clowns?"

"Not at all. Clowns exist, cherubs don't. At least not the cute little angels filled with baby fat and dimples, except maybe for Rachel. What did you feel like when you saw her transform?"

"I shit my pants—that's not metaphorical, I actually did," he confessed.

"I can't blame you. Rachel is my best friend in the world but when she is transformed I drop to the ground in sheer terror. I can't help it. I feel so—dirty around her when she's in her true state. She keeps telling me not to be afraid and all of that calming patter they must learn in angel school, but I'm still face-flat on the ground and shaking in awe."

"Hey," Gavin said after a pause, "I miss you."

"Sure it's not just fear of having table service tomorrow?"

"Nope. I just keep thinking of you."

"I know," Trudy replied as she stretched out on the bed. "I kept thinking as I made my way to the room that I wish my beau would save me from the maniacal deer marauders."

"Huh?"

"Long story, kiddo. Let's just say that I really miss you too."

———

Masters had just finished putting his schedule together for tomorrow; it was shaping up to be a busy day. He had over forty calls to respond to, all requests for interviews. He needed to hit the ground running with the callbacks, and the breakfast and tour with Trudy was going to cut into an already hectic day.

But, oddly, he was looking forward to it. He also made a mental note to call his lawyer first thing in the morning.

He decided to go downstairs and see what Holly had done with the display area for the Hodag. Holly's choice of fashion confirmed that she had no taste, but he hoped that hadn't flowed into the display area as well.

As he entered the room he was pleasantly surprised. On one wall was a pictorial history of the Hodag myth. The center area was occupied by a grouping of six large posters derived from his photos. Under the spotlights and dark background they looked quite impressive. Conveniently placed around the room were dispensers for barf bags. He was a bit worried that the display—depicting, as it did, the Beast in full fury and lording its might over hapless, bloody victims—would cut into the café's profits as tourists lost their appetites but he was confident that he'd make up for it in souvenir sales.

"It looks very nice," a voice behind him said.

Masters turned around to see Azael. "How did you get in here, you sneaky bastard?"

"Really, Jay, I thought we had progressed beyond that point. Tell me, have you bonded with your little girl yet?"

"We had a nice conversation on the drive down," Masters lied. "I'm taking her out for breakfast tomorrow, and then I'll show her around the Mysterium."

"Very nice. Very nice indeed."

"Why is it you are so interested in this Gavin kid anyway?"

"Let's just say he has a certain skill set that will prove useful to us."

"You mean the healing thing?" Masters said, and seeing Azael's avid expression, immediately regretted it.

"Healing, you say? That is very interesting. The boy is multi-talented then—all the better. Are you certain of this?"

"Your pet ran a horn through my shoulder. I almost died, but Gavin healed it better than new."

"Oh, yes. I must apologize about that. It is not a totally controllable entity. I can make suggestions or threats on how it should behave, but ultimately it does what it desires to."

"Well, it nearly killed me."

Azael ran his hand across one of the posters of the Beast. "Then it was showing restraint, because if it wanted to kill you, it would have. Which reminds me," Azael continued as he reached into a black bag that was near his feet, "I have a present for you, something from the Beast. We had to discipline it for disobedience."

He pulled out a tail spike from the creature and held it out to Masters. It was about two feet long and came to a sharp point. The other end was a bloody mess, looking like it had been ripped out of the creature by force.

"We do not tolerate disobedience, just so you are aware," Azael coldly said. "Consider this an apology from the Beast. Keep it. Put it on display. Even have scientists look at it. They will pull their hair out attempting to identify it."

"How do I say that I got it?"

"Don't be a dolt. I can think of a dozen explanations off the top of my head. Say it tried to swipe its tail at you and that it broke off on a tree. You grabbed it and ran. Be creative. Oh, one more detail," Azael added. "You need to change your signage. It is not to be called a Hodag. The Hodag has too many shyster connotations, and besides it really isn't that well known outside of Northern Wisconsin."

"Well, what do I call it?" Masters asked.

Azael smiled at him in a way that sent a chill down his spine. "Call it what it is my friend. Call it a demon."

"Nobody will buy that. Hell, I believe it, and I wouldn't even buy it."

CHAPTER TWENTY-ONE

Sheriff Winston and several other officers huddled near their cars just outside of one of Creekside's ubiquitous campgrounds. It was five in the morning, and the chill of fall caused them to grip their coffee mugs for warmth. The campground was fit to burst with Hodag hunters of every describable—and indescribable—stripe.

"There's no way we'll be able to control these yahoos," Winston grumbled as he puffed away on a Marlboro. "Another hour and the crazies will scatter into the woods in full cry, most of them with rifles." He couldn't tell the other officers what he knew, and the inability to express the true danger that stalked through the woods was causing him to chain smoke.

"Should we shut down the campground?" an officer suggested.

"I'm looking into it," Winston replied. "The Department of Natural Resources is conferring with the State to see what our options are. It's really their ballgame. Besides, they'll just set up camp someplace else."

Winston pointed over to a pop-up tent. A fifty-something man with a wild gleam in his eyes followed a dowsing rod through the opening. "Dowsing for Hodag," Winston commented bemusedly. "That's new."

The sheriff brought his coffee mug to his mouth but was finding it difficult to connect. "What the—?" he said as the mug sloshed out most of its contents.

"Earthquake!" one of the campers yelled as the tremor increased. Winston grabbed the side of his truck to steady himself as the ground bucked underneath him.

Panic gripped the campground as RVs shook on their springs and tents swayed in rhythm to the shaking ground.

As quickly as it had begun, it ended.

"What the hell ..." Winston said, nervously planting another Marlboro in his mouth.

———

Jonathan stood at the edge of the Morgan quarry. A pit over a quarter mile around, the bottom had long ago filled with water when the miner's pumps were shut off for the last time so many decades ago. It was now a lake with only the jagged cliffs ringing half of the expanse. Near the shore the foundations of long abandoned mining structures stood in silent sentinel as the only reminder of the quarry's glory days.

Several other members of the Morgan community approached him.

"They have begun to arrive," Jonathan said to the group as he pointed towards the center of the lake. "Azael has been summoning them into the light."

A glow had formed at the bottom of the quarry that was visible even from the surface a hundred feet above.

"We will fan out into the forest," one of the group said. "We can contain them."

"Let us see what we are up against first," Jonathan said, holding out his arm. "Wait."

Around the lake, little waves formed as beings rose out of the water and made their way to shore. Some resembled the Beast in the forest, others appeared more like goats walking on their hind legs, and others crawled on their bellies like snakes, rising out of the water and crawling onto shore to seek the darkness of the forest. None appeared as men.

"See how their contempt for humanity causes them not to even take the human form, even though it would be preferable for their task," Jonathan said.

"He once, many ages ago, called them bright morning stars," one angel commented. "To think what they have lost."

"There are so many. They could not separate us from our friends in Creekside, so they seek to destroy by force," Jonathan sighed as he turned to

Tomas, the elder who had spoken during the community meeting that now seemed so long ago.

"It brings back memories of another time, Jonathan," Tomas replied. "One that I do not wish to repeat."

Jonathan turned to the others. "Go now. The newly arrived will stay with the ladder. Our community will fan out to Creekside and the campgrounds. We will also need some of our numbers in the forest. Stay in your current form unless life is threatened. Remember, we are visitors in this world and do not want to cause undue distress to our human friends."

—

Trudy sat up in bed, flipping through television channels while waiting for her father to pick her up for breakfast. A headline ticker crawling across the bottom of the screen on CNN caught her eye: *Mysterious creature in northern Wisconsin labeled a "biblical demon" by controversial "Reverend" Jay Masters.*

"What!" Trudy yelled, lobbing the remote at the TV. The hapless device bounced off the screen with a dull *thunk* and fell onto the stained carpet while the rusty metal motel room door rattled under a firm knock.

Trudy jumped up and snatched open the door, not bothering to ask who was knocking.

"Good morning," Masters said in all cheerfulness until he was dragged into the room by his lapel and pushed against the wall.

"You sick fuck!" Trudy yelled at him. "What did you do?"

"Hey!" Masters shouted as he pushed her away. "This is no way to treat your father."

"What did you do?" Trudy said again as Masters looked over to the television to see one of his photos of the Beast.

Masters smiled at the television coverage. "What do you mean?" he mumbled back.

Trudy was livid. "You're telling people that there is a demon in the forest, how do you *know* that?"

Masters incuriously grabbed the remote off the floor and turned the volume up. "It's clearly not a normal animal. It's pretty obvious it's something else."

196

"Bullshit!" Trudy replied. "Tell me the truth. How do you *know* that?"

He sat on the foot of the bed, mesmerized by the stock photo of himself in front of the Mysterium. He flipped the channel to Fox News, where the same story was being reported with Masters again figuring prominently.

He smiled. He nearly drooled.

"Hey! I'm talking to you," Trudy said as she reached down and unplugged the TV.

Masters scowled as the screen turned black. "A man came to visit me. He told me what it was."

Trudy stood with feet apart, arms akimbo, head cocked belligerently. "Let me guess. He was a middle-aged guy with a well-tailored suit and spit-shined shoes?"

"Yeah," Masters said as he stood up. "You've met him?"

"Mr. Azael! You're doing business with a demon?" she cried and turned away from him.

"So you have met him," Masters said as Trudy shrugged off his hand on her shoulder.

"He stopped by the diner to say hi," Trudy said as she turned to face her father. "You really don't know what you're screwing up with your publicity stunt."

"Why don't you enlighten me?"

Trudy fell silent.

Masters gave a smug smile. "I thought so. We all have our little secrets, don't we, Trudy? Look, I'm not doing this to hurt anyone. The guy wants publicity. I guess demons are sliding off the brand recognition charts. Anyway, I can give it to him. It's a win-win for both of us."

Trudy continued to glare at him while Masters moved closer and pinched her cheek. "You're really quite attractive when you're pissed off. You got that from me."

She slapped his hand away. "Are we getting breakfast or what?"

"So you'll be seen in public with your father?"

"I just want to get it over with so I can get out of this crummy tourist trap and go home."

She picked up her jacket from the chair where she had tossed it the night before. The right corner of the jacket near the zipper was a crumpled wad of fabric and dried deer slobber. She reached down to pick up her bag but it was intercepted by her father, who offered to carry it.

"There isn't any money in there, if that is what you're going for," Trudy said.

"You are so jaded," Masters observed as they stepped out into the sunlight. "You're more like your father than you want to admit."

———

Josh Barber was emptying the trashcans next to the pumps when a family in a Volvo station wagon pulled up.

"Hi, there," Josh said amiably to the worried-looking husband. "Bathroom's in the back."

"Yeah, well," the man said as he got out and walked over to the pumps, "I'm not going to the back of anything with a demon out there in the woods."

"Did you say ... demon?" Josh said.

"Yeah, that's what I said. You might want to watch the news this morning. The guy—Reverend-something—who took those photos of the Hodag is now saying that the thing in the woods is a bona fide, fire and brimstone-type demon."

Josh couldn't believe that the truth was being circulated and feigned incredulity. "You must have heard wrong, mister."

"I know what I heard," the man said as he shakily swiped his card at the pump and grabbed the gas handle while looking off into the forest behind the Citgo. "There's something out in the woods that isn't of this world. It's freaking my wife and kids out, so we're out of here."

The man came up close to Josh and whispered, "An unknown animal is one thing, something of flesh and blood, but something from the spirit world? No thanks. There's no protecting yourself against that. The boy here wanted to use his Winchester I got him for his birthday to shoot the thing, a really nice 94 trapper, but you can't shoot a demon no matter how good your firearm is."

"Well, I imagine it is all a hoax," Josh said to calm the man down. From the back seat he heard one of the kids cry, "Daddy, let's go. Please! I don't like it here!"

"I doubt it," the man said as he finished fueling and waited for the pump to spit out his receipt. "The Reverend guy has a horn or something from the thing. He's invited scientists to study it. He sounds pretty confident. It's on display down at the Reverend's place—his Mysterium, I think they called it on TV—in the Dells. We're going down there now to take a look."

As the man got back into the car he hollered over to Josh, "Take my advice and close up shop. Take a long vacation someplace other than here. You can lock your doors but that won't keep a spirit out. They'll walk right through it."

As the Volvo sped away, Josh had a vision of the beginning of the end of a dream, an ideal, a way of life.

———

Rachel pounded her fists on the back door to the Cluck and Grunt when she realized that she had locked herself out.

"Gavin!" she shouted. "Bill! The door's locked. I can't get in."

After a few minutes the door opened.

"I was wondering where you were." Gavin said.

"I forgot to prop open the door when I took the trash out."

"Why do I have to shout out the orders to Bill?" Gavin complained. "I can just put the order up on the wheel and he can read it. Or even if I just call pancakes, something less unusual than 'blowout patches'—I've got it—we can call them pancakes!"

"He's very set in his ways," Rachel said as she stepped inside. "He always wanted to run a true diner like you see in the movies. You need to humor him. When I started, I made a cheat sheet and taped it next to the register. Use that."

"Thanks, you're a lifesaver," he replied as they walked into the dining room. "Have you noticed how all the tourists are sort of agitated today?"

"Yes," Rachel said. "Like they want to get in and get out quick. One man left me a twenty-dollar tip for a cup of coffee and a donut to go."

"Well, maybe I'll just try asking one of them what's up." Gavin said, and then he looked at Rachel. "They don't bite, do they?"

Rachel grinned. "Amateur."

As Gavin started towards one of the customers Maggie was coming in the front door, her expression worried as she headed straight towards Rachel.

"I probably should buy a television," she began. "I heard this secondhand from Josh."

"What's happening?" Rachel said as she steered Maggie into the back room with Gavin following behind.

"He said that some tourists were saying that Trudy's father has pronounced the thing in the woods a demon." She looked at Rachel while biting her lip. "They did the same thing in Nepal. First there were sightings of a monster—a yeti—and then some deaths. Then the real terror began. They came out in the open and displayed themselves for what they were. That's when the villagers sought to drive the community out. They blamed them for bringing the demons to their land."

Rachel thought for a moment. "Well, in a way they were right, Maggie. Without the community the Fallen would have ignored the area, or at least stayed covered to deliver suffering, unseen by the people, as they usually do."

"It's happening here too," Maggie cried.

Rachel grasped her hands. "This is different, Maggie. We stay here because Creekside has asked us to. We fight together, human and angel as one force, because we love each other. That's the difference. From what I heard of the Nepal community, the ladder was much smaller and glowed less brilliant. The relationships were simply not there to withstand an attack from the Fallen. I pray that someday you will be able to see the ladder as Gavin and I do."

"It is beautiful," Gavin added.

"I envy you two." Maggie smiled. "Someday, perhaps."

Masters let out a loud belch as he exited the Chubby Cherub Restaurant, causing a tourist to step back a pace as they tried to enter the building. "Trust me, girl, I've eaten in some of the worst chuck buckets in the country," he opined, "and that was championship awful."

"I'll never make fun of the Cluck and Grunt again," Trudy said in agreement. Her eggs were the consistency of snot and the bacon was burnt beyond recognition. "Old Bill is a gourmet chef compared to that."

"Ready to see the glory of the Dells?" Masters said. "The Mysterium beckons just on the other side of the hill. I'll drive."

"What's wrong? Can't take the Trudymobile?" she mocked as they approached his SUV. "Mmm, a BMW," she whistled. "The flimflam gods have been good to you."

They drove for about fifteen minutes and made it a quarter of a mile. The miniature golf courses and the amphibious ducks loading area had some tourists but not enough to explain the gridlock. "Are the roads always this crowded?" Trudy asked.

"In summertime," Masters replied, "but this sure isn't summer. It's something better!" He pointed up ahead.

Trudy could see the Mysterium's garish sign looming in the near distance with a policeman in the street, directing traffic. Slowly they inched up to the driveway and were greeted by a harried parking attendant. "Five bucks," he said distractedly while simultaneously attempting to text on his phone.

"Hey, asshole," Masters said. "Do you want five bucks or do you want to be employed?"

The kid looked up with a start. "Oh, sorry Mr. Masters!"

"*Reverend* Masters," he corrected as he accelerated and swerved around the line, hitting several orange traffic cones in the process.

"Always the charmer," Trudy said.

"Can you believe this?" Masters said in wonder as he surveyed the nearly full parking lot. "It's not even ten a.m. and the place is packed."

Trudy looked at the front of the building where a large banner now proclaimed See THE DEMON OF CREEKSIDE. In front of the Mysterium an improvised queue line had been set down with stanchions and nylon rope that wound its way underneath the metal piping that held up the black fiberglass circus tent panels.

Huddled around the back of the building were a half dozen news trucks with their dishes pointing up to unseen satellites. Trudy looked over at her father as he parked the car in the back of the building. He was grinning from ear to ear.

"You really eat this stuff up, don't you?" Trudy asked.

"What's not to love?" he replied as they got out of the car. "I did ten interviews this morning before meeting you for breakfast. I've got another thirty scheduled for later." He slapped the roof of his car and let out a self-satisfied holler. "Plus, get this—*The Today Show* is coming tomorrow. How neat is that! We're going to have some of the researchers who are looking at the tail spike, and I'll give my story. It's unbelievable—the fucking *Today Show* coming to interview little ole me!"

They entered through the back office and Masters walked over to the auditor, a timid little man with a bad comb-over and owlish eyes behind thick glasses. "How are we doing today?"

"I'm doing better. It's been a daily struggle for me since Betty passed away, but thanks for asking, sir."

"Not you!" Masters grumbled. "The *take* today, how are we doing?"

The man looked up sadly at Masters, obviously disappointed—but not surprised—with his lack of concern. "So far we've had more admissions in the first hour this morning than in a normal week of operation."

"That's what I wanted to hear," Masters smiled and walked off.

Trudy left the auditor with a sincere "sorry for your loss" before running to catch up with her father.

"Over here," Masters said as he entered the museum area and nudged his way through the crowd. "I want to show you the new exhibit."

Trudy could hear the exhibit before she could see it. Screams issued from just beyond a black velvet wall, sort of like the haunted house the Jaycees had every October in Minocqua. Masters went towards the rear of the wall, where a hidden door was located. "Come on," he whispered. "I want to stand in the back here for a bit to see what the customers think."

Trudy stood with her father in the dark recesses of the exhibit area behind the display posters. She could see a wall banner proclaiming the Demon of Creekside; although the posters were facing the wrong way for her to see the face of the demon, she could see its effects. People would walk into the room and attempt to adjust their vision to the muted lighting. They would read the information posted on one wall and then proceed on to view the enlarged photos. She could hear one older gentleman as he raised his reading glasses and stuck his nose close to the poster. "Photoshopped," he pronounced and turned away. Other reactions were more severe; one woman with three kids in tow took one look and screamed while her children grabbed her hands and pulled her quickly out of the room. A couple that may have been honeymooners in matching "I Love You More" T-shirts shared a barf bag in the back of the room.

"Isn't it amazing?" Masters whispered over the smell of vomit. "Watch when they round the corner from the photo area to the display case."

"What's in the display?" Trudy asked.

"A tail spike from the demon," Masters said nonchalantly. "Azael gave it to me for display."

"You're an ass," Trudy said as she watched patrons make their way around a ten-foot high black wall and into the display area. The tail spike was placed in the center of the area under Plexiglas, illuminated by a bright spotlight shining down from the ceiling. It was there that a number of the tourists seemed to accept that such a thing was possible, that they were actually looking at a hunk of demon, and the mood turned dark. While a few raised their cell phones and snapped photos, most just stood there in a daze as if they were unable to process what they were seeing.

"It's like they're at their own funeral," Trudy said sadly.

Masters patted her shoulder, "They'll snap out of it when they hit the gift shop."

CHAPTER TWENTY-TWO

Elder Tomas sat in a folding chair next to the bridge that spanned Mill Creek just to the south of Creekside. A drooping hat shaded his eyes as he lightly gripped a fishing pole. His mind was not on a trout supper though; instead he scanned the tree line on the other side of the creek for any sign of activity.

Seven of his kind were around the perimeter of Creekside, watching for anything out of the ordinary, any sign that the Fallen were on the move.

He looked up as a Channel Seven News van crossed the bridge and pulled up beside him.

"Hello," said the woman in the passenger side seat, peering at him over her shades. "Catch anything?"

"No," Tomas replied. "I think they are all swimming south for the winter."

"Do you live around these parts?" the woman asked. "We're trying to get the opinions of residents in the area about the rumor that there's a supernatural being in the woods."

"Supernatural being…" Tomas said. "Well, this is an unusual area Miss. You're liable to run into a supernatural being at any time." He looked up at her with the well-practiced addled expression he reserved for the overly curious. "Might not even realize you're seeing one."

The woman smiled the way someone smiles when they think you're nuts but do not wish to offend. "Have you seen any?"

"Supernatural beings?" he grinned. "Sure, every day. I can honestly say that a day does not go by when I don't see one."

"Then you believe that there is a demon in the woods?"

204

He shrugged lazily. "What's not to believe? The real question should be, are there more than one out there? The woods are probably chock-full of demons right now."

The woman gave a look that could only be read as condescending. "Well, thank you, sir, for your time. Hope you catch a big one."

"A fish or a demon?" he asked as they were already driving away.

———

Ben Logan, the driver of the van, who was also the sound technician on the team, said to Barbara, "Let's try to find someone who isn't a loon next time."

Barbara flipped down the visor to examine herself in the mirror, "Yeah, if we can. These small towns are full of local color like him—pea-brained shitkickers who come out of the woodwork like moths to a flame whenever something out of the ordinary happens. Let's go right up the main drag and park over by the church," she added. "We'll set up shop there, then Jim can grab his camera and we'll take a little stroll."

As they drove up Main, Barbara was surprised by the amount of traffic. "Most of these towns are dead this time of year. This place looks like Disney World."

"Most of them are tourists," Jim said from the back. "It might be hard finding a local for this human interest story."

"Well we'll interview some of the tourists as well," Ben said. "If we can't wring anything worthwhile out of the locals, we'll have to switch it up a bit and make a tourist story out of it."

"There's the local hangout," Barbara said as she pointed to the Cluck and Grunt. "That's going to be our best chance."

"We'll rely on you to sweet talk the management into letting us tape there," Ben said as he turned left on State and pulled up about a half block from the church.

Barbara noticed a man working on the church sign, stepping back every so often to see if the lettering was correct.

"You guys get set up," Barbara said. "I'm going to go talk to the Bible thumper over there at the church. See what they think about demons in the woods!" she laughed.

"Hello," she said as she walked over to the man. "I'm Barbara Kern from Channel Seven—"

"How does this look?" The man said as he stepped back a couple feet to let her examine the sign.

"Uh …" The letters were straight but the wording was not what she expected: STAYING IN BED AND SCREAMING OH GOD! IS NOT THE SAME AS GOING TO CHURCH. "Hmm … looks good to me," she declared at length.

"Good, glad to hear it," he said, holding out his hand. "I'm Reverend Brustad. How may I help you?"

"Reverend? I didn't—"

Brustad smiled warmly. "Yeah, Reverend. Plain clothes division."

Barbara smiled back, but not so much that her Botoxed face would break. "Glad to meet you. We're in town doing a human-interest story about how the residents feel now that they're in the national spotlight. The rumor that a demon is in the woods has piqued everyone's interest."

"We do have a lot of visitors now," Brustad replied. "As you know, there have already been deaths. I'm just praying that no one else will be hurt."

"Do you believe there is something supernatural in the forest?" Barbara said as Jim, her cameraman, came up beside her. He hefted the heavy camera onto his right shoulder and put an eye to the viewfinder.

Brustad cleared his throat and said, "I really prefer not to be on camera."

"Why not?" Barbara asked. "The public would like to hear from a man of the cloth at a time like this."

Brustad motioned to Jim to lower the camera and then took her by the arm and walked her a few paces away. "You'll find, Miss," he said sotto voce, "that the people in this town are not going to be very talkative."

"Why's that?"

"We are a very close community, with like interests and goals. We do not share those with, pardon the term, outsiders."

Barbara smiled. "Well, I like a challenge."

She walked back to her cameraman as she ran a finger across her neck and motioned for him to follow. "Well, strike two," she said. "Let's go to the diner and see what happens."

Azael stood just inside the tree line on the far side of Mill Creek. From his vantage point he could see most of the town: buildings drifting down towards the river while others fought their way up the sloping hill. In the distance to the south he could see the bridge that crossed the river and an indistinct figure with a fishing pole.

The Beast came up beside him and sat down.

"Hello, my friend," Azael said as he patted the creature's mottled flank. "I see your tail is healing nicely."

The Beast gave a disgruntled snort.

"Surely you are not still upset about that?" Azael said. "You realize that disciplining you was for your own good."

The Beast let out an aggrieved growl that called to mind the characteristic cry of a Wookiee, but infinitely more hair-raising.

Azael gave the creature a firm love tap. "Well, be that as it may. We also reward those who do well, and you, my associate have done very well overall. Today, you will receive a reward."

He smiled as he pointed over to Creekside.

"You will do the following, as I specify, or face another discipline," Azael continued. "But I assure you that you will find my plan very enjoyable. Our goal today my friend is to instill terror. Pure, sharp, cutting terror in the souls of the ones He loves."

The Beast's rotted out human face was still capable of expression and it now looked upon Creekside with anticipation.

"Take your hatred out on the sedate village of Creekside."

The Beast rotated its bull head to the front and snorted loudly through wide nostrils.

"But, here are the conditions," Azael continued. "You are paying attention I trust. You must not hurt the boy or his mate. Besides, he is being guarded by a protecting loyalist that you, I am sad to say, are in no way a match for."

The Beast gave vent to a mournful cry; its moist eyes showed its wounded pride.

"Do not carry on so, and heed me!" Azael scolded. "Be careful for others who have not rebelled." He pointed to the distant fisherman. "They are also protecting the town.

"Finally, and this may be the hardest for you, my friend: Do not kill on purpose. You are to injure as many as possible but do not kill—of course, if a few should die accidentally…" Azael shrugged. "What can we do?"

———

Maggie sat at a table near the diner's front window, her hands gripping a cup of coffee while Gavin and Rachel stood nearby behind the counter. Gavin was wondering what to do when Rachel put a hand on his arm.

"Leave her be," she said. "She needs time to think."

"I can't imagine going through this twice," Gavin replied. "How does she cope?"

"She's a strong woman. Strong in her faith. She'll make it through."

"Well, if anyone can cheer her up," Gavin said as he watched a figure approaching the diner in a waddling gait, "that guy can."

Sheriff Winston came into the diner and smiled as he saw Gavin and Rachel. Gavin gave a head nod towards Maggie, which caused the sheriff to look over by the window.

"Maggie," Winston said with a smile as he sat down opposite her. "What's the matter?"

"Clarence," she said, looking up at him grimly, "so much for our motto of Protecting Light. I've failed them."

"Don't be silly," he said as he put his hand on hers. "You did all you could here."

A smile flickered on Maggie's face and died. "I brought them here. I'm the one that told Jonathan that this was a safe place to build, a safe place to live side by side with us so we could learn from each other. I brought the people of the town into the circle and they pledged themselves to the same cause.

"I remember the day we had the town meeting and voted to change our motto to *Tutela Lux Lucis* because that was our purpose now: to protect the light that the angels brought to us. Everyone was so joyous. We had finally found our purpose on this earth.

"Whatever happens now," she said as she pulled her hand away, "is because I started it many years ago."

———

Barbara Kern and her cameraman walked into the diner and noticed the sheriff sitting with his back to her. She felt a nudge in her side from her cameraman, which she knew was Jim's signature way of warning her to be on her best behavior. She scanned the rest of the diner and decided the best place to start was with the petite blonde waitress at the counter.

"Hello," she said as she approached her. "I'm Barbara Kern from Channel Seven News, I was wondering if I might speak with the owner?"

Rachel turned around and shouted into the kitchen. "Bill, you have visitors."

After a moment of gagging and throat-clearing, Bill shouted back. "What do they want?"

Barbara raised her voice so that it would carry back to the kitchen. "We'd like to interview a few of your regular patrons about the attacks in the woods."

"Are you going to show the name of my place on the news?" Bill hollered back.

"Of course," Barbara yelled. "We'll mention it several times."

"Okay, you've got a deal." Bill said with a laugh. "Go ahead and interview Rachel there first. That should get your story moving right along."

Rachel looked back and forth between Bill and the reporter with a worried expression. "I, I—"

"Don't be nervous, honey," Barbara said with seasoned mock solicitude. "It's just like having a normal conversation. Ignore Jim over there, just look at me." She took out a pen and paper. "May I have your full name?"

"Rachel…" she said, shooting a pleading look at Gavin.

"Young. Rachel Young. I'm her brother, Gavin," he said, extending his hand.

"Nice to meet you Gavin, Miss Young," Barbara said, shaking his hand and then gesturing to Jim to start taping. "This is Barbara Kern reporting from Creekside with siblings Gavin and Rachel Young, employees at a local eatery. As our viewers know, there are rumors circulating that the mysterious creature in the woods that has so far claimed the lives of four hunters is in fact a demon. Miss Young, do you believe that there is a demon in the woods outside of your town?"

Rachel stared at the camera with a blank look. "Uh— " Then she blew out her cheeks and exhaled. "Yes," she said quietly.

"I think my sister is finished with the interview," Gavin said, sticking his palm in the camera and pushing it back.

"Watch it, kid," Jim warned. "This camera cost more than you'll make in two lifetimes working at this dump."

"Decorum, Jim, decorum," said Barbara through gritted teeth. "We'll cut all this out in editing." She smiled at Rachel and continued. "It's long been known that demons and angels are myths created by primitive humans in order to explain things beyond their comprehension. Miss Young, you can understand why so many find it difficult to comprehend why someone would still believe in such things."

No sooner had she finished the provocative statement than the diner's plate glass front window blew inward with astonishing force, creating a hailstorm of flying glass. Barbara instinctively held up her arms to protect her eyes as all heads turned toward the source of the chaos.

"No!" Gavin screamed even as Maggie was grabbed around the torso by a mammoth paw of the Beast and dragged into the street through the shattered window. The sheriff lay motionless under a table with shards of glass jutting out of his chest and face.

"You better be filming this," Barbara said to the cameraman, who was crouched near the floor. "This is our Peabody."

Rachel hopped over the counter and stepped to the front of the diner. "Start healing the injured!" she yelled, then the room went white.

———

The Beast knew that it had made a mistake but it could not help itself. It had been so long since Nepal, but even now it burned with hatred for the human that was struggling under its claw. When it had noticed the female in the window, no threat of discipline would keep it from what it was about to do.

It never understood before why it couldn't kill the frail thing that squirmed beneath it. Then, for the first time, it realized Who had stayed its claw and burned with an even greater hatred. The thought that this human was kept alive by the One they rebelled against—and that, because of this human, the ladder was formed and a community grew up around it—was too much for the Beast to bear.

Roaring in anger, it dug its claw into her side to test her reaction. She screamed in pain as blood pooled on the street. But even as the Beast could see that she was wracked with agony, her face showed only peace. Perhaps she, too, understood the part she had played, and was content. To the Beast, this was the final insult, one it could not brook.

Confident now in its abilities it brought another claw down and underneath her ribcage, penetrating the heart and killing her instantly.

Then the Beast saw a blinding light coming from the diner and realized it beheld its doom.

———

Rachel transformed in front of everyone in the diner, resident and tourist alike, causing all to fall to the floor, paralyzed with fear. Gavin saw the reporter crouched down near the counter and the cameraman face down on the floor, crying, but still managing to point the camera in the right direction.

Only Gavin had all his wits about him as he rushed to Sheriff Winston's side. The injuries were so severe there was no time for him to think. He thrust his hand down on Winston's chest and was immediately knocked back across the room by the bolt that shot between them.

Rachel, now in full angelic cry, had made her way through the shattered window and onto Main as the diner shook and car alarms blared ear-splittingly all down the street.

"Who—*what* is that?" Barbara said, shielding her eyes from the glow.

"That's your myth," Gavin said as he left Winston and scampered to attend to another customer with a bad gash on his head.

———

The protecting angel's wings unfurled, casting a shadow over the Beast. As her shield spun up, sparks pounded the roadway, melting the asphalt. The Beast looked up and snarled in hatred towards the loyalist who dared interfere. It attempted to flee but was grabbed by the tail and dragged back before the divine being and its accursed light.

In the distance the Beast noticed the fisherman that Azael had pointed out earlier was now running up the center of Main Street towards the fight. A mist began swirling around him that quickly turned into a rotating cloud that continued to brighten. The Beast watched the man as he was enveloped in the whirlwind. Lightning crackled across the boulevard, bouncing between streetlamps as thunder shattered shop windows, raining glass upon the ground. Accompanying the storm was the sound of the roadway being reduced to rubble under the rhythm of a syncopated pile driver. Over the din another sound could be heard, one that it had forgotten about for so long—the battle cry of the cherubim. The cloud parted and the Beast realized that all hope was gone.

The cherub radiated light as it ran with feline grace, its lion-like body now the size of a Kenworth big rig. The shadows on Main Street evaporated under the brightness of the cherub who now possessed four heads and four wings. One of the heads was that of a man, the other a lion, the third a bull, and the fourth an eagle, all with the complexion of molten steel.

The battle cry that reverberated down the street was one the Beast had once uttered itself, back in the age of supplication and groveling before the throne. A choir issued from the cherub as four voices in unison chanted, "Holy, holy, holy is the Lord." The Beast recognized this one; they once called themselves brothers back before the creation of this cursed planet. When the rebellion began, this one continued his stupid loyalty to the one who calls Himself King. Millennium of being relegated to this decomposing ball of dirt had weakened the Beast, it knew. It was no longer the mighty cherub that it had once been. Against the protecting angel it had little chance, but against Tomas it had none. Like a weightless thing, it was lifted up by the angel and slammed into the concrete. Before it could recover, it was carried aloft again and tossed into the side of a building, shattering the façade and sending bricks cascading into the street. Dazed, the Beast cowered underneath the rubble, acquiescent of its fate.

By the time the protecting angel had pulled it out from under the debris, the cherub was alongside. The Beast wailed in agony as the two angels grabbed opposite ends of its body and started to pull. It could feel its flesh starting to rip, pumping blood onto the street, and its spine beginning to separate.

The Beast made one last feeble and ignoble attempt to escape as it bit down on the protecting angel's glowing arm. It was its last act of defiance as it felt its own flesh give way and separate in two.

As one pain ended another began as it felt itself spin, picking up speed as darkness enveloped it. The pain was unimaginable as it heard others screaming nearby; it knew that it was not alone, that others had traveled this way before it. The Beast felt like it was falling but it knew that it wasn't going down, but drifting out, to the outer darkness: the place they all knew of but would never discuss. Many ages ago the Beast was once a cherub, capable of eloquence and wisdom, kindness and humility. It thought briefly of those times as it continued to drift into darkness. It was a world that it had almost forgotten; the time before the rebellion against the hated One. Now it could only bellow in rage as it was sent to the cursed place known as the abyss.

———

Maggie dreamt. Nepal seemed a million years ago, yet she remembered everything, every last detail. The smells, the sounds—it was all there, every minute of it, even the awful things, but strangely they no longer hurt. *She* no longer hurt.

She felt a cool breeze touch her face; it was so different than the hot breath of the Beast that it brought her around. She opened her eyes to find herself on her back on a bed of grass, not in Creekside but in Morgan.

"Maggie, dear one—rise!" a familiar voice said as a shadow passed over her.

"Jonathan!" she cried as she gazed upon him. He wore glowing raiment, carrying a staff of lightning in his right hand. "What happened? Why am I here? Why are you in angelic form?"

Jonathan bent down and, with a wing, scooped her from the ground and placed her upon her feet. "Usually when a human makes the transition they go immediately to their appointed place," he explained. "An exception was allowed for me to show you something before that happens." With that, he moved aside and she gazed upon it for the first time in her life.

"The ladder," she gasped as she watched the churning column of lightning rise into the sky. "It's so beautiful. I see now what Gavin means."

She turned to face the woods. Her vision and hearing were now far superior to anything she had ever experienced before. She could hear battles far off in the deep forest. "The Beast is still in town. Gavin and Trudy need our help."

"Rachel is there and others from Morgan—don't be afraid," Jonathan reassured her. "Your journey here has ended, but I have a feeling there is still much for them to accomplish."

They approached the church. The doors to the building were open, along with the doors to the narthex. They entered and approached the ladder.

Maggie stood, arms outstretched, basking in the electric sensation, like the sting of thousands of bees, absent the pain. A branch of light formed and moved towards her. It touched her palm and then wrapped itself around her hand. It felt cool to the touch, nothing like what she expected.

She could never before discern the features of a transformed angel's face; now she could. She looked upon him and was not afraid. His face was gentle, that of a shepherd of a flock. A hint of the One he served. Jonathan smiled. "I've never seen that happen before. It obviously knows its mother."

"Mother?"

"You planted the seed that grew into this. It stands today because of you. You protected the light, and this is the result. Now is the time, Maggie. I will visit you soon— Gavin and Trudy in their own time."

"And Clarence?" she asked.

"He knows the truth. He just needs to take it to heart."

"He will in time. He has a very big heart." Maggie regarded her corporeal self; she looked the same, but she pulsed with a vitality that surely belonged to another dimension, not the vale of dross and tears men call earth.

"I'm actually dead then?" she said tentatively. "I feel more alive than I ever have before."

"The demon killed you true, yet you live. Your work here is done, let others fight these battles. Your Lord has other duties for you. Step through when you are ready."

She looked into the column that still held her hand. "It is so bright."

"No darkness will be found where you are going. We all see and are seen. Go now, Maggie, He awaits you with joy."

CHAPTER TWENTY-THREE

Masters motioned to Trudy. "Let's go up to my office. I've got a surprise for you."

"So, what's the plan?" Trudy said as she climbed the stairs to the second level of the Mysterium. "Azael doesn't give out freebies, and I can't imagine that he wants to be on the cover of *People*."

"He hasn't told me—why? Should I be suspicious of the motives of a demon?" he laughed.

"Jerk," Trudy groused as they entered her father's waiting room. The television on the wall was blaring Channel Seven News while a bored receptionist sat at her desk, filing her nails.

"They're going to have a feature story on Creekside," he said. "Don't want to miss that. There's someone I want you to meet. Holly, let me introduce you to my daughter, Trudy."

Holly stood up with a tight smile and tighter dress and held out her hand. She looked like she had just seen a rat.

"Let me," Trudy said, trotting over to shake her hand. "I imagine its slow going in that thing."

"Come on into my office, we need to talk," Masters said to Trudy.

She followed her father into the next room, all the while feeling Holly's eyes tossing invisible daggers at her back.

When they entered the office and closed the door, Trudy couldn't help but ask, "What's with Jessica Rabbit out there?"

"Oh, she just senses competition. Holly doesn't handle competition well."

Trudy crossed her arms. "But I'm your daughter, remember?"

"That's why you *are* the competition."

"Come again?"

Masters put a guiding hand on her shoulder. "Over here. Take a look out the window."

Trudy walked over and was surprised by how beautiful the view was. The lake was sparkling under the fall sun, and the leaves were all turning a golden brown with hints of red. The idyllic scene was worlds different than the strip of neon and miniature golf from the front of the building.

"I scrounged up all the money I had to buy this land and put this building on it. I didn't have any backers, nobody to help me out. Nobody wanted to." He turned to Trudy. "You think I'm a terrible person." He paused and again admired the picturesque view. "Perhaps I am, but I wanted to build something grand. Something lasting that would continue beyond my mere existence."

"I think it's called a legacy." Trudy said.

"Exactly!" He smiled. "A true and lasting legacy." He motioned for her to have a seat. "The problem I have, and I've been thinking about this for a while now, is: What happens when I'm gone?"

"Hold on there," Trudy said, waving her hands. "I think I know where this is going ..."

"Just have a seat for a moment and hear me out," Masters insisted. "You have my name. You are a Masters, like it or not; the last of the line as far as I know. Anyway, I'm having my lawyer draw up a new will. You are listed as my sole heir."

Trudy was shaken. "I don't want to be. I don't want to be part of some, some—what the hell kind of place is this again? You profit off of freaks of nature one moment and now you're ramping up to profit off of evil. As far as I can see it is all based off of taking money from gullible people who shouldn't be wasting their money in this tourist trap."

Masters smirked at the obviously spot-on assessment of his craft. "You need to continue my legacy, Trudy. Someday I'll be gone and I need someone I can trust. Frankly, you're the only one I think I *can* trust. That loud trap of yours always tells me exactly what you think."

"Well, after that episode in Creekside with your hunter friend, I can see why you've been thinking about death, but I'm not the person you're looking for. Will it to Holly. She looks like the loyal sort. From that painted-on dress I would imagine you two have more than just a working relationship."

"She's a dim bulb," Masters scoffed. "To put it in the vernacular: body by Fisher, brain by Mattel. No, Trudy, you're the logical—"

Holly broke into the office, screaming, "Jay! Oh God, Jay! Get out here now!"

As they ran into the next room Trudy gasped when she saw the time-delayed video feed from Creekside on the TV. There, unmistakably was the diner, its front window shattered. And the limp body being pulled out of the building by the Beast … it was Maggie.

"Oh God …Oh God …"

She thought she could make out Sheriff Winston, sprawled underneath a table, as she scanned the screen for—"Gavin!" He stood to the left of the frame, frozen in indecision and shock.

Then, in the middle of the screen, she saw Rachel beginning to transform. "No, Rachel!" she cried as the screen filled with light. "No …!"

The camera stayed focused on Rachel as she glided through the window frame and into the street. She could also make out Gavin running across the screen, she assumed to help the sheriff.

As the surreal scene unfolded, Trudy made out the lifeless body of Maggie near the sidewalk, and the Beast being tossed around like a rag doll by the powerful Rachel. Then she noticed another being enter the frame. This one was larger and more glorious than even Rachel in her angelic state. The two took the Beast and tore it in half. Then, while the camera continued to record, the scene changed to the human Rachel and an old man in a fishing cap she recognized as Tomas, standing next to the gory remains of the Beast.

Masters stood next to her and croaked, "You've been holding out on me."

———

Gavin jumped over the broken glass of the diner's front window and ran to Maggie. Rachel was already standing by her side; the tears in her eyes said everything.

"You can't heal her Gavin," Rachel said. "She has transitioned. Her work here was finished."

Sheriff Winston came up beside them, obviously weak, but the glass had pushed itself out of his body and his wounds had healed completely, although his uniform was a bloody, tattered mess. He looked dazed, not knowing what had happened, but then looked down at Maggie and seemed to comprehend.

"Maggie!" he cried as he threw himself to the ground next to her, putting his hands to her forehead. He looked up at Rachel and then at Gavin, and pleaded. "Do something. Please! For God's sake, help her." He started to wail, the pained sound echoing down the now silent street. "Gavin, heal her like you did me." Then he looked up at Rachel. "You're an angel. You can do anything."

"We can't, Clarence," Rachel said as tears streamed down her face. "It's too late for Gavin to do anything, and angels aren't all-powerful beings. There's only One who is."

She knelt down next to the Sheriff and put her arm around him.

"She's home now," she said quietly. "Do you remember how I said that I am just a visitor here? That it's really your world? Well, that is only partly true. This shouldn't be your world either. It wasn't for Maggie. She always lived in another in her heart; it's the one she always wanted to share with you. She was here for exactly the amount of time she needed to be. Now she lives elsewhere, but she *lives*, Clarence; she lives.

"You believe in angels because we showed ourselves to you. You believe in me because I levitated your truck. There is a difference, Clarence, between what you know as fact and what is in your heart. That is what Maggie always knew, and what she so desperately wanted to share with you, even when what you believed was so obviously contrary to reality. What she once saw as a dim vision here in Creekside, where humans and angels coexist in unity of purpose, heart, and worship, she now sees face-to-face. She has worlds to explore and ages to do it in. New friends to make and duties to perform. Time to spend with old friends when they come her way in due time. We grieve *our* loss, Clarence, not hers."

Rachel looked over to another from Morgan, who now stood nearby. "I'm going to put you into Beth's care," she said to the sheriff. "She is a ministering angel and will be with you as you grieve for your loss."

Tomas saw Josh Barber drive up in his tow truck and walked over to speak with him.

"You're all over the news," Josh said as he got out of the truck and glanced at the Beast's severed carcass. "Man, and I thought that thing was ugly when it was in one piece." He looked over to those gathering around Maggie, and his expression changed to one of grief.

Tomas put a hand on Josh's shoulder. "You know where Maggie is now, so along with your grief, be happy for her. She is with the One that she loves. Our concern here now is to put your tow truck to good use and get the demon out of the middle of the street."

"Yeah," Josh agreed, "it's not doing much for property values. But what do we do with it? Normally, with road kill, I'd suggest eating it ..."

"The longer it stays recognizable, the more it will pique curiosity among the demon-seekers," Tomas observed. "Human fascination with evil is something the Fallen ones crave."

"I think I know what to do with it," Josh said. "Just don't tell the DNR."

———

Barbara Kern and her cameraman stumbled out of the Cluck and Grunt, along with the other patrons. What had been a peaceful thoroughfare through a sleepy northern Wisconsin town now looked like a war zone.

The center of Main Street contained a crack about two feet wide and three feet deep that ran down the entire road, heading south. The State Farm insurance agent's office on the far side of Main was a mass of rubble and shattered glass. A shallow crater in the asphalt was directly in front of the news team, with the Beast's gory remains on the far side.

"They just took us live, Barb," Jim said as he communicated with Ben in the van.

"Okay," Barbara said as she tried to compose herself. She had known pure, unadulterated, swear-to-go-to-church-on-Sunday-from-now-on fear for the first time in her life, and she was pretty sure she had wet herself. A furtive glance at her slacks assured her it didn't show. She spied Rachel, back in her "human guise," and walked over to her. Shitty as Barbara felt, she wasn't about to let the story of the century get away.

"You saved us, Rachel," she said, "but what are you *really*? You're obviously not the shy waitress that I met earlier."

Rachel gave a panicked look to Gavin as he stepped between them.

"She has no comment," Gavin said.

"Well, she better start commenting," Barbara said. "We have just broadcast the entire thing. People will want to know what happened here."

"This is Creekside business," Gavin snapped. "You're not welcome here."

"Listen, kid," Barbara said as she cut the mic. "You're going to need to tell us what happened here. This is big news. *You're* big news. You and your little sister are going to be famous." Then she turned the mic back on and smiled at the camera.

"The young man here," Barbara said as she fought to remember his last name, "Gavin, er, Young, healed a number of the injured before my very eyes. I believe we have captured some of that on tape as well. Unfortunately, one woman was beyond even his amazing power to heal." She motioned for Jim to pan down to Maggie's body.

Sheriff Winston exploded. "You get that fucking camera out of here and back off! This is a crime scene."

"It's *news*, sheriff," Barbara said, unfazed. "The First Amendment guarantees freedom of the press—"

"You back away from my Maggie," he said, shaking in anger as his beefy hand reached up to wipe his tears. "I want you a hundred feet back now, or I swear I'll arrest the lot of you."

"Certainly, officer," Barbara conceded. "But we're going to find out what happened here. The public will want to know. It is their right to know. And my right to report it."

"Just get the hell out of my crime scene until told otherwise."

———

"Thanks for driving," Trudy said to her father from the passenger seat of the Corolla.

"You're in no shape to drive," Masters said. "Any luck getting Gavin?"

"No," Trudy said in disgust, tossing the phone onto the dash. "You'd think someone who is going to be an engineer would have a better understanding of the on/off button on a cell phone."

"It would be a faster drive if we'd taken my Beemer. We may have to pull over to the side of the road and shoot this thing before we get there."

"Don't worry," Trudy said, patting her door fondly. "This old girl has gotten me through many a winter up here." She turned and looked out the passenger window. "Guess my driving you down to the Dells to get rid of you didn't work so well."

"Trudy," Masters said. "I'm sorry for what happened in Creekside. The woman who died, were you close to her?"

"She was a good friend," Trudy said with a tear in her eye. "She was a square peg in a round hole, just like me. She didn't quite fit into the scheme of things. Guess we bonded because of that."

Masters paused for a moment. "So there *are* angels in Creekside? I wouldn't have believed it if I hadn't seen it on television."

"What did you expect? Demons are fallen angels. I guess Azael didn't give you full disclosure after all."

"So, the girl from the restaurant ..."

Trudy laughed. "The one you wanted to hit on? Yep, she's an angel of the non-fallen variety." She slumped into the seat and put her feet on the dash. "I told you she wasn't your type."

"That's amazing."

"Just another day in Creekside. See what you missed by running out?"

"And your boyfriend, is he one too?"

Trudy had to laugh. "Gavin? No, he is one hundred percent human."

"Then what's with the healing? You said he doesn't know how he does it."

"Okay, Pops here's the CliffsNotes version for you to get you up to speed. Guess you can't fuck things up any more than they are already."

"Watch your language, young lady," Masters scolded.

"Yes, Daddy," Trudy said sarcastically. "The town of Morgan is a community of angels that came here to learn what it is like to be human. It helps them in dealing with us to understand how truly screwed up we are, I guess. In Morgan, they have a portal to their home. I'm told it looks like a giant ladder of lightning rising into the sky, although I've never seen it."

She looked at her father. "The only human who can is Gavin."

Masters glanced over at Trudy. "So he has another gift besides healing?"

"I doubt he would consider either a gift. He has violent headaches when he is far from the ladders, and it gets better as he moves closer to them. The angels believe that the demons would like to use him to find the ladders around the world. He will move towards the next one when this one closes—he can't help himself."

Trudy sighed. "And this one will certainly be shut down. This is so screwed-up," she said as she pounded her hand on the armrest and glared at her father. "Partly in thanks to you."

"Trudy," Masters said slowly, as if weighing the pros and cons of speaking further. "I knew that Azael wanted Gavin."

"What?" Trudy said. "He *told* you?"

"He didn't say why, only that he was of interest to them and did not mean to hurt him. Azael also wanted me to get to know you so that you would keep in touch, and that way I'd know where Gavin was."

Trudy pulled her feet off of the dash. "*What?* You mean you only came to the diner because you wanted to use me? *You piece of shit!* All that garbage about you wanting to see me, it was just bullshit? You were going to use me to help demons? What the hell is wrong with you?" she screamed as she started to cry.

"Trudy, I—"

"Stop the car!" she yelled, pummeling his arm. "Stop the fucking car and get the hell out! *Get out!* I don't want you in my car or my life."

Masters somehow kept the Corolla on the road. "Not until you hear me out," he said evenly.

"I don't want to ever hear another lie that comes out of that cesspool of a mouth of yours," she said as wiped her eyes with her sleeve. "Why didn't you just stay away like you did when I was growing up? That wasn't much, but it's a hell of a lot better than this."

"Look, kid, I've done nasty things throughout my life. I'm good at it, and fortunately my conscience doesn't seem to be operational. At first I was using you, I admit that, but things changed on the way down to the Dells. I started to realize that my legacy isn't just the Mysterium."

He looked at her and Trudy thought she could see tears in his eyes. "My legacy is also you."

"I don't want to be a legacy," Trudy spat as she continued to wipe her eyes. "When I was little I wanted a father like the other girls had. Sure, some of those fathers came home drunk at two in the morning and beat their wives senseless, but I didn't understand that as a kid. I just knew I was missing out. Now I just want to be left alone. My life sucks, and you're not helping it any."

"Hell, your life is far from sucking, Trudy," Masters said with a laugh. "I've known plenty of losers, and you're not one of them. You're too strong-willed and cocky to be one, and besides, you're a bit of a bitch. Personally, I like that; it adds character. Creekside is my definition of a hellhole, and you lived there and survived. You talk to angels every day—how amazing is that? You have a boyfriend. You have a future. One day you will have the Mysterium."

He looked at her. "Masters are not losers. You know I could have not told you about Azael's plans. You would never have known."

"Then why did you? Another sick mind game of yours?"

"I just told you why," he said quietly as he watched the road in front of them. "You're my legacy."

"Legacy ... great," Trudy said in disgust as she crossed her arms. "Most daughters are told that they are loved. I'm a legacy."

"For me," Masters said, "a legacy is the highest compliment I can give. And if you never believe anything else I say, believe this: I fiercely protect my legacy."

———

Josh pulled up to the lake at the Morgan quarry, his several ton load of demon carcass still securely strapped down to the bed of the truck under a tarp.

"Nobody comes out here," Josh said to Tomas in the passenger seat. "The water isn't used for drinking or anything. And it's deep."

Tomas nodded. "It's appropriate. The Beast shall descend back to the depths."

As they got out of the truck Josh noticed lights off in the distance, along with a distant roar like a tornado.

"What's that?" he asked Tomas, as he pointed off into the forest.

Tomas walked over and gazed with Josh at the flashes that turned the tree-tops to ominous silhouettes. "It is a skirmish between an angel and one of the Fallen. It's happening now throughout the forest."

"They can't win can they?" Josh asked. "The demons can't possibly win."

"No. They have already lost the war and are doomed to the pit, but they do win battles, and that is my fear."

The elder patted Josh on the back. "Come on, my friend. Let's return this foul carcass to the deep."

———

Gavin surveyed the chaos along what was once a sedate Main Street.

Josh was able to remove the Beast before the first wave of police, fire, and ambulance arrived, leaving only a giant congealing puddle of blood in the middle of the street, but the rest of the devastation remained.

Television news trucks rumbled into town and set up their mobile studios at the south end of Main. Police tape crisscrossed the street to keep them at a distance. The formerly injured, that Gavin had healed, clumped together near the restaurant, whispering amongst themselves while Bill surveyed the damage to his diner and the shattered Cluck and Grunt sign that flickered above the counter.

Rachel and Gavin watched as Sheriff Winston gently tucked in the sheet that covered Maggie's body as she was wheeled by stretcher to the ambulance. He could also feel multiple telephoto lenses pointed at them from the eager reporters in the distance.

"Well," Gavin sighed, "got any ideas?"

"Not really," Rachel said as she looked towards the assembled media. "But we can't stay here, it isn't safe. You need to move to Morgan with me until we figure this out."

Out of the corner of his eye Gavin noticed an aged shit-brown Corolla pull up in back of the television trucks. "Trudy!" he smiled.

Gavin ran toward the police tape and jumped over it, not even acknowledging the gaggle of media that fairly salivated over his every move.

Trudy met him and jumped into his arms, her legs wrapped around him as he struggled to keep his balance and kiss her at the same time. "I was so worried about you," she said as she took a breath.

"I have bad news," Gavin said as he put her down. "Maggie's dead."

"I know," Trudy replied. "It was on the news."

Gavin noticed Masters walking up from one side as Rachel approached from the other. The news crews turned their attention to Rachel. For every step she took, the intrepid journalists took two cautionary steps back. They were incapacitated from doing their jobs by an all-consuming fear, quickly turning to terror, of the petite blonde strolling past.

Masters looked at Rachel for a long moment before speaking. "Is there anything I can do to help?"

Rachel was looking at the sea of cameras, and Gavin could see her panic was growing even as the reporters were becoming agitated by the silence. They expected some profound utterance from the being that had revealed her divine essence mere hours ago.

"Uh, no, thank you," Rachel croaked.

"Here," Masters said. "Let me try." He turned to the media and raised his voice in a commanding baritone. "I am the Reverend Jay Masters of Masters' Mysterium in Wisconsin Dells."

The cameras moved in unison off of Rachel and onto Masters.

"I am the one that discovered the demon that once lived in the woods, but which, thanks to this young lady, has now been destroyed. I'm sure that you have many questions about what took place today. I will take questions for the next twenty minutes."

As the reporters converged on Masters, he motioned to Gavin to take Trudy and Rachel and leave.

"I never know what that huckster has up his sleeve," said Trudy as they crossed the police line and walked back towards the diner. "Did he do that to help you, Rachel, or was it just for some easy publicity? He may be my father but he's still a slimeball."

Rachel smiled. "I think it was mostly for you."

"How's that?"

"Like I've said before, Trudy, you're not very observant sometimes," Rachel said uncritically. "I've been studying human nature even before I came to Creekside. Even when your dad was addressing the crowd, he kept looking back at you. He wanted you safe, and that meant keeping Gavin and me safe as well."

"Oh, I guess you're right," Trudy admitted begrudgingly. "But get this, he told me that I'm his *legacy*."

Rachel took Trudy by the arm. "There are worse things to be."

———

Trudy took a seat with Gavin and Rachel at the back of the debris-littered diner. After they were seated she heard heavy crunching on glass and looked up to see Sheriff Winston walking towards them.

"Well, you were right, Trudy, the shit has hit the fan this time," he said as he grabbed a chair and sat down with a look to Rachel.

"Clarence, I'm so sorry about Maggie," Rachel said. "I wasn't fast enough."

"It wasn't your fault," Winston said. "Like you said, you're not all knowing. Hell, I was sitting right next to her, right in front of the damn window, and I didn't even see it coming. Maybe when I was younger I could have gotten a shot off, but I couldn't manage it today."

Masters entered the Cluck and Grunt and walked back to the gathering.

"Well, Reverend," Winston said, "seems like when things go to hell, you're not far behind."

"I was with my daughter in the Dells when this took place," Masters said as he pulled up a chair, "if you need my alibi."

Gavin asked Masters, "What did you tell the reporters?"

"I told them the truth," he said as he leaned back with a satisfied smile.

"How much of the truth?" Trudy asked, not sure she wanted to hear the answer.

"All of it."

"Well, this is a fine time for you to turn honest," Trudy said.

"I told them what they needed to hear," Masters replied. "You can't hide this place any longer. It's out in the open. Did you see how full of fear the reporters were? They didn't know what was going on, or why. Their whole world is getting tossed upside down." He paused. "And if it is happening for the reporters, you can sure as hell know it is happening for Mom, Pop, and Skippy watching the thing happen live on television."

Masters looked around them and shook his head. "Look, we all agree that angels are good and demons are bad—right?" They continued to look at him, only Rachel was nodding her head up and down. "Do I need to draw you guys a picture? Think of your typical John Wayne movie."

"Oh, I love John Wayne," Rachel chimed in. "He was so good in my favorite, *McLintock!*" They watched as she got into character and did her best impression of the Duke: "Somebody oughta belt you in the mouth. But I won't. I won't. The hell I won't!"

The group erupted in laughter. "There you go, little lady!" said Masters. "In a John Wayne flick, you know instinctively who the good guy is and who the bad guy is. Well, Rachel is the one in the white hat who just gunned down the villain in the black one. She's a hero." Masters smiled. "It also doesn't hurt any that she's cute as a button. In my job, spin is everything. They're still curious but they've calmed down."

"Rachel suggested that we move to Morgan until things cool down," Gavin put in.

"It ain't my place to correct an angel," Masters said. "But I say we don't hide. We stay in the open. People will need to get used to the idea that angels exist in our world."

"It's going to become a damn Disney World here," Winston grumped.

"Like it wasn't before?" Masters replied.

Winston eyed Masters and crossed his arms. "Tell me, Reverend—and I use the term loosely—what's in it for you? You have to be playing some angle."

"My demon exhibit in the Dells is old news," Masters replied. "Angels are the new growth industry. Like it or not, Sheriff, I'm still at the center of this. Anything out of the ordinary here is only going to grow my legend."

"So, you're in it for television gigs and book signings, is what you're saying?" Trudy hissed.

"Not at all," Masters replied. "That is a residual benefit of the situation, and we've got here the perfect team"—he waved his arm around the table—"to pull this off. We have our angel, our officer of law and order, our master healer over here, and I'm the showman."

"And then there's me," Trudy added sadly.

"We'll find something for you to do, honey," Masters said, patting her on the knee.

Trudy noticed a piece of silverware starting to rattle on the table and instinctively looked over at Rachel, who for her part was staring intently at the far end of the diner.

The silhouette of a well-dressed man stood just inside the broken window.

Trudy reached over and put a restraining hand on Rachel's arm.

"Please, please, Rachel my dear," said Azael. "No need to get up. I think you managed to redecorate enough for one day."

"How did you get across the crime scene barrier?" Winston demanded.

"With ease, obviously," said Azael glibly. "I just dropped by to chat with the good Reverend Masters here. I listened to that fabulous speech you gave to the media. Very touching. I was moved."

Azael stepped forward and adjusted his tie. "Unfortunately, that speech wasn't part of our deal. Promoting angels is not your line of work, Jay; your hands are too dirty for it."

"I always go with the winners," Masters replied.

"Well, that is unfortunate for you. And your daughter."

Masters stood up at that moment. "Leave Trudy out of this. This is *our* business."

"I'm just saying that it would be unfortunate if she knew what our arrangement truly was."

Masters didn't blink. "She already knows."

Azael smiled. "You are more daring than I thought, Jay." He looked over at Trudy. "Dear girl, you still sit at the same table with your father, even after you heard how he was going to use you?"

"He uses everyone," Trudy said. "Why should I feel special? Guess he even used you."

At that Azael turned chilly. "Rachel, you poor misguided one. You realize that keeping the ladder open is only prolonging the inevitable. Our forces are already gathering around Morgan."

Trudy dug her nails into Rachel's arm.

"What would be your punishment," Rachel calmly asked, "if you are unable to close this ladder? You once commanded legions into battle and ruled over human cities Ages before that, you were honored by our kind and allowed to approach the throne of the Most High as one of the sons of light. Now you command mere dozens in a forest far from everything. Azael, how very far you have fallen."

"Enough!" Azael shouted, his anger now fully exposed. "We will crush you and your pathetic pets that you gather around you."

Azael composed himself and continued unctuously. "Pardon my outburst, young lady," he said to Trudy, bowing gallantly.

He turned to Gavin and said, "Young man, your star has risen. Your feats of healing the injured looked very impressive on television. I imagine Trudy is very proud of you. I think you will find your life quite changed now. You will be followed and filmed wherever you go from now on. There will be no need for us to ever wonder where you are, my boy—thanks to the paparazzi, we'll always know."

Azael fixed his gaze on Masters. "I guess that means we no longer have a need for you, or your daughter."

Rachel stood up and took a step towards Azael, her skin already beginning to glow.

"Oh, put your claws away," Azael said with disgust. "I know when I've overstayed my welcome."

With a quick salute, Azael said to Winston, "Officer, a pleasure. I'll see my way out."

CHAPTER TWENTY-FOUR

Holly was relaxing in the tanning booth when her "Lady Marmalade" ring tone rudely fetched her back from a tropical daydream. She pushed up the coffin lid-like cover of the bed and reached for her phone, outside the machine on the floor.

She looked at the incoming number and answered, "What is it, Jay, I'm nude!"

"Yeah, so? You can't answer the phone when you're in your birthday suit?"

"I'm getting a tan since you refuse to take me to St. Thomas."

"You'll get skin cancer and die, and then I won't have to take you anywhere."

Holly gave a loud huff that she hoped Masters heard.

"Listen, I need you to get Stan and redo the exhibit," said Masters. "Demons are going to be just a small part of the space. I need you to create a new area devoted to angels in Creekside."

"How am I supposed to do that? I don't have anything."

"Leave that to me. Just get Stan working on the new floor plan and signage, and I'll deliver the goods."

———

Masters hung up the phone. He was in Trudy's apartment, looking at the built-up array of trash.

"How can you live this way?" he asked.

"Easy—just push the shit to the side when it's bothering you. So, you're going to make an angel exhibit now?"

"Yeah," he said as he kicked some of Trudy's dirty underwear under the bed. "Demons are so last year."

"Well, I can't argue with the fact that angels are a much better subject, though I'm afraid to see what it looks like after its been Mastersized."

"Mastersized? I like that."

"It wasn't a compliment."

"Why do you have to be such a ball buster?" Masters carped. "I'm really trying to be a father."

"Too little, too late. But I do appreciate the effort."

"Are you sure it's okay that I bunk here?"

"A little bird told me Carol doesn't want you around. You got blood all over her carpet last time."

"If I remember correctly, you did that."

"Your room, your fault. You get the futon. Try not to snore."

"So," Masters asked as he pushed his hand into the futon to test its firmness, "you really like this Gavin guy, I take it. Have you? Uh …"

"Had sex?" Trudy replied, turning towards him with her mouth hanging open. "You're not gonna give me the birds and bees talk, I hope?"

"Well, I …" he mumbled.

"The answer is no, although we did have a smokin' hot tomato bath once. It's a little too late for the father/daughter talk thing, anyway. Mom had that one with me a long time ago." She pulled back the covers to the bed and removed a half-eaten bag of Skittles. "I think she said something to the effect of never falling for someone like your father."

"Words of wisdom," Masters said as he plopped down on the futon.

———

Rachel stood near the kitchen table in Maggie's house while Gavin paced back and forth.

"I feel like I'm in a cage," he said. "I thought it was hard just being confined to Creekside—now I can't even get out of the house."

"The police have things well under control," Rachel said. She always respected others in a protecting role and the police were doing their duty. "They will keep the house secure tonight."

Gavin was restless and his eyes showed it. "I can't stay here. It doesn't feel right. Whenever I look at that Kathmandu wall hanging, I start thinking about her. This whole place reminds me of her."

"I know what you mean," Rachel said. "I have many fond memories of her. Trudy and I would come over here and play cards and talk. Maggie always managed to cheer Trudy up when she was in one of her moods. I think they understood each other."

"But that's the difference between us," Gavin said morosely. "You can actually visit her if you like. I can't."

"Not yet. But someday you will see her again."

"It sounds good, but sometimes it is difficult to believe," Gavin said as he sat down at the table. "It just seems like good never wins out. That we struggle our entire lives and it amounts to nothing. That life ultimately has no purpose."

"You and I may be very different," said Rachel, joining him. "I'm an angel and you are human. I've lived much longer than you and have seen much more. What you're saying I would have found very difficult to understand before joining the Morgan community. How could someone doubt? How could someone not believe? After all, I've spent my entire existence before the throne, but the more I am in this body, the easier it is to understand the pressure this life puts upon you—with all of the pain and suffering that goes with it as a result of the fall. By joining the community, I gave up some of the things that I've taken for granted. Now I become tired easily. I hunger and become cranky if I don't eat. I want to avoid the hard things that are put before me because they become painful to me.

"Gavin, I am a protecting angel," Rachel continued, pained but wishing to present her situation honestly to him. "My purpose is that of a warrior: I was created to do battle, to defeat any foe. Why, then, does a group of reporters throw me into a panic? Why do I become afraid if someone doesn't like their eggs? Why does a simple thing like ordering from a menu throw me into an unreasoning panic?"

Rachel looked at Gavin with moist eyes. "I know that people in town put up with me. They cover for my mistakes and treat me with kindness. They realize that I'm not human, that I'm unsure of myself in this form. I am only an approximation of human, but I see now why He became fully human yet still fully God. It makes sense to me now."

———

Jonathan stood in the central square of Morgan as lights flashed throughout the deep forest. Many angels had come through the ladder to offer assistance as the battle intensified in the woods.

The abandoned church at Morgan would erupt in a blaze of light as the ladder opened, only to return to calmness as another figure exited the building and made their way into the woods.

Elder Tomas approached Jonathan and said, "We have skirmishes throughout the western and southern areas of the forest. The dumping of the Beast's body in the quarry lake only gave more impetus to them, I'm afraid. They seek to overrun us by sheer numbers and stumble upon the ladder in the process. If they continue the assault, they will most likely succeed."

Jonathan considered this and said, "As long as the battle is in the area surrounding Morgan, we are fine. I just do not want this to spread into Creekside. We have delivered too much grief to them already today."

"Maggie was a warrior," Tomas said as he looked at Jonathan. "She died nobly and was greeted by her Lord as a good and faithful servant. I only wish I were there when she was welcomed into the communion of the saints."

"Faithful servant, that is true," Jonathan sighed. "It's interesting, Tomas, that when we are not in these bodies it is so easy to make light of human death. Do they not understand that it is just a transition? That they really do not cease to exist; that once created, they will always be? That this is only a brief phase in their existence? It's only after being here, and feeling what they do, that I understand the dread and fear that goes along with the possibility of ceasing to continue in this form, and the mourning when they lose one they love. It is truly frightening, Tomas, the thought of death."

"I, too, have had these thoughts," Tomas replied. "But, we must remember where we come from and what our purpose is. If we identify too closely with them, we will make foolish mistakes that may lead to disaster."

"But that is what we were sent here to do," Jonathan insisted. "We are here to identify with them. To live as they do. To suffer as they do. I cannot help but feel the heartache they do."

———

Azael waited as patiently as he could outside of the Oneida County Jail. It was nearly midday, and he was growing impatient at the delay in processing the bail request. He had to call in a number of favors just to persuade the court to do it at all. He couldn't blame them, as his new hire was a considerable flight risk.

Finally, a scraggly man with a mullet walked out the front door, squinting in the bright sunlight. He spotted Azael and walked over to him. "Are you Azael?" he asked.

"Yes." Azael said as he held out his hand. "Theodore, nice to meet you."

Theodore didn't make a move to shake it. "Why'd you bail me out? I don't know you from Adam."

"We have a mutual friend. Someone I would imagine you would like to become reacquainted with."

"Yeah? Who's that?"

"A Reverend Jay Masters. I understand that he's the one that put you in jail to start with."

"That fucker would be dead now," Theodore spat, "if it whutn't for that brat kid of his who beaned me right before I could slit his throat."

"Well, both of them are in Creekside now if you wish to pay them a visit," Azael offered.

"Why are you so interested in me running into them?" Theodore said, eying his dapper benefactor suspiciously. "Does the guy owe you money? It don't look like you need any."

"The man disappointed me in a business transaction. I do not take such things lightly."

"So, you bail me out to do the job for you? Why do I feel like I'm the sucker here?"

"Not at all, my friend," Azael cooed. "I'm doing you a favor. If I were to kill him, it would be clean and emotionless. If you kill him it will be with hatred and malice in your heart. Those are very enjoyable feelings to have. The exquisite feeling of you fulfilling your rage would give me pleasure far above anything I could accomplish on my own."

Theodore grimaced. "So, what, you want to watch? What the hell are you, some kind of sicko voyeur?"

"Your command of French is impressive," Azael mocked. "Theodore, I do not need to be there, physically, to relish the emotions that will attend the act. Just think of me as being there with you in spirit."

Theodore thought about it for a moment. "Well, I would like another chance to slit that bastard's throat."

"There you go, my boy," Azael said with a smile. "Might I suggest you also take care of the one that hit you on the head?"

"That spiky-haired bitch? Yeah, I'll enjoy that kill. It'll be nice and slow too. No knife for her—I'll dip my wick in her and then treat her to a long, slow strangle to give her a good send-off to the graveyard—"

"Spare me the details!" Azael grinned. "I knew that I made a good choice when I covered your bail."

———

Rachel and Gavin made their way to the Cluck and Grunt, surrounded by a police escort consisting of three officers and a bored German shepherd. A group of reporters and religious pilgrims trailed behind as they walked down State Street and onto Main, which was packed with bystanders, along with a road crew busy filling in the gash that ran down the center of the street. To their right a demolition crew was removing the building crushed by the Beast.

"You should be ashamed, Rachel," said Gavin. "Look at this mess!"

"I'm sorry!" Rachel gasped as she surveyed the damage. "I shouldn't have thrown it into the wall. I imagine the owner of the business is mad at me."

"I'm kidding," Gavin smiled. "You did good."

The first thing she noticed about the exterior of the diner was the plywood over what used to be the window. Stepping inside, Rachel could see that the floor had been swept clean and tables put back into place, although the Cluck and Grunt sign had suffered a mortal wound when a foot-long piece of plate glass shattered the brittle plastic into shards of bacon and eggs.

Masters and Trudy were there to greet them.

"This is our base of operations." Masters said. "We are here to stay."

"It's so dark and dingy without the window," Rachel said sadly.

"Right now it works to our advantage." Masters said. "It keeps prying eyes at bay."

"I don't like hiding," she grumbled.

"Angels hide every day or this would be old news," Masters replied. "You're just hiding in a different way."

"We're always in the world, working," Rachel said touchily. She felt hungry and realized crankiness was setting in but was unable to stop herself. "The effects are seen every day if you would bother to look."

Trudy apparently sensed her needs and yelled back to the kitchen. "Bill, can you fix something for Rachel? She's starting to sound like me."

"Sure," Bill replied, "anything for the little lady."

"Thanks, Bill." Rachel said. "Are you mad about your diner? I can't blame you if you are."

"Hell no," Bill said. "I get to redecorate on the insurance company's dime. Plus, I'm picking out a new name for the place. How's this sound? Pigs in Heaven."

Trudy groaned. "There goes my resume again."

"Don't worry, kid, I'll have a talk with him," Masters said. "So, here's what's going to happen. I've handpicked a select group of media that will be setting up for interviews. I have also selected ten average Joes to come in to ask a few questions." He looked over to Rachel. "Can you handle it?"

"I don't like speaking for the community," she replied. "It is not my position. I would prefer if Jonathan or Tomas spoke."

"Can you get them here?" Masters asked.

"I think they already are ..." Rachel said. She turned her attention to the sounds coming from the street, as brilliant light filtered through the cracks in boarded-up window.

The group from the diner opened the front door only to find a crowd of about five hundred people—police, reporters, bystanders—prostrate on the ground, all humbled before the presence that was moving towards them down the north end of Main Street.

A mighty cherub flanked by two angels in their transformed states approached the humans. Their immense wings spanned the entire width of Main, and the street was shadowless under the brilliance of the triumvirate.

"Do not be afraid," the cherub said in a voice suggestive of a roaring waterfall, the words being felt in the mortals' hearts more than heard. "We are but servants of the Most High. Do not bow before us."

Slowly, the gathering raised their heads. Their awe had not diminished, but now they were now able to look upon the angels. The media recovered their wits and started recording as news helicopters buzzed overhead, capturing the event from the sky.

The cherub continued. "We come to you in our corporeal forms today to speak of battles that have waged unknown to you for millennium. Indeed, one such battle is taking place as we speak, not far from here.

"There was once war in heaven and the Anointed Covering Cherub was cast down to earth. Today he roams this world, accusing and seeking to destroy. His wrath is severe because he knows his time is short."

The angel to the right of the cherub spoke. "The angels that fell with him are known by you as demons. They are attempting to circle the town of Morgan in hopes of driving us out of this world. In the past we have always retreated so as not to bring suffering to our human friends."

The cherub spoke again. "A sister left this world yesterday who taught us more about what it was to be human by the example of her life, than what we could learn in an eon of living in community. To honor Maggie, we will not retreat.

"Do not enter the woods surrounding Morgan!" the cherub commanded. "War has begun."

CHAPTER TWENTY-FIVE

Theodore sat on the edge of the plush Sleep Number bed at the Holiday Inn Express in Rhinelander. It felt good to be out of jail and surrounded by luxuries. In the pokey he always felt that weird guard's eyes on his package when he was in the shower, and a more-gorilla-than-human inmate/primate that could have snapped his spine like a wishbone controlled the television in the rec room.

All that shit was behind him now as he flipped channels between CNN, NBC, FOX—it didn't matter, they were all continuously looping the same surreal events in Creekside and the warning of the cherub that "war" had begun. The president was due to speak in fifteen minutes, but Theodore didn't care.

He never received his knife back from the police and had to purchase a new one from a local pawn shop. It was a skinny switchblade that felt awkward in his hand; he would have preferred Buck's big old Bowie, but that too was gone. He sharpened it the best he could with the cheap whetstone he bought from the Wal-Mart, all the while cursing Azael for being a cheap sumbitch and only giving him three hundred bucks and a hotel room. Theodore was planning to skip after he finished his business in Creekside, so Azael could just eat the bail costs. He felt that was only fair for doing that fancy prick's dirty work for him.

While watching the news, he began to feel nauseous. The food from the George Webb Restaurant never used to affect him, and he wondered if he had eaten a bad egg.

The pain struck him without warning, causing him to drop his knife onto the floor. His head felt like a mainline train just ran through it, and then he felt something else. It was as if another person was attempting to pick the lock to his brain.

The unseen entity entered and began pushing Theodore's psyche to the back of his skull. He could feel himself losing control over his body and becoming a mere spectator of his own actions. He fought the loss of control but could not overcome the entity that was taking over.

The one now in control of Theodore's body reached down and picked up the switchblade. Theodore could feel his body doing it but was not responsible for the actions. He did recognize the voice that ricocheted through his brain like a cluster F-bomb, in dozens of languages at once. Somehow Theodore was able to understand the cacophony of words which he was being bombarded with. They were all curses towards God.

Theodore was then forcibly pushed to the back of the bus.

The driver, he realized with abject terror, was Azael.

———

Sheriff Winston was surrounded by caskets. He wanted the best he could afford for Maggie, and the Rhinelander Funeral Home had a vast selection. The gloomy strains of a church hymn filled the selection room, doing nothing to improve Winston's melancholy, and he thought he would choke on the cloying smell of flowers, flowers everywhere.

"I understand that she had no relatives," the funeral director said as they traversed the spotless, over air-conditioned room. It was so cold, in fact, that Winston wondered irreverently if some of the samples didn't contain bodies.

"No children or husband," he rasped. "She has a brother and his wife down in Milwaukee, and a nephew that was staying with her. They don't have any money and neither did Maggie. I just want to see her receive a proper send-off. One she deserves."

"Of course," the director said. "She was lucky to have a good friend like you."

"I was never a good friend to her," he sadly replied.

Winston noticed as the funeral director deftly changed the subject. "As you can see, we have a nice selection of wood and metal caskets, in varying price points for every budget."

"I think Maggie would be horrified to be buried in metal casket," Winston said. "She had simple tastes."

"Well, we have a variety of wood types: cherry, mahogany, walnut, or oak. Linings can be velvet or silk. We have a special currently on the Bracondale mahogany veneer one to your right. It features a cream velvet interior, and we can add an embroidered head panel of your choosing at no extra cost."

"Do you have one of angels?" Winston whispered. "She always loved angels." And then he began to cry.

———

"Sorry the angels ruined your big media day," Trudy said to her father as they once again sat around the table in the back of the diner. The plywood across the windows made the normally dreary diner look even more depressing.

Masters sat there, staring at the floor tiles for a moment, before replying. "It's for the best. The big angel—what's his name, the guy with four heads and wings?"

"We know him here as Elder Tomas," Rachel said.

"Yeah, he said about all there was too say." Masters paused. "Perhaps the days of the old-time showman are over, when something like that happens in broad daylight. Who would want to pay to see a giant stuffed horse or a magic trick or a sideshow when something miraculous happens right out in the open? When angelic beings battle, and a damn kid"—he glanced at Gavin—"no offence, can heal the injured?" He looked back to Trudy. "We can't compete with that. I don't even think World Wrestling Entertainment can."

"It's a new era," Gavin said. "I can only imagine what's going on all over the world as people try to grasp this … miracle."

Masters looked at Trudy. "I wanted to leave the Mysterium to you, Trudy, to carry on, but I'm afraid that my life's work will go the way of Betamax and bag phones."

Trudy looked at her father, who was obviously heartbroken. The master showman, formerly so glib of tongue, quick of sharkish smile, slouched in his chair in an uncharacteristically subdued way, and the life seemed drained out of him.

"I never wanted the Mysterium," Trudy said. "At first I never wanted to be your legacy, either. Let's face it, you're still a total ass, but it was my mother you knocked up, and I'm the result. I'm a Masters, and I want you to know I'm with you."

Her father looked up for the first time and met Trudy's eyes. "You'll never know how much that means to me."

Trudy turned towards the sound of a pounding on the door as a policeman's head poked in. "Miss—you, the angel—you need to come out here quick!"

She accompanied Rachel to the door as Masters, Gavin, and even Bill followed along to see. "What's happening?" Rachel asked the officer, whose discomfort being in the company of an angel was written all over him. "It's okay, I'm a friend," she reassured him, patting his arm.

"The people," he said, pointing to the street. "They're picking up weapons and heading for the forest. They want to defend your people."

"Oh no," Rachel said. "They can't. It's far too dangerous for them. Tell them to come back!"

The officer shook his head woefully. "I can't. They ran right through our line. We can't throw them all in jail."

"But they'll be hurt," Rachel said. "With the war raging, the woods are a death trap."

"Fools rush in ..." Masters said, earning Trudy's best stink eye.

"Trudy, you and your father should stay here with Bill—you'll be safe," said Rachel. "Gavin, come with me; I may need you to heal. We need to get to Morgan quickly. I'll carry you!"

Trudy heard Gavin utter, "You'll *what?*" and then was practically blinded by Rachel's transformation. The angel picked him up and tucked him to her side like he was a football and glided off towards Morgan. Trudy watched the glowing angel disappear over the bridge and then across the trestle into the forest.

She shook her head. "I wonder if the Packers need a new running back?"

———

Sheriff Winston heard the call for assistance over the radio and drove hell for leather towards Creekside. He had department business in Eagle River but now regretted being so far away from Creekside. He knew the officers on the front line were unprepared for the mob that burst through their ranks and ran recklessly into the forest, but he was still mad as hell. He should have anticipated something so human to happen.

He was within two miles of Creekside when traffic came to a stop. Cars were parked along the gravel shoulders of the highway and even off in the weeds. Traffic was not moving at all, and no amount of sirens or flashing lights would change that fact. Disgusted, he got out to walk.

The cars were abandoned, and he could only imagine that their former occupants were out in the forest trying to help the angels, get a photo, hunt a demon, or some other stupid stunt. Though he respected their dedication, he feared what the results would be.

The National Guard was supposedly on the way to help contain the exuberance of the people and keep them out of harm's way, but he feared it would be too little, too late. He expected the White House and military to be all over this by now, but they remained strangely silent and non-committal as yet. In an era of flash mobs, YouTube, and TV reality shows in which every damn body got to be a star for a few seconds, Winston believed the feds still considered the televised spectacle to be some super-elaborate prank perpetrated by some media-savvy joker, as no power could be greater than the US government—and Uncle Sam didn't appreciate being "punked."

He guessed that he was two miles from Creekside but only half a mile from Morgan. Taking a deep breath, he ducked into the woods.

Jonathan had made a command center out of his kitchen, with a map of the area spread across the table. Elder Tomas was with him as they attempted to create a proper battle plan.

"They keep advancing from the south," Tomas observed. "I think that is our most vulnerable side."

"We have fifty of our number on the south already," Jonathan replied. "I fear that they will loop around and attack from the north, where we are scattered and few. It would also allow them to reach the ladder without going through town."

"Assuming they know where it is."

"I think they must have a good idea by now. Besides, with their numbers they can sweep every square inch of town in a matter of minutes."

The door burst open and Rachel and Gavin ran into the room.

"We have news from Creekside," she said.

"What is the news, sister?" Jonathan asked.

"The humans wish to fight alongside us. They have entered the forest."

Jonathan sat down in shock. "I admire what they are trying to do, but their weapons would have little effect on the Fallen. The best we could hope for is that they are ignored. The worst …"

"Slaughter," Tomas said, "outright slaughter."

———

Theodore saw his life unfold as if he were watching it at a matinee. The young woman getting into her car on a side street didn't even have time to react as he covered her mouth with one hand and drove the knife between her ribs with the other. It wasn't him, he kept reminding himself. It wasn't him leaving the dying woman on the ground, gasping her final gurgling breaths through blood-covered lips as he got into her car and drove off, but yet it was. The more he tried to push himself to the front, Azael pushed back. He was no match against the demon and resigned himself to being a spectator.

The sun was sliding below the tree line and causing the road to darken, but Theodore knew where he was going and what was about to happen; yet, he had no power to change it—not that he wanted to.

He hoped that Azael would allow him more control when it came to the slaying of Masters and his offspring. He especially wanted to enjoy raping Masters' brat daughter, and then savoring the feeling of her convulsing body under his as he strangled her to death. If he had to sit in the back row during that, he would indeed be mad as hell.

———

Jonathan walked out onto his porch. The sun was setting, and all he could see were flashes of light in the distance to the south. He looked over to Rachel.

"We need to bring the Fallen into Morgan. If the battle stays out there, humans will be killed."

"I agree," she said. "I will call our lines back."

"No, your place is in Creekside. I do not want another incident to occur there." He looked at Gavin. "Son, you need to stay in Creekside as well. If there are injured, we will bring them to you. Our healers are few in number, as we were not expecting human assistance in the woods."

They looked as one as a man stumbled into view, approaching from the east.

"Clarence!" Rachel shouted as she ran over to Winston and gave him a hug. "You shouldn't have risked going through the forest."

"The road's jammed with do-gooders' abandoned cars," he panted, drenched in sweat. "I had to get to some sort of civilization, and hoofing it to Creekside didn't agree with my rickety knees." The Sheriff looked around. "So that's the new gathering hall? I like what you've done with the place, Jonathan."

"Thank you," Jonathan replied. "Although I don't know what it will look like by morning. We're inviting the Fallen to a party."

"I love a good shindig," Winston said. "May I stay?"

———

"We need to go back to my apartment," Trudy said, leaning on the counter. "This place is depressing. Even Bill took off."

"Yeah," Masters agreed. "They're not coming back tonight. Best to get some sleep so we're useful in the morning."

"I wish I knew what was going on out there," Trudy said as she grabbed the keys and motioned her father to the front door. "Cell coverage is iffy at best out by Morgan. I think the ladder messes with the reception in the area."

The showman grinned. "You like to be in the middle of things. You're a Masters all right."

Outside on the sidewalk, as Trudy locked the door, she asked, "I'm just curious, what made you the person you are? I'm serious. What happens to someone where they end up like you?"

"I hesitate to ask, but what do you mean, like me?"

"A charlatan. A huckster. A narcissistic, money-grubbing, self-serving ego-maniac with no regard whatsoever for the feelings of other people."

Masters for once looked ashamed. "Whew. I guess that covers it. Do you think I started out as a kid wanting to be the way I am? They didn't teach this in elementary school. If people screw with you long enough, then you end up like me."

They started to walk down the street towards Trudy's apartment. "Now you see," she said, "what is really going on in the world: Can you really be the person you are after all of that?"

"You make it sound like I am such a terrible person," he said as he ran his hand along the window of the dry cleaners. "Am I really that bad?"

"You've grown on me, I admit," Trudy admitted as she smiled at him. "But that's only because I have a high tolerance for douchebags."

Masters laughed. "You are one major ball buster. Have I told you that before?"

"I think you mentioned something to that effect," Trudy smiled. "So, what's up with the Mysterium? Is your hot girlfriend getting the exhibit on angels ready?"

"She's doing what she can, but I really need someone competent to assist me." He stopped and studied Trudy. "I'd like you to come aboard as my right hand."

Trudy didn't know what to say. "I'm a waitress at a crap diner in the middle of nowhere. How could I do that job?"

"Because you're my daughter," he said. "That's how."

———

Sheriff Winston stood on the porch of Jonathan's house, becoming genuinely terrified of what was taking place just outside of Morgan. The angels had brought the line back to just outside the town proper. In the darkness, the angels' lightning flashes lit up the woods like tracer rounds of human warfare. He could see an angel nearby holding a staff of blue lightning, swinging it above its head as a weapon as three goat-like creatures approached. With one swipe it decapitated all three, but in the distance he could see five more approaching. Soon even the mighty angel would be overpowered. Winston felt helpless to assist. He glanced at the Glock on his hip, as useless as a peashooter against a rampaging rhino, in this epoch-making scenario, as Jonathan had told him—in less colorful terms.

Beth approached him. "This isn't a safe place to be, Clarence. Come with me to the basement. It is the most secure place for you."

At that moment, a house on the other side of the square exploded into a fireball as a propane tank ruptured.

"I'd rethink that statement," Winston said. "If I'm going to get killed here, I'd at least like to see it coming."

"Then we should move to the church. It's the closest to the ladder and will be the last area to fall." Beth tried to comfort her charge, but Winston could see she was having difficulties of her own. "I wish Rachel were here, or one of the other protectors. They are much more powerful than I am."

Beth and Winston ran towards the church as a thirty-foot length of birch tree flew just over their heads and crashed into Jonathan's porch.

"That was too close," Winston panted, and picked up his pace.

They made it inside the building and closed the door.

"So this is the Rookery?" Winston said, taking it all in between gasps. "It's not what I expected. Guess the birds have all been scared away." He turned to Beth. "I take it this is where the ladder is supposed to be?"

"Yes, it is just over there"—she pointed to the center of the building—"where that circle of clear ground is."

"Can you see it now?" he said, squinting in the gloom.

"Yes, it is a column of light about twenty feet in diameter. It pulses and glows, and when one of us comes through it flares into brilliance before returning to its former state."

"Sounds beautiful, but I guess I'll have to take your word for it," Winston said. "What would the demons do if they reach it? Can they destroy it?"

"Demons have been cast down. They are forbidden access onto a ladder. They cannot see it, but I imagine they know by now that it is in this building. They will wait and observe the area. When they see one of us come through, they will know exactly where it is. Then they can focus their advance in one specific direction. One touch of a demon is all that is required to close the ladder … forever."

Wailing cries, mournful but carrying a final note of lingering hate, came from the east and reverberated through the empty Rookery.

"What the hell was that?" Winston asked.

"The hell indeed," Beth replied. "It is the cry of one of the Fallen being cast into the abyss."

Winston shuddered. "I've been in law enforcement for thirty years. I've never heard such a mournful sound in my entire career."

"Sad it is. They were once my brothers and sisters, until they rebelled. Now they are twisted and corrupt shadows of their former glory, doomed by their own pride to an eternity in separation from the Light."

They both peeked out the door and could see a host of angels, some twenty strong, locked in combat with hundreds of demons just on the other side of the square. One angel was on his back with six beast-like creatures tearing at his neck until another angel swung his sword of lightning across the length of them, disemboweling all in one blow. While this was happening fifty more demons ran past them and into the square.

"They have breached the town!" Beth cried. "I must join the fight." She walked over to Winston and took his hands in hers. "You've been through a lot. You know the truth now; take it into your heart before it is too late."

Winston looked at Beth. "Maggie told me many times how I was missing something. That is what kept us apart. She couldn't be paired with me because we were so different. Now we are the same; I just wish she knew that."

"Stay here, Clarence," Beth said as she gently kissed his cheek. "If you transition today, be certain that I will visit you and Maggie in Paradise."

CHAPTER TWENTY-SIX

Rachel and Gavin emerged from the forest and walked towards the rusty-girder span bridge that crossed over to Creekside. She had passed this way hundreds of times before, but now it felt so very different. She thought back to the time when she first met Trudy. Jonathan had told her that a human had volunteered somewhat unwillingly to look after her and show her how to live in this world. Trudy had stood there in the middle of the bridge in an old U2 Vertigo tour T-shirt and worn jeans, arms folded and with that been there, done that look of world weariness on her face. But beyond the imposing façade, she could feel Trudy's loneliness as it seeped out of her. Now, as she walked across the bridge with Trudy's boyfriend, she couldn't help but smile.

The police milled about, looking off towards the fires and sparking lights of Morgan. When they spotted Rachel, they grew silent and backed up a few paces.

"Shouldn't you be gathering up the civilians?" Rachel said as sternly as she could. She always grew upset when someone in a protecting role was not doing their job.

When no one answered, one young officer screwed up his nerve and stepped forward. "Guess I just elected myself spokesman, Your, uh, Angelicness," he said nervously. "We're under orders not to leave Creekside until the National Guard are in place and can secure the town."

"Secure the town?" Gavin said, pointing towards Morgan. "The fight is out there, in case you've forgotten. It's kind of late to secure the town after everyone has left."

248

"Yes sir," the fidgety officer said. "You're the one that heals, aren't you? I saw you on television along with the little lady here. We all thank you for what you did." Turning to Rachel he added, "I've never spoken to an angel before. It is quite an honor, Your Angelicness, but, well … some of the guys here fear what someone with that much power is capable of."

Rachel gasped. "They're … they're afraid of me?"

The officer stepped back a pace. "Well, yes, pardon me for saying so. You put on quite a show back there."

"Yeah, you are kind of scary when you're in angelic kick butt mode—or just hungry," said Gavin to break the tension. Rachel frowned at him, then managed a smile.

Emboldened, the officer said, "My orders are that after you enter Creekside, you will not be permitted to leave again." His face was grim now as some of his fellow officers began to step forward.

"And how would you propose to stop an angel?" Gavin said, becoming visibly angry. "I'd just like to see you try—"

Rachel put a comforting hand on his back. She did not want a confrontation with these nice men that were only doing their jobs to the best of their ability. "We will certainly obey your request, officer. Come on, Gavin, let's find Trudy and her father."

Gavin was still complaining as they walked down Main Street. "Of all the ungrateful ways to treat you after what you did."

"Pride is what started this," Rachel said to calm him. "It's because of the pride of one of our kind that war began so many ages ago. I can only do what I know is best and not expect any kind of reward or gratitude. You'll need to learn this as well because of your gift."

As they crossed over to Creekside, they saw a couple of National Guard trucks arrive, brimming with troops.

Gavin watched the trucks drive by, waving idly at the Guardsmen. "It really is a war zone."

"Let's go to the diner and see if Trudy and her father are there," Rachel suggested.

"I hope they went home," Gavin said. "They need rest."

Rachel looped her arm around his and smiled. "So do you, 'big brother'."

Gavin laughed. "Sorry, it was the only thing I could think of to get that reporter off your back. Don't they give angels last names?"

"We're created, not born." Rachel replied. "There's not much of a family tree for our kind."

They walked together down Main Street. "I think this is the quietest it's been around here for some time," Gavin remarked about the nearly deserted street.

"It will start again in a few hours," Rachel said as she took out her keys to the diner and opened the front door. The room was dark when they entered.

"Looks like they went back to Trudy's," Gavin said as he surveyed the empty restaurant. "We should let them sleep, I guess."

"Wait," Rachel said. "I feel something."

"What is it?"

"*Shhh!*" she said, holding up her palm. She felt one of the Fallen not far from their location. It was further down Main Street, and it felt like …

"Rachel? What's wrong?"

"We need to go to Trudy's now."

"Why?"

"*Now!*" she yelled as she ran towards the door.

———

The battle had consumed the gathering house as more propane tanks exploded and fire crept through the town. Winston looked through the doorway to see angels a mere forty yards away, fighting against the demons. As strong as they were, the demons outnumbered them and continued to push them back towards the Rookery. He saw one angel run a sword of lightning through a red-hued satyr, but for every one destroyed, five more took their place. Another angel with wings made of what looked to be swords impaled a demon on the tip of its wing while at the same time giving an anguished cry as a snake-like creature bit into its leg.

Despite the angels' best efforts, Winston figured it was only a matter of minutes before they were on him. He went into the sanctuary and waited for the end.

———

Seeing a bright light forming in the middle of the church, a fallen cherub entered the building through the destroyed west side and bounded into the sanctuary, its four faces from hell observing every inch of the deteriorating structure. Although the ladder was invisible to it, the activity indicated it was about to open. The demon could not believe its luck that an angel coming through the ladder would point out its location like a beacon.

As the creature started to run towards the angel it felt hot metal pierce its flesh. The pain was minor, but it turned to see what had caused the aggravation. A puny human wielding some ineffectual weapon was squeaking strange protests and gesticulating comically. Inwardly it laughed at the rotund little blob of flesh and vowed to kill it after it had finished its mission.

The Beast reached out a claw and swiped at the empty air, knowing that the ladder was there.

Its aim was perfect, and even though it could not see the ladder, it saw the effects as what was left of the east and west walls of the church were blown twenty yards out, with the final remnants of the roof collapsing inward.

The Beast had little time to glory in its accomplishment as it realized that the last of the loyalists through the ladder was an archangel.

———

Winston was knocked on his ass by the blast of the closing ladder and then blinded by the being that emerged. Even through the billowing dust cloud, Winston could tell that the angel before him was easily twice the size of the other angels Winston had witnessed just outside the church doors and wore armor of molten gold that flowed with the movements of the glowing white being underneath. The angel's breastplate was decorated with the embossed head of a lion as a halo of lighting arced around his head. The angel clutched a spear of lightning in his left hand even as it picked up and crushed to pulp the demon with its right. Dropping the carcass like a filthy rag, the angel bent down and regarded Winston. "Do not fear," the voice commanded. The words of the angel cascaded around him like a thousand voices as one, a complete choir in one being. "I am Uriel. You are under my protection."

Winston cowered against the floor of the church as Uriel took flight, his massive glowing wings illuminating the dark recesses of the church, and soared off towards the center of Morgan.

———

Theodore could only look on in silence as Azael, using his borrowed body, climbed the claustrophobic stairway to the second level of the almost abandoned brick structure. Apparently the demon knew the door that he needed to find and when he did, he gave a gentle knock.

He could hear footsteps and then the sound of prey stirring. "Rachel, it's five friggin' a.m.—just like clockwork," an annoyed voice grumbled within.

As soon as the door was unlocked, Azael leveled a kick that sent it swinging against the wall, where it cracked in two. Azael knocked Masters' kid onto the bed and pulled out Theodore's switchblade.

Theodore was still a helpless spectator but sensed that the events unfolding were distracting Azael's attention, weakening his hold, as he concentrated on his grim task. There was renewed promise of possibly regaining some of his control. He hoped so, as he wanted to be one who snuffed this bitch.

With terrible speed Azael rushed toward the bed and pinioned Trudy's arms with his knees. He pressed the button on the handle and the blade sprang out with a chilling *snick*. Theodore wished he could applaud as Azael sliced open the bitch's sleep shirt. He gouged the tip of the knife between her breasts, drawing blood.

Wham!

"I should have killed you when I had the chance!" Masters yelled, leaping upon Theodore's body, knocking him to the floor, and punching him in the face. The knife went flying. To Theodore's delight Azael's flailing arm grabbed it and swung it at Masters' midsection, opening a deep wound. Theodore heard the bitch yell out "Father" as Masters slumped to the ground.

Azael got to his feet and brushed himself off in a very meticulous, un-Theodore like way. His fist went out, hitting the slut between the eyes when she foolishly tried to get off the bed. She lay in a daze as Azael prepared to slit her throat.

Theodore couldn't stand the idea that Azael was going to waste such an opportunity. The body of Theodore/Azael began to flounder about the room, upsetting the furniture and Trudy's quartet of guitars, as the two fought for supremacy. Theodore's malice proved strong. He caused Azael to drop the knife, and willed his right hand to reach out and pull down Trudy's shorts.

Enraged, Azael fought back, recovering the knife. Theodore could feel his left hand gripping the switchblade and, through force of will, caused the hand to spasm open. His confidence fortified, he was able to take both hands and pull Trudy's shorts and underwear off of her and spread her legs. He reached down and attempted to unzip his pants. He couldn't feel his pecker, but he knew it was down there someplace, and he intended to use it, Azael or no.

He could hear Azael screaming in anger within his brain and echoing through his skull. It was the last thing he heard as blackness engulfed him; then he began to spin down into a world he had heard about but never believed existed.

———

Gavin stood over the prone body of Theodore, broken Stratocaster in hand. Part of Theodore's skull and brain matter had landed on Trudy's stomach. He stood gazing in mute wonder at the macabre tableau until he heard a frantic yell from Rachel.

"Gavin! Get out of the way—I only have a few seconds now that he's dead."

As she pushed him aside, she flipped Theodore over and put her hand to his chest. Her right hand began to glow and appeared to liquefy as she pushed her arm into his ribcage. Theodore's corpse jerked and convulsed until Rachel removed her arm, and then he fell still. In her hand struggled a worm-like creature about two feet long. It appeared shriveled from age and the skin was peeling off of it in long translucent strips.

"Shit!" Gavin yelled, jumping back a foot.

"It's Azael," Rachel said. "This is what he truly looks like. He was once a protecting angel as myself. This is what he's become since the time he was cast down. His sins degraded him, tearing him apart a little at a time. What a tragedy for one of the Sons of Morning to become a vile thing such as this." Without another word, she grabbed the shriveled, writhing creature with both hands and twisted until, with a hate-filled wail, it was crushed under her grip.

"I'll take care of Trudy," Rachel said as she moved to the bed. "Gavin, check her father."

Gavin kneeled down besides Masters. "He's still breathing," he said as he grabbed the bookcase for support and put his hand to Masters' chest.

Nothing happened.

"It's not working," Gavin said in a worried tone as he tried again.

Rachel wrapped a blanket around Trudy's waist as she cradled her in her arms. "Morgan has fallen," she said with tears in her eyes. "The ladder has closed."

———

Trudy sat on the edge of the bed, shaken and dizzy as paramedics attempted to stabilize her father for transport. She had pulled her shorts back up but still kept the blanket tightly around her as another paramedic inspected her pupils with a light.

"You need to go to the hospital as well," he said. "You got a pretty nasty hit to the head from the looks of it."

"Will he be all right?" Trudy asked about her father.

"It's a bad wound, I won't lie to you," the paramedic said as he stood up. "But he has a fighting chance."

Trudy stood up with the help of the paramedic as Gavin came over to her.

"Well, guess you've seen the goods," Trudy said with embarrassment.

Gavin looked away embarrassedly. "Sorry about your guitar," he said, pointing to the shattered Strat on the floor.

"Shit, I never play the thing," she shrugged. "Glad it came in handy for something."

"Rape's nothing to joke about, Trudy."

"Yeah, tell me about it." She paused and smiled wryly. "To tell the truth, I was kind of hoping that you would be the one to deflower me."

Gavin blushed. "Yeah, all the girls tell me that after they've had a demon possessed hillbilly trying to get in their pants." Bending down, he kissed her cheek.

———

Jonathan inspected the damage to Morgan with Sheriff Winston. Jonathan's house was missing its porch and a thirty foot long tree trunk was sticking out of the living room window. "Pity I don't have insurance," he said.

"Yeah, and if you did, it probably would have an 'acts of demons' clause," Winston replied.

The rest of the town didn't fare any better. The gathering house was still burning, its roof having collapsed sometime before, while other houses were either crushed under the weight of the battling titans or pushed off of their foundations to lean at crazy angles against the few remaining trees.

"Are they gone for good?" Winston asked as he scanned the surroundings. "The demons?"

"Yes. The ladder is closed. They have no need to return to this area again. They expect us to disperse as we always have done."

"Then you can rebuild?" the sheriff said as they walked over to the burning gathering house.

Jonathan held out a palm to one of his kind that was carrying a pail of water towards the building. The man understood and put down the bucket, turned, and walked away.

"I don't think it is our place to rebuild," he said. "Morgan has fulfilled its purpose. It's time to let her sleep."

"Then what will you do?" Winston asked.

Jonathan looked at the sheriff and smiled. "It's a new era. One of those exceptional times in human history when the paradigm changes forever. What once was hidden has now been revealed."

CHAPTER TWENTY-SEVEN

Trudy put a pillow over her head to try to drown out the drone from both the military helicopters circling overhead and Rachel's snoring. Admitting defeat, she sat up in bed. Rachel lay curled up on the futon with her mouth open and drool staining the pillowcase. It had been two days since the destruction of Morgan, and Trudy's first night sleeping in her own bed after being released from the hospital and escorted under military protection back to Creekside. The angels had moved in with their friends in Creekside as their own homes were destroyed, and she had found Rachel busily scrubbing away blood stains in her apartment when she arrived back. Trudy appreciated her new bunkmate but made a mental note to buy her some Breathe Rights.

She stood up with a wobble, her head still hurting from what the doctors said was a mild concussion, and went over to the window. The National Guard cordoned off Creekside after the battle when it became inundated with the curious and the faithful. A few Guardsmen patrolled the street while helicopter gunships circled overhead. The town had become an angelic internment camp while the government tried to figure out what was happening.

Trudy heard a loud snort and then a yawn. "Good morning," she said to Rachel, who was stretching like a cat.

Rachel sat up in bed. "Futons are very comfortable," she said, pawing absently at her eye boogers.

"Glad you like it, since we're probably going to be prisoners here for years to come."

"They're just afraid. Their entire world has turned upside down. Today the president is coming to Maggie's funeral. I'm sure he will straighten things out."

"It's the vice president who is coming, and he's a flake. If he were in charge he'd probably start World War Three," Trudy carped. "I guess we're not worth the president's time. That, or he's scared of you so he sent someone expendable."

"The president needn't fear me," said Rachel. She hardly looked fearsome as she slipped on her muskrat slippers and shuffled over to Trudy to look out the window, all the while scratching her derrière. A tank rattled the windows as it rolled down Main Street. "I hear the military set up a cafeteria in back of the church."

"Poor Bill can't compete with Army rations," Trudy said. "Are you hinting that you need to be fed?"

"Maybe," Rachel sheepishly replied. "Let's get dressed and find some breakfast. Maybe Gavin will be there. Have you heard from him?"

Trudy shook her head. "I think the area's only cell tower was a casualty of war. I'm not getting any signal at all. Land lines are out too. Maybe the government doesn't want any communications going in or out of this area."

"Well, then, we can walk to Maggie's house," Rachel said, then quickly added, "After breakfast."

"Okay," Trudy sighed. "You get to clean up first. I've got to get some coffee brewing or we're not going anywhere."

As Rachel went to the shower, Trudy sat down on the bed and looked around her apartment. Random thoughts started to dance around in her head: *Who left all the trash around? I need to wash the windows. Did something move over in the corner? I don't even like AC/DC. Why have I let myself go to hell?*

Glancing over at the three remaining guitars in the corner, she said a quick prayer of thanks for the Fender that gave its life to protect her. She realized the guitars were the only items that she bothered to dust; if she were honest with herself, she knew they were her pride and joy.

She walked over to the blue Rickenbacker 360 and picked it up. The instrument glistened in her hand. John Lennon had played one, back in the day. Putting the strap over her head and plugging in the cable, she turned on the Marshall amp. The powerful thrum of the amp stoked her inner rock star as she grabbed a pick off the shelf and ran it over the strings. Slightly out of tune but not bad, she thought, as she tuned it up.

Strumming softly, almost afraid to begin, she whispered the lyrics to a classic Dylan song. The instrument felt comforting in her grasp; an old friend. The music that was part of her was lying dormant all these years, waiting to be reborn. Her fingers had not forgotten how to use the guitar and she grew in confidence. *How was it the chorus went? Yeah, G, D, Am7. That was it. Sweet.* She raised her voice and switched from Dylan's melodic take to Guns N' Roses' version of the same song, taking a stab at Slash's solo that rattled the windows and caused a blonde head to poke out from the bathroom.

Trudy gave Rachel a big grin. She sang "Knockin' on Heaven's Door," but she realized she was finally knockin' on the door to her life.

———

Gavin sat with Sheriff Winston at the funeral home. Winston was able get him past the road blocks to the viewing but no one else from Creekside would be able to attend. They sat there alone in the front row, directly before Maggie's open casket.

"They did a wonderful job," Gavin mumbled to be polite.

"Too much makeup, She hated makeup," Winston replied. "And you don't have to make nice with me. She just looks dead. Like all dead people. In my day I've seen scores of dead folks and there's nothing these mortuary cosmetologists can do to make 'em look alive again. But they try. I'll give 'em credit, they try."

Gavin turned embarrassedly away from the sheriff and looked at the silk embroidery of Angels that adorned the interior of the lid. "Well, the angels are nice."

"Yes, they're nice."

"I wonder what she's doing now?"

"Probably chastising some angel for tracking mud into heaven," Winston said with a slight smile.

Gavin smiled back. "You know, I've learned a few things since you found me in that campground. I've learned that angels can be annoying. Skunks should never, under any circumstances, be jerked back from the jaws of death, and what we see here is just a fraction of what we have yet to experience."

"Now you're talking like Maggie."

"Brother Jonathan told me that the ladder was placed at Morgan because of Maggie. She planted the seed that everything here has grown from."

Winston sat in silence for a moment. "That's good to know. I hope Maggie knows that as well."

Gavin looked towards the coffin. "I'm sure she does."

———

Trudy and Rachel stood in line at the mess tent, plastic trays in hand. The soldiers who kept watch around the perimeter kept glancing at them, Rachel in particular. Although there were angels mixed in with the group currently seated and eating their breakfast, they were not prominent on television and therefore blended in with the humans.

"I've had this uneasy feeling in school, but it was usually just before someone threw something at me," Trudy said.

"Don't be afraid," Rachel said, "I'll—"

"Protect me," Trudy finished. "Yeah, I know. They're mostly looking at you anyway, little miss television angel. How does it feel to preempt *The Beverly Hillbillies?*"

Rachel gave a pained expression. "I didn't mean to!"

As they shuffled through the line, selecting their food, Rachel startled the cook by taking half a dozen waffles.

"Kicking demon ass takes energy," Trudy said as they moved on.

They found seats on a bench near Reverend Brustad.

"Hi, Rev," Trudy said. "How's it going?"

Brustad slid over. "Top o' the morning, young ladies. Well, I'm not looking forward to the funeral, it is going to be a circus, and Maggie doesn't deserve that."

"What do you mean?" Trudy asked.

"Haven't you seen the other side of the bridge, beyond the military line? That entire area is filled to overflowing with tourists that have just come to gawk. I've heard they ripped what was left of Morgan down to its foundation for souvenirs."

"I did manage to rescue my fuzzy slippers," Rachel said with evident pride.

"Good girl," said Brustad, patting her knee.

"Well, Rev," Trudy said, "you always complained that you were preaching to the choir here in Creekside. Here's your chance to reach a lot of people all at once, and you can do it in Maggie's honor."

"I haven't thought of it like that," he said. "She would like that."

Trudy noticed Jonathan walking up to their table, "Where's my man?" she asked.

"He's at the funeral home with Sheriff Winston. Winston sneaked him out of town early this morning."

"How are his headaches?"

"Not bad, so far but I believe it is a residual effect from the ladder. They will eventually return, and I fear they will be bad."

"So there's no hope for him?" Trudy asked. She was trying to be strong but she felt like crying.

"There is always hope," Jonathan said as he sat down with them. Leaning close to the group, he whispered, "A seed has been planted even as we speak. It will need care and watering with loving relationships to grow, but it is in fertile soil, and it is on this continent."

Rachel beamed. "A baby ladder!"

Jonathan looked at Rachel and then at Trudy. "Gavin will need help to get there," he said, "from both of you."

CHAPTER TWENTY-EIGHT

Trudy watched as the hearse, with a police escort and an Oneida County Sheriff's Department pickup, pulled up in front of the boarded-up Cluck and Grunt, the official staging area for the procession to the cemetery. She and Rachel were waiting outside on the sidewalk as the vehicles came to a stop before them. Trudy ran her hands down her black dress in an attempt to smooth out some of the wrinkles. She had last worn it to her mother's funeral four years earlier.

Gavin got out of the pickup and ran over to Trudy, giving her a kiss while Rachel grinned from ear to ear.

"I've missed you," she said.

"I was so worried about you and your father, but they wouldn't allow me to contact you. Are you both okay?"

"Dear dad's out of ICU and expected to make a full recovery. The old bastard—and I mean that endearingly—will be barking orders to poor Holly in a couple days. And I'm fine, just a concussion. If Aaron Rodgers can play with one—"

"Who?" Rachel broke in.

"Football. Never mind," said Trudy. "If he can play with one, then I guess I don't have an excuse. How about your noggin there, mister?"

Gavin placed an exploratory hand on his forehead. "Some pressure but nothing major yet. I'm not looking forward to this—it's crazy out there. My parents are stuck down in Rhinelander. It's impossible for them to get up here, what with the crowds. You can't see it from here, but about a quarter mile out there is a military zone that cuts through the woods. Fire breaks, barriers, razor wire—you name it, they're building it. Funny thing is, they don't seem to know which way to face. Some guns are pointing out while others are pointed towards Creekside."

Rachel looked pained. "We're not a threat!" she complained.

"Maybe they heard you snore," Trudy replied. She glanced over at the sheriff, who had pulled his truck over to the side, away from the procession area. "How's he doing?" she asked Gavin.

"He's heartbroken, but I think he understands that it was Maggie's time to leave us. She put all of this in motion. Now it is our turn to continue with it."

Trudy looked up at him and smiled. "Well, I'm not entirely sure who you are! You sound so different than that bedraggled boy who wandered into town and tried to hit on me in the diner."

"I was successful, if you remember."

"That you were, you stud-muffin you," she said and jabbed a finger into his side.

"Please," Rachel moaned as she walked off, "that's too much even for me."

———

The procession started to move north on Main, led by five Oshkosh Defense light combat vehicles. The hearse with Maggie's remains followed. In back of the hearse the human population of Creekside and the angelic population of Morgan, in their human forms, walked together.

Trudy looked up to see three Marine helicopters heading towards the cemetery and surmised it was the vice president and his delegation.

She took Gavin's hand in hers.

As they crossed the bridge, police on motorcycles, along with armed soldiers, created a cordon around the party as they proceeded towards the cemetery.

Trudy noticed a strange mix of reactions among the crowd as the procession made its way along the narrow two-lane road. Some in the back were obviously treating this as a perfect opportunity to get snockered. She could hear the whoops and hollers and noticed with sadness their total obliviousness that they were at a funeral. Those closer in were more solemn as befitting a funeral, although she spied a number of Masters' Mysterium T-shirts and Hodag plushies amongst the camera-coated group. She wasn't surprised that even from a hospital bed her dad could still turn a buck. The scariest sub-set was at the front, reaching out towards the procession or prostate in worship. When they recognized Rachel, one of the few identifiable angels in the group, owing to the TV coverage, cries of petition rang out as others tossed rose petals at her.

Rachel looked horrified and grabbed Trudy's arm. "They shouldn't do that! They shouldn't worship me! Make them stop."

"It's a natural reaction, Rachel," Trudy said. "Remember when you first transformed in front of me? I was flat on the ground and ready to worship you myself. It was only later that I realized what a ditzy blonde you really are."

Rachel hesitated. "Uh ... thank you?"

"You're welcome."

"This is crazy," Gavin said. "It's like a warped state fair."

Trudy scanned the familiar cemetery that now was ringed by military vehicles and troops. Snipers were positioned in strategic locations throughout. She imagined that some of it was protection for the vice president. Further out another phalanx of soldiers formed a barrier between the cemetery and the citizens that came to see the angels. Grouped in a semi-circle near the front entrance drive, she estimated the gawkers to be tens of thousands strong. Behind the crowd sat an odd midway of souvenir tents, deep-fried Twinkie stands, and Porta-Potties that backed up against Mill Creek.

"My father would be proud," Trudy said.

As they made their way to the entrance gates of the cemetery, the angels still in human form broke off from the group and moved around the perimeter, following the fence line until one was spaced every ten yards or so.

"Looks like we have our own security detail," Trudy said to Gavin.

The burial site was on a slight rise, not far away from Trudy's mother and Mrs. Brustad's resting place. The hearse came to a stop and Gavin went to be one of the pallbearers, along with Sheriff Winston, Josh, Bill, Mr. Hansen, and Mr. Graff. Television news crews had positioned themselves just behind the rows of chairs, and Trudy could make out Barbara Kern being shoved roughly to the back by CNN and the other big boys of broadcasting. She couldn't help but smile.

As they brought the casket to the site, Trudy felt sadness for the sheriff; there was so much love that he never was able to show Maggie.

Trudy and Rachel then made their way to the first row of folding chairs and were directed by the White House staff to sit next to the vice president.

Holding out his hand, the vice president greeted them. "Thank you for inviting me; we've heard a lot about you, young lady," he said to Rachel. "You managed to grab the headlines in an election year."

"Sorry," Rachel sheepishly replied.

Trudy huffed and didn't shake his hand. "You've got nothing to be sorry about; I didn't see the government helping out in any of this. They're just making us prisoners in our own homes."

"Sometimes the best way to get a handle on things," he replied softly, "is to put everything in a box and come back to it later. People tend to forget about those things tucked away in the attic. But don't worry, you may be in the attic for now but that won't last forever."

"I should introduce you to my father," Trudy said with all the sarcasm she could muster. "You'd like him."

Reverend Brustad began to speak. "We come here today to lay to rest our sister, Margaret McKenzie. As our friends from Morgan have taught us so well, her valiant battle to protect the light may be over, but her personal journey is far from over. She made the transition to a better life with her Lord. We, the living, can only imagine the wonders that await her discovery as she enters eternity. We will follow her one day and share in her joy.

"It remains for us to comfort each other now in our time of loss. She is gone from our midst, this fine person, but let us find succor in the firm knowledge that we will see her again.

"We are honored to have with us today the Vice President of the United States who will share words of comfort with us." Brustad lifted his arm in a gesture of welcome to the dignitary.

The vice president approached the lectern and with an obviously well-rehearsed solemnness began to speak. "Fellow Americans, today we pay tribute to Margaret McKenzie. Maggie, as she was known by her friends, grew up in the Midwest and lived a life that was filled with the values we as Americans cherish—family, friends, and the ability to worship as she pleased. To some it would be looked upon as an ordinary life, a cycle of mornings and evenings as time passages moved her along through the seasons and years. It was only in death that we realized how extraordinary her life truly was.

"We have all seen the news footage of the incident in this area. We have unfortunately also witnessed the death of this dedicated woman along with many others. Now I realize that some of us have sincere questions about what the cameras captured and in these days of video editing and manipulation the entire event has been brought into question. Theories abound as to what really happened, from a gas main break to aliens from outer space." He paused for dramatic effect. "I've actually have heard some folks say it was an invasion from Canada! First, let me assure you that the President has committed himself to finding out the truth and presenting it honestly to the country. But let me point out that a healthy dose of skepticism in no way diminishes the one who we come to honor today.

"We also understand that the residents of the area have lost homes and businesses, and what better way to pay tribute to those who lost their lives here than to assist in the rebuilding of Creekside and the surrounding area. Working alongside FEMA, the Small Business Administration, and other government agencies, we will insure that small towns such as Creekside not only survive, but thrive.

"Again, I thank you for this opportunity to speak before you today. God bless Margaret McKenzie and America."

The vice president returned to his seat and whispered to his aid, but loud enough to be heard by Trudy. "This is a new world. Like when the Spanish came to the Americas. Only this time we're the fucking Indians."

Trudy was about to blurt out something totally inappropriate until she noticed Brustad motioning Winston to the dais.

"Someone very dear to Maggie has a few words to share with us," Brustad said.

The sheriff walked over and stood stiffly behind the wooden podium, grabbing it with both hands. Looking down at the polished oak surface bereft of notes, he could feel the eyes of hundreds upon him. *How very many friends she had*, he thought as he attempted to pull himself together.

"In my job, I'm often lied to and I've learned over the years to believe only what I can see; to trust no one and to doubt everything. It's always served me well. I've dodged a few bullets in my time because of my skepticism. It may have kept me alive, but I realize now that I didn't really *live*. I was struggling after my wife died and Maggie came into my life with exuberance, even though she was going through a very similar situation. She didn't let the hardships and loss bring her down. She always stayed above it in a way I could never understand. She attempted to tell me what she believed with all her heart, but I wouldn't listen. After all, who could believe something so unbelievable? Angels living with humans? Miracles? A God that actually cared?

"My unbelief drove a wedge between us. I would find myself criticizing and mocking her," he said while wiping away a tear. "Soon we were spending less time together, my visits to Creekside only for official duties." He paused and turned towards Rachel. "Then an angel came along with a flying pickup, and a wayward college kid I met in a campground healed my wounds when I lay bleeding to death. But Maggie healed me the most. She taught me that the world was more wondrous than what my limited perspective could see. She taught me to trust. She taught me to believe.

"I miss my Maggie," he began to openly cry, "but I trust the angels who have told me she is not just the body that we bury today, but a spirit who lives on."

Brustad approached Winston and put a hand on his shoulder. The sheriff returned it with a bear hug as he wept.

———

After Winston returned to his seat, Brustad stood before the assembled media. Trudy could see that he was realizing that millions of eyes around the world were on him as he started to perspire. It was a far cry from a few hundred members in a run-down old church. She hoped he remembered that the words he spoke now were for Maggie.

Brustad opened his Bible and said, "Let us remember these words from Romans 8:35–39:

Who shall separate us from the love of Christ? Shall trouble or hardship or persecution or famine or nakedness or danger or sword? As it is written: 'For your sake we face death all day long; we are considered as sheep to be slaughtered.' No, in all these things we are more than conquerors through him who loved us. For I am convinced

that neither death nor life, neither angels nor demons, neither the present nor the
future, nor any powers, neither height nor depth, nor anything else in all creation, will
be able to separate us from the love of God that is in Christ Jesus our Lord."

As Reverend Brustad finished, the sky brightened as seventy-seven angels began to transform in unison. Rachel also began to glow and grow as she stepped away from the vice president and towards Maggie's grave.

She approached the foot of Maggie's casket as Jonathan's rapidly brightening figure glided towards the head. The Secret Service moved in front of the vice president to shelter their man as Rachel's shield and sword hissed with raw power, throwing off blue strobes of light. Jonathan glowed bright in silver robes as he held a crooked staff of lightning in his right hand. Both angels knelt before the casket. Rachel spread her massive razor-sharp wings, the sound of a thousand knives scraping together, and brought them up and forward over her head so that they formed a V-like canopy over Maggie's casket. Jonathan's softer and less imposing but equally majestic wings did the same.

As the tips of their wings met together over Maggie's coffin, covering and protecting it, Rachel thrust her sword into the soft earth. The ground shook in response as the two angels paid their final respects. The seventy-seven beat their wings in unison, mimicking the report of cannon as sonic booms crisscrossed the cemetery.

Trudy noticed that the crowd in the distance was silenced and fell to their knees, even the drunk ones, by the spectacle in front of them. Meanwhile, the vice president was being pushed back by the Secret Service towards Marine Two while they reached inside their coats for weapons. As quickly as it had begun, it was over. The petite blonde Rachel stood by the grave, while the residents of Morgan in un-tailored suits and simple black dresses ringed the cemetery.

Slowly the casket was lowered into the ground, as Sheriff Winston continued to weep. Beth put her arm around him in an attempt to comfort.

As the funeral concluded with Mr. Graff giving a catfight bagpipe solo of "Amazing Grace," the vice president was already being whisked back to Washington.

"He's left already?" Rachel pouted. "He seems like a nice man."

"I think your reenactment of the Ark of the Covenant from Indiana Jones spooked him," Trudy replied. "He didn't want his face to melt off or something…"

"Our wings are part of us; they help us express ourselves much as you do with your hands."

They stood there next to the grave watching Mr. Graff gently place his bagpipe into a nylon bag as Gavin and Jonathan walked up beside them.

Trudy asked Jonathan, "What will you do now that the ladder is closed?"

"We will stay in Creekside. Your government thinks they have control, so who are we to tell them otherwise?" he said with a smile. "We'll truly become part of this community. We will work here, and share our lives with those around us. We can also grow old here, in a fashion, so that we do not stand out, even as our friends also age."

"What about the media and the pilgrims?" Gavin asked.

"They'll eventually grow bored with us," Jonathan said. "The human attention span is minute, I'm afraid. Until that time we will show hospitality to all who come."

Trudy and Rachel both held onto Gavin, as he seemed unsteady on his feet.

"Are you okay?" Trudy asked him.

"Just a little headache coming on. Guess I need to get used to them."

"Not necessarily." Rachel looked up at him, grinning.

"What do you mean?"

Trudy took his hand. "How would you feel about a road trip?"

"I don't understand?"

Jonathan said, "You remember that I told you there are always seven ladders? When the one here at Morgan closed, a new one was created, and it happens to be in North America. I imagine you are already starting to feel the pull of it."

"Vaguely," Gavin said as he concentrated. "It's off to the southwest, right?"

"Correct," Jonathan replied. "Rachel will show you the way and protect you during your trip."

"But what about the Fallen?" Gavin asked. "They'll follow us."

"They will probably try," Jonathan replied. "The media will also follow you. You will be stalked by more than one hunter, Gavin. Rachel will help you avoid the Fallen but you must be wise enough to avoid the Beast with many eyes." As he said this, Jonathan looked out to the assembled media with their telephoto lenses. "They watch you even now. But even if they are able to track you to the next ladder, we are stronger now for having been here, and having lived along-side the people of Creekside. Through all of the difficulties, the ladder never wavered, never grew dim. Let them follow."

Gavin looked at Trudy. "Will you come with me?"

"Well, I don't know ..." Trudy said with mock indecision. "My father is just out of ICU. I'm the second in command of the most popular tourist attraction in the Midwest. Plus"—she poked him in the chest with her index finger—"you'll need to make an honest woman out of me, Gavin Young, since you've already seen me without my bloomers on."

"Marriage?" he asked.

"Glad you asked. I'd love to."

Gavin picked Trudy up by the waist and kissed her as he spun her around in front of Maggie's grave.

"So, where are we going?" Gavin asked Rachel mid-twirl.

Rachel's freckled face broke into a wide grin. "I hear Nevada is beautiful this time of year."

The End

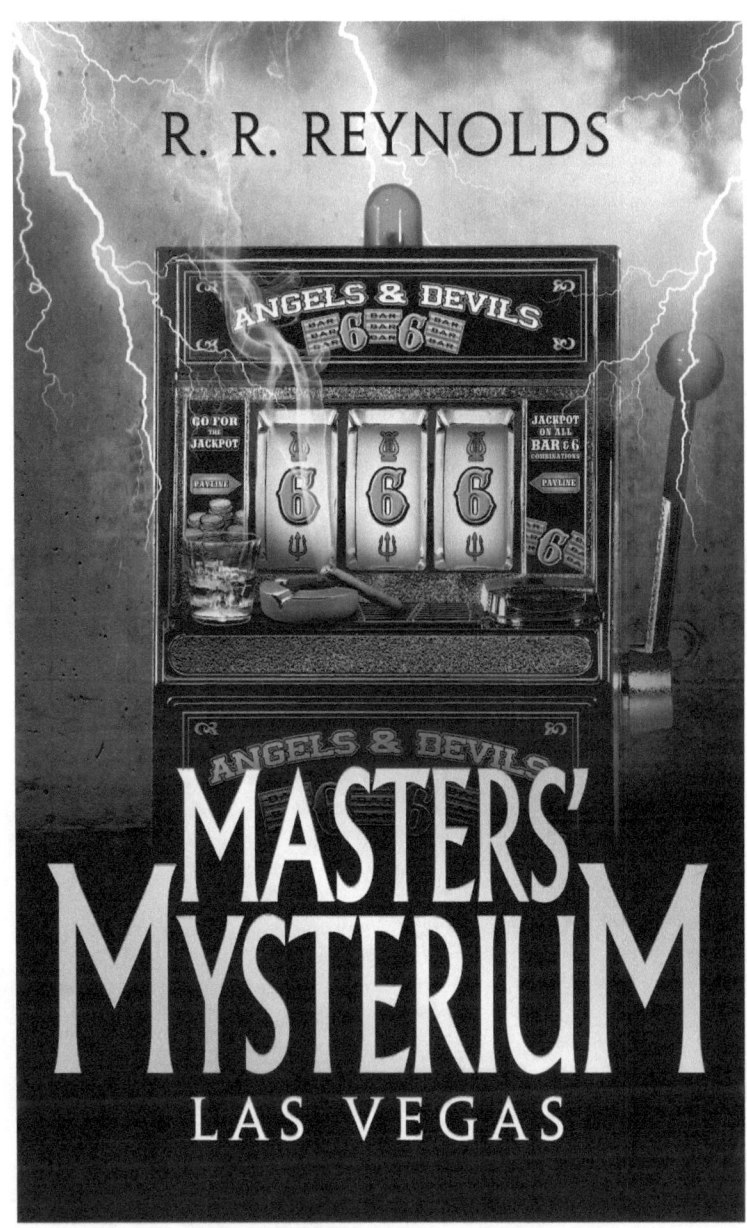

Kirkus' Indie Books of the Month Selection.

"Like Charlaine Harris' Midnight, Texas saga this is cutting-edge genre fiction that will appeal to genre fans as well as mainstream fiction readers. It's a storytelling tour de force no matter the categorization." – *Kirkus Reviews (starred review)*

www.MastersMysterium.com

Cluck and Grunt

Creekside, Wisconsin

www.ingramcontent.com/pod-product-compliance
Lightning Source LLC
Chambersburg PA
CBHW020736250626
47155CB00003B/781